THE
UNVEILING

THE
UNVEILING

PAUL D. TURNER

HIDDEN
ROOM
BOOKS

www.pauldturner.com

Paperback ISBN: 9781739436216
E-book ISBN: 9781739436209

Cover Design: SelfPubBookCovers.com/Addydesign

Hidden Room Books
www.hiddenroombooks.com

Chapter One

Session One

Anna's taxi arrived at the giant, imposing Grimwald House, which looked like it had broken free from the cover of a creepy children's book, and as she stared and wondered what dark secrets it might hold behind its decaying walls, she imagined the house peering back at her, eager to learn her own secrets. *What an ugly old eyesore you are,* she thought. *You really ought to have been torn down years ago.*

Looking out through the windows of the taxi, she saw nothing but woodland surrounding the house: tall trees clumped closely together, defending their secrets from prying eyes like hers. Anna imagined wolves creeping around out there, waiting to pounce as soon as she left the safety of the vehicle.

She could hear the wheels of the taxi crunching the gravel on the path up to Grimwald House. This house was in the middle of nowhere, isolated from the world. Anna had no idea where she was, and when she tried to check the location on her phone it appeared similarly clueless. The route to reach this house had been long and convoluted. Her driver had navigated countless twisting roads that snaked through fields and farmland, and some of those country roads were very narrow and carried the promise of a sudden death if a big truck suddenly came the other way at speed. She wouldn't be too surprised if she were to find out that the driver had deliberately chosen the most confusing route, and had perhaps even circled back around a few times, simply to ensure that his passenger would lose her bearings.

In Anna's hand, she held the mysterious invitation letter that had brought her here this evening. She unfolded it and read it again:

Dear Guest

You are invited to witness something incredible that few have ever seen. Escape your life for a moment, and take part in something extraordinary.

On the back of this letter, you will find details of the date and time that you are expected to attend a special event at Grimwald House. You will not find the house on any map. You will be picked up from your home and brought to us. You will join a select few other invited guests for an unforgettable evening of mysteries, good company, and fine food and drink.

In the interest of preserving the exclusiveness of this special event, we ask that you do not show this letter to anyone, and do not reveal your full name to your fellow guests when you attend.

You only have this one chance to uncover a fantastic secret, and what are any of us made of, if not our secrets? Whether you attend or not, be in no doubt, secrets will still be revealed, but if you choose to accept this rare opportunity then we guarantee that your life will never be the same again.

We look forward to seeing you very soon.

Yours sincerely
H

A mysterious letter from an unknown sender, promising excitement and mystery to liven up her life, how could she resist an invitation like that? Of course, there was also another reason that Anna felt compelled to attend. She could read between the lines of the thinly-veiled threat near the end of the letter that suggested if she didn't want certain things that she'd done to be revealed to the world, then she had to come. That part of the letter had haunted her since she'd first read it. She dropped the letter on the seat beside her and stared out of the window again.

'We're here,' the driver announced, as if imparting some specialist knowledge to his ignorant passenger. She waited for him to open the door for her, but instead, he sat there in his seat, not moving, as if his gloved hands were stuck to the steering wheel. Shaking her head in dismay, Anna opened the door herself. She swung her legs out and stood up, her high heels digging awkwardly into the gravel. Anna closed the door, slamming it to make a point. Before she could muster up a polite – if undeserved – *thank you* to the driver, the taxi was pulling away from her, almost as if it couldn't bear to remain near this house for a moment longer. Perhaps it knew something that she didn't?

With a sense of foreboding, Anna turned her head and allowed herself to take in Grimwald House. At first glance it appeared to be a typical English country house, though a rather unloved one judging by the state of the exterior. Its skin was pale and blotchy: the brickwork was painted white or left bare and the walls were riddled with holes, with green mossy hair sprouting from odd places. The dead vines that snaked up the walls looked like veins that intertwined across its giant body. The house kept its mouth closed for now: two large wooden doors blocked entry to whatever lay inside. All its eyes were closed too, as if the house were sleeping: large glass windows with lattice frames, made impossible to see through by the closed curtains beyond. So many windows, and yet not one of them seemed to be doing its job; the house was giving up none of its secrets just yet.

The house seemed to have two floors and an attic in the roof. High up on top of the roof, the house reached out its ears: small towers that stretched upwards to the darkening sky. Smoke was rising from a chimney, blowing slowly across the roof, creating a sort of eerie mist, and out of that mist came the gargoyles, stone demons that perched on the roof, frozen in place. They leered down at Anna, with their mouths wide open, keeping their wings folded in and seemingly content to remain where they were, at least for now.

Anna shuddered, then chided herself for letting her imagination take a sprint. It was only a house, and it was hardly the strangest thing that she'd ever seen or experienced in her life. She stepped back and took a photo of the house on her phone, preserving it forever, although she suspected that the house had always looked like this, and would do so for hundreds of years to come. It seemed like a house that was out of place and out of time, like it didn't belong here but it had taken root and now refused to leave.

It was early in the evening and the sun was only just holding on, soon to plummet down and disappear behind the hills on which the twisted trees had spread like an infection, creating a barrier that surrounded Grimwald House. There was an orange glow to the sky, as if it were on fire, but Anna didn't feel warm. She was shivering in her thin dress in the cold air. All that time that she'd spent planning what to wear for this event, and now she thought that she ought to have chosen something warmer. But she'd dressed to impress, practicality and comfort be damned. She'd picked a golden dress, one of her own designs that had worked wonders for her in the past, along with a pair of matching high-heeled shoes.

Anna had wanted to make a good impression on the other guests sharing this evening with her. It had been a while since she'd put this much effort into a social occasion. Over-exerting herself with her work, drowning in deadlines and emails and meetings, and suffering through a couple of bad first dates, had led to her avoiding social situations, but she'd told herself if she didn't want to keep feeling so lonely and disconnected from the world, then she had to try.

The wind had started to pick up, and it was messing up her hair like some invisible poltergeist determined to undo all of her hard work. Carried by the wind, a strange scent invaded her nostrils and almost made her gag. She checked her shoes in case she'd trodden in something, but they were thankfully free from squished dog poo. She wanted to turn heads for the right reasons this evening.

Anna heard a loud crack and turned her head, too quickly, and it made a cracking sound of its own. She looked towards the woods. There was a low stone wall and a small iron gate standing between the house and the woods. She couldn't see anything moving between the tall trees, but that didn't necessarily mean there wasn't anything out there, eyeing her with its hungry eyes...

The house suddenly seemed the less dangerous option. Her shoes fought the gravel as she made her way up to the grand front doors. On each door there was an iron knocker with an unpleasant, almost demonic face, its teeth biting down on the hinge. She took hold of one of the knockers, and banged it against the door.

She waited a couple of minutes, but no one answered the door. She went to knock a second time, but hesitated. Did she really want to go through with this? She had her phone, so she could call for a taxi to come and rescue her, assuming that they'd be able to find this remote place. She knew that she ought to have asked the driver of the taxi that had brought her here for his contact number in case she needed to make a quick escape.

As if someone had heard her wish and chosen to grant it, a taxi pulled up behind her, but it was dropping off, not picking up. Anna turned to see a handsome man exit the vehicle, wave off the driver, then walk towards her. She had to admit, she'd been secretly hoping that there might be at least one good-looking single man here tonight. Or maybe even a not-so-single man; she couldn't afford to be too fussy.

The man gave her a big grin and extended his hand to her. He waited patiently for her to take it and shake it. 'Hi there, I'm Mark.'

She shook his hand. 'I'm Anna. Just Anna, since apparently we're not allowed to share our full names.'

'It's very nice to meet you, Just Anna.' He held her hand for longer than seemed necessary before he finally released it. He was staring at her, and Anna felt like she was being studied, or appraised. What was she worth to him, she wondered?

'You know,' Mark said, 'I wasn't sure what kind of company to expect at this thing. I've been to far too many parties where you're lucky to see a single attractive young woman, often it's just old crones hunting for toyboys, so I'm pleasantly surprised so far, and I think this could turn out to be a very interesting evening.'

'Oh,' she said, unsure of how to respond to that. After an awkward pause, Anna asked him, 'Do you know how many other people are supposed to be coming tonight?'

Mark shook his head. 'No, but not many, I wouldn't think. This is meant to be quite an exclusive event. The invitation letter I received made it seem that way, anyway.' He took out a letter from his pocket and showed it to Anna.

'That looks like the exact same letter that I got,' she told him. 'It's so vague, it doesn't say anything about what exactly we're going to be doing here, what this place is, or who invited us.'

'You're right, the invitation *was* very cryptic... and yet you still decided to come here anyway,' Mark noted.

'Yes, well, so did you.'

'I had my reasons.'

'And so did I,' Anna said, but she had no intention of telling Mark exactly what those reasons were.

'Perhaps there isn't anyone else coming and it is just going to be you and me, Anna, in this big old house, all by ourselves?' Mark smiled at her. 'I don't think that would be so bad, though, do you?'

'Honestly, I'm not so sure.'

He grinned. 'Come on, I promise you, once you get to know me, you'll like me.'

Anna smiled. 'We'll have to see about that. Something tells me I might need to watch myself with you.'

Mark laughed. 'Ah, sounds like you must have been speaking to one of my exes... Honestly, I swear, anything bad you might have heard about me is only *partly* true.'

'No, actually, you're lucky, because I genuinely have no idea who you are. I know nothing about you other than your first name. If I am supposed to know you, if we're supposed to have something in common, some reason why we've both been invited here, then I'm sorry, because I don't know what that would be. I don't recognise you at all.'

Mark nodded. 'Yes, and I know for sure that I'd remember if we had met before, because there's no way I'd forget a woman like you. I don't know who you are, Anna, or what brings you to Grimwald House, but all I can say is I'm very keen to find out.'

Are you? Anna thought. *You ought to be careful what you wish for.*

'By the way, that's a nice dress,' Mark said, taking the opportunity to look her up and down. 'It's very impressive. You look amazing.'

'Thank you, I actually designed it myself.'

'Really? Now I'm even more impressed! Good-looking *and* talented, that's a very powerful combination.'

I'm impressed too, Anna thought, *I've known you all of five minutes and yet you've somehow managed to flirt with me more than the last man I dated did in the whole two weeks that we were together.* She knew that this one was going to be trouble.

Anna rubbed her cold arms. Now the night was growing colder, she was feeling foolish in this flimsy dress. She was aware that she was exposing far too much flesh to the cold air, and she envied Mark in his warm-looking jacket. He seemed to notice her shivering, and he offered her his jacket. When she automatically declined, he tried again and said, 'I'd be no gentleman if I stood here allowing a damsel to be in distress, especially in that dress. Come on, you must be freezing. Please, take it.'

Reluctantly, she allowed him to place his jacket around her shoulders. She hadn't actually given him permission to touch her bare arms as he did so, but that hadn't stopped him.

'That's better,' he said, 'you don't look so cold now. Shame to have to cover up that lovely dress, and everything else, but at least you won't freeze to death out here now.'

Anna was keen to have Mark's eyes on something other than her body, and decided to try to move the conversation away from herself. 'I tried to keep track of the route on the way here but it was so confusing, and I've no idea where we are. I hope they're planning on bringing those taxis back for us later, or God knows how we'll get home.'

Mark looked back at the gates and the road beyond, then back at the house. 'I've been to a lot of parties and events but I've never been invited to Grimwald House before, in fact I'd never even heard of this place before tonight, so this is a new one for me. I'm intrigued, for several reasons.'

'I just want to get this over and done with,' Anna said, sighing.

Mark examined the doors to the house, and the strange door knockers. 'So, have you tried knocking on those doors to see if anyone's home, or do you want me to do it?'

Still cold, and still fed up, Anna rolled her eyes at him and answered, 'You know, that never even occurred to me... thank God you're here! Yes, of course I tried knocking, do you really think I'd be standing out here in the freezing cold if someone had answered?'

Mark frowned at her, as if unsure how to respond. He turned his attention back to the door, stepped forward, took hold of one of the knockers, and banged it against the door three times, rather forcefully.

'I'm beginning to wonder if there's actually anyone here at all,' Anna said. 'What will we do if nobody's home?'

'I'm quite happy to share a taxi ride back with you, and I know some nice restaurants, this evening doesn't have to be a total waste. We could still have a good time, just the two of us.'

Anna shook her head. 'If turning around and leaving is an option, then I'm going straight back home and I don't really have any desire to see either this house, or you, ever again. No offence.'

'Oh. I see.' Mark looked hurt.

Anna wondered whether she was being a little harsh with him. She had only just met Mark, and had immediately formed an opinion of what kind of man he was. Perhaps that was unfair. She started to worry that she'd made things awkward with the first handsome stranger that she'd spoken to in a long time. He had only been joking around, and flirting a little, if badly, but she'd shot him down and his plane was currently a burning wreck on the ground. She opened her mouth to say something nice, to make an effort to rescue him, but she couldn't think of the right words.

So instead, they waited in silence.

A few minutes later, they heard an awful creaking, groaning sound, like some horrible creature waking from the dead, as the house's jaws opened: the doors parted and swung slowly back into the interior of the house, which was ominously dark inside.

Anna and Mark glanced at each other. They waited, but no one came out to greet them, so Mark decided to take charge. 'I'll go first, just to check that it's safe. You should wait here.' He walked through the doorway into the house. Anna ignored his instruction and followed him, but prepared herself to be ready to turn around and run at the first sign of anything that might leap out of the dark to attack them.

'Candlelight,' Mark noted, indicating the dim lighting and glowing walls. 'Somebody should tell them to upgrade to electric lighting, it is the 21st century, after all.'

'I assume it's for effect,' Anna said, feeling even more anxious now. 'I think whoever's brought us here to this bloody house, they want to scare the shit out of us, and they're doing a good job of it so far.' She noticed that Mark winced at her swearing, and she found that amusing. *I'm so sorry, am I spoiling the image of the sweet, polite, naive rich girl that you hoped I might be?*

It was a little warmer inside the house, so Anna handed Mark his jacket back. Her high heels clacked on the shiny black and white chequered floor. She looked around. The interior of the house was no less imposing than the exterior. On the left and right sides of the long hallway there were closed doors hiding several rooms, and against the far wall was a grand staircase with wooden rails and a carpet that rolled down towards them like a tongue, and if you were to allow that tongue to pull you up those stairs then you'd reach a wooden wall on which hung a dead animal, a stag's head with long sharp antlers like the horns of the Devil. Long, darkly-patterned curtains flanked the long-dead creature, hiding it from the world outside those windows. Anna looked up. Elaborate patterns were carved into the wooden ceiling over her head, curving and swirling to create an almost dizzying effect. She wondered how many more rooms there might be on the floor above.

She breathed in through her nose. The air in here smelled of dust and age – when it didn't smell almost overpoweringly of a man's cologne. Anna was certain that she couldn't have applied her own perfume anywhere near as liberally as Mark had his. She took a step away from him.

To her immediate left, Anna saw two doors, one with the sign *LADIES* and the other *GENTLEMEN*. This old house had indoor bathrooms, then, so at least she wouldn't be expected to relieve herself in some little wooden hut outside in the garden. It was a sign of some degree of modernisation in this otherwise archaic house.

Further along the wall there was a portrait of an austere-looking family: a well-dressed man and woman standing behind a handsome younger man who might've been their son, and a pretty girl, who seemed to be staring back at Anna. As her eyes continued on past the portrait, Anna found herself distracted by an elliptical mirror that had caught her attention and her reflection. While she thought Mark was looking the other way, she straightened her hair, undoing the wind's damage, checked her makeup, and stared at herself for a moment. *Not perfect, but it would have to do.*

'Quite a breathtaking sight, isn't she?' She turned to catch Mark smiling at her again as he added, 'The house, I mean.'

Anna ignored his flirting. 'There has to be someone else here other than the two of us,' she told him. 'There must be some staff, at least, because someone opened the front doors for us. They didn't just open themselves, did they?'

'Hello? Is anyone there?' Mark called out, but he didn't get any response. 'This is all very strange.'

'Yes,' Anna agreed. 'I'm starting to wonder if this is some elaborate ruse? Maybe they intend to kidnap us and hold us for ransom, and if they don't get paid, then they'll murder us in some horrible fashion?'

Mark raised an eyebrow at her. 'You have quite an imagination.'

'I suppose that's just one of my many quirks that make me so fascinating.'

'Yes, you're certainly that.'

Anna gave him an unimpressed look.

'Perhaps we should explore this place together?' Mark suggested.

'No, as tempting as it is to go off wandering around this creepy old house in the dark, risking bumping into whatever ghouls and ghosts might be hiding here, I think I'm happy to stay put for the moment and wait to see if anybody else arrives.'

Mark nodded. 'Alright then, we'll wait here. Together.' He flashed her a smile. 'I'll keep you company, and then you won't have to worry about any big nasty monsters. I'll protect you.'

'Great. Thank you so much, now I feel so much safer.'

What a gentleman you are, Anna thought, *and like all supposed gentlemen, I know exactly what your game is, but you're going to lose.*

They waited for the next guests to arrive, which they did around ten minutes later. Anna watched with curiosity as Mark opened the doors to allow them into the house. A tall, older woman entered first, followed by an overweight, middle-aged man. The older woman looked at Anna and at Mark, and then announced, 'My name is Vivian. It's a pleasure.'

Something about the woman immediately made Anna feel that they might not get on. But she told herself that wasn't fair, and she ought to stop being so quick to judge people. She should at least give her a chance.

The man beside Vivian coughed and it seemed to rattle his chest. He sounded like a smoker. He adjusted his glasses as he introduced himself. 'Good evening. I'm Harold.'

Anna and Mark introduced themselves, before Anna added, 'We've been here for a while but we've not seen anyone else, not even any staff. Presumably somebody's home, but they haven't bothered to reveal themselves to us yet, and I'm getting a little tired of waiting around. Perhaps we ought to leave?'

Vivian smirked. 'Now, come on Anna, try and have a little patience. I've travelled quite far to get here and I assume that you have, too? Do you really have such a hectic social life that you can't spare an hour or two to *"witness something incredible"*, as we were promised in that invitation?'

Anna folded her arms across her chest. 'Maybe I do have a busy life? Maybe I'm not just some lady of leisure who can afford to travel for hours and then sit around doing nothing. I could be at home, getting on with my work, so if this is all going to be some big waste of my time, then I'd rather just go.'

'I see.' Vivian smiled back at her, with a knowing look on her face. Anna didn't like the thought that this woman believed she knew everything about her and was judging her, having only just met her.

The group began chatting. The conversation started with mundane topics like the weather and what their journeys to get here had been like, but eventually progressed to finding out what each other did for a living, although they all remained vague on the details and also avoided revealing any other personal information such as their full names, as per the instructions in the invitation. Anna told them a little about her fashion business, and then Harold explained that he was an accountant with various clients. Vivian did not work, and Anna suspected that she probably never had. Mark said that he was "between projects", which he seemed slightly embarrassed to admit, and was quick to change the subject.

'If we're going to be waiting a while, do you want me to go look for some chairs for you all to sit on?' Mark offered. 'There must be some in one of these rooms, and you don't want to be standing around like this all night, do you?'

'I'm fine,' Anna replied.

'She might be fine,' Vivian said, 'but yes please, if you wouldn't mind, Mark. My body's not as young and strong as it once was.'

Mark then looked at Harold, who smiled and told him, 'No thank you, Mark, I'm alright as I am. I have two perfectly good legs, and I've been sitting in that taxi for two hours, so I'm quite happy to stand. Perhaps I'll come with you, and then we can—'

The appearance of the final member of their group proved enough of a distraction to bring their conversation to a sudden end.

The woman surprised them by descending the staircase rather than coming from the front doors, and also by the fact that she was un-deniably a striking beauty. She had a young, very pretty face, and her

dark skin contrasted pleasantly with the white dress that clung to her
slim figure. She wore shoes that were long and narrow and ended in
little bows above where her toes would be, with glittering straps that
wrapped around her tiny ankles. Anna suddenly craved both those
lovely shoes and those lovely long legs that went with them too. She
decided that she would happily trade her own body for this girl's body
in a heartbeat, especially when she saw the way that Mark reacted to
the new arrival. As the young woman approached the bottom steps,
she looked directly at Mark and gave him a smile that seemed to nearly
knock him off his feet. 'Hello, my name is Katarina.'

Mark's voice wavered as he said, 'That's a lovely name. It suits you.
I'm Mark. I'm very happy to meet you.'

Anna couldn't stop her eyes from rolling; it hadn't taken him long
to forget all about her. She might as well not even be in the room
anymore. Anna suddenly decided that she didn't like this new arrival,
and was convinced that they weren't going to get on.

Vivian appeared unimpressed with their new companion too. She
looked at Harold and prompted him with, 'Well? Introductions?'

'Oh, yes, of course,' Harold said. He smiled at Katarina. 'Good
evening, my name is Harold, and this is Vivian. That's Mark, as you
know, and that's Anna over there. It's a pleasure.'

Mark offered Katarina his hand, as if to suggest that she might not
be able to manage the final steps by herself, but she declined his help
and he looked disappointed. She then looked at the others and said,
'I'm happy to meet you all.'

'Yes, likewise,' Vivian said, with little trace of enthusiasm.

Katarina then turned her head and locked eyes with Anna. The way
that she was staring at her so curiously made Anna feel uncomfortable,
so to break the awkwardness of the moment, Anna told her, 'I love
your dress. It's gorgeous.'

Katarina seemed to be lost in thought for a moment before she
replied, 'Thank you, it's my favourite dress, I wear it all the time. I'm

sorry if I was staring at you, Anna, but... I haven't seen a dress quite like yours before.'

'Thanks, I actually designed it myself,' Anna said.

'Did you really? You must be very talented. Very special. I'm quite jealous.'

Anna took the compliment, even if she didn't believe that anyone would be impressed by her, not once they'd seen Katarina. She changed the subject. 'So it looks like you were the first of us to arrive, then?'

Katarina nodded. 'Yes, I'd been here quite a while before you all arrived, and since nobody else was here I started getting restless, so I decided to explore this strange house, but there's not a lot to see as most of the rooms appear to be locked for some reason. Perhaps they don't trust us? I haven't seen any staff yet, which seems odd. I had started to wonder if anyone else was actually coming tonight. I certainly wouldn't want to be here in this house all by myself for very long.'

'Did you receive a letter inviting you here, like we all did?' Mark asked.

Katarina nodded. 'Yes, it was a very odd letter. I wasn't quite sure what to make of it, with all those promises of mysteries and secrets, I thought perhaps—'

'Look, this is all fascinating,' Vivian said, rudely interrupting her, 'but I'd like to know whether our host is going to finally reveal his or herself, and if not, then what are we supposed to be doing here? Is there some purpose to all of this?'

'Earlier on, I thought I'd heard some noises coming from behind one of those doors,' Katarina said, pointing in Anna's direction.

Anna turned around. She tried turning the doorknob on the next door along from the bathrooms. 'This room seems to be unlocked,' she told them. 'Maybe we're meant to go in here?' The door opened with a groan, and as Anna tentatively stepped through the doorway,

the rest of the group huddled together behind her, curious to see what
lay beyond.

Fine, she thought, glancing back at her followers who were urging
her forward. *If I'm to be the sacrifice, the one that gets killed first in this
house of horrors, then let's just get it over with...*

To Anna's relief, there was nothing too terrifying behind that first
door. It was simply a cloakroom. She continued on to the next door
and tried that one, and it was unlocked too, and when she opened the
door, the room behind it was a little more impressive.

She led the group through into a circular room, at the centre of
which stood a round dining table encircled by five chairs. The room
was quite bland otherwise: its curved walls were bare and free of dec-
oration, there were no paintings or furniture, and not even a carpet
on the floor. Oddly, it had no windows at all, and there seemed to
be only one door in or out of the room. The room's odd circular
shape and lack of windows made the room feel more oppressive, more
claustrophobic, than it should have.

'No candles in here,' Mark pointed out, and then he pointed upwards. Anna looked up and could see that a set of five lights hung from
the ceiling, and in each one a bulb shone brightly behind its spherical
glass prison. As Anna approached the dining table she saw that it was
bare except for five envelopes, one placed in front of each chair. Each
of the envelopes had a name written on it – *their* names.

'That's not ominous at all,' Anna said.

Harold circled the table until he found the envelope with his name
on it. 'I feel a little like a knight invited to King Arthur's Round Table,'
he said, with a smile.

Vivian seemed amused by that. 'In that case, Sir Harold, why don't
you take a seat first?'

As Harold accepted her suggestion and sat down in his chair, Mark instead played the gentleman again, first pulling out Vivian's chair for her, and then doing the same for Anna. When he approached Katrina, however, she put her hand up and told him, 'I can manage, but thank you.'

Again, the young woman had disappointed Mark. *Good for her,* Anna thought, *maybe she's immune to his smarmy charms?*

Once Mark had taken his own seat, they all sat facing one another, and it wasn't long before the giggles broke out as they all realised how ridiculous the situation was.

'I mean, this is crazy, what are we doing here?' Anna said, shaking her head.

'I do hope that our host intends to serve some food at this little party of theirs!' Vivian announced, rather loudly, in a voice that she seemed to hope would penetrate the walls of the dining room and spread throughout the rest of the house. 'Especially since I've starved myself and have barely eaten a thing all day!'

Anna caught Katarina glaring at Vivian. Considering how thin Katarina was, Anna suspected that joking about starving oneself was not something that the young woman would find particularly amusing. But even though she was perhaps a little too skinny, she was still gorgeous, and Anna found that she envied her, especially her lovely smooth skin and her lack of wrinkles. At work last week, Anna had been told that she was getting old. Not directly, but via a few not-so-subtle comments from an employee of hers named Connie. She knew that Connie was always reaching out her greedy fingers for Anna's job, but if she wasn't careful then one day she might find those grubby digits of hers getting cut off...

Unlike Vivian or Katarina, who Anna suspected were likely to have come into wealth by marrying a rich man or by being born to rich parents, Anna had had to work very hard to make her money. She'd often gone above and beyond to make her fashion business a success.

She'd done things people wouldn't believe, not that she'd tell anybody about them. But she was proud of what she'd accomplished, and even prouder of her bank account balance. She still found it hard hobnobbing with people like Vivian and the rest of this group, wealthy people that would have looked down on Anna and her family when she was younger, back before she'd made a success of herself, but she'd learnt to wear a mask and play the role that they wanted her to play.

The mysterious letter inviting her to Grimwald House, sent by someone whose name was apparently simply "H", had been extremely vague about the purpose of this evening. Anna had briefly wondered if it was one of those secret sex parties for the rich that she'd heard rumours about, but had so far failed to be invited to. If that was the case, then the present company was a little disappointing; Harold was not very good-looking and rather overweight, and as for Mark, while she could admit that he was rather handsome, he was a bit too full of himself, the stereotypical rich playboy type – although Anna had certainly done worse in the past, if she was being honest with herself. Vivian seemed a little old to be indulging in naughty things like that, although Anna wouldn't put it past her, and as for Katarina, well, she was harder to read. Several times so far this evening, Anna had caught Katarina staring at her and it had made her feel uncomfortable. Perhaps it was just that Anna was the only real female competition Katarina faced tonight and she was sizing her up? It wasn't as if Anna hadn't been doing the exact same thing herself. But right now, if Katarina's eyes burned into Mark's body any more than they already were, then his skin would be charred. For some reason, it bothered Anna that Katarina was looking at him so intensely.

Anna turned her attention back to the envelope that had her name on it. She wondered what it might contain. Deciding that whoever had left these envelopes probably wanted them to open them, she took hers off the table, opened it and found inside a letter and also a pen – and, strangely, a needle. Anna unfolded the letter and read it:

Dear Guest

Thank you for attending this evening. We promised you something special, and in a short while, what that is will be revealed. Before that happens, there is something you must do.

We require a commitment from you to attend a similar evening on the Friday of each week for the next four weeks. If you feel you cannot make this commitment, please leave now. However, should you do so, then you will not be invited back again for any future event.

Should you decide to continue, you must agree not to speak of what you see here to anyone else, and not to try to contact any other members of your group outside of these sessions.

On the table in front of you, you will find a pen and a needle. Please use the pen to sign your name on the dotted line at the bottom of this letter.

In the hollow circle beneath the dotted line, please place a drop of your blood. You can use the needle provided. A small drop will suffice. When finished, please fold this letter and place it in the envelope and then seal it. When each of you has done the same, then the evening's events will begin.

Once again, thank you for being a part of this very special evening.

Yours sincerely
H

Anna watched as the others opened and read their own letters, and she suspected that they all had the same message. She could see that each of them had their own pens and needles too.

When someone finally broke the silence, it was enough to startle the group. 'Well!' Vivian said, putting her letter back on the table. 'How very interesting.'

Mark spoke next, and he sounded annoyed. 'Is this supposed to be some kind of joke, do you think?'

Harold frowned. 'This is a little odd.'

'Just a little?' Anna said. 'It sounds completely crazy to me.'

'Before you all go ahead and sign anything,' Harold said, 'I think you should all understand that what we're doing here is signing a contract, even if the method is rather strange. We're promising to attend each week and to follow their rules about not speaking about whatever happens here. I don't know what the consequences might be if you break this contract, so don't sign it if you're not sure you can make this commitment.'

Vivian smiled. 'I've been to parties where far odder requests have been made of their guests than this, believe me. I'm quite intrigued, and I've come all this way, so I'm signing it. You only live once, after all.'

The rest of the group watched as Vivian leaned forward, picked up the pen from the table, and signed the contract. Then she picked up the needle, and jabbed it into her finger. She winced as she squeezed a drop of her blood onto the paper. 'There, all done,' she said, then she folded the letter and put it into the envelope. She placed the envelope back down on the table and sucked on her finger to stop the bleeding. With a grin, she said, 'Who's going next? Come on, live dangerously!'

'I'll do it,' Katarina said. She slowly and carefully signed her name, then didn't wince as she picked up the needle and pricked her finger with it. She pressed her finger against the paper and then put the letter back into the envelope. She sucked on her finger as Vivian had done, and as she did so, she stared at Anna.

Anna turned away from Katarina's stare and told the others, 'I'm not sure about this.'

She heard a cough and then Harold picked up his pen and needle. 'I'll go next, then. I may be going against my better judgement here, but I suppose I ought to see this through.' As he jabbed himself with his needle, he cursed, 'Christ!' and that made Mark laugh nervously, before he too picked up his own pen and needle.

'I'm sure this is all a bit of harmless fun,' Mark said, looking at Anna. 'What have we got to lose? It'll be fine.' She didn't find him very convincing.

Once Mark had finished and put his envelope back on the table, Anna felt four pairs of eyes on her, waiting expectantly. She felt a familiar pressure again – to fit in, just like at work, and before that at school. Pressure to do things that she wasn't comfortable with so that she could be part of a group, and not be the coward, the loser that gets cast out. She knew that this could be a moment that she ended up regretting. But lesser men and women than herself had had the courage to sign that contract and stab their fingers this evening, so what was she waiting for? Was she seriously going to stand up, declare herself a coward, and leave now? Or did she want to find out what this whole mysterious evening was really all about?

'Oh bloody hell, fine, I'll do it.' Anna picked up her pen, and signed her name. Then she picked up the needle, and jabbed her finger. It didn't break the skin the first time, so she jabbed it harder, and then the blood began to spill.

A tiny crimson dot landed in the middle of the circle under her signature. She folded the letter, placed it into the envelope, and then put the envelope on the table. She sucked on her finger.

'So, it looks like we're all in, we're all committed,' Vivian said. 'Once a week for the next four weeks, we'll all have to meet here.'

'Yes, but meet here to do what exactly?' Harold said, taking off his glasses to rub his eyes. 'I mean, we still don't know why we're here, do we?'

Anna noticed that Katarina was staring at something on the table in front of her. Mark noticed too and asked her, 'What's the matter, Katarina?'

'There's a note on the table, a message,' Katarina replied. 'It was hidden underneath my envelope so I didn't see it at first. It says "*Look under the table*".'

Mark eased his chair backwards and then knelt under the table, and Katarina did the same. The other three members of their group waited for the two of them to resurface, which they did a few seconds later, and Mark had something in his hands.

'It was stuck to the bottom of the table, it's a book,' Mark told them, as he lifted the book up for them to see. It had a brown cover with the word *Journal* at the top. He examined it and flicked through all the pages. 'It's empty though,' he declared. 'There's nothing written in it. What's so special about an empty book?' He looked at Katarina. 'It was under your side of the table, and you had that message underneath your envelope, so I'm guessing this book is meant for you?'

Mark attempted to hand the book to Katarina but she told him, rather forcefully, 'No! I don't want it. Get it away from me, please.' She was staring at the book in a way that seemed to suggest she recognised it. She seemed almost scared of it.

Mark put the book down on the table, surprised by her reaction. 'Sorry. It's only an empty book, that's all. It's nothing to be afraid of.'

'Please, Mark, just leave it alone.'

Suddenly a scraping sound came from somewhere within the wall. They all stared in amazement as a door revealed itself in the wall. It slid open, not fully, but just enough that there was a narrow gap that they could see through, but whatever was on the other side was so dark that nothing was immediately visible through this new doorway. The group glanced at each other, sharing a look of surprise.

'Where on earth did that come from?!' Vivian gasped.

They waited to see what would happen next, but when nothing did, one by one they each got to their feet, warily, and walked towards the strange new door in the wall. 'Should we have a look inside?' Mark asked, as he took hold of the door handle and pulled it to slide the door fully open. They still couldn't see anything in the dark room that lay beyond the door. Mark took a step forward but then hesitated, and stepped back. He looked at Katarina and said, 'Ladies first.' He stepped aside for her, but Katarina seemed very reluctant to enter the mysterious room, so instead Vivian went first. She was followed by Anna, who encouraged Katarina to come with her, and then finally the two men followed them.

Once Mark had entered the room, the door slid shut behind him all by itself. Anna wondered who might be magically controlling this door; she imagined they might find a man behind a curtain somewhere in this house who was working the controls.

They found themselves in a small, dark room, which had soft candlelight that illuminated some sort of statue that stood against the far wall. Anna had never been particularly claustrophobic, but this tiny room had a good chance of changing her mind. She noticed the others had gone quiet, and were all staring at the statue.

Anna moved closer to the statue, and then realised that it wasn't a statue at all – it was a body. It was stood up and wrapped from head to toe in bandages. It looked like a—

'It's a goddamn mummy!' Mark exclaimed. 'This is some kind of tomb!'

'This is rather exciting, isn't it?' Vivian said. 'Not much surprises me nowadays, but I have to hand it to our host, this isn't at all what I expected to find here.'

Anna couldn't quite believe what she was seeing. When she looked around at the rest of her group, she saw that Harold wore the same confused but intrigued face as Mark and Vivian did, however Katarina looked terrified and clearly didn't want to be here. She was edging herself back towards the door.

'I wonder how old this thing is and who it might have been?' Harold said, peering at the body. 'I'm assuming that there is actually a body underneath all those bandages and it isn't just a mannequin, a dummy or something like that. I suppose there's no way to know for sure, well, not unless...' His voice drifted off.

'That's it!' Vivian said suddenly, startling them. 'I think I might now have an idea what we're all doing here.'

'Go on then, enlighten us, because I haven't a clue,' Mark said.

'Alright, I will. In Victorian times, they would hold parties where they would invite a group of guests to get together to witness the unwrapping of an ancient Egyptian mummy – for fun!'

'That's awful!' Katarina said.

'This particular mummy has been stood up, rather than lying down, I suppose to make it more impressive. Its arms are straight down, not crossed over its chest like you often see in pictures of mummies.'

'It appears to be a woman,' noted Mark, 'judging by the chest area, anyway.'

'Yes, I see you noticed that,' Vivian said, smiling at him. She turned to the others and said, 'Did you know, sometimes at those parties they would set up the body in such a way that it'd look like it was dancing while it was being unwrapped... I wonder if we can expect something like that here?'

'That's so disrespectful to the dead,' Katarina moaned. 'I'm sorry, but this whole thing is revolting. I think I'm going to be sick.'

Vivian shook her head at Katarina. 'Then point your mouth away from me. You all have to understand, this was back before mobile phones and TV and the Internet and video games, so let's not judge the Victorians too harshly for their choice of entertainment on those long evenings, shall we? If that's why we're here tonight, to unravel this body, then I don't know about the rest of you, but this would certainly be a first for me. Who knows, maybe as we unwrap all that linen we'll find that it's wearing various bits of jewellery that could be worth a fortune. Is no one else just a little excited to see what might lie underneath?'

Vivian seemed disappointed by the reactions of the rest of the group, who appeared less enthusiastic. Harold and Mark moved closer to get a better look at the body.

'If you're right,' Mark said, looking at Vivian, 'if that's the reason that we're all here, then what happens now?'

Vivian laughed and then told him, 'I suppose now you get to undress your mummy, Mark. Oh, how very Freudian!'

He frowned back at her. 'Hang on, what do you mean? You want *me* to unwrap this thing?'

'Yes! Come on, I don't see anyone else here who's going to do it for us. So don't be scared, be a big brave boy and take hold of a strip of bandage and start pulling, and see what your prize is. Then each of us will take our turns to go next. Oh come on, don't look so mortified, it's only like a game of Pass The Parcel! Perhaps start carefully, though – who knows how fragile it might be? And let's hope the bandages haven't fused to the body.'

Mark eyed the corpse dubiously. 'I'm not sure I'm too comfortable with doing this. Katarina's right, this all seems disrespectful to this poor dead woman, whoever she was.'

Vivian smiled. 'Come now, Mark, you don't mean to say that you've never wanted to undress a lady at your very first meeting?'

Mark looked down at his hands, choosing to avoid the eyes of the women in the room. 'Um...'

Vivian rolled her eyes and said, 'Oh, for heaven's sake, get out of the way then.' Harold and Mark stood aside as she stepped closer and examined the body. 'Where should we start? From the bottom and work our way up, I suppose. Katarina, come over here, don't be shy. Let's show these boys how brave us girls are, shall we?'

Katarina reluctantly edged closer to the body. To Anna she looked like a mouse approaching a piece of cheese that might suddenly spring a trap to break its neck.

Vivian pointed at the body. 'Do you see that trail from its right foot, almost as if somebody's indicating a starting point? I assume that's where we're meant to begin. Start pulling from there.'

Katarina bent down and reached out her shaking hand towards the mummy's right foot, and took hold of the bandages and started pulling, but she did it extremely slowly, much to Vivian's obvious annoyance. It seemed to take the young woman a tremendous amount of effort to perform this relatively simple – if macabre – task, and Anna suspected that Katarina was doing all that she could to stop herself from suddenly fainting in front of them all.

Anna felt both repulsed and fascinated as the first bandages came away in Katarina's hands to reveal a brown, decayed foot beneath. The dried skin that was barely covering the bones of the foot was thin and wrinkled, and it looked a little like the bark of an old tree as it stretched its way up to just below the ankle.

Katarina jumped back, letting out a gasp of disgust. 'I can't do anymore, someone else do it, please!' She quickly put her hand over her mouth and turned away.

Vivian seemed to find Katarina's reaction hilarious, and after she stopped laughing at her, she knelt down and unwrapped the ankle and some of the lower right leg.

Anna suddenly became aware of a faint ticking sound reverberating around the room. She realised that it hadn't been there when they'd first entered, it had started the moment that they had begun pulling at the bandages. The others hadn't noticed it yet, as far as she could tell. They all seemed transfixed by the sight of the almost skeletal foot.

Vivian released the bandages and stood back. 'So, who's going next? Harold? Come on, step on up. Go on, try the left foot.'

Harold coughed and then got down on his knees, a little awkwardly, then proceeded to unwrap the left foot. 'Oh my word, look at that!' he gasped. As Mark helped Harold back onto his feet, the group were all shocked to see that the left foot was far more misshapen than the right – in fact, it was missing its middle three toes.

'It's not a complete foot!' Mark remarked, unnecessarily. 'Perhaps it was broken in transit from wherever it came from? Or perhaps some animal got in and chewed those toes off – rats, maybe?'

'Perhaps this poor woman, whoever she may have been, lost these toes when she was still alive?' Harold suggested. 'It could have been an accident, I suppose. Or else someone chopped them off deliberately, and, I would imagine, painfully.'

Katarina made a sound of disgust from the corner of the room.

'I suppose I'll go next,' Anna said. She knelt down and her bare knees touched the cold floor. She looked between the two feet of the dead body and decided to choose the less deformed one. She took a deep breath, and then began pulling the bandages away from the corpse's right lower leg, and continued up to just below the knee, at which point the bandages seemed to have become much tighter, and resisted her attempts to go any further, so she abandoned her task with little reluctance. Anna couldn't help but retch as the smell hit her nostrils. 'You know, this is not how I usually like to spend my Friday evenings.'

'How *does* a woman like you spend her evenings?' Vivian enquired, with a smile.

'I'm not sure that's any of your business,' Anna answered. She rubbed her head, feeling a headache coming on.

'Then I'll have to rely on my imagination, or base it off what I used to do when I was your age, which was longer ago than I'd care to admit.'

'I really don't like the air in here, or the smell,' Harold announced, before he started coughing again. 'Mark, I think it's your turn.'

'Right.' Mark knelt and pulled the bandage away, revealing the left lower leg, and stood back up. He rubbed his arms. 'Is it me, or is it getting colder in here?'

'Do you all hear that sound?' Harold asked. 'Like a ticking clock?'

'Yes, I noticed it the moment we pulled the first bandages off,' Anna told him. 'It seems to be getting louder now.'

The others stopped to listen to the ticking.

Then there was a loud gong, at which point Katarina almost jumped out of her skin, and the ticking suddenly stopped. Vivian had her hand on her chest and complained, 'Was that loud noise really necessary? Almost gave me a bloody heart attack!'

An awful groaning sound made Anna's body go cold. She thought at first that the mummy was coming to life, furious about being awoken, enraged by their disrespectful pulling at its wraps, but then she realised that the sound was coming from behind her, and she turned to see the door slide open again, by itself. The dim lighting of the small room had faded away and now they couldn't see the corpse at all.

'I guess this means we're done for now?' Mark said. 'Time to leave this tomb?'

Katarina was first to leave, in a hurry, as if she couldn't bear to be trapped in that small dark room with that decaying body any longer, and the others swiftly followed. Mark was the last one out, after encouraging Harold and the ladies to go first, and as he exited the tomb the door slid shut behind him, locking the room and the mummified corpse away from their view. The door had now blended into the wall so well that it was almost as if it had never even been there.

They each returned to their chairs at the dining table. They glanced at one another, before taking in the sight that greeted them. The table had been laid. The signed and bloodied contracts, as well as the book that had unnerved Katarina, had been removed and were now replaced by plates and cutlery, glasses for water and wine, and patterned nap-kins. A cruet held a little army of silver pots for salt, pepper, vinegar, and oil. There was a decanter with a golden liquid inside blocked by a stopper that resembled a glass egg, and a jug of water, and in the centre of the table, flanked by two long candles, was a large silver serving dish covered by a dome. Anna's stomach grumbled as if anticipating what might be revealed should she lift the cover off the dish.

'Finally!' Vivian said. 'It appears dinner has been served. Shall we see what's on the menu?' She grinned as she leaned forward and took hold of the cover, and raised it off the dish. She revealed a cooked turkey on a bed of peas, green beans and carrots. 'It smells delicious! Everyone, sit down and I'll serve. Allow me to be your host for a while.'

The rest of the group proceeded to sit at their seats while Vivian reached across the table and picked up a sharp knife. Katarina looked at the knife-wielding woman warily, and then turned to look at the rest of her group. 'I don't know how any of you can think about eating after what we just saw in that room!'

Vivian laughed, finding amusement in Katarina's discomfort. She waved her knife at the rest of the group. 'What about the rest of you? Who's hungry?'

They held up their plates as Vivian served – all except for Katarina, who put her hand on her stomach and looked like she was about to throw up at any moment.

'I'm actually feeling quite hungry after all that excitement,' Harold said, tucking in.

'Me too,' Mark agreed. 'I seemed to have worked up an appetite.'

Anna tried not to think about the decaying body that she'd just seen, and focussed her attention instead on the food in front of her. She picked up her knife and fork, and started cutting at the meat. She cautiously took a bite, and told them, 'It's pretty good. If it is poisonous, at least it tastes nice.' She offered a piece to Katarina, who shook her head and turned away. Katarina didn't seem to have the stomach for any of this. *Fragile little thing, isn't she?* Anna smiled to herself.

Katarina suddenly got up from the table and went to stand near the door. The rest of the group continued to eat their food. They ate as if they'd not eaten for a week, and Anna guessed that was due to nerves and excitement. Mark and Harold were talking with their mouths full, impolitely, and discussing theories about who the mysterious body in the tomb might have belonged to.

Vivian took a few sips of wine and then commented to Anna, 'I have to say, I have no idea who that dead woman is in there, but I'm just happy not to be the oldest woman here this evening, nor the one with the worst skin! Oh, but to be young again, like you, Anna... I bet you have your pick of handsome men, don't you? I'm not exactly drowning in offers these days. You should enjoy it while it lasts.' She said it with a grin, and when Anna didn't smile back, Vivian added, 'Oh, lighten up, dear!' She looked across the room and said, 'You too, Katarina! This is all just a bit of fun. You young ladies need to learn to relax and enjoy things.'

Anna put her knife and fork down for a moment. 'I'm just wondering if we really came all this way just to peel bandages off a dead woman?'

Vivian shrugged. 'What's to complain about? Unique entertainment, decent company, alcohol and a meal? I've had worse evenings.'

The group continued eating and chatting. At one point Anna caught Mark's eyes, and he nodded his head towards Katarina, who did not look well at all. Anna slid her chair back away from the table. She stood and approached the young woman cautiously, and then asked, 'Is everything alright?'

Katarina put her hand up to indicate that Anna shouldn't come closer. 'Please, leave me alone. I'm sorry, I'm not feeling very well.'

'Perhaps if you had something to eat?'

Katarina shook her head. 'I don't think I could keep anything down.'

'It's probably being here in this strange place, seeing what we saw in that room, and the god-awful smell of it too.'

'It's not just that,' Katarina said, with a sigh. 'A while ago, I lost one of my best friends, her name was Jane. At her funeral I saw her body in the coffin, of course she didn't look anything like that body we just saw in that tomb, thank God, but still... it's a very painful memory for me.'

'I'm sorry,' Anna said.

Katarina looked back towards the dining table. 'That book that was hidden under the table, the empty journal... I used to have one just like it. My father gave it to me. The same size, the same cover, everything, although mine wasn't empty, it was nearly full. I used to write all kinds of things in it, including personal things, secret things, not just about myself, but about other people too. There were things in there that I wrote about Jane, my friend, things that I... regret. What a strange thing to find here in this house, and under my side of the dining table, as if it had been put there for me to find, as if someone knew what it would mean to me.'

'That is quite strange,' Anna agreed. 'I wonder why anyone would do that?'

'I don't know. Anna, I really don't feel well at all, and I'm so tired.'

Mark got up from his chair and joined them. He looked concerned. 'Perhaps we ought to see about calling a taxi to take Katarina home?' He took out his mobile phone, and frowned at it. 'Odd, I don't seem to have a signal.'

Anna tried her own phone, but had no luck. She sighed. 'Of course there's no signal. Well, that's just great.'

Vivian and Harold confirmed the same with their phones. 'I could take a walk around and try to find our elusive host,' Harold offered, standing up from the table. 'If I find anybody, I can let them know that we require assistance.'

'Good idea,' Vivian said. 'I'd like to come with you. I quite fancy exploring this house. I wonder what other secrets it might hold?'

'I think I'll stay here with Katarina,' Anna said. She hoped that would come off as caring and considerate, and not in any way cowardly.

'Then I think I'll stay and keep these young ladies company,' Mark said, smiling at Anna and Katarina.

Vivian followed Harold and they walked towards the door that led back to the hallway. Harold reached for the doorknob to open the door—

The door suddenly seemed to open itself. Harold and Vivian stepped back as a tall man with a long face entered the dining room, wearing a black suit, white shirt and a black tie. He greeted them with, 'Good evening, ladies and gentlemen. Thank you for coming. My name is Handsworth, I'm the butler here.'

As his eyes roved the room, they lingered briefly on Katarina, but even longer on Anna. After a moment, Handsworth turned away from her and asked them all, 'I trust you're enjoying your meals?'

'Oh yes, very good,' Vivian said, with a smile. 'Compliments to the chef, and all that.'

'I'll pass on your compliments, Vivian. I'm sure they'll be appreciated.'

'You know our names then?'

Handsworth smiled. 'Oh yes, I know all of you.'

Harold coughed for Handsworth's attention. 'Katarina here's not very well, so I think perhaps we ought to call it a night.'

Handsworth looked at Katarina. 'Yes, I can see that she appears rather unwell. Perhaps something she ate disagreed with her?' He pointed behind him and told them, 'You'll find the bathrooms are just down the hall, by the front doors.'

'Actually,' Anna said, 'she hasn't touched the food. More likely it's from being trapped in that tomb over there with that dead body. That's not something any of us signed up for.'

Handsworth took a step towards her. 'That's not quite true, is it? You all signed the contract and agreed to be here.'

Anna folded her arms. 'We didn't know *what* we were agreeing to. Who arranged all this, anyway? Was it you? Are you "H" from the letter?'

Handsworth shook his head and laughed. 'No, no, I'm merely the butler. My employer sent you those letters, and arranged for you all to be here on this special evening.'

'Your employer? Who might that be?'

'I'm afraid that they wish to remain anonymous, at least for now.'

'There was an empty book, a journal, stuck to the underside of the dining table, on Katarina's side,' Mark said. 'Who put that book there, and why?'

'I have no idea,' Handsworth replied. 'Perhaps someone left it there by mistake?'

'Taped to the table?' Mark said. He seemed dubious. 'And there was a note too.'

Anna caught Katarina glaring at Handsworth. She didn't seem to think it was just a mistake, and neither did Anna. That book had been put there deliberately, she was sure of it.

'Look, Katarina is obviously quite poorly,' Harold said, 'so would you please call a taxi to take her home?'

Handsworth approached Katarina and looked at her more closely. 'No, I think rather than send this girl on a long journey, it might be better if I took her upstairs to one of the bedrooms and let her sleep here for the night. If her symptoms don't improve by the morning, then I can call a doctor to come and take a look at her.'

Anna looked at Katarina, then back at Handsworth. 'I'm not comfortable with leaving her here by herself. I think one of us should stay with her.' When she saw no one else volunteering, Anna sighed and then said, 'I suppose it'll have to be me then.'

'That's not necessary,' Handsworth said. 'I can look after her. She'll be quite safe here.'

'Look, I don't particularly like the idea of spending the night here, but I know if it was me in that state, I wouldn't want to be left alone in some strange house with some strange man I didn't know – no offence.'

'None taken,' Handsworth replied, but Anna suspected that to be a lie. 'Does anyone else wish to spend the night?' he asked the others. 'If so, arrangements can be made.'

Harold answered first. 'No, thank you, I think I'd rather head home.'

'Yes, me too,' Mark agreed.

Vivian looked a little disappointed as she said, 'I suppose if this evening's entertainment has ended already, then I might as well be heading back too, since it's quite a journey.'

'Very good,' Handsworth said. 'I'll call for taxis to take you home. The front doors are unlocked and you may all leave at any time.' He turned to Anna. 'Now, shall we see about taking this young lady upstairs? You can help me, just so there can be no false accusations of any impropriety.'

'Does she need someone to carry her up the stairs?' Mark offered, stepping forward.

Katarina then spoke up, which surprised them all. 'I can walk, I don't need to be carried, thank you. Just show me to the room, and I'll manage.'

'Very well. Ladies, whenever you are ready...' Handsworth indicated that Anna and Katarina should follow him. To the others he said, 'Please remember that you have all agreed to return one week from today, for the next session.'

'Katarina, I hope you feel better soon!' Mark called out.

She gave him a sweet smile and replied, 'Thank you, Mark, I appreciate that. I look forward to seeing you all again soon. I'm sorry if I spoiled your evening.'

Anna said her goodbyes too, and accompanied Katarina as she followed Handsworth, who led them out of the dining room and into the hallway.

'How long have you worked here, Handsworth?' Anna asked.

'Oh, all my life. I've barely known anything *but* this house.'

'So are there other staff here?'

'Yes, of course. This house doesn't look after itself, and I couldn't manage it all on my own. Currently we have three housemaids employed here.' He paused to think. 'Yes, that's right, three. We lost the fourth just recently, she moved on. I sometimes forget their names, so many have come and gone over the years. One of our maids is also our cook, she's quite a talented woman. She'll be preparing all the meals for your sessions here. Now, let's see, I think I'll put you in the master bedroom, Katarina. And Anna—'

'I think we ought to share a room,' Anna said. 'I'd like to keep an eye on her.'

After a pause, Handsworth answered, 'Yes, of course. The master bedroom is large enough for the both of you. Katarina can take the bed, and I can bring you a pillow and blankets, if you'd like to sleep in a chair or on the floor.'

'That'll be fine.' Anna thought she could survive roughing it for one night. When she was young, she'd sometimes slept on the floor rather than having to share a cramped bed with her sister or brother. She could've asked Handsworth for a separate room, but she wasn't happy to leave Katarina alone in a room here, not in her vulnerable state.

They started to ascend the stairs, and Anna caught Katarina staring at her again. 'Thank you for staying with me, Anna. You seem like a good person.'

Anna chose not to argue with her. If this girl wanted to believe that, if it was going to make her feel safer, then fine, let her.

At the top of the staircase, the stag's head stared down at them. Giant antlers protruded from the top of its head. 'I don't like that thing,' Katarina commented. 'It makes me think of death.'

'I think it looks like some fearsome monster who could burst into life at any second and attack us...'

'You have quite the imagination,' Katarina said, smiling at her.

'So I've been told already tonight,' Anna replied.

'His name was Gerald and he was a gentle creature,' Handsworth told them, spoiling Anna's fantasies. 'He used to roam the woods out there, almost as if he was guarding this house. He was such a familiar sight that those who lived here gave him that name, and after he died, it was decided that his body, or at least his head, should be brought in here. And now he continues to watch over us all.'

Anna and Katarina exchanged glances as Handsworth led them away from Gerald. They turned left at the top of the stairs and walked along a corridor until they came to a door. Handsworth took out a key and unlocked the door, and they entered into a large bedroom. Inside was one of the most unusual beds that Anna had ever seen, a four-poster with strange markings running through the wood and a frilly fringe, with curtains tied to the back two columns. The canopy above bore a small image of a bird-like creature with outstretched wings.

Positioned against one wall was a wooden cabinet with a candelabra atop. The candles were already alight. In the corner of the room was a folding screen that would offer some privacy if Anna or Katarina wanted to change out of their clothes, although Anna had no intention of disrobing – after all, she couldn't be sure that they weren't being watched. There could be hidden cameras in the walls. Or she could be letting her over-active imagination loose again.

With some effort, Katarina lowered herself onto the bed. Anna offered to help Katarina take her shoes off but she declined, and when Anna reached out to pull the sheets over her, Katarina held up her hands and told her, 'Please, Anna, stop fussing over me! I'm not a child or an invalid. Leave the sheets off, I'm so hot now.'

Anna wondered if Katarina might be coming down with some kind of fever. She turned to Handsworth and said quietly, 'I think you should call that doctor you mentioned, I don't like the look of her.'

He nodded. 'Very well, I'll try, but there's no guarantee that he'll be available to see her tonight. I'll call him and then I'll bring you your blankets and pillows. Oh, and there's a jug of water and glasses on the chest of drawers over there, should you be thirsty. If you need anything else, at any time during the night, please pull the chain on the wall there and it will ring the bell for my attention.'

'Thank you, Handsworth,' Katarina said from her bed.

Handsworth returned to the door. He gave Anna a nod, and then left the room, closing the door behind him. Anna put her ear to the door and waited until she couldn't hear Handsworth's footsteps anymore, then tried the doorknob. She'd half-expected to find that they'd been locked in here, but no, the door opened freely. She closed it again and found a chair that she brought closer to the bed so that she could sit and watch Katarina, who lay on her back with her eyes closed already.

Katarina seemed to drift off to sleep quite quickly, but occasionally she would let out a moan, as if she was having a nightmare.

Anna sighed. This was going to be a long night.

As Katarina slept, Anna read the Bible, the only book that whoever lived here kept in their bedroom, although he or she kept it hidden away in a drawer in the cabinet along with a flimsy-looking wooden crucifix, and both were covered with dust. She needed something to help her stay awake, but the Good Book wasn't working very well, and she kept nodding off. She had tried her phone, but was unsurprised to find that the centuries-old Grimwald House had no Wi-Fi.

There was a soft knock on the door that at first she thought she'd only imagined, but then the door slowly opened, and Handsworth crept inside. Anna stared at him as he said quietly, 'I'm sorry, I wasn't able to reach the doctor, he must be unavailable this evening. How is Katarina?'

'I think she's alright,' Anna answered. 'She's still sleeping. I just want to keep an eye on her for now. To tell the truth, I'm having trouble staying awake.' She demonstrated this with a yawn.

'Perhaps a brief walk would help?' Handsworth offered his hand to Anna. She got up from her chair by herself, and followed Handsworth out of the room. As she closed the door behind her, Anna looked towards the bed where Katarina was sleeping and whispered a promise. 'I'll be back soon.'

In the corridor, Handsworth told her, 'Please feel free to wander around the house by yourself, but I'm afraid that you won't be able to enter most of the other rooms as the doors are locked for the evening, for everyone's safety.'

She decided to take him up on his offer, partly because she was anxious about Katarina and needed a distraction, and partly because Handsworth's company made her uncomfortable. She watched him leave and then she started walking, the dim candlelight doing nothing to dispel the oppressive atmosphere of the house.

As she walked, Anna saw several rooms with closed doors, and when she dared to try opening a few of them, she found that they were locked. There were so many corridors that it created a maze-like effect. She followed one short corridor that led to a long curtain blocking a window to the outside world. She pulled back the curtain to take a peek outside. She could see only endless woodland, the twisted silhouettes of the trees that guarded the house. It was deathly quiet here, and she suddenly felt very alone. She started to wish that the other guests had stayed in the house with them, rather than going home. A little joke or flirtatious remark from Mark to break the silence wouldn't have been unwelcome at that moment. She hoped that Katarina would recover from whatever ailment she had, but even if she did feel better, she wouldn't be travelling tonight, which meant Anna was stuck here until the morning.

She continued exploring, passing by more rooms. At the end of one corridor she found a grandfather clock, with the hour hand poised at the *IX* on its face. Anna was sure that the clock must be slow, but when she checked her phone, the times matched. It just felt like she'd been here a lot longer than she had.

In one corridor, she noticed a panel in the ceiling that she thought must lead to the attic. There was a handle to pull it down, which presumably would drop a ladder for her to climb up. But Anna decided to leave it well alone; there was no way she was going to climb up into some dark, dusty, bug-infested old attic on her own. She wasn't that stupid.

In some ways, Grimwald House reminded her of the grand old houses that she'd visited as a child on trips with her family, back when her father had still been alive. She and her brother and sister would marvel at huge houses like this one and joke about someday earning enough money to afford one themselves. Anna was the only one for whom the idea wasn't so ridiculous anymore, as neither of her siblings had been anywhere near as successful in their careers as she had, and she had fallen out with both of them several times over the years, usually because they had come to her asking for money, "*Sucking at your teat until it's raw!*" as her recently-divorced financial advisor had once so graphically described it. It had eventually reached the point where she'd started thinking of herself as an only child – it was better that way.

Yes, Anna could probably afford to buy a large house like this one if she wanted to, but she much preferred her luxury apartment on the tenth floor of the Thornton building. She liked her mod-cons. A big, modern open-plan apartment suited her better than a place like this with its endless dark, twisting corridors, where something nasty could be waiting for you around every corner. No, when she opened a door to a room in her home, she wanted to find nothing more intimidating behind it than her one hundred inch TV. You could keep your secret tombs and hidden corpses, thank you very much.

Still, she had to admit that the strangeness and mystery of this evening had intrigued her, even excited her, just a little. She could try to see this as a refreshing change, something to enjoy, if only she didn't feel so unnerved by it all. With the occasional exception, her life could often be quite samey and boring, working long hours for her business rather than doing anything more adventurous. She was the boss of her company, but the work she did was often just as mundane as those beneath her. On those days, she felt ordinary, and not special at all, although Anna knew that anyone who was privy to her best-kept secrets might question that statement – not that anyone was, of course.

Anna stopped suddenly. Was that a baby's cries that she could hear? It sounded like it was coming from around the corner, from the next corridor. She must have imagined that, surely?

No, there it was again: a kind of whimpering sound. *What is that?*

She glanced back the way she had come, and then decided that she really should have left a breadcrumb trail to help her find her way back, because right now she was lost. She wondered whether she should try to call out for Handsworth, but she realised that she wouldn't feel any safer with him by her side – more likely, the opposite. No, she was going to have to go and investigate the creepy noise in the creepy old house by herself, as insane as that idea might seem.

Anna crept cautiously around the corner, squinting, ready to squeeze her eyes shut if she didn't like what she saw.

A beast stared back at her with big, droopy eyes, long ears, and a long nose. Drool was coming from its mouth.

She stopped and stared at it, not sure whether to back away or to stay standing still. The decision was taken out of her hands when the creature waddled towards her on its four short legs. She knelt down, and cautiously gave the dog some fuss. It wagged its tail. 'Good girl!' she said, rubbing behind its ears. 'What's your name, then, you odd little thing?'

Unsurprisingly, it didn't reply to her question, but when she managed to take hold of its collar she found a name there: *Ebony*. Stroking the animal helped Anna feel a little calmer. It was nice to have a friend in this unfriendly place.

The dog suddenly started growling and bared its teeth. Anna withdrew her hand and then froze. Ebony had seemed quite content, why was she turning on Anna now?

The animal backed away from her, then turned, and began to waddle away.

A hand then touched Anna's shoulder, making her jump, and she spun around to see Handsworth's angry face. 'Silly bitch,' he muttered. He pointed at the dog. 'Her name is Ebony. Roams this house like she owns the place, forever getting in places she shouldn't and causing trouble. She should know better by now.'

'It's alright, she's fine,' Anna told him. 'I actually like animals more than I do most people, to tell the truth.'

'I expect you do. Shall we return to Katarina now?'

Anna nodded, and walked behind Handsworth as he led her back to the master bedroom. He seemed to have no trouble navigating the maze of corridors. She glanced back as they walked, but she saw no sign of the dog. As they passed by an adjoining corridor, Anna glanced down that corridor and at the end of it she could see a large black door that she hadn't seen before. She stopped and stared at it for a while, before Handsworth told her, 'Keep moving, please.'

As they walked, she caught Handsworth looking at her curiously. 'I have to say, Anna, you seem rather familiar to me. Where do you think I might have seen you before?'

She shrugged. 'I don't know. I design clothes, so if you're a keen reader of fashion magazines then you might have seen me in an article or two. I have done a couple of interviews on TV too. Otherwise, I have no idea.'

'It doesn't matter. Perhaps I'm mistaken.'

Eventually they reached the master bedroom. Handsworth knocked softly then entered first, with Anna following. They found Katarina sitting up on the bed. She looked a little brighter than she had done before. 'How are you feeling?' Anna asked her.

'A little better, thank you. I'm sure I'll be fine by the morning.' Katarina glanced at Handsworth and then back at Anna. 'If it's not a bother to you, Anna, I'd still like you to stay in here with me tonight. Is that alright?'

Anna nodded, and approached the bed. 'That's fine. That's why I'm here. I'm not going anywhere.'

Katarina lowered her eyes. 'When I woke up and saw that you weren't here, I was worried that you'd left me here alone and might have decided to go back home.'

'No, I went for a walk, that's all, and I got a little lost until Handsworth found me,' Anna explained. 'This house is like a labyrinth. But anyway, I'm back now, and I won't leave you again, I promise.'

Katarina gave her an appreciative smile. Handsworth pointed to a pile on the floor that included a pillow and blankets. 'I hope those are sufficient. I'll leave you two ladies alone now. I hope you're both able to get a good night's sleep.'

'We'll see,' Anna replied, as Handsworth left the room, and closed the door behind him.

'I don't think he likes me,' she told Katarina, 'and the feeling's mutual. He's seriously odd, but I suppose he fits right in here, in this godforsaken place.'

Katarina frowned at her. 'Do you really hate this house that much?'

Anna shrugged. 'It has far too many rooms, and it doesn't seem to want me to see what's inside any of them. But it does have a funny little dog named Ebony. That's the nicest thing I can say about this place. I prefer cats to dogs, and I've seen no cats here so far, but who knows what kind of creatures roam these halls? At home, I have this little devil of a furball named Jelly. I miss that stupid cat.'

'Jelly? What an odd name for a cat!' Katarina exclaimed.

'Well, he's an odd cat. I got him as a kitten and he was this timid little thing, so Jelly seemed like an appropriate name at the time, and it stuck.'

'I never had a pet as a child,' Katarina said sadly. 'My father wouldn't allow it.'

'Then you should meet Ebony, I think you two would get on. Anyway, is there anything you need?'

Katarina shook her head. 'Just some sleep, I think, and also to know that you're here, watching out for me, and that you're not going to leave me again. It means a lot to me that you're here with me.'

Anna felt uncomfortable with the gratitude. 'It's no problem. I just want you to get better.'

'I'll try. Goodnight. Sleep well, Anna.'

'You too.'

As Katarina lay her head back down and closed her eyes, Anna picked up the Bible again, and sat back in her chair. Occasionally she glanced up from the text and watched Katarina sleep for a while. She watched her chest rise and fall, and occasionally Anna had moments of irrational panic when that chest suddenly stopped moving for a whole four or five seconds, before it then resumed its movement, and Anna could breathe again too.

The young woman didn't look quite so sickly while she slept. She looked calm, peaceful, and beautiful. Annoyingly beautiful. Sometimes Katarina's lips moved as she slept, like she was having a conversation in her dreams. Anna wondered what she was dreaming about, and hoped that it was something pleasant.

She could do with some nice dreams herself. On more than one occasion in the past few months, Anna had woken up to find her sheets wet, her skin sticky, and her mind still hanging onto the fading embers of a nightmare, one that she could never recall by the time she got out of bed and went to the bathroom to wash the sweat off her body. She put it down to working too hard and too late too many times. She knew that it wasn't a great idea to be staring at her computer screen until the early hours right before going to bed. But the work needed doing. If she wanted to keep that bank balance looking so good then she had to keep working hard. She had her team, but at the end of the day, it was her vision that had built her company, and she was the only one that truly understood what made her clothes so special, and only she knew what it took to make her business so successful.

Anna had once had a boyfriend who'd criticised her about her working hours, telling her that she was working herself into an early grave, and to be fair to him, he was not wrong; she usually felt like a zombie on those late nights in front of her computer, and her health had sometimes suffered.

Back at home in her apartment, Jelly would often try to sit on her lap while she worked on her newest fashion project. She'd stroke the cat to relax herself while she planned her world domination, just like a James Bond villain, although occasionally she'd have to tell him to get off if his sharp claws were digging into her legs. Sometimes, he'd sit himself at the foot of her bed while she slept, as if intending to protect her from any dream demons that might come for her in the night. She missed that big lump of fur right now, but he probably wouldn't even care that Anna was gone, at least not until he needed feeding again. If she just closed her eyes and pictured her apartment in her mind, she could put herself back there with Jelly, and the two of them could be sitting on her comfortable sofa, or curled up on her big soft bed, where it was safe, and warm, and she wouldn't have to worry about scary tombs with dead bodies...

Anna opened her eyes as she heard the chime of the grandfather clock somewhere out in that maze of corridors, which reminded her that she was still here at Grimwald House, somewhere much less warm and much less comforting. She sighed as she stared down at the floor, which didn't look very comfortable. She could sleep in this chair, but she was bound to wake up with a stiff neck and other aches and pains if she did that. She raised herself from her chair, ever so carefully, hoping the creaking of the wood as she moved wouldn't wake the sleeping princess on the bed. She opened the blanket out onto the floor, then positioned the pillow at one end, and lay herself down, careful not to bump her head on the chest of drawers. Her head appreciated the softness of the pillow, and her body the warmth of the blanket as she wrapped it around herself as tightly as the wraps that had bound that dead woman's body—

Stop it! She didn't want to remind herself of that hideous thing in the tomb downstairs. As she lay there, the flickering of the candles from the candelabra cast odd shadows about the room. Anna closed her eyes. She hoped she wouldn't have any nightmares tonight, since she was without Jelly to comfort and protect her. She didn't want to wake up having drenched the blanket with sweat and then have to hand that over to Handsworth and the maids come morning, along with an apology.

She told herself to think pleasant thoughts, yet she struggled to think of any. She heard many odd creaks and groans, some far off in the distance, some disturbingly close, as the old house settled in for the night.

Sleep! You need to sleep!

An hour later, she finally drifted away.

Waking up, getting her bearings, she found herself in a strange, un-familiar place, but worse still, she suddenly realised that something crucial was absent, and when the fog of sleep had finally cleared from her mind, she knew what it was – or more accurately, *who* it was – that was missing. Katarina was gone. Her bed was empty.

There was a tiny sliver of daylight invading the darkness through the curtains. It was morning. Standing up and stretching, feeling her body aching from lying on the floor all night, Anna looked around, wondering why Katarina had left and why no one had thought to wake her. She wondered if she should go looking for her? She rang the bell to summon Handsworth, and waited impatiently for him to arrive, and when he finally did, she demanded to know what had happened to Katarina.

He informed her that Katarina had recovered and had felt well enough to go home, but that they had decided not to wake Anna and disturb her sleep. She was reluctant to take Handsworth's word for it but she wasn't sure that she had any other choice. Feeling drained, she wanted to get out of this place and go home. She was hungry so she took breakfast in the dining room downstairs by herself. Handsworth brought her bacon, sausage, egg and toast. She devoured it all, leaving behind only an empty plate.

When Anna had finished her breakfast, she heard a car arrive at the house. She opened the front doors and saw a taxi waiting for her. She recognised the driver as the same one who had brought her to the house, but when she waved at him, he didn't wave back.

Anna looked back inside the house. She could try to find Handsworth to say goodbye to him, but she had no desire to stay in this house a moment longer than she needed to. She stepped outside and closed the doors behind her, then made her way to the waiting taxi to begin her long journey home.

Anna was startled when the taxi driver woke her from her sleep and told her that her journey was already over and that she was home. She felt relieved. It was almost like a form of time travel or teleportation, to close your eyes in one place and then wake up somewhere else entirely without even noticing the time pass. She yawned as she looked out of the window and up at her apartment building. Somewhere up there, her bed and her cat were waiting for her.

She stepped out of her taxi and into the warm morning sunshine. She entered the building and rode the elevator up to her apartment. She grunted a greeting to another resident, a snooty woman who eyed Anna's shiny but rather rumpled dress and clearly thought she had been up to no good last night.

Anna fumbled with her keycard to unlock her apartment door, and wandered inside unsteadily. She bumped her shin on her coffee table, swore, and tried to ignore the growls and dirty looks from Jelly, who was only a cat and had no right to judge her like this. She gave him some food to shut him up.

She closed the door to her bedroom, took off her dress, then tumbled onto her soft, familiar bed, face forward into her pillow, wondering how she still felt so tired even when she'd slept for most of the night and during the taxi ride this morning as well. She heard Jelly scratching at her bedroom door, and yelled at him to stop it, and eventually he did.

Even though it was a Saturday, she had some work that needed doing, so she couldn't allow herself to sleep all day, even if that was all that she felt like doing at that moment.

Anna told herself that she'd only rest for a few minutes, maybe half an hour, and that she wouldn't allow herself to have any thoughts about creepy old houses and long-dead mummies, but she soon found that she could think of nothing else.

CHAPTER TWO

KATARINA

After that bizarre experience at Grimwald House, Katarina had struggled to get the horrible image of that bandaged body in the tomb out of her mind.

As per the instructions in the invitation letter that she'd received, she hadn't told anyone else where she'd gone or what had happened, not even her parents, and that was fine with her, because she didn't want to think about it. She'd told her parents only that she'd been invited to an exclusive event with some important people, and that it might be a good way for her to make some contacts that might benefit the family.

She was not looking forward to having to return for the next four sessions, but she'd signed an agreement in ink and blood and felt that she had no choice. However, she kept finding herself back there at that house prematurely, unwillingly, whenever she allowed her thoughts to drift. She'd desperately needed a distraction, and she'd hoped that this evening would provide one.

Katarina had tried to continue with her life as normal, and that meant things like attending parties such as this one where she would be expected to socialise with her father's friends. There was a time not so long ago that the idea of going to lavish parties like this one with so many people all mingling together in such a carefree fashion might have seemed like a fantasy, but they seemed to have become even more frequent now, as if everyone was making up for lost time.

She couldn't even remember the name of the woman whose party this was, only that she was the daughter of a friend of her father's, and that it was her birthday. Katarina's father had insisted that she attend, and when her father insisted on something then he always got what he wanted. She knew better than to argue with him.

Her stomach had suddenly taken a turn for the worse after eating something unrecognisable from the buffet table. Or perhaps she hadn't fully recovered from that strange evening at Grimwald House? She made her way upstairs to a bathroom. She went inside and locked the door behind her. She stared at her reflection in the mirror, willing herself not to be sick. She knew that she mustn't show weakness, or else her father would be displeased with her. She told herself that she only had to stand a few more hours of this and then she could go home and wrap herself up in her bedsheets and hide away from the world. The question then was whether she'd be able to sleep or whether she'd have more nightmares about that body in the tomb.

Katarina cupped her hands and took a drink of water, and then cupped them again to splash cold water on her face. There was a knock on the bathroom door. 'Just a moment, please!' she called out. She checked herself in the mirror and then unlocked the door. An older woman in some discomfort pushed past Katarina as she exited the bathroom. Perhaps she too had eaten something that had disagreed with her?

Katarina descended the red-carpeted staircase to rejoin the party. This house was smaller than Grimwald House, and it was a far more brightly-lit and welcoming place. She didn't fear the corridors and rooms of this house, just the people in it and their expectations of her.

Although she had no particular desire to attract attention, she found that sometimes she couldn't help it. It was almost as if people had never seen someone with darker skin like hers, which she thought was ridiculous in this day and age. However, considering the circles that her father usually travelled in, perhaps it wasn't so surprising; she knew that there was a rich white elite whose exclusive ways she felt ought to have died out by now. It was one of the reasons that Katarina's mother, who was born in Africa, often avoided attending these kinds of parties. But Katarina's mother and father had told her often that despite what anyone might say about her parentage, it didn't mean that she was any worse – or any better – than anyone else. The problem was that people who met her often seemed to expect her to be exotic and interesting, and when she disappointed them, they soon turned their attentions elsewhere. Despite the best efforts of her parents and tutors, Katarina still found it hard to fit in with these people, and she always feared that she'd say the wrong thing.

One thing that she'd always been good at, however, was gossip. She loved finding out little secrets, which she wrote down in her journal, and then she'd share them with other people, and it made her feel powerful, and appreciated. It helped get people to like her – at least for as long as it took her to finish disclosing the things that she'd discovered. However, since the awful incident with her friend Jane, Katarina had sworn to herself that she would stop getting involved in other people's lives and spreading their secrets. But as she stepped aside to avoid a trio of young women near the foot of the staircase, she couldn't help but overhear their conversation and take an interest in it.

'It's horrid!' one woman said, shaking her head.

'I heard the police have no idea who this awful man might be,' another said.

'Those poor women!' the third woman said.

Intrigued, Katarina hovered closer to the women, pretending to be busy examining a beautiful and probably very expensive vase.

'Do you think he used a knife, or scissors?'

'Perhaps it was one of those nasty shears people use for gardening?'

'I don't want to think about it, it will give me nightmares.'

'I heard he has his wicked way with them first, before he kills them.'

'Oh, don't believe every scandalous thing you hear! The rumour mill does love to embellish these things.'

'I don't think there's any need for embellishment, I think having a part of your body cut off before you're murdered is quite horrifying enough!'

Katarina stifled a gasp and kept her eyes on the vase, as another of the women said, 'Let's hope that awful man remains fixated on killing only foreign girls, and not girls like us, so we can all sleep soundly in our beds. I would expect—'

Katarina heard one of the women shush her, and realised that the trio had now spotted her. She didn't look at them as she moved away and went back to the main room. She picked up a glass from a tray and started drinking. Was this true? Was there some killer out there, hunting and murdering "foreign" girls like herself? Should she be worried? Especially if the police had no idea who he was. He could be anyone...

She was suddenly aware of someone watching her from the crowd of people mingling in the room. There was a young man staring directly at her, with a tiny smile on his lips. She looked away, but when she looked back, he was still there, and still staring at her.

She told herself not to jump to conclusions. This was just another young man eyeing her up, and she should be used to that. There was no reason to think that he had any worse designs on her than most men did.

Katarina suddenly wanted her father. Normally at events like these she would try to avoid him unless her presence by his side was absolutely necessary. Her father was not a kind man; the nicest thing that he'd ever given to his daughter was her name, which was taken from a picture of a beautiful woman named Katarina in a book that he'd acquired during a journey across Europe as a young man. Right now, though, she desperately wanted to see a familiar face, so she made her way through the crowd, careful to avoid getting too close to that odd young man, thinking that once she'd found her father she might feel a little safer.

She thought that she'd spotted the back of her father's head, so she adjusted her direction to head towards him, when suddenly a hand caught hold of her arm and spun her around. She was about to cry out for help until she saw who it was. She wasn't too surprised to see William here at this event, and she also wasn't too unhappy about it either.

She'd first met William in rather unusual circumstances. It was the day of her friend Jane's funeral, and Katarina had made her escape straight after the service, unable to face Jane's family or anyone else. She had believed that each pair of eyes on her during the service had been judging her, condemning her, even if none of them could have known what she'd done. Earlier that day, she'd taken her journal and had burned it in the fireplace at home, destroying all of the personal thoughts and secrets that she'd written in there about herself and others – including some things about Jane.

Katarina had wandered through the cemetery, wanting to be alone. The heel of her left shoe had suddenly broken, and in anger, she'd thrown the shoe away and it had bounced off a gravestone. She'd then heard a gasp and a handsome man had stepped out from behind a tree. He had seemed as surprised to see her as she was to see him. He'd noticed her one shoe and her other bare foot, and he'd seemed amused and intrigued. He'd then brought her missing shoe back to her, remarking that she had lovely feet as he did so. He'd introduced himself as William Taylor, and she had told him her name, and then they'd talked for a while. She'd been unable to stop the tears flowing, and explained to him that she was upset due to her friend's death, and he'd comforted her. She had thought that she'd wanted to be alone, but she'd quickly realised that what she really needed was someone to help her feel better and to take her mind off her grief and her guilt.

Katarina had found William interesting and attractive, and after they'd parted that day, she'd thought about him often, and it wasn't long before they encountered each other again, at a party for one of her father's business associates. Since then, they'd bumped into each other several more times, and had become friends – and even, for one special night, something more. William was intelligent, polite and kind, and paid her more attention than anyone ever had before. He was around ten years her senior, but with a boyish, handsome face. He had once told her what he did for a living, but she'd been lost in the warmth of his bedsheets at the time, and the information eluded her when she tried to recall it now.

Katarina's father liked William and had encouraged her to become his friend, although her father did not know quite how friendly the two of them had become.

Her friend Jane's death had hit Katarina very hard, and it was strange for her to think now that something so tragic had led to something so good.

William smiled at her. 'Hello again, Kat. I was hoping to see you tonight.'

She smiled back. 'Hello, William. How are you?'

'Very well, thank you. All the better for seeing your lovely face again.'

She averted her eyes, feeling embarrassed. 'I was looking for my father, have you seen him?'

He leaned in closer to her, gently put his hand on her arm, and said softly in her ear, 'Now, do you really want your father, or would you rather I kept you company?'

'William, please, not here.' She took a step back from him, her eyes darting around the room, fearful of what others might think.

He held up his hands. 'I happen to be speaking to the most beautiful woman that I've seen all evening, and I'd like to spend more time with her. Is that a crime?'

'No, of course not,' Katarina replied. 'I'm sorry. There are just so many people here, and there's all this noise...'

He reached out and took her hand. 'Then let's go somewhere quieter, where we can talk.'

She caught that strange young man staring at her again. He didn't seem to move at all. He was frozen in place, almost like a statue, and that thought suddenly reminded Katarina of that strange body standing up in the tomb at Grimwald House. She shuddered and turned back to William and said, 'Yes, I think I'd like to get out of here now.'

'Great,' William said, as he put his hand in hers and then led her out of the main room and into the garden, where she could look up and see the night sky, which was dotted with stars.

'Mmm, breathe that air, would you?' William said, closing his eyes and taking deep breaths.

She kept her eyes open and breathed in deep. 'It *is* nice.'

He opened his eyes and looked at her. 'It's wonderful. And so are you. You look incredible this evening.'

'William—'

'I know, I know. I can't help myself! You're twice the woman of any of that lot in there. They're all bitter old hags or dumb young gossips, the lot of them. But you're different. You're unique.'

Katarina felt herself go hot in the cheeks, even more so when he moved his hands to her waist and told her, 'Let's dance out here by ourselves for a while, and see what happens.'

She frowned. 'I can't hear the music out here, and without that, we can't dance.'

He laughed. 'We don't need music.' Then he took her hand, and twirled her around. She couldn't help the smile that filled her face. He hummed a pleasant tune in her ear as they danced – it was her favourite song. He'd remembered it.

'I'd very much like to see you again,' William said, 'but just the two of us, perhaps tomorrow night? Could I come calling around eight o'clock?'

'I'm not sure that would be such a good idea. What about my parents?'

'Sneak out of the house if you need to, I know it wouldn't be the first time you've done that.'

'Where would we go?'

'I have a place in mind, but it's a surprise. You'll have to trust me. Do you trust me?'

He stroked her bare arm with his fingers, and she felt a tingle through her body. She nodded at him. 'Yes, I trust you.'

'Wonderful!' He beamed at her. 'You won't regret it, I promise you. I'll show you the night of your life!'

'You ought to be careful about making promises that you might not be able to keep,' she teased him.

'Ah, you'll see. I might surprise you.' William looked away from her for a moment, his attention drawn back to the house. 'You know, I think I may have some competition. It seems I'm not the only man with eyes for you this evening. Hardly a surprise, really. Is that man over there a friend of yours? Don't say he's your lover, because I think hearing that might just kill me. Or else I'd have to kill him.'

Katarina followed his gaze. That strange young man was staring at her again from behind a window at the house. What was wrong with him? What did he want with her?

'I don't know who that man is,' she told William, 'but he keeps staring at me, and has been doing so all evening. It is bothering me, especially after some of the stories that I've heard tonight.'

'Don't worry about him,' William said, glaring at the other man. 'You're with me, and if he wants trouble, then he'll get it, and he won't like it.'

Katarina put her hand on his arm. 'No, William, please don't start fighting again, you remember what happened before. If it wasn't for my father intervening, you would've been prevented from attending any more events like this. I don't think he would be very happy if he found out you'd got yourself into that kind of trouble again.'

William sighed. 'Fine. You know that I've no desire to anger your father, I admire him, and I've certainly no intention of getting on his bad side – I've seen that rather nasty-looking sword that he keeps in his study...' He grinned. 'Besides, I'd much rather dance, than fight, any day.'

They continued dancing, Katarina trying to ignore the man staring at them and choosing to look at William and the stars instead. William gradually moved his body closer to hers as they danced, and his fingers interlocked with hers, sealing the two of them together, and then she could feel the warmth of his body pressed up against her own, and it was comforting in the cool night air. Since they couldn't hear the music anyway, they could decide when the dance should end, and for the moment, she was quite happy for it to continue forever.

Katarina spent much of the next day thinking about William and their dance, and their upcoming meeting. Irrational thoughts had entered her head, crazy thoughts about marriage proposals. She'd always felt an attraction towards William, but despite that one intimate night that they'd spent together, she'd never considered having a serious relationship with him. But the magic of last night's dance had swayed her. She couldn't seem to concentrate on anything – a fact that her father had pointed out repeatedly during their brief conversations earlier that day.

She took her dinner and rushed through it, then went back to her bedroom to get ready. From seven o'clock onwards, she spent most of the hour staring at the clock and willing it to advance. Finally it approached eight and she crept downstairs carefully, avoiding her father, who she knew by now would be in his study with a drink in his hand, the first of many. Once, as a child, she'd made the mistake of opening the door to his study and had found him swinging his antique sword around, drunkenly slurring the words of a song, and he had only narrowly missed lopping off her head. It was best not to disturb him whenever he retired to his favourite room.

Katarina knew that her mother would be in bed already, having taken whatever pills she was taking nowadays, so she was much less of a threat. She opened the front door slowly and carefully, wincing at any sound it made, fearful that she might be heard, then stepped through and closed the door behind her.

At the far end of the path that meandered from her father's house to the street, she could see William standing there, flowers in his hand, and a car parked behind him. When she reached him, Katarina accepted the flowers and also a kiss on the cheek. She pressed him for clues as to their destination but he wouldn't give anything away, saying it would spoil the romantic evening that he had planned if he did.

She was determined not to let anything ruin this evening. She was going to enjoy herself, wherever the evening might take her.

The car deposited the two of them on a hill overlooking a river below. William's driver remained in the car as they stood and admired the view, which even in the dark was breathtaking. There was no one else around, and it was as if they had the whole world to themselves.

'It's beautiful!' Katarina exclaimed, beaming at William.

'I'm glad you like it. I've always thought this was a very romantic spot. You can see for miles. The boats down there on the water with their little lights, mirrored in the stars shining brightly in the sky... I find it all rather magical.'

'Can I assume that you bring a lot of women up here, then?'

He looked offended. 'Of course not! You're the first. The only.'

'I'm sorry, I find that hard to believe.'

'Alright, you've caught me, there may have been one or two before you. But not many, and I only bring the most special ones here, I swear. You can believe me.'

Katarina smiled. She didn't even care if he might be lying.

They sat down on a blanket on the grass, and for several minutes they said nothing, just staring at the view, and then into each other's eyes.

'God, I love that smile,' he told her. Then he placed a kiss on the knuckles of her left hand. 'I love these fingers too.' He gently stroked her fingers, then he reached down and slowly took off her left shoe. 'But I especially adore these gorgeous toes of yours... you have no idea how much.'

She giggled as he caressed her foot with his fingers. 'Oh, stop it, they're only toes, they're nothing special. You can be so silly at times!'

Katarina was happy here, in this place, with William by her side. That horrible evening at Grimwald House felt like a bad dream that was gradually fading away.

William reached for her hand, and squeezed it. 'I need to be honest with you, I do have an ulterior motive for bringing you up here, beyond showing you this wonderful view.'

Katarina suddenly felt very nervous. *Was this it? Was William going to propose to her?*

'Oh yes?' she said. 'And what might that be?'

He took a deep breath. 'Kat, I've never stopped thinking about you and that night that we spent together. I go to those parties, always hoping that you'll be there. I have tried to put you out of my mind, and I'll admit there have been other women, but I've rarely found anyone as interesting as you. I think you've captured my heart, Kat. I think I love you.

'Ever since I first saw you, it's like you've cast some spell on me. Whenever I see you, I then can't stop thinking about you for days. I dream of you, and your body, and all I can think about is what I'd like to do to you...'

Katarina swallowed hard, as she felt William's hand touch her cheek, then work its way slowly down her body. 'What exactly is it that you want to do to me?' she asked, trembling.

Then he leaned in, and kissed her on the lips. She closed her eyes and allowed herself to become lost in the moment. When he finally took his lips away from hers, it pained her.

'Wait here, and keep your eyes closed, I have another surprise for you. I'll be back in just a minute.'

'Alright, but don't be too long,' Katarina said, smiling at him. She closed her eyes and heard William walk away, and wondered what he might have planned for her. She pictured him getting down on one knee, and holding out a ring to her.

She heard a strange noise and resisted the urge to open her eyes and peek, but she wasn't sure how much longer she could wait. She was desperate to know what William was up to, and also desperate for him to be beside her and touching her again.

She heard some footsteps approach her. She kept her eyes shut tight, knowing that it must be William returning with whatever her big surprise was.

'William, you are terrible, keeping me waiting like that!' Katarina called out, trembling with anticipation. 'What are you up to?'

There was no answer.

Suddenly she felt something touching her lips, and then her nose – it was odd, it felt like a cold, wet cloth, and it had a very unpleasant smell. *What is that?! It's horrible!*

When she opened her eyes again she found that the night sky had somehow lost all of its stars and that the river had faded away, and then she could only barely make out a blurred face staring down at her, and she tried to cry out but couldn't, and then that face disappeared too, until eventually she could see nothing at all.

Katarina awoke to a blinding light.

When her eyes could finally focus, she found herself in a bright white room, lying on a bed, with an unfamiliar man standing over her. He looked down at her and said, very slowly, as if speaking in slow motion, 'Hello, Katarina. I'm a doctor. Please try to remain calm, you've had quite an ordeal. Your father is outside waiting to speak to you, but I wanted to talk to you first to explain what has happened to you.'

'I don't understand,' she said groggily, 'what's going on?'

'This is all going to come as quite a shock, I'm afraid, and there's no easy way to tell you, but I believe you should know the facts. You were attacked by a man the police believe has mutilated and killed several young women.'

Katarina heard the words but they did not sink in. 'What?'

'Yes, you were attacked, and if your friend hadn't returned and frightened the man off, then there's a good chance that you would have become just another victim, and you wouldn't be speaking to me, or to anyone. William was injured in the struggle with this man – your friend is fine, not to worry, but he was unable to prevent the man from, well, taking a "souvenir", as the police have called it.'

'What does that mean?'

The doctor slowly pulled the bedsheets away from her body.

Katarina stared down at her left foot. There was a gap where her three middle toes should have been.

'No!' she cried out.

'Now please calm yourself, young lady, I think you have to count yourself lucky. Thankfully William was able to bring you here to the hospital – if he hadn't acted as quickly as he did, then it could have been far worse. I heard that he gave a description of your attacker to the police, so there's no need to worry, I'm sure this man will be brought to justice soon enough. Now, try to compose yourself, and I'll bring in your father to see you.'

His voice faded out, and Katarina couldn't drag her eyes away from her incomplete foot. She tried to close her eyes but found that when she did, she couldn't get the image of that horrible mummified corpse at Grimwald House out of her mind, so now she was afraid to close her eyes, and even more afraid to open them. She wanted to cry, but the tears would not fall.

Katarina placed a shoe on her right foot, and then carefully placed the other shoe over her left foot. She knew that it wouldn't be long now before the bandages would be removed and she would be free of them, but then she would have to face the sight of her damaged body. She would be forced to see her now incomplete foot and the stitches where her three toes ought to be.

She walked over to her dressing table, where she sat and stared at her reflection. She had this odd sensation of not recognising herself in the mirror anymore. She told herself that she was being ridiculous and that the woman staring back at her was still Katarina. A few missing toes didn't change that. She glanced at the walking stick that had been given to her when she'd left the hospital, but she was determined not to have to use it tonight.

She'd chosen this particular dress to wear because it was the same one that she'd been wearing on that terrible night when she'd been attacked. She wanted to wear it tonight to show William that she was still the same woman that she had been, the one that he'd said he'd fallen in love with, and that her attacker hadn't taken everything away from her, only a small part of her. She glanced at the clock on her wall; it was a quarter to eight. William would arrive here at her father's house at any moment, so she needed to be ready. She stood up, and walked out of her bedroom, then along the corridor, pausing outside her mother's bedroom. She placed her ear to the door and waited there just long enough to hear her mother's snores. She hoped the pills her mother took would keep her dead to the world for the rest of the night, so it wouldn't matter what noises might come from downstairs.

Her father was out at another party and hadn't invited Katarina because he was embarrassed by all the fuss that she'd caused with her little "accident", as he'd called it. In fact, he'd barely spoken to her at all since she'd returned from the hospital, except to insist that she write an apology to William for "putting him in danger". She'd also overheard him telling her mother that this was Katarina's own fault and that if she would just dress and behave properly then things like this wouldn't happen to her.

Katarina had worked up the courage to send a message to William, telling him that she was desperate to see him again, and after she'd awoken from another difficult night, she'd discovered a card had been left on their doorstep with a picture of a heart on the front, and inside it simply said: *Eight*.

Katarina waited in the hallway, her eyes never leaving the front door. She took deep breaths, and wished her body would stop shaking. It would be extremely embarrassing, and would spoil all her plans for this evening, if she were to faint the moment that she opened the door and saw William's face again for the first time since that night.

She froze when she heard a knocking at the door. Through the obscured glass, she saw a tall dark figure standing outside, waiting to be let in. One more deep breath, and a quick prayer to God to help her be strong tonight, and then she opened the door.

She saw William's eyes immediately crawl down her body, hesitating on her feet, before he looked up and said, 'Good evening, Kat. You look wonderful, as ever.' He looked a little awkward as he asked her, 'How are you feeling?'

'I'm well, thank you,' she replied, and she gestured for him to enter. She closed the door behind him and took his coat. 'It seems quite chilly out.'

He smiled. 'Yes, I suppose it is. I take it you're here alone tonight?'

She nodded. 'My father's out, and my mother's... indisposed. We have the house to ourselves.'

'That's good. That's very good.'

She led him through the hallway, and could feel his eyes watching her as she hobbled along.

'So, how is your foot?' William asked, rather suddenly and bluntly. 'I'm sorry, I had to ask. What that awful man did to you was terrible. It's a miracle that you weren't more seriously hurt. I shudder to think what may have happened if we hadn't brought you to the hospital as quickly as we did.'

'I know. And thank you. And will you thank your driver for me too, when you have the chance? But I promise I'll be alright. I have adapted to my situation.'

William put his hand on her arm. 'Kat, I do sometimes wonder if what happened to you might have been my fault.'

Katarina stopped and turned to face him as he released her arm. 'What do you mean?'

'At the party, when you told me about that man who'd been watching you all evening – if only I'd have confronted him then, perhaps I could've stopped him, and this would never have happened to you. I should have done more.'

Katarina shook her head. 'No, William, you did enough.'

'I had hoped that the police would have identified that man and caught him by now, but they're bloody useless, aren't they? I gave them his description, what I could remember, but it was dark that night. If I'd only had a better look at him, then perhaps—'

'William, please, it's alright. I know that the man who hurt me won't be able to hide forever, and he'll be punished for what he did to me. Now, let's talk about something else, shall we?'

When they entered the drawing room, Katarina offered him a chair and then asked, 'Would you like something to drink?'

William grinned as he sat down. 'I would, yes, thank you – but none of the weak rubbish that you keep in here. Does your father still keep a special collection in his study? Why don't you get me something good from there?'

'Yes, of course,' Katarina said. 'William, I just wanted to say, I'm so glad that you're here. I thought you might not want to come. I know it's only been a few days but I haven't stopped thinking about you – about the things that you said, and the things that you did. I still don't remember very much about that night and what happened to me, but I know that I have you to thank for me being here. I know that I could have died.'

He smiled at her. 'I've missed you too, Kat, although I have to say that I feel like a part of you is always with me. I think we're connected, you and I, more so than ever now after this experience that we've shared.'

William reached out and took her hand, and she told herself to be brave, but she was struggling to hide the fact that being this close to William again – feeling his touch on her skin, his warmth, the smell of him – was killing her. She had to fight the feelings rising inside of her, the desires that she had, the things that she knew that she wanted to do to him, *needed* to do to him...

She knew that she had to control herself. She gently eased her hand away from his and said, 'I'll fetch our drinks, and then we can talk.'

'I was hoping we might do more than talk,' he said.

Katarina gave him a smile. 'Let's just see what the evening brings, shall we?'

She closed the door behind her, and steadied herself against a wall.
Then she straightened herself up and made her way to her father's
study.

Katarina stared at the liquid that she'd poured into the glass she held
in her hand. She'd already downed her own drink, knowing that she
would need courage for what was to come. She looked up when the
door to the study opened and in walked William.

'Sorry if I startled you,' he said, 'but I was growing bored, and
wondering what was taking you so long to pour me a drink. I thought
you'd forgotten about me.' He slowly closed the door behind him and
looked around. 'I always liked this room, you know. Your father has an
impressive collection. And he's an impressive man.'

'Yes, and he's always liked you, too. You know that.'

'I do, and I'm very grateful for that.' William grinned as he told her,
'You might think it an odd thing to say, but I've always found this room
rather romantic.'

Katarina raised an eyebrow. 'You think my father's study is *romantic*?'

He chuckled. 'I did say you might find it odd! But come on, you
must find the idea a little enticing – you and me, together, in the most
forbidden part of your father's house? No one would ever know what
we do in here...' He took several steps closer to her. She was breathing
hard and as his eyes lowered towards her chest, he reached out his
fingers and gently caressed her.

Katarina tried to ignore the pleasant sensation and remind herself
of what the purpose of this evening was meant to be. She held out the
glass to him and said, 'Here you are. Have your drink, and then we can
talk about anything you want. And we can do anything you want. I
promise. Here, take it. Drink it. Please.'

William stared down at the glass that she held out to him in her shaking hand. She could see his eyes examine it with curiosity. Then he looked up at her, smiled, and said, 'Did you really believe that I'd be that stupid?'

Katarina was trembling as she looked at him with wide eyes. 'What... what do you mean?'

He shook his head at her, and then in a sudden swift motion he smacked her arm hard, causing her to fling the glass across the room where it struck the wall, shattered, and spilled liquid down the wood. She gasped in shock as he grabbed her wrists, and as he squeezed them, he said, 'Did you think you could drug me? Poison my drink?'

'No, of course not!'

'Don't lie to me, Katarina! I know what you're trying to do. I know why you invited me here. You remember everything that happened, don't you? You know what I took from you. I see through your little act.'

'I... I don't...' she stuttered.

'You ungrateful bitch! Don't you realise that I could've let you die out there, but I didn't, I saved you by bringing you to the hospital. I never did that with any of the other girls. You should've just accepted what happened to you. But now you've made things so much worse for yourself. What do you think I'm going to have to do to you now?'

Katarina managed to pull herself away from his grip, but she tripped and fell backwards onto her father's desk. William then leapt forward, placing his body on top of hers, pinning her to the desk. She struggled but couldn't get him off her, so she reached out and grabbed a paperweight from the desk and swung it at his head as hard as she could. As he staggered backwards from the blow, she pushed herself onto her feet and threw her body towards him, causing him to topple over and crash to the floor.

William lay on the floor, dazed. Katarina stood over him, her heart pounding, the blood rushing through her face. 'You're right!' she shouted at him. 'I did know that it was you that attacked me that night! You drugged me, and then you mutilated me! *You* took my toes, you cut them away from my body, it wasn't some other man, despite all your lies to the police. Did you think I wouldn't remember those times when we've been together and you would talk about my body in such odd ways, especially your strange obsession with my feet? I always tried not to let myself think anything of it, even when it made me feel uncomfortable, and to just allow myself to believe that you were simply a silly, passionate man in love, but it wasn't ever love, was it? You just wanted to take something away from me, to own it, just like you did with those other girls. You're a monster, William, and you have to be stopped!'

Katarina had never felt more alive than she did right now. There were no more secrets, no more lies. Everything was crystal clear, and she knew what she had to do. She dropped the paperweight and then looked up at the wall on which was her father's most prized possession. She reached out her arm, tightened her fingers around the grip, and pulled the sword from the wall.

'What are you doing?!' William gasped.

Katarina thrust her foot down onto the palm of his right hand, digging in hard with the heel of her shoe, forcing his fingers to spread outwards. As he cried out in pain, William stared up at her, his eyes bulging in fear – and then she brought the sword down across his fingers.

A crimson line now divided his fingers from the rest of his hand. Katarina kicked away the severed digits. William stared at his missing fingers in disbelief, before letting out a pathetic moan.

'Shut up!' Katarina shouted at him. 'This is the least you deserve after what you did!'

'Please... don't kill me!' he begged.

She pointed the sword towards his face, her hands shaking. 'I'm not going to kill you, William. I'm just going to stop you from being able to hurt anyone else. You're going to tell everyone that this was just a terrible accident, that you were drunk and you were foolishly trying to impress me by playing about with my father's sword, and you injured yourself. Yes, it might sound ridiculous, but my parents and everyone else are far more likely to believe that story than they are the idea that a weak girl like me could somehow maim a big strong man like you, aren't they?'

'You're crazy!' William spat at her, his eyes streaming. 'I'll tell them all what happened, they'll know you did this to me, and they'll have you locked up...'

'No, you won't! Because if you don't go along with my story, then I'll tell everyone what you did to me and to those other girls. I'll go to the newspapers too. Yes, perhaps people won't believe me, but there will always be that doubt in the back of every woman's mind whenever they see you, and they'll all stay away from you.'

Katarina looked down at William's bloody hand, and sighed. 'That's not enough though, is it? You still have one good hand. Enough to do some damage with.' She could see in his eyes that he was starting to fade away but she didn't want to grant him the peace of unconsciousness, so she trod down hard with her other foot onto his still-intact left hand. He turned his head to look at it with dread, then looked back up at her and begged, 'Please, no, Kat, don't—'

Katarina swung her father's sword a second time.

She stood over William and stared at the damage she'd wreaked, before she dropped the bloodied sword and it clattered to the floor.

William's eyes were dopey and he was shaking, staring at his hands, which each now had only a thumb remaining. Katarina regarded the mess that she'd made of her father's floor, and wondered what he'd think when he saw all this blood...

Calm down! she told herself. *You'll say this was a terrible accident, just like you planned to. They will believe you. You can do this.*

When she'd planned this evening, she had thought about all the other women that William had hurt, and she had decided that there was only one way to make sure that he couldn't do anything like it again, short of killing him: she would drug him by crushing up some of her mother's pills and putting them into his drink, and while he was unable to fight back she would take away the tools that he used to commit his monstrous acts.

She took deep breaths to try to calm herself down. As she stared down at William's pale, inert body, Katarina suddenly found herself thinking of that horrible bandaged corpse at Grimwald House, and with a sudden sense of dread, she realised that William hadn't moved or said anything for far too long...

What have I done?! Is he...

She quickly knelt beside William and put her ear near his mouth and nose. Relieved to discover that he was still breathing, she allowed herself to breathe again. He was alive, for now, but she knew that she would have to hurry to stop the bleeding and fetch bandages to wrap those parts of his body that were now incomplete, or he soon might not be.

Katarina's whole body was shaking now, and a cold wave suddenly came over her and she dropped to her knees and vomited on the floor. When she had no more left to give, she wiped her mouth, and stood back up. She couldn't stay in this room, the sights and the smells were threatening to overwhelm her. She had to get out of here and try to compose herself. Then she would need to get cloths and bandages and come back to this room and dress William's wounds and then rehearse again what she would say to her mother and father. There was so much to do, so much to do...

She opened the door and left her father's study and closed the door behind her, and then turned around—

'Katarina, what are you doing in there? What was all that damn noise?'

She froze. 'Hello, Mother. I was just... wandering around. I was restless.'

Her mother stood before her in her nightdress, looking half-awake. 'You shouldn't be wandering around in your father's study, you know how he gets about that.'

Katarina gently eased herself back to block the door. 'Yes, Mother, I'm sorry.'

Her mother yawned and wiped her eyes. 'I thought I heard someone shouting down here?'

'Oh, that was me. I caught my bad foot on something and I tripped. It was quite painful. I'm sorry if I woke you.'

'Hmm. You really are becoming quite accident-prone, aren't you?'

'I know. I'm sorry, I will try to be more careful. Go back to bed, Mother.'

Her mother stared at her, and for a moment Katarina was terrified that she might notice the smell of blood and vomit from inside the room, and demand to look inside. She didn't want her mother to know what had happened, not just yet, she wasn't ready. Once she had tended to William and prepared herself properly, she would make her way upstairs, rush into her mother's room in tears, distraught, and tell her about this awful, horrible accident that had occurred in her father's study, and beg for her mother's help to make sure that William would be alright. But for the moment, she needed to get her mother far away from this room.

'Alright,' her mother said, with a sigh, 'I will go back to bed, but I had better not be disturbed again. Please behave yourself, and for God's sake, be quiet. Sometimes I don't know what to do with you, Katarina, and nor does your father. You can be so selfish. You know I already have enough things to worry about.'

As Katarina watched her mother go back upstairs, she thought about what she'd done. But she also thought about what William had taken from her, and what he'd taken from all those other women, and she called out, 'You don't need to worry about me, Mother. Everything's going to be alright now.'

CHAPTER THREE

SESSION TWO

'Anna, wait there! I'll come and get you!'

She heard Mark's voice a moment before she saw him emerge from the doorway of Grimwald House bearing an umbrella and a smile. He protected Anna from the rain as she made her way from the taxi to the house. She'd decided to wear a warmer outfit this time, and since the sky was grey and it was raining and cold, she didn't regret that decision.

'It's great to see you again, Anna. Let's get you inside and out of the rain.' Mark had one hand on his umbrella, one on the small of her back, as he led her into the house, where she discovered that she was the last one to arrive.

As Mark put the wet umbrella away in a box by the front doors, Anna found that the other members of their group were standing in the hallway, studying the portraits of the family that must have once lived here. As Anna approached, Harold was quick to greet her, followed by Vivian, but Anna was far more interested in finding out how Katarina was doing. The young woman seemed distracted though, and didn't answer Anna when she asked her if she was well. Anna was keen to know whether Katarina really had recovered after that last session, as Handsworth had claimed.

Speaking of the devil, Handsworth appeared now, coming down the stairs towards them. Anna noted with some amusement that Ebony was waddling down after him. Handsworth greeted the group but his words were overshadowed by the whimpering of the odd little dog, who wandered between each member of the group, stealing their attention away. It hovered by Katarina but seemed to decide that she was unlikely to give it the attention it craved, so instead it settled in front of Anna, lying down and looking up at her forlornly. Anna bent down and stroked the dog behind the ears.

'He seems to like you,' Mark noted. 'He's got good taste.'

'He's a she,' Anna replied, 'and yes, she does. I'm normally more of a cat person, but this little gal's got character.' She stroked the dog's back and told it, 'Nice to see you too, you little monster.'

Anna stood back up as Handsworth announced, 'If you'd all like to proceed through to the dining room as before, and take your seats, then the evening can begin.'

'We were just admiring those family portraits on the wall,' Mark told him.

Handsworth nodded. 'Yes, this house has quite a few stories to tell. But please, if you could all move through into the dining room now, thank you.'

As the group went into the dining room, Handsworth picked up Ebony and kept her in the hallway with him. Anna saw him whisper something indecipherable to the dog.

The door closed behind them. The dining room was laid out with a table and chairs, as before, except this time there were no contracts waiting to be signed in ink and blood. They took their seats. The group chatted as they waited, all except Katarina, who merely nodded or shook her head at any questions thrown her way, until eventually people stopped throwing them at her. Anna noticed that Katarina didn't look quite so pale and sickly this time, just rather melancholy. Had something bad happened to her since their last session?

'I don't know about you, but I've been looking forward to tonight,' Vivian said, interrupting Anna's thoughts. 'I found the previous session rather exciting, I wonder what they have in store for us this time?'

'I suppose we'll find out soon enough,' Anna replied. Would they all go into that tomb again and peel a little more off the mummy, and then retire for a meal? Or did their unseen host have something else planned for tonight?

Anna looked towards the wall where the hidden door had revealed itself last time. It really was well-hidden. She couldn't see anything that suggested there might be a door there.

Vivian followed her gaze. 'I see you're as eager as I am for that door to open again. I wonder how much longer we'll have to wait?'

Harold had overheard their conversation. 'Perhaps they've forgotten about us?' he said.

Anna allowed a smile on her face. 'Or perhaps Ebony, the dog, is running amok and Handsworth is trying to catch her, so he's too busy dealing with her to pull the lever that opens the magic door for us. What a shame, perhaps we'll all have to go home unsatisfied.'

Vivian laughed at that and said, 'You think Handsworth's behind all of this?'

Anna shrugged. 'I doubt the dog's the mastermind behind it all, and I didn't see anyone else the last time I was here.'

'Oh yes,' Vivian said, 'you spent the night here, didn't you? How was that?'

'There's not much to tell. Katarina slept, I took a wander around the house, I met that daft dog, I came back, fell asleep, and when I woke up, Katarina was already gone. Apparently she was feeling much better, but nobody had bothered to tell me that until the morning.' Anna waited to see if that would trigger Katarina to say anything, but she remained silent, seemingly content to stare down at her shoes.

'That's all that happened?' Vivian said, seeming disappointed. 'I'd hoped for something more exciting, I thought this place would hold more mysteries, perhaps even more tombs with more dead bodies... Are you sure you saw no ghosts or ghouls wandering around, no monsters roaming the halls late in the night?'

'No, not unless you count Ebony the dog,' Anna replied. 'Sorry to disappoint you. I'd tell you if I had seen something, I swear.'

Vivian smiled. 'At least it's good to know that you aren't keeping any secrets from us.'

'Well, I never said that.' Anna held Vivian's smile for a moment, until the older woman turned away to talk to Harold.

For the next few minutes the conversation between the group took in subjects such as the weather, certain recent events in the news, what everyone's favourite holiday destination was, and how much longer they might be kept waiting. When there was a lull in the conversation, Vivian leaned herself closer to Anna and said, quietly, 'I do find myself wondering about that Katarina. So sickly last time, so very quiet this time. I don't understand their type very well, perhaps you might have an idea of what's wrong with her?'

'I'm fine!' Katarina shouted out suddenly, startling everyone, particularly Vivian.

Then they heard a ticking sound that seemed to swim around the room. Anna couldn't see where it was coming from. Perhaps there were hidden speakers behind the wall?

'There's that ticking again, like last time,' Harold said.

'Like a countdown,' Mark suggested.

'Yes,' Harold agreed, 'but last time it was counting down while we were already in that tomb unwrapping the dead body. But we haven't even gone into the tomb yet, so what's it meant to mean now?'

Mark stood up from his chair. 'Perhaps we're supposed to try to find that hidden door ourselves this time? Come on, Harold, give me a hand, I'm sure it was somewhere around there...'

The two men went towards the wall and began touching it, moving their hands up and down and in circles, hoping to find a hidden handle or a switch that would activate the door.

Vivian smirked. 'Boys, you're making us ladies all hot and bothered the way you two are stroking that wall so very intimately.'

Harold looked embarrassed, and returned to his chair at the table, but Mark was unperturbed and insisted, 'I know that door's here somewhere, and I'm going to find it.'

While Vivian continued watching Mark with amusement, Anna noticed that Harold was fidgeting in his chair. 'Is something wrong, Harold?' she asked.

'It's this damn chair,' he grumbled. 'It's so lumpy, I can't get comfortable.'

Now that Harold had mentioned it, Anna realised her own chair was more uncomfortable than it had been in the previous session. Harold seemed to decide that he'd had enough of it, and he got to his feet and started picking at the seat of his chair. 'Bloody chair!'

'Leave it alone, Harold,' Vivian warned, but Harold ignored her and pulled at the material, and there was a loud tearing sound as the fabric came away in his hand.

'That's torn it,' Mark said with a grin, but his grin then turned into a look of surprise as Harold lifted up his chair, tilted it forward, and a pile of money – coins and notes – spilled out across the dining table.

Harold stood back from the table and shook his head. 'What is all this about?'

Mark returned to the table and checked his own chair. He tore a hole and showed the others; there was money inside his chair too. 'Looks like we're all sitting on a gold mine,' he said, grinning again, as he poured the money onto the table.

Harold started counting all the money from his chair. 'Seven hundred and twenty-six pounds and thirty pence,' he concluded.

Mark had also been counting his. 'Yes, I think it's probably about the same amount for me. That's a strangely specific amount. What does it mean?' He looked at the women. 'I wonder if you ladies all have the same amount of money under your seats?'

'It's seven hundred and twenty-six pounds and thirty pence exactly, though,' Harold repeated, lost in thought. 'No more, no less.'

Mark frowned at him. 'Is that supposed to mean something to us?'

'Not to you, but it certainly means something to me.' Harold looked around at the group. 'It's exactly the same amount that I had in my savings account on the day that I interviewed for my first accounting job, an apprenticeship position. I remember feeling so embarrassed when the woman who interviewed me asked me how much money I had in my bank account, because she wanted to use that figure as an example in a test of my numerical skills.' Harold stared at the money in his hands. 'I got the job, and I ended up doing very well there at that company, before I started my own business. If I hadn't got that job, then I'm not sure what I would've done. I probably would've just given up and chosen to do something else with my life. So I suppose my whole career, and all the money that I've made, can be traced back to that day, when I had that exact amount of money in my account, and I didn't know what my future held. When I didn't know what would become of me. Or what I would become.'

Harold let the money fall through his fingers, and sighed. He stared down at the floor, not saying anything more.

'How strange this is,' Vivian commented, as she and Katarina stood back from the table to allow Mark to tear open their chairs. They were not surprised to find money inside their chairs too. Mark tipped the chairs and the money poured onto the table.

Anna had started ripping a hole in the seat of her own chair, so Mark returned to his position by the wall and started touching it again, still hoping to find a way into the tomb. Anna lifted her chair over the table and then poured the money out. She wasn't going to bother counting it, she knew that it would be the same amount as Harold and Mark and the others had found in their chairs.

There was a yelp from across the room. Mark was excitedly pointing at the wall, and Anna could see that the hidden door to the tomb had now manifested. 'I found it!' he exclaimed. 'Told you I would! Must have been some kind of pressure panel in the wall, you just have to touch it in the right way in the right place.' Mark beamed at them with pride, but Anna suspected that the door's sudden appearance was nothing to do with Mark. She eyed the money on the dining table. She wondered if there might be some kind of sensor in the table that had activated the door once they'd emptied the contents of their chairs onto it? She'd put money on that being the real reason the door had suddenly opened, rather than Mark randomly finding the exact spot to touch to activate it, but she decided to keep quiet about her suspicions and allow Mark his moment of glory.

Mark slid the door open as the group joined him. He then led them through into the tomb.

Anna grimaced when she saw that the mummified corpse was still there, although she knew it wasn't as if it was likely to have got out and wandered off anywhere, was it? So they had some more unwrapping to do. As before, the door slid to a close behind them, sealing them in with the veiled body. They could hear that ticking sound, louder now, but the clock it was coming from remained unseen.

'I suppose we should get started then,' Harold said. 'I think I'd like to go first this time, unless anyone has any objections?' He bent down, adjusted his glasses, coughed, then took hold of the end of a bandage and started pulling, revealing the decayed left knee and upper leg of the woman. As he stood back up, his own legs seemed to momentarily lose their strength, and Mark had to right him. 'Are you alright?'

Harold nodded. 'Yes, yes, I'm fine. I think it's the air in here, it's a little hard to breathe. Someone go next.'

Mark went for the right leg, and carefully pulled off the bandages. At least no parts seemed to be missing from either leg, unlike the left foot and its missing toes.

The ticking continued as Vivian told Anna, 'Now for the fun part! Come here and help me unwrap the groin area...'

Anna wrinkled her nose, but forced herself forward, and with Vivian's help, she began peeling the wraps from around the corpse's groin and buttocks. A sudden hiss of stale air made her jump back.

Vivian stifled a laugh. 'Oh dear, did our ancient friend here just break wind?'

'I hope not, this tomb has a bad enough stench to it already,' Harold said. 'There's no window to let any air in or any smells out. I don't know how you all can stand it.'

Anna smiled at him. 'Oh, I've smelled far worse things than this room. Mark's cologne, for example.'

'Sorry, what was that?' Mark asked, frowning at her.

'Nothing,' Anna replied. 'Whose turn is it next?'

Vivian turned to look at Katarina. 'Come on, girl, don't just stand there like some useless ornament. It's your turn. Finish this delicate area for us.'

Katarina had squeezed herself into the corner of the room, as far away from the corpse as possible. 'No, thank you, I don't think I could handle that.'

Vivian lost her temper. 'Then what is the point of you even being here? Fine, I'll do it all myself! You really need a stronger stomach or you won't last five minutes in this world.' She pointed at the corpse. 'Just think of what this poor woman must have gone through. Your discomfort pales in comparison, yet here you are acting like some spoilt little child, afraid to get her hands dirty.'

Katarina glared at Vivian as she finished unwrapping the groin area.

'Whoever this was, they were definitely not male,' Mark declared.

Vivian stood back and said, 'Yes, obviously all signs point to this being a woman, although did you know that with male mummies they would sometimes remove the penis?' Harold and Mark looked uncomfortable as Vivian continued, 'They sometimes replaced it with an artificial one so that it would appear more impressive. The real thing could be stored separately, it was not always attached to the body. Perhaps we might find it lying around somewhere in this room?'

No one in the group appeared particularly keen to go searching for it. Trying to change the subject slightly, Anna said, 'Vivian, you seem to know a surprising amount about ancient mummies.'

Katarina agreed. 'Anna's right, you *do* seem to know a lot more than the rest of us do about all of this. Why is that?'

Vivian gave Katarina a frosty stare. 'That's because I read books, dear. You should try it sometime.'

The ticking suddenly ceased and a gong sounded. The candles went out, and the door opened.

'Oh. I suppose that's it for tonight, is it? That's all we're going to get?' Vivian sounded a little disappointed. 'Oh well, never mind, I'm ready for my dinner now anyway.'

They exited the tomb, and the door closed behind them. They returned to the dining table, and noticed that the money was all gone and the chairs that they'd ripped open had been replaced.

'Someone's cleaned up in here and taken all that money away,' Harold observed. 'That was quick.'

'That's disappointing,' Vivian said, 'but more importantly, where's our dinner?'

Mark smiled at her. 'Perhaps tonight we should order in then, instead. Chinese, anyone?'

They took their seats again, and waited, hopeful that dinner was on its way and was simply running a little late.

'I am starting to feel like the service has gone downhill since last we were here, and it wasn't exactly five-star then,' Vivian said, with a sigh. 'Perhaps I ought to go onto the Internet and leave a bad review?'

'I'm not sure it would make a difference,' Anna said. 'If there's a website for the world's creepiest houses, then I'm sure this place gets rave reviews.'

Suddenly the lights in the room went out, leaving them in the dark, unable to see each other. From nowhere in particular there came the sound of music: a piano being played. The piece played for several minutes, and then stopped just as suddenly as it had started. The lights came back on.

Someone was missing.

'Where the bloody hell is Harold?' Vivian exclaimed, staring at his empty seat.

Katarina pointed out that the door to the hallway was open. 'Perhaps he got scared and ran out?' she suggested.

'Perhaps he went to order that Chinese food,' Mark said, but the usual confidence and levity in his voice seemed as absent as Harold was.

'We need to find him,' Vivian said, standing up and making her way over to the doorway. She stopped when she realised that the others weren't following her. 'Well, come on then, Harold might need our help!'

The others got up and followed her into the hallway and looked around, but there was no sign of Harold. They watched as Mark tried the front doors, but they wouldn't open. 'Nobody's getting out that way,' he told the group.

'Mark, why don't you try looking for Harold in the bathrooms?' Vivian suggested. 'Go on, have a look, I shouldn't be surprised to find him in there. When you have to go, you have to go, and that only gets truer with age, believe me.'

Mark did as he was told, and they waited as he checked both of the bathrooms. When he returned, the look on his face told them that he'd been unsuccessful.

'I think we ought to split up and search the rest of the house for him,' Vivian suggested. The others didn't look too pleased with her suggestion, so she added, 'We can go in twos. Mark, why don't you come with me and we'll search downstairs? Anna, you can take Katarina and have a look around upstairs. I'm sure you're both a lot fitter than I am and can manage those stairs better than I would.'

'I see you've put yourself in charge, then?' Anna said.

Vivian shrugged. 'Nobody else was being particularly proactive, so yes, I stepped up. Let's just go and find Harold, I'm worried about the poor man. It's very strange how he disappeared like that all of a sudden. And what was that music that we heard? It's a mystery that needs solving! Come along, Mark, you can be my bodyguard. We can talk as we walk, and get to know each other a little better.'

As Mark and Vivian began to check around downstairs, Anna and Katarina headed up the stairs.

'I do hope Harold is alright,' Katarina said to Anna as they walked. 'Between you and me, I have the feeling that he's not a well man.'

'He seems alright to me, other than that nasty cough of his,' Anna said. 'What about you – how are you feeling tonight?'

'I feel better than I did last time we were here together. Anna, I'm sorry we didn't wake you before I left that morning, but you seemed like you needed a good night's sleep too.'

Anna noticed that Katarina looked like she was concentrating hard, as if each step she took was an effort. When they reached the landing, Anna stopped beneath the stag's head and said, 'Katarina, you still don't seem one hundred percent to me, are you sure that you're alright? Has something happened since the last time I saw you? I can see that you're in pain.'

'I already told you that I'm fine!' Katarina replied, testily. 'You don't need to worry about me. Please, let's just get on with what we need to do. Let's find Harold.'

'Alright, I'm sorry.'

'No, I'm sorry, I didn't mean to be so rude. I appreciate you caring about me, I really do.'

Anna decided not to pry further. If Katarina didn't want to talk about whatever was wrong with her, then it was no business of hers.

She indicated to Katarina that they start by taking the left-hand corridor, which she knew should lead them to the master bedroom that
they'd spent the night in last week.

When they reached the door to the bedroom, Anna tried the doorknob, but the door was locked. 'Where's Handsworth when you need
him?' Anna muttered. 'Or maybe I should try calling for Ebony, the
dog, and see if she can hunt down Harold for us? Ebony! Ebony! Here,
girl!'

No small beast came running towards them, so they carried on
along the corridors, and Anna tried a few more doorknobs, but had
no success with those either. As they continued walking, Katarina
suddenly asked, 'Anna, are you married?'

'Why are you asking me that right now?'

'It's just that we didn't talk that much last time, of course that was
my fault because I was too busy being ill, but I don't feel like I know
you that well, and I'd like to. I feel like maybe we could become friends
if we spent more time together.'

'I'm not so sure about that,' Anna replied distractedly. When she
looked at Katarina she noticed that the younger woman seemed disappointed, so she quickly clarified, 'What I mean is, I doubt we'll have
much chance to get to know each other if we only meet once a week to
unwrap a dead body. Remember, we're not allowed to see each other
away from this house, for fear of upsetting our host, whoever they are.'

Katarina nodded. 'You're right, of course, I'm being silly.'

'No, it's not silly, it's just... Look, if we'd met in some other place
and some other time, then maybe we would have become friends. I
don't know, I don't make friends all that easily, and if you got to know
me, then you might not even *want* to spend time with me. Anyway, to
answer your original question, no, I'm not married. I don't even have
a boyfriend right now.'

'I'm surprised to hear that. I was sure that you'd have someone. I'm
sorry, it's just that you seem so confident, and strong, and beautiful.'

Anna laughed. 'You think *I'm* beautiful? You should take a look in the mirror. *You're* beautiful. Surely you know that?'

'No, I don't feel beautiful,' Katarina sighed. 'Not anymore, anyway.'

'What about you, then?' Anna asked. 'Are you married? Do you have someone special? A boyfriend, or a—'

'There was someone,' Katarina answered, avoiding Anna's eyes, 'but he wasn't who I thought he was. It's hard for me to talk about.'

Anna's attention was caught by something moving at the other end of the corridor. 'Wait, I think I see something down there, what is that?'

There was someone standing there in the dark, not moving. With a glance at Katarina, Anna started cautiously walking towards the strange figure. 'Harold, is that you?' she called out.

The figure suddenly turned and disappeared around the corner.

'Come on,' she told Katarina, and they walked more quickly. They reached the end of the corridor, and turned the corner.

There was no one there.

'Look over there!' Katarina hissed at Anna. She pointed at the door to one of the rooms. The knob on the door seemed to be moving, slowly.

Feeling brave, or at least trying to appear that way in front of Katarina, Anna stepped towards the door, and knocked twice. She gave it a second before she turned the doorknob and opened the door to reveal a small bedroom, and stood in front of the bed was a tiny young woman in a nightgown with red hair and a pale, freckled, frightened face.

'Hello,' Anna said. 'Who are you?'

The girl didn't answer, and eyed the doorway as if judging her chances of escaping past them. Anna noticed the look, and closed the door behind her. 'I asked you a question – who are you? What's your name? What are you doing here?'

The girl seemed to deflate. 'My name is Louise, miss. I'm sorry, I'm not supposed to talk to any of the guests, not without permission.'

'Are you part of the family that owns this house? We saw some portraits on the wall downstairs. Are you related to them?'

Louise shook her head. 'Oh no, miss, I'm only a maid. I work here, and some nights I sleep here too. I was going to the staff bathroom down the hall before coming to bed to get some sleep, as I have an early start tomorrow, you see. That family you saw in the paintings, they're long gone now.'

'Can you tell us who currently owns this place? Who do you work for?'

Louise glanced between Katarina and Anna. 'I'm sorry, I'm not allowed to tell you that. I could get in trouble, and I can't afford to lose this job. I would help if I could, but I can't. I'm sorry. Please, I—'

'Alright, never mind then,' Anna said. 'But you must be able to tell us something about this place and its history. What do you know about that family in the pictures? Who were they?'

Louise looked unsure. 'I shouldn't, it's not my place.'

'It's alright, you can tell us,' Katarina said. 'I promise you won't get in trouble.'

The maid nodded, and sat down on her bed. 'I *can* tell you a little of the history, but I don't know much. I can tell you about the Gray family that used to live here, long before I started here. Mr Gray was quite religious, and he liked to travel the world, teaching about Christianity, and he would often bring back treasures from his adventures, all kinds of strange and unusual objects from places like Africa, Egypt and China. There's a room up here on this floor of the house that's full of all sorts of odd things that Mr Gray collected and brought back with him from his travels. His wife, Mrs Gray, looked after the house and raised the children. I'm sure from looking at those portraits you will have noticed their handsome son Robert, and there was also their adopted daughter, Helena. Mr Gray found Helena and took her into his family. Mrs Gray began to educate her in the schoolroom up here, and she learnt to play the piano in the music room. She'd had a difficult past, so it was fortunate that the Grays accepted her into their family. But then there was that one terrible, awful night...'

'Go on,' Anna said.

'I don't know the full story, but... they say that this old house was taking quite a beating from the fierce winds and the snow, but there was worse to come; a fire broke out, and when the maids went to check on Mr Gray, his wife and his son, she discovered that they were all dead!

'It must have been an awful sight for her to see those bodies like that.' Louise shuddered before continuing. 'Thankfully none of the staff working here at the time were hurt, and as for the daughter Helena, well, she couldn't be found at all, that poor girl seemed simply to vanish, never to be seen or heard from again. It's such a tragic story.'

Louise played with her fingers. 'Most of the rooms that were damaged by the fire were eventually restored. But oh, I don't like to think of those deaths happening right here in this house, in these rooms, it would give me nightmares! I know that it all happened a long time ago, but I still find that I'm afraid to go into certain rooms here. I know I'm being foolish, I suppose I get scared easily.'

Anna had a disturbing realisation. 'Last time we were here, Katarina and I stayed in the master bedroom – is that one of the rooms where...?' She looked at Louise, and as the girl opened her mouth to answer, Anna told her, 'Actually, never mind, I don't think I want to know.'

'That is quite a story,' Katarina said. 'Those poor people... I wonder whatever happened to that girl Helena?'

'Speaking of missing people,' Anna said, 'we're actually looking for someone ourselves, right now.'

'Oh? Who's that?' Louise asked.

'His name's Harold,' Anna said. 'We don't know his surname. He arrived here earlier tonight, like we all did. And now he's gone missing. Is there any chance you've seen him wandering around up here?'

'No, I'm very sorry, I haven't,' Louise said, shaking her head. 'You could try speaking to Mr Handsworth, he might know where Harold is. He knows everything that goes on inside this house.'

'Yes, I bet he does,' Anna said. 'I *would* like to have a word with him.'

'Most of the main rooms here have a chain,' Louise explained, 'and if you pull it, it'll ring one of the bells in his office, and then he'll come to that room. Otherwise, you can find his office if you go down the stairs and turn to your left.'

'Thank you for your help, Louise,' Katarina said.

The maid bowed her head and replied, 'Of course, miss.' The girl was blushing, unable to look Katarina in the eyes, as if dazzled by her beauty. Anna noted that her companion seemed to have that effect on people, and clearly not just on men like Mark. Louise had had no such reaction to Anna.

'We'll leave you in peace now,' Anna told her. 'Sorry for barging into your room like this.'

'That's quite alright, miss. I hope you find the man you're looking for. I'm sure he'll turn up soon, one way or another.'

'Thank you,' Anna replied. 'Come on, Katarina, let's go.'

The two women left Louise in her room and returned to the corridor. The door closed behind them.

'She seemed nice,' Katarina said.

'Yes,' Anna said, 'nice, but not particularly helpful, other than that little history lesson, and I don't know about you but to me that almost sounded rehearsed – like the kind of thing a tour guide might say, a scary tale that they'd tell to unnerve the tourists. Anyway, I think we should finish looking around up here and then go back downstairs and look for Handsworth's office. I'm sure we'll bump into Vivian and Mark downstairs, and who knows, maybe they've found Harold already?'

Anna led Katarina back along the corridors, hoping that she'd be able to find her way back to the staircase. She stopped when she noticed a large black door, possibly the same one that she'd seen when wandering the house on her first night here. She indicated the door to Katarina and said, 'I wonder what they keep behind there?'

Katarina looked at the door. 'That door's very ornate. And rather ominous-looking. I think we ought to leave it alone. We should go find Handsworth.'

'Alright, fine, don't be adventurous, then.' Anna shrugged, and they continued walking.

Anna was relieved when they eventually found the staircase again, and they began to descend. The windows *tat-tat-tat*-ed with the sound of raindrops hitting them. Anna was glad to be indoors and not outside in the cold and the rain where she'd be forced to seek shelter under those tall trees, which would mean venturing into that dark woodland, and who knows what might be creeping about out there? No, in here was safer – but it was all relative.

Anna didn't want to have to spend any more time in this house than was absolutely necessary, but she wasn't going to leave until they had located Harold. If their roles were reversed and she was lost somewhere in this labyrinthine house, she hoped that Harold wouldn't leave until he'd found her and made sure that she was safe. But then again, did she really know any of the rest of her group well enough to assume that they'd put themselves out for her? Maybe they'd just decide to abandon her and leave her to her fate.

Her stomach grumbled, reminding her that their host had failed to provide dinner this evening. Another thing to question Handsworth about once they located him.

'If you're very hungry, perhaps we can look for the kitchen and find something for you to eat?' Katarina suggested, and Anna went red with embarrassment on behalf of her noisy stomach. 'I don't have much of an appetite myself at the moment, perhaps it's being here in this strange house, but food is the last thing on my mind.'

Anna doubted that Katarina ever had much of an appetite, she was so skinny. She probably lived on rabbit food, unlike Anna, who liked her food. It didn't even need to be anything that fancy; she would kill for a beef burger right now.

When they reached the ground floor, Anna tried a few more of the doors downstairs, but only the bathroom, cloakroom and dining room opened for her, the rest of the rooms she tried remained stubbornly closed. So many rooms, so many possibilities. Knowing that she was being denied access to these rooms piqued Anna's curiosity. Her imagination tried to fill in the gaps as to what exactly was behind these doors; perhaps every room contained a different horror – not just mummies, but ghouls, ghosts, werewolves, and vampires? Or maybe there was nothing at all behind these doors, and the whole thing was just a facade, like being on a movie set?

Anna noticed that Katarina was staring at her again, and then she realised that Katarina had been speaking, but she hadn't been listening to her. 'Sorry, did you ask me something?'

'Oh, it was nothing important,' Katarina replied, with a smile. 'It's funny, you seemed to drift away. You were here one moment, and then gone the next.'

'I'm sorry, I do that sometimes, I get lost in my own head and let my imagination get the better of me. Although, I don't think I'm imagining that smell, am I? Do you smell it too? Something's cooking.'

Someone must have been eating tonight, even if it wasn't the guests. They followed the smell to the room next to the dining room, and when Anna tried the door it opened into a kitchen. Anna's stomach growled appreciatively at the smell of cooked meat that hung in the air. Also hanging in the air were various pans above their heads, and on one wall she saw some kind of meat hanging from a hook. On the edges of the room Anna could see a large black stove, a sink, and a cabinet holding rows of plates and pots, and a large clock on the wall.

Katarina looked around the room in wonder. 'Anna, don't you think that stepping into this room is a little like stepping into the past?'

'What do you mean?'

'Well, look at all these old things around us,' Katarina replied, sweeping her arm across the room.

Anna had to agree. 'It does look like a kitchen that you'd see in a stately home, something from Victorian times or maybe even earlier.'

'I quite like it,' Katarina said, admiring all the crockery on the shelves. 'Wouldn't you love to be able to go back in time and see what life was like in those days, Anna?'

Anna shrugged. 'I don't know, I think I prefer my kitchen at home, and all of its mod cons. For me, this is missing a few essentials – like a microwave, for example. Or a fridge-freezer. Or a television. To be honest, with me and cooking, I usually can't be bothered with anything that takes much more effort than pressing a few buttons. I wouldn't know what half of this stuff is used for. Maybe this is all just for effect and somewhere hidden away in the back they have more modern appliances?'

Katarina smiled at her. 'I expect that you have a lovely home. I'd love to see it.'

'I don't think our host would like you popping round to mine for tea,' Anna replied. The wooden floor creaked under Anna's feet as she walked towards the long table that dominated the centre of the kitchen. On the table she found a chopping board with a knife, a rolling pin, and what looked like a jelly mold. Her eyes were drawn to a single silver serving dish, possibly the same one that had contained the turkey during their previous session. Anna approached the dish with trepidation. Her overactive imagination insisted that she would discover something nasty underneath the dome, but when she lifted it off, it was just an empty dish. Anna sighed with relief, but her stomach rumbled as if disappointed.

'What exactly did you think you were going to find in that?' Katarina asked, amused. 'You seemed afraid to open it.'

'It doesn't matter, my imagination's running wild at the moment. Let's carry on.'

'Hold on, I think I can hear voices!' Katarina suddenly declared.

Anna tensed up but then relaxed when she saw Mark enter the kitchen, followed by Vivian, who wore a puzzled expression. 'Did you find Harold?' Anna asked them, at the exact moment that Vivian asked the same question.

'No, we found no sign of him down here,' Vivian told them. 'I take it you had no better luck upstairs?'

'No,' Anna answered, 'we couldn't find him either. But there are so many locked doors in this place, who knows if he might be behind one of them?'

Mark stood with his hands on his hips, shaking his head. 'He must be around here somewhere, a man doesn't just disappear into thin air like that!'

'I don't know about that,' Vivian said, 'my first husband did. I came home one day to find his wardrobe empty and his favourite car missing from the garage. Not even a goodbye note. He just abandoned me and our children. I found out later that he'd moved to Italy with some twenty-something blonde that he'd met at a bar.'

No one seemed to know how to respond to that revelation. Vivian waved her hand. 'Never mind, I'm not sure why I shared that. The point is, none of us really knows Harold, and perhaps he had a good reason to dash out of that room. Or maybe he's simply scared of the dark.'

'Let's head back to the dining room, maybe he's come back by now,' Mark suggested.

They returned to the dining room, but there was no sign of Harold there.

'This is getting tiresome,' Vivian said, exasperated. 'We should—'

'Shush!' Anna interrupted her. 'Everyone, please, be quiet for a moment!'

Vivian did not look happy at being silenced. She watched as Anna raised a finger, pointing to the heavens. 'Does anyone else hear that?'

They all listened. From somewhere out in the hallway, the gentle tinkling of a piano drifted towards them. 'It's the same melody that we heard when the lights went out earlier,' Katarina observed.

'Yes, I think you might be right,' Anna agreed. 'I'm sure it's coming from upstairs.'

'Hang on,' Mark said, 'I thought you ladies just told us that you checked upstairs and didn't find anything?'

Anna winced at the accusatory tone, then Katarina told him, 'We didn't hear any music when we were up there, and we didn't find Harold, but we did see someone – a maid, her name is Louise. We found her in one of the bedrooms. Perhaps that's her playing that piano?'

'She did mention there's a music room upstairs,' Anna said. She turned to Mark and Vivian. 'Did you see Handsworth at all? We came down here to find him, but we got distracted. We thought Handsworth might have an idea where Harold's gone.'

Mark shook his head. 'No sign of Handsworth, but there's that door across the hall with his name on it, and we tried knocking, but there was no answer. Most of the rooms are locked, and I doubt Harold's got lockpicking skills. Then again, who knows, maybe he does? We did find a small conservatory at the back of the house, filled with odd plants, but Harold wasn't there. I did have a good look, in case he was hiding behind one of those plants for some reason, maybe as a prank. But there was no one there.'

Vivian let out a loud sigh. 'Well, if we're going to have to go upstairs to find the source of that music, and hopefully find Harold too, then let's get on with it. It could take me a while to get up those stairs, so you'll have to bear with me, I'm not quite as fit as I once was.'

Anna took the lead as the group made their way out into the hallway and then across to the staircase at the other end of the hall. The journey upstairs was more slow-going than before, since they had to wait for Vivian to catch up with them, but eventually the group reached the top of the stairs. Gerald the dead stag got a few odd looks from Vivian and Mark, before they all continued along the corridors, following the sound of the piano music.

They found the maid's room again, but when Anna held her ear to the door, the only sound that came from within was snoring. They continued on. The rain outside had become even fiercer now, almost drowning out the sound of the piano, but as they walked along one particular corridor, the music began to grow much louder. They were close now.

Katarina pointed at a door. 'I think it's coming from that room!'

'Try the door,' Vivian suggested. Anna took a step towards the room, but Mark quickly moved to place himself between her and the door, telling her, 'Wait. I think it's best I go in first, just in case.'

'In case of what, exactly?' Anna asked him.

Mark didn't answer, and knocked gently on the door. 'Harold, are you in there? I'm coming in.'

There was no reply from within, but the music kept on playing. Mark glanced at the others, then took a deep breath, and turned the doorknob. The music suddenly stopped. Mark entered the room, then let out a gasp.

Anna couldn't see what he'd seen. With a sense of dread, she followed him into the room. She pushed past him and saw an old grand piano gathering dust in the corner of the room, and a few other musical instruments on the floor, along with a couple of worn music books and scattered pages of sheet music.

'I don't understand it,' Mark said, 'there's nobody in here.'

Vivian and Katarina entered next, looking around the room, appearing equally bemused. Mark was right, there was no one here, and in fact the room looked like it had been vacant for years, judging by all the dust and cobwebs.

'It's quite eerie, isn't it?' a voice said from behind them.

The group turned in surprise to see Harold standing in the doorway, his hand resting on the doorframe, clasping his glasses in his hand, his eyes far away.

'Harold!' Vivian exclaimed. 'There you are!'

'Yes, here I am.'

'Are you alright?' Mark asked. 'We've been looking for you. Where did you go?'

'Here. I came here, to this room.' Harold entered the music room, and stood in front of the piano. He put his glasses back on and then ran his fingers along the keys. 'I heard the music when we were downstairs in the dining room, and I saw the door open, and I followed the music up the stairs, and I ended up here.'

'But there's no one here,' Katarina said, 'so where was that music coming from?'

Harold stared down at the piano keys as he said, 'It only plays when the door's closed. I tried it. You come in, the music stops, you go back out and close the door, and it starts up again. It's like there's a ghost of a musician in this room who's too shy to play in front of others.'

'I don't like this room,' Katarina declared, and promptly went back out into the corridor.

'We finally agree on something,' Vivian said.

'It's probably just some silly trick,' Mark suggested.

Harold gave a sad smile. His fingers touched the keys, and Anna realised that he was trying to recreate the melody that they'd heard. 'I know that melody,' he said, 'it's one my father used to play. I also used to sing it to... Never mind.

'You know, when I was a child my father tried to teach me how to play the piano, but I was always more interested in other things, things like numbers and sums, they made more sense to me than anything else. I think back to it now and I wish I had taken the time to let him teach me. He died about ten years ago. He'd been very sick and hadn't told me. So I missed my chance. I haven't heard that melody for a long time, and I haven't thought about my father for a while, but now the memories are all coming back to me. What I don't understand is how and why it's playing here, in this house?'

Anna reached out and touched his arm. 'Harold, it's someone playing tricks, most likely Handsworth or whoever this "H" character might be, if it's not him. It's probably all part of the entertainment. Ours or theirs, I'm not sure yet. I'm sure it's a recording and it's automatically set to turn off and on when people come in or go out of this room. Don't let it upset you.'

'I'm not upset,' Harold said.

As Mark went back out into the corridor, Anna looked at Vivian for help, and she moved forward and took Harold's arm. 'Come along now, Harold, let's be going. I'll need you to help me down the stairs. My legs aren't what they once were, and yours are still strong. Be a gentleman and help a lady in need.'

'Yes, of course,' Harold said, and allowed himself to be led out of the room.

Anna followed the others out, casting worried glances back at the piano. She then closed the door behind her, and just as Harold had said, the music from within started up again. She reopened the door, and it suddenly stopped. 'That's incredibly creepy,' she commented, and she could see that the rest of the group seemed to agree with her. As she closed the door and walked away, the music continued playing.

Vivian then made a suggestion. 'Since it appears that none of us will be getting fed this evening, I suggest that once we leave this house, we go and find somewhere to eat. Perhaps our taxi drivers can suggest somewhere nearby?'

'Remember that we're not allowed to see each other when we're not here at this house,' Katarina reminded her.

'Yes, she's right,' Mark said, 'it's a stupid rule, but I don't feel like I want to get on the wrong side of our host, especially if he – or she – is the type that likes to play pranks.'

The group found their way back downstairs, after a few wrong turns, and were relieved to find that the front doors were now unlocked and that they could leave. They could hear the heavy rain outside and decided to take umbrellas from the box by the front doors.

Vivian took out her phone and told the others, 'Since our host is seemingly absent and not considerate enough to arrange for our transportation back home tonight, then it falls to us to sort ourselves out. Let me do it. There are some perks to having been married to a well-connected man, I'm sure I can get us something a little fancier than those cramped little taxis that brought us here.'

'I think I can still hear that music,' Harold said softly. 'I feel like I should go back up there.'

Anna tried to listen but she couldn't hear any music now, and she suspected that Harold might be imagining it.

'No,' Vivian said, shaking her head, 'you definitely shouldn't be doing that, we don't want you getting yourself lost again.'

'I wasn't lost,' Harold protested.

'You need to come outside with me,' Vivian said, 'and you can keep me company while we wait.' She took hold of his arm. Harold looked down at her hand and then placed his hand on top of hers. 'Alright, I will,' he replied.

'I think I'd prefer to wait outside too,' Anna said. 'I don't fancy staying in this house any longer than I need to.'

Mark stood beside her and said, with a grin, 'Then I'll keep *you* company.'

Anna caught Katarina frowning at Mark, before the young woman announced, 'I think I'd rather stay inside where it's warm and dry, at least until the rain stops. I don't want to catch a cold standing out in the rain.'

Vivian rolled her eyes at Katarina, and then led the rest of the group out into the rain, wielding their umbrellas. She looked at her phone and told the others that she had a signal, but only a very faint one.

Anna became aware that Mark was standing too close to her. He looked at her and said, 'Anna, has anyone ever told you how beautiful you look in the rain?'

'No, because that's a very weird thing to say to someone that you barely know.'

'Sorry. Did you know that my father proposed to my mother on a rainy day like this, in front of the Eiffel Tower? I've seen the photos. They were both soaking wet. Apparently he got down on his knees and sang her favourite song and then at the end he proposed, and she said yes.'

'Well, we're not in France, and I barely know you, so there'll be no proposing of any sort tonight, if that's what you're thinking.'

Mark looked mortified. 'No, no, I just meant – Oh, forget it, it doesn't matter.'

'It's forgotten. Let's just stand here in silence and wait while Vivian calls our rides to come, shall we?'

Mark nodded, and didn't say any more. Harold had started humming to himself, and Anna realised that he was humming the same melody that they'd heard in the house.

Vivian had managed to reach someone on her phone, but the conversation didn't seem to be going well. She took the phone away from her ear for a moment to explain to the others, 'Taxi company's never heard of Grimwald House. What a surprise.'

Anna checked the map app on her phone, but all it gave her was an apology that it still could not identify her current location. 'That's great,' she muttered. 'It's like we're in the middle of nowhere.'

'Hold on, I hear something. What's that?' Vivian pointed and they saw headlights coming along the road. A taxi drove up to the house, and when it stopped, the driver wound down his window and called out, 'Alright, who's going first?'

Anna looked at the others. So their host, or Handsworth, had actually bothered to call them a ride home, after all. Shame he'd forgotten to let his guests know that they hadn't been abandoned.

'Hah!' Vivian said. 'It's as if someone read my mind.' She then spoke into her phone and told the person on the other end of the call, 'Never mind, it looks like we already have transportation this evening.'

She hung up and persuaded Harold to take the first taxi. He got in reluctantly, and as it moved away, he waved at them through the rear window before he disappeared from their sight.

When the next taxis arrived, Anna went back to the house to let Katarina know. Vivian took the second taxi and Mark took the third, while Katarina told Anna that she should take the fourth.

'Are you sure you're going to be alright by yourself?' Anna asked her, reluctant to leave Katarina alone here at the house.

'I'll be fine,' Katarina assured her. 'I'm sure the next taxi will be along any minute. Go on, don't worry about me.'

As Anna's taxi pulled away from the house, she settled back into the seat. She found herself humming Harold's tune. She knew she was going to have that tune stuck in her head now, and it would remind her of that room with the piano and no one playing it, which annoyed her because she didn't want anything to drag her mind back into that house. She just wanted to go home and forget all about it.

Anna had dozed off on the ride home, just as she had last time, and the driver had to wake her when they arrived at her apartment building. Inside, she took the elevator to reach her apartment, and when she entered, she found Jelly waiting by the door for her. He sounded hungry.

'Give me a minute, will you?' she told the cat. 'I haven't eaten anything myself yet.'

She went to her fridge and found some slices of ham she could put into a sandwich. That would have to do for dinner tonight.

She fed Jelly and then sat on her sofa, eating her sandwich, with her feet up on a footrest, watching television and trying to distract her mind from this evening's events. She rolled her eyes during the lead news story about the latest government cock-up, another politician caught with his pants down. The story had taken priority over seemingly less important news such as a disastrous earthquake and a war going on in some small country that she'd admittedly never heard of. Ghostly pianos and ancient corpses seemed somehow less dramatic when compared to the crazy stories on the news.

When the news had finally finished and an episode of the latest hit crime drama started, Anna's eyelids became heavy again. She said goodnight to Jelly and got herself ready for bed.

Wrapped up in her bedsheets, Anna stared up at the ceiling. Another seven days until the next session at Grimwald House. Seven days until she'd have to go back into that tomb and see that hideous corpse again. She could still hear that piano melody in her head, even now. She wondered if Harold was still thinking about it.

Stop it! She needed to stop thinking about that creepy house so much, or she'd be right back there again, and she didn't want that. She needed to think of nicer things. For the next hour, she tossed and turned and desperately tried to fill her head with more pleasant thoughts, like interesting places she'd been or had always wanted to go to. She imagined herself at the Eiffel Tower, but Mark was there, with his cheesy grin, asking her to marry him, and that brought her mind back to Grimwald House again. She buried her face in her pillow and groaned in frustration. This was going to be another long night.

CHAPTER FOUR

HAROLD

If you don't change your ways, then you won't live past fifty.

Those few small words, drummed into Harold's head by his doctor, had changed his life.

Since Harold had not had much of a family for several years now and had few hobbies on which to spend the money that he'd earned from being an accountant for several wealthy businessmen, instead he'd spent most of his money on food and drink and cigarettes. He'd dine in the finest restaurants, order whatever he fancied from the menu – cost and calories be damned – and he'd smoke after meals, and also during the rest of the day, whenever he got that itch and needed a little relief.

He didn't need a house any bigger than the one that he currently owned, and he already had an expensive car. He'd already found that his skills with money had not translated very successfully to gambling so he had given up on that after it had left him with nothing but debts and regrets. So there was not much else to spend his money and freetime on other than alcohol, food, and cigarettes.

So when his doctor had told him that he would only have a few years left to live if he didn't give up those things that still brought him some pleasure in his life, it had initially made Harold very depressed, which had led him to want to drink more, to eat more, and to smoke more, to fight that misery inside of him. But when he forced himself to take a good look at himself in the mirror and saw how big his belly was, how bad his skin was, and how tired his eyes looked, Harold decided that he had to follow his doctor's advice and do something about his life before it was too late.

He knew that there were plenty of good reasons to cut back on his extravagant lifestyle, not just for the sake of his own failing health, but for the health of his bank balance too, which in his professional opinion deserved its own less-than-optimistic prognosis.

Things would get better soon, though. He'd been exercising more and had started cutting back on a few of his indulgences, as difficult as that was to do, and he'd also made plans to try to turn things around financially too.

The two evenings at Grimwald House had provided a welcome distraction from the stress of sorting out his life. He'd met some unusual people and seen some unusual things, not least the mysterious mummy in the tomb. He could picture himself unwrapping that leg, recalling vividly its unpleasant odour. He was intrigued to know who the unfortunate woman that died so long ago might have been. Perhaps when they reconvened to continue unwrapping the corpse, they might discover more clues as to who she was.

He had to admit to having felt a little apprehensive during the unwrapping. As a child he had watched many classic horror movies from between his fingers while curled up on the sofa. His father would sometimes like to turn the sound off on the TV and play the piano to add his own dramatic soundtrack to the film while Harold watched it. He had seen some films where ancient mummies would come to life to take their revenge on the living. Yes, it was all make-believe, but he couldn't deny that while peeling the wraps from that body at Grimwald House, he had half-expected the dead woman to suddenly reach out and try to grab him by the throat...

Harold had certainly had other memorable company on those evenings. The two younger women, Anna and Katarina, were both quite attractive, but Harold found himself more drawn to Vivian, who wasn't the first older woman that had ever caught Harold's eye. Vivian was intelligent, confident, forthright, and seemingly quite fearless; she'd been very eager to start unwrapping that body in the tomb even when the rest of the group had been rather more reluctant.

Harold had also enjoyed chatting with Mark. Despite his rather forced bravado with the ladies, he seemed like someone that Harold could see himself having a few drinks with. Well, perhaps just the one drink.

Since the last session, Harold had found himself humming the melody that he'd heard playing on the piano with no player, the tune from his childhood. It had been many years since he'd heard that particular tune. He knew that it couldn't be a coincidence that a song that had meant so much to him just happened to be playing at that house that evening. Similarly odd was the very specific amount of money that his group had discovered hidden in their chairs in the dining room – seven hundred and twenty-six pounds and thirty pence, the same amount that he'd had in his bank the day of his interview for his first accounting job.

How had their mysterious host found out these personal, private things about him? And why arrange these elaborate tricks, what was the point of it all?

Right now, Harold was sitting in a corridor outside a meeting room at the lavish offices of one of his clients, waiting for that client to finish a previous meeting so that Harold could present his report on the accounts that he'd been examining for most of the week. It was important to Harold that his client be impressed and happy with his work.

This particular client, Mr Timothy Edwards, was one that Harold had known for many years. He was a wealthy man who owned a number of businesses, and Harold didn't begrudge the man one or two errors here or there in his accounts, especially when Timothy gave a good amount to charity, which guilted Harold into making the occasional donation himself. Like most rich men, Timothy had more money than he knew what to do with.

Harold could hear the murmur of voices from behind the closed doors of his client's office. They appeared to be getting louder – or closer. He took off his glasses to rub his eyes and then quickly replaced them as the doors opened. He sat up straight in his chair as a striking young woman with dark hair wearing a short skirt came out of the room. As she walked by, he recognised her as Zara Edwards, the daughter of his client. She did not look happy. Harold knew from conversations he'd had with Timothy in the past that Zara and her two older brothers were always fighting over who would eventually take over the reins of the family business from their old man. Timothy had tried putting them in charge of certain smaller companies that he owned, to see how they would get on with running their own businesses, but he had grumbled to Harold that so far he'd been unimpressed with their efforts. They seemed to prefer to spend most of their time – and their father's money – enjoying themselves in the U.S., where their late mother's family lived, rather than here in England helping to run their father's businesses. Harold doubted that any of them had a good enough understanding of their father's businesses to be able to take over from him, or to manage all of his money properly. Timothy was one of Harold's wealthiest clients, and Harold had a vested interest in making sure that the man's money went to the right places.

Zara's eyes caught Harold's just as she entered the lift and the doors closed. He waited until his name was called, and when it finally was, he got to his feet, straightened his suit, and entered the room. His client stood behind a large desk, resting his hands on the surface, and shaking his head. Harold noticed that there appeared to be a storm brewing on the man's face. 'Take a seat, Harold,' he commanded.

Harold lowered himself onto the chair and said, 'Thank you. It's good to see you again, Timothy.'

Timothy Edwards remained standing, which struck Harold as odd, as well as the fact that normally he would have been offered something to drink by now. Nevertheless, Harold placed his report onto the desk and opened it, ready to start going through it. He looked up to see Timothy glaring at him, and hesitated. 'Is something wrong?' Harold asked. He glanced at the door. 'Is everything alright with Zara?'

'This has nothing to do with my daughter. No, I'm afraid it's to do with you, Harold.'

'Me? Sorry, I don't know what you mean?'

Timothy rubbed his beard as he started circling around the desk. 'Confidentiality, that's what I'm talking about, or the lack of it. It seems *someone* has been leaking certain financial details to a rival of mine, and I'm very disappointed.'

Harold went cold. 'Timothy, I've worked with you for years. You don't think that I would do something like that, do you?'

'Somebody bloody has, and it wasn't me. The information that has got out includes things that I thought only you and I were aware of. So it must be you or somebody at your office.'

'I swear I don't know anything about that,' Harold protested. 'You know that there's only me and my assistant Susan, and she doesn't have access to your financial information, and frankly doesn't have the wherewithal to do anything like this. Besides, she's a good person and I trust her.'

Timothy sighed. 'Then we come right back around to you again, don't we? So what is it, am I not paying you enough? Somebody come to you with a better offer?'

Harold shook his head. 'No, no, I'd never do that to any of my clients. Timothy, please, you have to believe me!'

'I think I'd prefer that you address me as Mr Edwards from now on. In fact, I think I'd prefer that we no longer do business at all.'

'There must be some mistake, some misunderstanding. I'm sure we can sort this out.' Harold held out the report that he'd prepared. 'I've spent days on this report and preparing my recommendations, why don't we sit down and take a look at it? I'm sure you'll be happy.'

'I don't give a shit about your damn report!' Mr Edwards yelled at Harold, making him jump. 'The only reason I called you in here today was to look you in the eyes and tell you, in person, that I no longer require your services. My assistant will also be sending you a formal notice in writing, and I *will* be considering legal action. Now please leave, and don't ever come back again. You can forget about references. In fact, I've half a mind to call your other clients and tell them what has happened, and advise them to never do business with you again.'

'Timothy – Mr Edwards – please, don't do that.' Harold's mind immediately went to trying to calculate how much income he could lose if that threat was carried out.

Mr Edwards pointed to the door. 'Show yourself out. I can't stand the sight of you anymore.'

Harold sat with his mouth agape, trying and failing to find some way to rescue this disastrous situation. Eventually, he made himself move. He stood, picked up his report from the desk, turned and walked back out through the door, which was slammed shut behind him, leaving him alone in the corridor outside.

Still processing what had just happened, Harold made his way to the elevator and rode it down to the reception area, before leaving the building through the front entrance.

When he stepped outside, he noticed Zara leaning against a wall, a cigarette on her lips, her phone in her hand. She was looking up and down the street, presumably waiting for someone. When she spotted Harold, she took the cigarette away from her mouth and called over to him, 'Need a smoke? You look like you might.'

Harold approached her and she handed him a cigarette, which he stared at as she lit it for him. He thanked her. *One cigarette won't hurt, just this once*, he told himself.

'Your meeting with my dad went that well, then?' Zara asked.

Harold was in a daze. 'Not really, no... he fired me, and I can't understand why.'

'Shit. I'm sorry. Dear old Dad isn't in the best of moods at the moment.'

Harold held the cigarette in his trembling hands as he said, 'Your father accused me of leaking financial information to a rival of his, but I would never do that to him.'

Zara raised her eyebrows. 'Wow. He really has gone off the deep end. I'm sorry that he's being such an asshole to you.'

'This could ruin me, if people hear about this. If my other clients find out, I don't know what I'll do.'

Zara took another drag of her cigarette and then said, 'I know what I'd do if I were innocent, I'd try and work out who stitched me up – assuming my dad's not just making it all up. I'd think about who might have access to my dad's financial records, and who might benefit from releasing them. Oh, and in case you start thinking it, no, it wasn't me. And I doubt it was one of my brothers, either, because they're both morons, and they haven't got the smarts or the balls to go up against Dad.'

Harold finished his cigarette while deep in thought. 'I'm going to head back to my office and try to figure this out. Thank you for the cigarette, and the advice.'

She shrugged. 'No problem. Good luck with clearing your name. I'd love to be there when Dad has to admit he screwed up and apologises to you, I'd like to see his face.'

Harold nodded a goodbye as Zara returned to her phone and busied herself doing whatever young women did on their phones these days. Harold walked down the steps to the street and found where he had parked his car, opened the door, and sat inside. He placed the report he'd written onto the passenger seat, and then took hold of the steering wheel. He could see his hands were shaking. What he wouldn't give for a drink right now...

Harold banged his fist on the steering wheel, swore, started the engine and then pulled his car out into the road—

Then the whole world changed around him. It turned, dizzyingly, it twisted, and became a blur.

He heard the deafening crunch of metal on metal, and then the windscreen shattered, but the glass didn't hit his face, because the airbag was in the way. Searing pain ran through his legs.

The world didn't stop spinning for several long, drawn-out seconds. By the time it had stopped, Harold couldn't see anything. He heard faded shouts, and then a familiar voice telling him that he was going to be alright, that she was going to call an ambulance, and that he shouldn't try to move.

He was vaguely aware of being in a car crash, but his mind didn't seem to want to fully acknowledge that. Instead, it sent him back to Grimwald House, where he imagined the strange piano playing in slow motion with no one's hands at the keys, and he thought he could now hear that melody from his childhood again, as if it was playing on the car radio. He found the music soothing as he drifted off into the darkness.

It had been two days since the accident, although time seemed to have lost all meaning. Harold no longer felt like himself anymore. He didn't feel whole, and he worried that he never would again.

His assistant Susan had come to visit him at the hospital. It would be nice to imagine that she'd done so purely out of concern for his well-being, but their conversation – as one-sided as it was – mainly revolved around what was happening to their business.

She was now imparting even more bad news.

'I've had the confirmation in writing from Mr Edwards and I've taken phone calls from two other clients who also now want to leave us. I'd say it's like rats abandoning a sinking ship, but I have no idea why we're sinking. I've explained your situation, and that you're still perfectly capable of working for them, but it doesn't seem to make any difference to them.' She let out a sigh. 'Harold, if this keeps up, I'm worried about whether I'll still have a job soon. I can't afford to go without pay! Not with the kids and their school fees and their clothes and the food bill each week... I just can't. What are we going to do?'

Harold was aware that Susan was waiting for him to respond, but he didn't much feel like moving his mouth to form words, nor in fact moving any part of his body that still functioned. He would, however, give anything to be able to move his legs again.

The doctor had told him that he had been lucky, that it could've been much worse, and that the damage to his legs was not permanent and that eventually he would be able to walk again. Harold wasn't so sure.

After all the worrying that he'd been doing about his eating, drinking and smoking, and what all that was doing to his body, he would never have expected something as dramatic as a car crash to be the reason that he'd end up in hospital. Not for the first time in recent memory, he felt like he was being punished.

Staring down at his legs, he couldn't help but think of that corpse at Grimwald House, with its own decayed, useless body. He started sobbing and Susan took his hand and squeezed it, and he appreciated her attempt to comfort him, but he could see from the expression on her face that she would rather be anywhere else but here.

Harold wiped his eyes and replaced his glasses as his nurse entered the room to check on him.

'Now, that's enough of that,' the nurse told him as she saw his face. 'Stop feeling sorry for yourself. You'll be back on your feet before you know it, you just need to be patient and work at it. As much as you might like my company, you can't stay lying in this bed forever, we've a shortage of beds, and only the people that really need them should have them.'

The nurse pointed at the contraption in the corner of the room that had been staring at him, that hateful thing that reminded him of how his life had now changed. 'Have you thought about giving it a try yet? I'd be more than happy to push you around for a while, I think it'd be good for you to see something other than these four walls.'

Susan took her side. 'She's right, you know. You ought to try it, Harold, you might feel better then.'

Harold forced himself to look at the wheelchair, and the tears came back again.

The nurse tutted. 'Now come on, all that blubbing's not very manly, is it? I'm going to come back and check on you later, and when I do, I want to see none of that, thank you very much. I'll tell you what, if I see nothing but dry eyes next time I come around, I'll see if I can snatch you a piece of Rosa's birthday cake, how does that sound?'

Harold nodded.

'That's a good man.' The nurse gave him a smile, then left the room.

Susan spoke again. 'Harold, I don't want to upset you more, but what are we going to do about these clients?'

Harold sniffled and finally answered, 'Timothy – Mr Edwards – has made a mistake, and he's taken it upon himself to speak to some of our other clients and convince them that I'm not to be trusted. If it wasn't for my legs, I would go see them right now and do something about it. I'm sorry, Susan. I don't know what the future holds, not for the business, and not for me.'

Susan nodded. 'Alright. Try and get some rest, Harold. Maybe give the wheelchair a go if you're up to it. Once you get out of here, we can sit down together and try to figure out what to do. In the meantime, I'll keep taking those phone calls. Maybe I can sweet-talk some of them into giving us another chance? I think it's worth a try.'

Harold watched as Susan got to her feet to leave. How he envied her. The simple act of standing up, which had once seemed like the easiest thing in the world, now seemed impossible, like some complex mathematical problem that he knew he would never be able to solve.

The promised cake for good behaviour hadn't been a lie, and it had tasted amazing, although it only had to clear the low bar set by the hospital meals that Harold had suffered through over the last few days.

The nurse seemed pleased with him, especially when he'd finally agreed to take the wheelchair for a spin. She helped him out of the bed and into the wheelchair, opened the door to his room and then pushed him through it and out into the busy corridor. He had a mild panic attack; he was unused to being surrounded by so many people all at once. He closed his eyes and took deep, slow breaths to calm himself down.

The nurse wheeled him along the corridor and when he reopened his eyes he saw that they'd arrived at a pair of double doors, beyond which was a small garden area. As he was taken through the doors and felt the cool air on his face, he looked around. The tiny courtyard was surrounded on all sides by the walls of the hospital building, and in the centre there was one solitary tree, faced by four benches, one on each side of the courtyard. The tree was a rather pathetic sight, but still somehow welcome after those four blank walls whose only comfort had been a window that he couldn't see much out of and an awkwardly-angled television set positioned too high up on one wall.

'A bit of fresh air, this'll do you good,' the nurse told him.

She wasn't wrong. It wasn't going to magically heal his legs, but it did make him feel a little better, a little more alive. The air was rather cold, but it felt good to breathe it in. He breathed in a little too deeply though, and it started a coughing fit that lasted nearly a whole minute.

'You really need to start taking better care of your health, don't you?' the nurse observed. Harold considered telling her about all the progress he'd made in that area over the past few weeks, the exercises that he'd started doing and the unhealthy things that he'd cut down on, but he was afraid that she might belittle his achievements and tell him that it wasn't enough, that it was too little, too late, and he couldn't take hearing that right now.

He heard the door behind them open and another woman, who had a younger, rather more feminine voice, told his nurse, 'Harold has a visitor, shall I bring her out here to see him?'

'Yes, that's fine, thank you, Rosa.'

Harold saw his nurse beaming down at him. 'Did you hear that, Harold? You have another visitor. You're popular today.'

It was probably just Susan again. Perhaps she had more bad news about another departing client to impart? He could do without that. He didn't want to think about work right now. He just wanted to be in this garden and stare at that wrinkled tree and forget about the rest of the world.

His nurse released his wheelchair and left to give him some privacy with his visitor. To his surprise, when his visitor entered his field of vision it wasn't his assistant and was instead a young woman in a short skirt. His foggy brain didn't recognise her at first until she said, 'I suppose I'm not allowed to smoke, or offer you one, am I?'

He recognised her now. It was Zara Edwards. The daughter of the client that had fired him. What was she doing here?

Harold saw Zara's eyes fall to his useless legs. 'God, I'm sorry about what happened to your legs. How terrible.'

Zara sat down on one of the benches, and crossed her legs. Another simple action that he could no longer do. 'I can still picture it in my head, you know?' she told him. 'Your car, all mangled up like that, you looked in such a state that I almost thought you wouldn't make it, but thank God you're okay, right?'

'Yes. Thank God.'

Zara reached into her handbag, presumably to go for a cigarette, but then stopped herself, and instead placed her hand back down on the bench. 'It happened so fast, didn't it?' she said. 'I mean, there you were, talking and smoking with me only a minute or two before it happened. That truck, it just came out of nowhere! Fucking idiot, not looking where he was going. I think these assholes drive those big trucks and they think they own the road and they're, like, invulnerable or something. They don't give a shit about what might happen if they hit someone else, like another car. Or even a kid, God forbid. I mean, as long as they're fine, that's all they care about. He could've killed you, you know? Maybe he was off his head. I couldn't believe it when that selfish bastard drove off and left you there. I wish I'd thought to take a picture of the licence plate on my phone, then the police could've caught the bastard. I'm just glad I was there so I could call you an ambulance, or who knows what might've happened.'

'Thank you for doing that,' Harold said. 'If you hadn't, I might've lost more than the use of my legs. I owe you.'

Zara waved her hand. 'Nah, you don't owe me anything, especially since my family's the reason you were there in the first place. If my dad hadn't asked you to come see him that day, if I hadn't offered you that smoke, if you'd only gone out to your car a few minutes earlier, then things would be so different for you right now. God, that's crazy, to think that all these tiny little decisions, they can change your whole life – just like that!' She snapped her fingers, which made Harold jump. 'It's mad, isn't it?'

'Mad. Yes.'

She uncrossed her legs, and stood up, making him jealous again. She circled the courtyard, then started fondling the leaves on the tree. She seemed unimpressed and released the leaves, and turned her attention back to Harold. 'How are they treating you here? The nurses are not too mean, are they? The one that I saw you with looked like a bit of a battleaxe.'

'She's alright,' he answered. 'They're looking after me. I suppose I should be grateful, it's just that I'm finding it hard to be positive, because of my legs, and with what's happening to my business. It's all such a mess.'

Zara nodded. 'Yeah, I get that. It sucks. Listen, I have to be honest, I didn't come down here just to check how you were. I mean, partly I did, but also because I wanted to talk to you about something.'

'What's that?' he asked, watching as the young woman circled the tree.

'It's about my dad,' she answered. 'I'm sure you know that he and I don't see eye to eye on some things. Most things, actually. Like what he does with his money, for example. My brothers feel the same way, but I wouldn't trust them to use it any more wisely than my dad. Sometimes I think the only person with any common sense in my family is me, at least since my mom died.'

Harold had a sudden coughing fit, which seemed to alarm Zara, but once it was over, he told her, 'It is your father's money, and until he's *non compos mentis*, he can spend it how he wishes. I've helped him over the years, and I've seen how the money's been managed. I would say he's done a reasonable job, barring one or two mistakes here and there.'

Zara sighed. 'Mistakes, yes, my dad's made a few of those in his life, believe me, I know that. As for being *compos mentis*, well, sometimes I wonder. You only have to look at the crazy thing he did to you, firing you like that for no good reason, just silly paranoia. Also, sometimes he forgets things, or starts a conversation with me and then drifts off. It's like he doesn't have the energy to continue. Like his battery's drained. It's a little scary, I have to be honest, seeing him withering away like this.'

Harold frowned. 'Is he really that bad? I can't say that I've noticed anything especially odd in his behaviour. At least up until he fired me, anyway.'

'Okay, but I see things. I hear things, too, from his housekeeper, his friends, even from his doctor. Little things, but they start to add up. And then I start to worry.

'Has he told you about this new startup company that he's invested a substantial amount of our family's money in? No? They make stupid little dolls, for God's sake! Kids' toys! Why the hell would we want to put so much of our family's money into that? I even asked him about it, and he told me this nonsense about it being some young woman that dazzled him with a great business pitch, blah blah, and what my dad described as, and I quote, "very impressive projections". Hah! What a joke! From what I've heard, the only impressive projections that girl has are her fake breasts... I can guess that greedy little bitch's game. She's trying to fleece my dad, and he's falling for it, like the old fool that he is. I doubt she's even that pretty, but you know how it is, all men are gullible idiots with one-track minds. No offence.'

Harold didn't take offence, however he did feel uncomfortable with the vicious way that Zara was describing that young woman, but he bit his tongue and didn't say anything. After a moment, he asked her, 'You don't seriously think your father would invest a large amount of money into a business just because some young lady comes along and flirts with him?'

Zara shrugged. 'I don't know, I really don't, not anymore. The thing is, Dad was never like this before. He was with my mom since they were teenagers, and my whole life I swear I've never seen him so much as look at another woman, not really, even when I know certain people have tried to tempt him. But he's changed in the past few months. It's like his brain isn't what it was. I mean, this is just one example, but there are others. Last month, for example, we couldn't find my mom's favourite necklace, the one that she wore all the time before she passed away. We looked everywhere, we even thought that one of my dad's staff might have stolen it. Then one day it turns up and – get this – it's only around his dog's neck! His dog, for God's sake! If that's not a sign he's lost it, then I don't know what is.

'You can see why I'm so worried. I've tried talking to him about it, I've even offered to get him some help, but he just denies it all, and we end up in another blazing row. I can't get through to him.'

'I'm sorry to hear all this,' Harold said, 'but I'm not quite sure what it is that you want me to do about it?'

Zara knelt in front of his chair, and placed her hands on his arms. She was very close to him now, and it made him feel a little uncomfortable. She stared at him with her piercing brown eyes as she said, 'I'd like you to help me prove that my dad is unwell and not capable of managing our family's money anymore. You've seen the financial records, you know them better than anybody, and right now I feel like you're the only one I can trust to help me. Will you help me?'

Harold considered her request. He wanted to help her, but Timothy was his client, not Zara, or at least that had been the case before Harold had suddenly been fired. She was asking him to go behind her father's back. Harold could be placing himself in the middle of a family feud, and that path could be fraught with danger. 'I need to think about it,' he said.

Seeing his indecision, Zara sighed, and then told him, 'Alright, look, Harold, there's one more thing I haven't told you yet, and I wasn't going to say anything, but I don't think I have a choice. And I'm sorry, I think it's going to be pretty painful for you to hear.'

Harold frowned. 'What is it?'

She took a deep breath and looked him in the eyes. 'I don't think your accident was just an accident.'

It took Harold a moment to process what she'd said. 'What do you mean?'

'It's all a little too coincidental, isn't it? You get on the wrong side of my powerful, wealthy, well-connected dad who we know has started to go off the deep end, and then all of a sudden you have this terrible accident right outside his office. You can't tell me that isn't a little bit suspicious?'

Harold was incredulous. 'What are you saying? You think your father arranged for that truck to hit me? No, that's insane!'

'Yes it is, but so is he. Look, I haven't told the police this, but I thought maybe I recognised the driver of that truck, I think I've seen him speaking with my dad before. I can't be sure, but if I'm right, then it means that this didn't just happen for no reason, it was done to you on purpose. Harold, I really don't know what else my dad might be capable of in his current state. That's what's got me so worried. What if I'm next, or one of my brothers? We don't exactly all get on. I'm frightened, and I'm not one to be easily scared.'

'This is unbelievable.' Harold stared down at his legs. Could this be true? Was Timothy Edwards responsible for what had happened to him?

Zara stared at her fingernails. 'Shit, maybe I'm wrong, and it is all just a bunch of coincidences. Perhaps I shouldn't have said anything, I've probably made things worse, haven't I?'

Harold shook his head. 'No, you did the right thing by telling me. I just never thought Timothy could be capable of something like this.'

'Do you see now why I'm so worried? We have to do something before anybody else gets hurt. I'm asking you to help me, Harold. Can you do that?'

Harold thought for a moment, then made his decision. 'Yes. Yes, I think I can. I'll help you. I don't want anyone else to get hurt.'

Zara looked pleased. 'That's good. Thank you, Harold, this means a lot. I promise you'll be taken care of, you know I have the money and contacts to get you help with your recovery, so you won't have to worry about any of that, and I'm sure you'll be up and about again before you know it. I'll also put in a good word with your other clients, too, and I know some of my dad's other contacts that we could send your way.

'Harold, I know this will be difficult, but remember you'll be helping my dad too, in a way, even if he isn't well enough to appreciate it. It's the best thing for everybody. Okay, look, I'll leave you in peace now. Here's my number, call me anytime.' She handed Harold her business card and stood up, placing her hand on his shoulder. 'I hope we'll chat again very soon. Things will get better for you, Harold, I know they will, and I'll do what I can to make sure of that. Goodbye for now.'

'Yes, goodbye, Zara. And thank you. Thank you very much.'

The young woman smiled at him, then left him alone in the garden and went back inside the hospital. His nurse then returned and said, 'I think that's enough excitement for now, don't you? No more pretty girls for you today! Let's get you back to bed, shall we?'

Harold allowed himself to be wheeled back to his room. As the nurse helped him back onto his bed, he thought about the conversation that he'd just had and what it meant. Had he really become a target for Timothy's growing insanity? If Timothy believed Harold had betrayed him and wanted revenge, then he was lucky he hadn't lost more than just the use of his legs.

The thought that it wasn't just an accident was hugely upsetting, and he had to try hard not to let it overwhelm him. Instead, he focussed his thoughts on Zara's offer. She was giving him the opportunity to restore his damaged reputation, not to mention the medical aid that could help him walk again, plus they could put a stop to Timothy's behaviour before anyone else got hurt.

Harold knew that even if he couldn't prove that Timothy was responsible for his "accident" then he could at least provide Zara with enough evidence to indicate that her father was making bad decisions and not capable of handling his finances properly anymore. Harold looked at the table beside his bed, on which his phone rested. He reached across and picked it up, then called Susan. He asked her if she would bring his laptop, on which he had a password-protected folder of files about the Edwards family businesses and finances. He also asked her to bring the paper copy of the financial report – Susan had mentioned that the police had recovered it from the scene of his accident. She'd seemed quite eager to do all this for him, and told him that he was starting to sound more like his old self again.

One thing that was particularly concerning to Harold was Zara's discovery of the odd investments that her father had made into that doll company. Harold would need to go through the records again and see if he could find a way to address Zara's concerns.

Susan promised to bring Harold what he'd asked for, so long as he promised to try and get some rest.

Harold's mind was racing, and it felt good to focus his mind on something other than his useless legs.

Harold rolled himself along the hospital corridors in his wheel-chair, making his way back towards his room, humming a song to himself. He felt like he was starting to get better at this and he wouldn't have to be quite as reliant on others as he'd feared. Thanks to Zara and her offer, he felt a little rejuvenated, at least mentally. He had a purpose again.

When he reached his room, he was surprised to see a woman with blonde hair with her back to him going through the report that Susan had brought him – the *confidential* report.

Harold gently closed the door behind him, then loudly cleared his throat to announce his presence. The young woman was startled, and dropped the document she was holding onto his bed. She put her hand against her ample chest and let out a deep breath. 'You made me jump!'

She looked at his legs. 'Wow, I see they weren't lying, that accident really messed you up. My, what nice big wheels you have.'

'Those files are about Timothy Edwards,' Harold told her. 'Put them down.'

She smiled at him. 'I know they are, and they're just as fascinating as the last records of his that I saw. For instance, I can see a mention here of a large set of payments to a company that allegedly makes little dolls. Isn't that interesting?'

Harold rolled himself closer. 'Yes, and his daughter Zara has found out about that, and is not too impressed. I think she suspects her father is being conned.'

She frowned at him. 'Oh, really? I wonder how she found out, I did try to be discreet. No, that's not true, I wasn't discreet at all. I flirted with Timothy in front of everybody at the restaurant. Tongues will wag.' She flashed a smile.

'Yes, Zara did mention that she thought you'd used your... feminine charms to convince her father to invest a lot of money into a business that he would otherwise have no interest in.'

She fluffed Harold's pillow. 'That wasn't what did it, though, not this time. I mean, usually it's very simple, I put on a tight dress, the right bra, a short skirt, come-to-me lipstick – it doesn't normally fail, not with any man. Some women, too. But Timothy Edwards, he was trickier. I had to figure out a different approach. I worked it out eventually, though. Zara, she was the key. Playing on his tricky relationship with his daughter, that was how I got to him in the end. I told him I'd set up that doll business and was desperate to make it a success because I was estranged from my father and would give anything to make him proud of me. Then I laid on the waterworks and Timothy fell for it, hard, like a lemming jumping off a cliff.'

'So you got Timothy to give you all that money by pretending that you loved your father?'

She smiled. 'I did.'

'What a very good liar you are,' Harold said, shaking his head. 'You don't care what your father thinks of you. You never have.'

She thumped her fist on the side of the bed, making Harold jump. Then she stepped towards him, waving her finger at him. 'No, I don't fucking care, because my father's a selfish bastard who wasted all the money he made on himself and his vices when he could've shared it with me and Mom! No, instead, he threw it all away and got fat, wrecked his health, and ruined his marriage! If Mom were still alive, she'd be so ashamed!'

Harold put up his hands. 'Calm down, or you'll have another one of your attacks.'

'Fuck you.' She was breathing hard and was bright red in the face. She closed her eyes, and walked over to the window, muttering to herself.

'You should know, Zara believes that her father's mental state is deteriorating,' Harold told her, 'especially since you planted his wife's necklace on his dog. Soon enough, she and her brothers will take control of their father's finances.'

She frowned at him. 'I didn't plant any necklace on any dog.'

Harold shrugged. 'Then perhaps Zara's right and her father really is starting to lose his mind. Anyway, the money that you convinced him to give to you for that doll business, it's now in a bank account for a company that doesn't exist. You should go to the bank, right now, and take out however much money you think you need, and then get as far away as you can.'

'What about your share?' she asked.

Harold sighed. 'Erin, that money was never for me. It was always for you.'

Erin looked at Harold like she didn't believe him.

'I want you to have a better life,' he told her. 'I want you to stop running any more of these scams, because I'm terrified that one day you're going to get yourself hurt. So take this money and make something better of yourself. With the state of my health, I don't know what my future holds anymore, so I want to make sure that when I'm gone, you won't have to worry about money. If I get creative with the financial records that I give to Zara, then I can make you and that doll business disappear. Zara has even promised to help me restore the reputation of my business and help with my medical situation too. Who knows, perhaps we could all still come out of this winners, in the end.'

Erin laughed. 'Except, of course, for poor old Timothy Edwards.'

'Yes, but you don't care what happens to him, do you?'

'No, I suppose I don't,' Erin replied, as she played with her hair.

'I should tell you something,' Harold said. 'Zara thinks her father might have caused my accident. That he might've arranged for that truck to hit my car.'

Erin stopped playing with her hair and stared at him. 'Shit, really? I wouldn't have pegged him as the type that would do something like that. I'm impressed. I guess you never know people as well as you think you do, do you? You know, it's your own bloody fault, selling off those financial records to Timothy's rivals, you were asking for trouble. I mean, why the hell did you do that?!'

Harold felt embarrassed. 'I just needed something to pay off a few of my debts, I was getting desperate, but I didn't want to take away any of the money that you were going to make, I wanted you to have all of that. And, if I'm being honest, I also thought it might not be a bad idea to have a backup plan, just in case—'

'In case I messed up? Oh ye of so little faith.'

'I did it for you, Erin, can't you see that?'

'I knew what I was doing! My plan was good, and it worked. I just had to adapt it a little. Timothy only needed a little nudge, just not in the way I'd originally thought. Do you know how bloody weird it was, though, flirting with a man who's old enough to be my father? I'm just glad that wasn't what Timothy seemed to want from me. But

God, the thought of kissing that wrinkled old face... ugh, it'd be like kissing you.'

Harold looked down, and said sadly, 'You know, you used to kiss me, when you were little.'

'Yes, on the cheek, and only because I was too young and stupid back then to realise what a useless bastard you were. Now I know better, and I can barely stand the sight of you.'

Harold lost his temper. 'Then, why don't you just leave, go take your money, and you'll never have to see me again, if that's what you want!'

Erin nodded. 'You know what? I think it is.'

'Erin, wait, I didn't mean—'

'No, you were right, I should go, I should leave you here. Thank you for letting me take all the money, I'm definitely going to do that, but I'm going to be generous with you too, I'm going to call us even. Because with that money, and with the bonus of getting to see you like this, in the pathetic state that you're now in, I think that's all I really needed. It's been a pleasure doing business with you, Dad.'

She mimed blowing him a kiss, and as she moved to leave the room she hummed a tune, a familiar tune, the same one that Harold had heard playing at Grimwald House. It was the melody that his father had used to play on the piano, and when Erin was a little girl Harold used to sing that same tune to her when she went to bed, to help her sleep. The memories hit him hard. She'd been such a kind child. It was difficult to see that sweet little girl in the hateful woman that he saw before him now.

Erin deliberately pushed Harold's wheelchair as she passed by him, and he rolled forward and banged into the bed. She opened the door and left her father alone in his room.

Harold stared at the window. Then at the report on the bed. Then down at his legs. He took off his glasses and cast them onto his bed. He gripped the wheels of his chair so hard that his knuckles went white.

Then he screamed out all of his frustration and guilt, rattled his chair, and cried out his daughter's name.

It was the morning of his next scheduled visit to Grimwald House, but Harold had no intention of attending, due to his extenuating circumstances. However, Harold had had enough of the hospital and told his doctor that he had decided to leave, and wouldn't take no for an answer. His assistant Susan had agreed to pick him up in her car and drive him back to his house.

Susan had seemed a little more optimistic since Harold had explained about Zara's offer, even if she wasn't particularly happy about the idea of going behind their client's back. Harold knew that Susan had no idea what he and Erin had done, and it was best to keep her in the dark.

While still in his hospital bed, Harold had already sent certain financial information to Zara from his laptop. She'd been very grateful, and he knew that he was doing the right thing, even if it hadn't felt like it at first.

Harold sat in the passenger seat, feeling frustrated as he waited for Susan to get out and then take his wheelchair from the boot of her car. She unfolded it and helped him into it, before she took his keys and opened the front door of his house and helped him over the step.

She then returned to her car and retrieved a pair of crutches. Harold looked around as he waited in the hallway for her. It was good to be back home again after those days spent in that cold, sterile hospital room, staring at those blank walls. There were unopened letters on the floor by the door, and Susan scooped them up and put them on a table in the hallway along with his keys.

'Let's get some air in here,' she said, and went off to open some windows. When she returned, she found Harold staring off into space.

She wheeled him into his living room before going through his mail. She picked up one letter in particular that had an elaborate scrawl on the cover with just his first name and no address.

'This one might be something important.' She tried to hand him the envelope. 'Harold, come on, please – your hands still work, don't they? Take it.'

Reluctantly, he took the envelope from her. Susan told him that she'd make him something to eat, and once she'd left him alone he opened the envelope, took out the letter inside, and began reading:

Dear Guest

This is a polite reminder that you signed an agreement to attend five sessions at Grimwald House. Attendance is mandatory. Please be advised that the agreement you signed is binding and must still be adhered to, no matter what change of circumstances may have befallen you in the meantime.

Yours sincerely
H

Harold stared at the letter in disbelief. Not only had this "H" somehow found out about his accident, but they still expected him to come and attend that ridiculous charade tonight. Did they really think he cared about pulling the bandages off some long-dead woman right now?

Harold angrily crumpled up the letter into a jagged ball and then threw it towards the bin. He failed to make the shot and it bounced off onto the floor.

Susan came back with a tray of food and a jug of water and set them down on the coffee table in front of him. She picked up the ball of paper from the floor and placed it in the bin. She glanced at the oversized clock on his wall and said, 'I will need to head off soon to pick up my kids. Do you need anything else?'

'No, I'm fine,' he told her.

'Call me if you have any problems, and I'll come straight over.' She stood in the doorway and looked at the staircase. 'We could get you a stairlift, maybe, until your legs get better. Oh, there's so much to think about now that you're – well, you know.'

'I know.'

She drummed her fingers on the doorframe. 'Have you thought about asking any family for help? Perhaps Erin could help?'

'No, Erin won't help me,' Harold replied bitterly.

'Perhaps you might consider hiring someone then? Just until you're back on your feet.'

'Zara Edwards has offered to help me pay for any medical care I need, so I could take her up on that offer. There's also that physiotherapist that the doctor recommended I see too. So there will be people to help me. But right now I just want to be alone, thank you Susan.'

Susan seemed reluctant to leave Harold alone, but she glanced at her watch and said, 'I do need to get going now, but I'll come back afterwards and check on you.'

Harold looked towards the crumpled-up letter in the bin and thought for a moment. Perhaps it would actually do him good to go to Grimwald House and be with Vivian and Mark and the others, it would certainly take his mind off his situation, if only for a short while. He wouldn't be the centre of attention there, not with all the other strange goings-on at that house. He looked at Susan. 'No, that's alright,' he told her. 'I have somewhere I need to be tonight.'

Susan frowned. 'What are you talking about?'

'I have an appointment, and apparently, non-attendance isn't an option. They'll be sending a taxi to come and pick me up.'

'That's ridiculous, you can't go anywhere in your condition, you're not up to it, you've only just got out of hospital. So don't be silly.'

'I'm not bloody useless!' he shouted back at her, and the outburst took her by surprise. 'I'm sorry, I didn't mean to shout. I promise, I'll be alright. I have to go.'

She looked dubious. 'I'm not happy about this, but alright. I'm coming back first thing tomorrow, though. And if you need anything at all, you call me.'

'I will. Thank you, Susan.'

Susan left the room and then the house. Harold listened to her car drive away. He looked down at his legs and sighed. He reached over to the coffee table to pick up the sandwich Susan had made for him, then ate it and drank some water. He wheeled himself to the downstairs bathroom, looked at his toilet apprehensively, decided that he didn't really need to go just yet, and wheeled himself back to the living room.

Harold picked up the remote and turned on the television, and allowed himself to get lost in sitcom reruns. He didn't laugh once. He took off his glasses and dozed off.

An hour or so later, Harold's phone rang and woke him. He put his glasses on, and despite not recognising the number shown on his phone, he decided to answer the call. 'Hello?'

The woman on the other end of the call sounded distraught. 'Hello, I'm sorry to bother you. I rang your office, it seemed to redirect me to a mobile. Your assistant answered and I'm afraid I lost my temper with her, but after I calmed down and explained everything she was kind enough to give me your home number. I hope that it's alright to call you at home? My name is Sally Farnham, you don't know me, but my husband... I'm sorry, he was the one that was driving the truck that hit you.'

'What?!'

'Please don't hang up. I know this is a bit of a shock. And I'm so sorry for what happened to you. I know my husband is too. I'm sure he is. The thing is... I don't know where he is. He's gone missing. He didn't come home from work, and it's been a couple of days now, and I'm very worried.'

'I see,' Harold said. 'Have you called the police?'

'Yes, I did, but they don't know anything yet.'

'Then there's not much else I can suggest at this point. I'm sure he'll turn up.'

'I know you have no reason to care about my husband, especially after what he did to you, but this isn't like him at all. He wouldn't leave us like that. I'm so worried about him. I can't sleep or do anything. I just want to know that he's safe.'

Harold started to get angry. 'Look, there's nothing I can do about it, I don't know your husband or anything about him, and frankly, after what he did to me, I don't know why I should care where he is, or what might have happened to him. So I think you should just—'

'I found something,' Sally interrupted him. 'I don't think he wanted me to find it, but I did. A payment into his bank account, from a week before your accident. It was an unusually large amount, much more than he usually gets paid for jobs.'

Harold frowned. 'Who is it from?'

'It's from a company called C.P.V.K. and I've never heard of them.'

'Oh... I see.'

'Does that mean something to you? Please, if it does, tell me.'

Harold was stunned. Yes, it did mean something to him. It was a small company owned by the Edwards family. He'd seen the name mentioned several times in various financial documents, but Timothy Edwards had always been a little vague about what the company actually did, he just said that it was to do with "problem solving".

'Is this something to do with the Edwards family?' the voice on the phone asked. 'I understand that you're their accountant, aren't you? My husband has done some work for them in the past, I know he has.'

Harold let the phone drop to his lap. The woman's voice was quieter down there, like a little mouse squeaking up at him. But he wasn't listening to her anymore.

It was easy enough to put the pieces together: this woman's husband, Mr Farnham, had been paid an unusually large amount of money, only days before he drove a truck directly into Harold's car just as he was leaving a meeting with a very unhappy Mr Edwards. And now Mr Farnham had mysteriously disappeared.

Zara's theory was correct then. It hadn't been an accident, after all. It had been deliberate. Timothy Edwards had wanted to hurt him, or perhaps even to kill him. Harold had underestimated Timothy. At least it didn't seem like he was aware of Erin's plot, and he hadn't tried to hurt her too, thank God. Still, this was uncharacteristic of Timothy, to say the least. He had always seemed like a good man. Harold couldn't quite believe that his mental state had deteriorated to the point that he would abandon his morals entirely and resort to attempted murder, not to mention whatever might have now happened to Mrs Farnham's husband.

Harold was vaguely aware that the woman had ended the call and was no longer waiting for Harold to respond. He rested his phone on the arm of his chair, deep in thought.

Why was the name of that company Mrs Farnham had mentioned still bugging him? There was something about it, a piece of the puzzle that he felt like he was still missing. Harold rolled himself over to a desk in the corner of the room and opened his laptop. He logged in and checked his records.

There it was: *C.P.V.K.* He now understood why his brain had been bugging him about it since he'd heard the name. He'd been correct in remembering that it was a part of the Edwards business network, but it wasn't registered under Timothy's name. It was under Zara's. It was *her* company, not her father's.

Of course! It made sense now. Zara was the one who had arranged for Harold's accident, not her father. She'd paid Mr Farnham all that money. This wasn't Timothy's doing, it was his daughter's. Timothy had on occasion mentioned how wilful and reckless Zara could be. It was much easier to believe that she might be capable of a deed like this than her father.

Harold thought back to when he was standing outside those offices, accepting that cigarette from her. What an idiot he'd been! She was stalling him. She'd been on her phone and must have been signalling Mr Farnham to drive his truck into Harold's car. She'd lied, she hadn't been surprised by the accident, she'd been waiting for it to happen. Planning it. Zara had acted like she'd saved Harold's life, calling that ambulance so quickly, keeping such a cool head, but she hadn't been his saviour at all – she had been his destroyer.

Zara's claims about her father's mental deterioration were undoubtedly lies too. She probably put her mother's necklace on his dog herself, just to make him appear senile. And as for Zara's promises that she wanted to help Harold, well, he knew now that the "accident" that she'd blamed on her father had given her a hold over him, and she'd exploited it. She didn't care about Harold at all. She'd used him. All she'd wanted was to steal the company away from her father, and Harold had given her exactly what she needed to do that. How could he have been so blind?

Now Harold knew what it was like to be deceived, and to be betrayed. Was the universe paying him back for what he'd done? He'd gone behind Timothy's back and sold information about his business to his rivals, as well as helping Erin with her own scam. He had thought that he would be able to get away with it, just as he had done before with other clients, but it had all gone wrong.

For all of Harold's scheming, for all that he'd suffered, he now re-alised that none of it had been worth it anyway – he'd still lost Erin, his daughter hadn't come back to him with open arms, wanting to reunite what was left of their family, as he'd foolishly hoped. No amount of money would be enough to heal all those old wounds, he could see that now. And his business was ruined, just like his legs were. He felt like he'd lost everything.

In a fit of rage, Harold picked up the plate from the tray and threw it across the room. It hit a wall and shattered. He stared down at the jagged pieces of plate scattered uselessly across the floor.

Broken. All broken now. Just like me.

CHAPTER FIVE

SESSION THREE

'Oh my God, what's happened to you?'

Anna stared in shock at Harold, who sat in his wheelchair in the hallway of Grimwald House, surrounded by Vivian, Katarina and Mark. Katarina rushed over to Anna and exclaimed, 'Oh, Harold's had an awful accident, it's devastating!'

Vivian shot Katarina a look and said, 'Now come on, let's try to be positive, please. I'm sure plenty of people recover the use of their legs after an accident like this, it just takes time and treatment.'

Katarina looked apologetic. 'Sorry, yes, of course, I didn't mean to sound so negative.' She turned to Harold and gave him a supportive smile. 'I'm sure she's right and that you'll be able to walk again very soon.'

Anna placed a hand on Harold's shoulder. 'I'm so sorry. How did this happen?'

'Car crash, a few days ago,' Harold said. 'The doctor said it should only be temporary, but it might take a while until I'm able to walk again properly. But with the way my health is, I'm not so sure... Anyway, I don't want to talk about it and I don't want this evening to be all about me and my situation. I'd rather take my mind off it all, as much as I can. So, how is everyone else?'

Katarina stepped forward and began, 'I'm quite well, thank you, although I have—'

Vivian interrupted her. 'Harold, I'm quite sure the rest of us have nothing at all worth complaining about.' She looked pointedly at Katarina, who chose not to say anything more.

'So, I wonder what fun things they have in store for us this time?' Mark said.

'Perhaps I'll hear that melody again,' Harold said, looking up to the top of the staircase.

Anna stifled a yawn. She'd been working late most nights this week to get some new designs she'd acquired ready for an upcoming presentation, and the stress was starting to take its toll. She couldn't trust anyone else with the job, so she'd had to do it all herself. It had meant long hours for her, and she'd woken up with her face stuck to her desk on more than one occasion this week.

Vivian noted the yawn and said, 'Oh dear, I think we're boring Anna.'

'No, no, I'm fine,' Anna told her, 'it's just been a busy week at work.'

'It sounds to me like you work far too hard,' Mark said, as he opened the door to the dining room for Harold, who wheeled himself in. The others followed him into the room, and as Anna closed the door behind her, she told Mark, 'If I didn't work so hard all the time, then I wouldn't be where I am today.'

He smiled at her. 'You mean here, at the wonderful Grimwald House?'

'No, you know what I mean.'

Anna noticed that this time there was no dining table, only a single chair in the centre of the room.

'Looks like they're playing tricks on us again. Perhaps we're going to play a game of musical chairs?' Vivian suggested.

'With only the one chair?' Harold frowned. 'Although I suppose it doesn't matter much anyway, since I brought my own.'

The others looked at him, trying to work out if it was alright to laugh at that or not. He broke the ice by laughing first. 'Sorry, I had this tough old bird of a nurse at the hospital who encouraged me to joke about things. I'm trying it out.'

'Good for you,' Vivian said with an affectionate smile.

'Unless the rest of us are planning on sitting on each other's laps, I can't see this arrangement working,' Anna said, crossing her arms.

'That actually doesn't sound so bad to me,' Mark said, that annoying grin back on his face again.

Anna heard the faint ticking sound coming from the wall again, and the others seemed to have noticed it too. 'That door to the tomb is still hidden,' she said. 'I wonder how we're meant to open it this time?'

'Hold on a minute, that's interesting, I'm sure that wasn't here before.' Mark walked over to the other side of the room, and glanced back at Anna. She couldn't see what he was looking at, not until he reached out and pulled at a small handle that he'd found in the wall. It didn't seem to want to budge, so he placed his feet against the base of the wall and then pulled hard with both hands, straining with the effort.

'Oh shit!' Mark gasped as he suddenly fell backwards onto the floor. The handle had come away in his hands, and something – a great many somethings – began to cascade down from a hole in the wall and pile on top of him. The rest of the group, mouths agape, tried to comprehend what they were witnessing. Hundreds of small shiny red packages had tumbled out of the hole in the wall, and Mark was almost buried in them. He managed to get himself up onto his feet and shake them off. 'What the hell?' he shouted. 'What is all this?'

Vivian bravely stepped forward and picked up one of the packages. Anna cried out, 'No, don't!', but it was too late, Vivian had already started unwrapping it, and popped whatever was inside it into her mouth and started chewing. Anna's imagination flew away and then returned with the idea that each package might hold a disembodied finger or a toe...

Seeing the looks that she was getting from the others, Vivian smiled at them and told them, 'It's alright, it's just chocolate. Tastes like strawberry flavour.' She took another one, unwrapped it and popped it in her mouth. 'Quite yummy, actually.'

Mark grinned. 'Looks like I found our host's secret sweetie cupboard! I suppose everyone's got one.'

'Must be a few hundred of those things!' Harold exclaimed, staring at the pile of sweets.

'I thought you told us you were an accountant?' Mark smiled at him. 'Shouldn't you be carefully counting each one to give us a more accurate figure?'

Harold gave a little laugh. 'That'd be quite difficult, especially given the rate that Vivian is wolfing them down.'

Vivian froze when she realised that everyone was staring at her. She finished chewing her sweet and swallowed it. 'Sorry, I got a little carried away. These are delicious! I've always had something a sweet tooth, I'm afraid.' She let the empty wrappers fall to the floor.

Anna bent down and picked up a sweet from the floor, unwrapped it, and ate it. 'She's not wrong, they do taste good.' She looked at Vivian. 'Probably not a good idea to eat too many, though.'

'Sammy Mitchell,' Vivian said suddenly, with a soft sigh. She took a handful of the red sweets and stared at them wistfully.

'Who's that?' Harold asked.

When Vivian replied, her eyes were far away. 'When I was a child, there was a boy I'd sometimes see on my way home from school called Sammy who liked me, and he kept bringing me these sweets, because he knew that I liked them. I suppose I should blame him for rotting my teeth, although he could blame me for getting him expelled from his school. You see, I knew that he was stealing those sweets for me from one of the local shops, but I didn't care, because I loved those sweets. However, a teacher at my school found out, she must have overheard me talking to a friend about it, and then Sammy got in a lot of trouble.

He was expelled from his school. And then, not long after that, he... Ah, never mind. You know, I haven't seen these particular sweets for, oh, must be a couple of decades, at least. I didn't think they even made them anymore. How bizarre to find them here, and so many of them!' Vivian let the sweets fall from her fingers.

Anna turned to Mark. 'I don't suppose you could do us all a favour and find the secret cupboard that contains a three-course meal? I'm getting hungry and I don't think gorging myself on sweets is the best idea. I need something more substantial.'

'Sorry,' Mark replied with a smile, 'I don't see any more handles that might open more secret cupboards, but maybe if we keep looking, we'll—'

There was a scraping noise and they turned and stared as the door to the tomb appeared in the wall again.

'Finally!' Vivian said.

'I don't understand how this works,' Mark said, examining the door. 'It's like it has a mind of its own.' He slid open the door and the group made their way into the tomb. Harold struggled with a slight step in the doorframe and Mark had to help him over it. 'Sorry, Harold, this place is not very accessible, is it?'

Once they were all inside the tomb, the door closed behind them. Vivian pointed at the bandaged corpse and smiled. 'Time to unwrap the tummy of the mummy!'

Vivian went first, pulling the wraps from around the stomach area. They heard the sound of the ticking clock growing louder. She helped Harold move closer, placing the end of one wrap from around the stomach into his hand so that he could pull it. Mark went next, followed by Anna, and they revealed more of the body, all the way up to the chest. Anna looked at Katarina, expecting her to be reluctant to participate again, but was surprised when she stepped forward. It looked like it took Katarina a lot of effort, and she didn't stop grimac-

ing as she pulled the wraps away, but eventually she unveiled the chest
of the corpse.

'Definitely a woman,' Mark commented. 'No doubt about that.'
He noticed Katarina glaring at him and said, 'What?'

'Do you have to stare at her body in that way? It's... disrespectful.'
Mark frowned at her. 'I was only—'

'It's very strange, isn't it?' Harold said, interrupting him.

'I think you'll need to be more specific, Harold,' Anna said. 'What's
strange?'

Harold pointed at the corpse. 'Do you see how the stomach and
chest aren't quite as badly decayed as the feet were? You would expect
the whole body to be in the same condition, wouldn't you?'

Vivian smiled at him. 'Harold, since when did you become such an
expert on ancient mummies?'

'I'm not. You're the one that told us about those Victorian unwrapping parties, and what the Egyptians used to do to the bodies. I'm just
using my eyes, that's all. You can clearly see a difference.'

Anna could see that Harold was right, the lower half of the body
had looked in a much worse state than the upper half did. There was
probably some scientific explanation for that phenomenon, but she
thought that was best left to someone who hadn't repeatedly failed
their Biology exams at school. Then again, they were dealing with
the body of some mysterious woman who'd been dead for possibly
hundreds or thousands of years, hidden away in a room behind a secret
door, in a house where pianos seemed to play themselves and sweets
poured from holes in walls, so perhaps it was foolish of her to expect
there to be a rational explanation for any of it. There were so many
things in this world and in her life that made no sense to her, so why
should she expect this to be any different?

The gong sounded then, to signify that their time was up, and the
candles went out and the door reopened, and they took their cue to
return to the dining room, which still had hundreds of sweets and

empty wrappers littered about the floor, and only that one single chair in the middle of the room and no other furniture. The door to the tomb slid shut behind them by itself.

'I feel like this would all be a lot more interesting if we had some kind of idea who that dead woman was,' Mark said. 'It's a shame our host hasn't provided at least some clues as to who she might have been.'

'I agree,' Vivian said, 'I think a bit of context would help to build the drama. Not that it isn't exciting peeling bandages from a dead body, but knowing a little of her history would make this more interesting. Imagine if she was a member of royalty, how fascinating would that be?'

'Personally, I don't much care who she was,' Anna said. 'I'm more interested to know who our elusive host is, and why they're going to all this trouble. I feel like we're being toyed with here. Why were the five of us invited, what's so special about us?'

'I suppose we must be the lucky ones,' Katarina said, with a humourless expression.

Harold drummed his fingers on the arm of his wheelchair. 'I can't say that I feel very lucky.'

Suddenly the room was plunged into darkness, prompting a chorus of curse words.

Anna tried to make out the others in the dark. She could see only vague shapes. There was a rustling sound as if someone was trampling through the pile of sweets.

'What the hell's going on now?' she heard Harold cry out.

Then came the sound of rushing water, and Anna felt her feet starting to get wet. *Where's all this water coming from?*

Someone bumped into her and Anna couldn't stop herself from falling over and splashing face-first into the cold water. She carefully eased herself back up onto her feet. She then heard a cry – was that Vivian? It was followed by a slightly more manly yelp that she guessed came from either Mark or Harold.

Harold! She suddenly remembered that he was in a wheelchair, so she had to try to find him and help him, but how could she do that when she couldn't see a thing?

There was a groaning sound from up above, and for a moment she wondered if the whole house was about to collapse in on them...

Anna was panicking now as the water rose up her legs, approaching her waist. She closed her eyes and tried to think of somewhere safe and warm and dry, but opened them again a moment later when she heard Mark call out, 'I think it's stopping!'

She heard the hissing of the water begin to die down, and was relieved to feel the water level start to drop. She tried to feel around in the dark, and called out, 'Where are you all?! I still can't see anything!'

Then she was almost blinded as the lights came back on.

The water was draining away through small holes she could now see at the base of the wall. A few odd sweet wrappers floated on the surface of the remaining water. She looked up towards the ceiling, expecting to see a gaping hole, but there was none. The ceiling was intact. So where had that water suddenly come from? She stared at the hole in the wall that had emptied those sweets all over Mark. Could the water have come in through there?

Anna heard coughing and was relieved to see that Harold was alright, but he was visibly shaken. He was gripping the arms of his wheelchair tightly. Mark was on his feet and trying to help Vivian up. Anna noticed that Katarina had managed to perch herself on the single chair in the middle of the room, clutching her knees to her chest, and was staring down at the wet floor beneath her with wide eyes. Safe up there on her little throne, Katarina looked considerably less bedraggled than Anna, who now had even more reason to be jealous of her. But Anna could see that she still looked very frightened, and as the last of the water drained away from the room, she decided to make her way over to check on her. 'Katarina! Are you alright?'

'No, I'm not!' Katarina replied. 'That was terrifying!'

'I think we're all alright now. You can come down.'

'I'm not alright!' Harold called out. 'I'm bloody furious! I'm in a wheelchair, for God's sake! If that water had risen up much higher, I could've drowned!'

Anna noticed that Vivian looked paler than usual, and was shivering violently. She wobbled precariously as Mark helped her to her feet. 'How is she doing?' Anna asked as she approached them.

'Something's not right with her,' Mark answered. 'Maybe it's shock. Vivian, talk to us.'

The older woman's legs seemed to give way and she collapsed to her knees, but she grabbed onto Mark and tried to pull herself back up. Her hand was on her chest and she seemed to be straining. 'You're alright, Vivian, it's over now,' he told her, but Vivian didn't seem to believe him. Anna knelt in front of her and tried to make eye contact with her wild eyes. 'Vivian, it's me, it's Anna. Can you tell us what's wrong? Are you hurt?'

Vivian's eyes finally stopped racing around the room and came to focus on Anna's face, and then she said in a weak voice, 'I'm not hurt, it was just all that water... I thought for a moment that I was going to drown.'

'You're alright now, it's over.'

'It's just the thought of almost drowning like that, it brought back some very bad memories. Sammy... Sammy Mitchell, that boy I told you about, who brought me the sweets... that's how he died. It happened a few days after he was expelled from his school, they found his body in the river, and he'd drowned.'

'I'm sorry,' Anna said.

Vivian waved her hand dismissively and said with a sad smile, 'It's all water under the bridge now. But please, give me a moment to recover.'

Anna stood back up and then looked around the room. 'This is utter insanity.' She then said more loudly, hoping their host was listening in and could hear her, 'Hey! You could've killed us! What the hell are you thinking? We have an invalid here!' She stopped and looked at Harold, and winced. 'Oh. I'm sorry, I just meant—'

'Don't worry about it,' Harold said.

Anna went over to the door that led to the hallway, turned the door knob and opened the door. She stepped out into the hallway and to her surprise she found that the floor out here was completely dry. Somehow the little flood they'd experienced seemed to have been contained to only the dining room.

'Oh, come on...' Anna shook her head in disbelief. On the floor by the door she'd found two piles of white towels and bathrobes. 'You won't believe this!' she called back to the group, and then she brought the towels and bathrobes through to the dining room and handed them out, and they seemed to be gratefully accepted. She used the towel she kept for herself to dry her hair, face, arms and legs. She took off her shoes and dried her feet. Her dress was still wet, and cold, clinging to her body, and she needed to take it off, but she wasn't going to do that in front of Mark and the others.

'I suggest us girls get changed in the bathrooms, while the boys get changed here in the dining room,' Anna said. She got no argument, so she led the other two women out into the hallway. They headed right, passing the cloakroom, and stopped outside the bathrooms.

'I'm not actually that wet, you two go on,' Katarina said. 'I was up on that chair so I managed to stay mostly dry. Honestly, I'm fine.'

'Good for you,' Vivian muttered, before she entered one of the bathrooms. Anna entered the other bathroom, leaving Katarina in the hallway. *Great*, Anna thought, *so Katarina gets to stay looking as perfect as ever in her lovely dress, while I have to embarrass myself by walking around in a bathrobe and looking like a total idiot. This evening just gets better and better.*

The bathroom was small, with only one cubicle and a full-length mirror on the wall above the sink. Anna started to undress and as she did so, she eyed the walls and mirror suspiciously, hoping that there were no voyeuristic cameras hidden there watching her. She wouldn't put it past their host to have secretly placed cameras in every room. She put on the bathrobe quickly and then came back out into the hallway, ignoring the looks that she was getting from Katarina, who put her hand to her mouth to stifle a giggle. Anna sighed and folded her wet dress and placed it on the floor beside the bathroom, her underwear tucked underneath, out of sight.

The dazed Vivian came out of her bathroom wearing her bathrobe, carrying her wet clothes in her arms, which Anna took from her and placed carefully in a pile next to hers. The three women then returned to the dining room, knocking on the door first before they entered. Inside, Mark was in his bathrobe and was finishing helping Harold put his on. Anna felt ridiculous wearing this bathrobe, and she noticed Mark's eyes tracking her as she walked across the dining room towards them. She couldn't tell from the look he was giving her if he was amused or aroused, or perhaps a bit of both. Harold coughed and Mark snapped out of it and returned his attention to helping him.

Harold looked embarrassed and didn't make eye contact with any of the group. When Mark was done dressing him, he placed his and Harold's clothes outside the room, and as he walked past her in his robe, Anna couldn't help but think what a comical sight this would be for anyone watching them: this group, almost complete strangers to one another, walking around in only their bathrobes. She'd put money on there being cameras hidden somewhere, recording all of this. Perhaps it'd end up on the Internet. If any of her staff at work found out about this, she'd lose any respect that they may have had for her, and then she'd have no choice but to threaten to fire them before they blabbed about it to anyone else.

Their host, "H", whether it was Handsworth or not, was making fools of them. Not only that, but someone could have been seriously injured, or worse. Anna had had enough. 'I'm going to find that bloody Handsworth and demand to know what the hell's going on.'

'Wait,' Mark said, 'I'll come with you. Will the rest of you be alright waiting here?'

'I'll stay with Vivian and Harold,' Katarina answered him. 'I'll keep an eye on them.'

Anna nodded. 'Alright, keep everyone here so we know where you are. Come on Mark, let's go and put an end to this madness.'

'I can't believe what just happened,' Mark said as he and Anna crossed the hallway. 'That whole room flooded, and then just as quickly as that water came, it all went away. The work involved to set something like that up, and all those hundreds of sweets too. Not to mention the hidden tomb and that corpse inside. Who would go to this much trouble, and why?'

'I'm beginning to believe that anything's possible in this madhouse,' Anna said.

Mark shook his head. 'It's all so elaborate, isn't it? What do they gain by making Vivian think about her past, with those sweets from her childhood and that boy who died, and nearly drowning us all? Or Harold and his mysterious piano, and that money that was hidden in our chairs?'

'They did the same with Katarina too,' Anna pointed out. 'Seeing that body in the tomb reminded her of her friend's funeral, and then there was that journal you found under the dining table, Katarina said that she used to have one just like it. Those things really upset her.'

'This is my point, all of those things seemed designed to bring up bad memories for each of us. So what's next? Is it going to be something from my past, or maybe something from yours?'

Anna looked away. 'I'd prefer not to have things from my past dredged up in front of everybody, thank you very much.'

'Me too. So what kind of secrets do you keep, Anna? What would you not want everybody to know about?'

'None of your business,' Anna replied. She tried to change the subject. 'You know, I feel completely ridiculous walking around this house in a bloody bathrobe.'

Mark laughed. 'You know, I won't lie, I did sort of hope that maybe one day I might see you in your bathrobe. Just not in these particular circumstances, obviously.'

She stopped walking and glared at him. 'You can't stop flirting for one second, can you? Even after what's just happened. You're ridiculous.'

He looked wounded. 'I wasn't trying to upset you. Sorry, I can't help it, it's just something I do.'

'Yes, I've noticed. And I'm sure Katarina has, too.'

Mark frowned. 'What does that mean?'

'Look, let's just stay focussed, shall we? Let's find Handsworth.'

They passed several doors and continued on until they reached a door with a sign that read: *HANDSWORTH*. Mark nudged Anna and pointed at the door. 'This is Handsworth's office.'

'I'm so glad that you're here to point these things out to me, I don't know how I'd cope without you, I'd be utterly lost.' She caught Mark giving her an odd look and asked, 'What?'

'Nothing,' he said, 'I'm just trying to work out whether you genuinely don't like me, or whether this bad attitude of yours is simply some kind of defence mechanism to keep people away. Or maybe you just enjoy insulting people.'

'No, not everybody, just people who say stupid things or continually point out the obvious. Why waste the words?'

He glared at her. 'Would you rather I kept quiet and said nothing at all then?'

Anna considered for a moment. 'Let me think about that.' She left him hanging for a while before she finally said, 'No, I suppose not. This house is far too quiet as it is.'

'Good, because I have plenty of things to say, stupid as they might seem to you. Sorry, I suppose you'll have to accept that I'm the talkative type. Speaking of which, shall we go in here and try to convince Handsworth to give us some answers?'

Mark knocked on the door five times, to the rhythm of *Shave and a Haircut*. 'That'll drive me mad if he doesn't knock back twice.' Mark grinned at her. She shook her head at him.

They waited, and after a few seconds, they heard a key turn in the lock, and then the door slowly opened inwards, creaking ominously as it did so.

'Come on in then, if you're coming in,' came a voice from inside.

Anna and Mark stepped through the doorway into one of the most cluttered offices that Anna had ever seen. Handsworth stretched out his arms and welcomed them in, before he walked over to a desk that was piled high with towers of papers that looked like they could give way at any moment. Along one wall of the room were rows of bells, each labelled underneath with the name of a part of the house. On the opposite wall hung rows of small portraits – all men, some in very old-fashioned clothing, and all bearing a resemblance to Handsworth. His ancestors, Anna presumed. On the back wall there was a partially obscured door leading to another room, and it was labelled *STORAGE*.

'Apologies for the mess,' Handsworth said. He tidied some of the papers on his desk, but it was a futile effort to make the room look less like a bomb had gone off in a library. He gave up after a while and turned around to face his visitors, frowning at their bathrobes. 'Is there something I can do for you?'

Anna laughed incredulously. 'You do know what just happened to us all, don't you? We almost drowned!'

Handsworth nodded. 'Yes, of course, and I must apologise about that, and I should have done so sooner, but I've been extremely busy. As soon as I realised what had happened in the dining room, I asked one of the maids to fetch towels and those bathrobes for you. There's a network of pipes that runs throughout the house, and it appears that one or more of those pipes must have burst, probably due to all the heavy rain that we've been having. It may have done damage to other rooms, and it'll take me some time to check them all.' He sighed. 'If only each room didn't have its own unique key, that would make the task considerably easier... Anyway, I've been trying to locate the number of a plumber that we've used in the past. I'll arrange for him to do a proper inspection of the house as soon as he's available. I suppose I'm going to have to get someone to check on the state of the roof too.'

Anna couldn't believe her ears. 'I'm sorry, are you trying to tell us that what happened to us was just some kind of accident?'

Handsworth frowned at her. 'Of course it was. What else would it be?'

Mark stepped forward. 'And that panel in the dining room that was full of hundreds of sweets, what was all that about?'

Handsworth smiled at him. 'Ah, now that was intended, I know that much. My employer likes their little tricks and games. I can't say that I care much for all that silliness, but it's not my place to complain, so I won't.'

'But did you know those sweets meant something very personal to Vivian?' Mark asked.

'I didn't, but I'm sure my employer did. They know quite a lot about each of you, and I expect this was simply an attempt to provide a little entertainment. I'm sure it was a pleasant surprise for Vivian.'

'It took her back to her childhood, for better or for worse. But I don't think any of us appreciated all that water then flooding into the room and almost drowning us. Especially Vivian.'

'Yes, I am very sorry about that,' Handsworth said, looking uncomfortable. 'I'll send a maid to collect your wet clothes if she's not done so already. In the meantime, could I ask that you both return to your group now? I'll be along shortly to take you through to the drawing room. We have a fireplace there, it will keep all of you warm and dry. I think that's preferable to you wandering around, as this house gets particularly draughty and chilly sometimes, and I certainly wouldn't want any of you to catch your death from the cold.'

'Speaking of death,' Mark said, 'that body in the tomb downstairs, can't you tell us who she might have been, or how she died? Where did the body come from, how did it get here? And why is it our job to unwrap it? What's this really all about?'

Handsworth turned back to the papers on his desk. 'Sorry, I'm not allowed to discuss that with you.'

'But—'

'Strict instructions from my employer. I have to obey them. I hope you understand. Now please, go back to your group, and I will be in to see you soon.'

'Mark, I'm freezing, let's just go,' Anna said.

Mark reluctantly agreed, and they left Handsworth's office, closing the door behind them.

As they walked back, Anna said, 'Warming ourselves by a fire sounds pretty good right now, doesn't it?'

'I suppose. Handsworth's lying to us, you do know that, don't you?'

'I know,' Anna replied. 'Broken water pipes? No, he's playing dumb, and I'm sure he knows a lot more than he's letting on. Did you see all those portraits on the wall in his office? I wouldn't be surprised if Handsworth's family has worked in this house for generations, so you can't tell me that he wouldn't know every little thing that goes on here. Perhaps it really was him who sent us those invitations, even if he denies it.'

'I don't know if I see Handsworth as some clever puppeteer working the strings here,' Mark said. 'I think there's someone else behind it all, someone he's working for. Someone very rich and bored and with too much time on their hands.'

'That could actually describe any one of us,' Anna said. 'By that reasoning, it could be me, or you, or any of the others. Oh, of course, I've worked it out now! It's Harold! He must be the mysterious "H" from the invitation letter, it's the only explanation. He's the mad genius behind it all. There you go, I've solved the case.'

Mark looked at her as if he wasn't sure if she was being serious or not. 'You don't really think Harold's involved in this, do you? He's suffered more than any of us.'

Anna sighed. 'No, of course I don't. Although, if I'm being completely honest, I don't know how well I can trust any of you. We're all strangers to each other here, aren't we?'

'I'd like to think that you and I know each other a little by now, Anna.'

'I'm not sure that we do.'

Mark stopped suddenly and put his hand on her arm. 'Come on, you don't suspect me of having anything to do with any of this, do you?'

Anna turned and studied his eyes for a moment. 'No, I suppose I don't. I think you're just as much a victim as all the rest of us are. Another unwitting pawn in some bored rich bastard's game, like you said.'

Mark looked relieved. 'Good. I'm glad. I don't want you thinking bad things about me. I want you to feel like you can trust me. Because you can, you know.'

Anna tilted her head. 'Why do you care so much about what I think about you?'

'Because... I like you, Anna. I thought that might be obvious to you by now. I think you're great.'

'Oh.'

'Also, you remind me of someone who was very special to me.'

'I see.'

They carried on walking, in an awkward silence, until they reached the dining room, outside which stood Katarina and Vivian, accompanied by Harold in his wheelchair. Vivian was fussing with her bathrobe, clearly uncomfortable.

'Did you find Handsworth?' Vivian asked as they approached. 'What did he have to say for himself?'

Mark answered her question. 'He's claiming that it was all an accident, that it was just some burst pipes due to the heavy rain.'

'Well, that sounds like a lot of nonsense to me,' Vivian said, 'and I don't believe it for one minute!'

'I think we can all agree on that,' Anna said. 'Anyway, Handsworth said he'll be joining us in a minute to take us through to the drawing room. He's promised us a fireplace where we can get warm.'

'Thank God for that,' Harold said. He then added for Anna and Mark's benefit, 'A young maid came down from upstairs and took away our clothes, to be dried.'

'It was Louise,' Katarina added.

Anna took a deep breath, let it out, and then said, 'Look, the flooding in that room was no accident, and it was bloody dangerous, someone could've been seriously hurt. We're all being played with here, and I don't know why, and I don't know what the connection is with that mummy in that tomb, but what I do know is that we're being lied to, and that bloody Handsworth knows a lot more than he's telling us.'

'Ahem.'

Anna turned, surprised to see Handsworth standing behind her. She couldn't tell whether he had heard what she'd been saying about him, but if he did then he didn't react to it. Instead, he told the group, 'I apologise for the ordeal that you've suffered tonight. If you'd all like to follow me through to the drawing room then we'll have you taken care of. I've asked the maids to bring you some food, and some brandy to warm you up a little more. You can rest by the fire for as long as you'd like. Please, come this way.'

Handsworth beckoned them to follow him across the hallway to a large door near to the front entrance and opposite the bathrooms. He produced a key and then unlocked the door. He opened the door for them and they went into the drawing room. Everyone made a beeline for the warm crackling fireplace with its dancing flames, all except Mark, who told the group, 'I think I'm suddenly in need of the bathroom. Sorry, won't be long, nature calls. Don't get into any more exciting scrapes without me, will you?'

Mark smiled at them, but Anna thought it seemed quite a forced smile. After Mark had gone, Handsworth picked up a poker from beside the fireplace and prodded at the wooden logs being consumed by the flames. Then he replaced the poker and said, 'Now, I hope you'll excuse me, I really must see about that plumber. The maids will be here shortly to look after you.'

Katarina sat in front of the fireplace, clutching her bare knees to her chin. She was staring into the flames, as if mesmerised. Vivian was similarly in a daze as she sat down while Anna helped Harold to get a little closer to the fireplace.

Anna looked up and noticed that on the wall above the fireplace was a coat of arms, a shield grasped by two bird-like creatures with long tongues. The shield itself had three parts to it: one had a sword, another an open hand, and the other a chequered pattern similar to the one on the floor in the hallway. Anna took a look around the rest of the room. There was a sofa, a coffee table, various bookshelves, and long curtains covering the windows. 'No TV, and no sign of a drinks cabinet, either,' she told the others, who she thought might empathise with her disappointment. She wandered over to one of the bookcases, unfastened the latch, swung it open and started perusing the selection of books. 'Not a lot of fiction here, mostly books about foreign countries and cultures. Someone here's obviously a traveller, or wants to be. Some of these books look very old.' She then noticed a small portrait hanging next to one of the bookcases, a similar picture to those out in the hallway. It showed the Gray family that the maid Louise had told her about, but this picture featured only the parents and their son, so it must have been done before the family adopted the girl Helena, and before they all succumbed to their tragic fates.

When she grew bored of exploring the room, Anna returned to sit by the fire. She rubbed her hands and then opened them, and felt the warmth of the fire on her palms. 'That feels nice,' she said, and Katarina nodded in agreement.

'It does,' Harold said, 'although I can't really tell if my legs are getting any warmer or not, they're still numb.'

They sat and waited by the fireplace. A few minutes later, Mark returned from his trip to the bathroom.

'Mark, why don't you come over here and get warm by the fire, you can take my spot if you want?' Anna offered. She could see the conflict in his eyes and guessed what it was. On the one hand, he wanted to act like a gentleman and appear to be putting the ladies' needs first, but on the other, he was clearly still cold, shivering as he stood there. 'Come on, sit here, before you freeze to death.'

'No, I'm fine,' he told her, with a polite smile. She shrugged and continued to warm her body by the fire.

There was a knock at the door and then a trio of maids entered. One of them was Louise, the young woman Anna and Katarina had encountered upstairs. Katarina suddenly jumped to her feet and called out, 'Hello again, Louise.'

The maid didn't respond or make eye contact, but she blushed a little. The other two maids were much older women, and they ordered Louise to tidy the curtains, while they carried trays of food which they distributed to the group.

'Oh, that's more like it,' Vivian said.

One of the older maids called out, 'Fresh towels, girl!' and Louise quickly exited the room. She returned a moment later with a pile of towels, which she laid next to the fireplace.

'Thank you,' Katarina said, sitting back down by the fireplace.

Louise nodded and said, 'You're welcome, miss.'

Anna watched the trio of maids take up positions in the corners of the room. They stood there, not moving, like robots awaiting their next instructions.

'Anyone else get the feeling that we're being watched?' Harold asked quietly as Anna came to stand beside him. 'Almost as if we're prisoners and those are our guards.'

'It's a creepy house,' Anna told him, 'so it stands to reason that it would have creepy staff too. And I thought Handsworth was bad enough.'

Vivian walked over to the closest of the older maids and asked her, 'When do you think we might be able to get our clothes back?'

The woman seemed to come to life and she answered, 'I'm sorry, I don't think they'll be ready until the morning.'

'You can't dry them any faster than that?'

'They're not only wet, but they're also quite filthy. The water in those pipes was not particularly clean, I'm afraid. But don't worry, they will be good as new by the morning, I can promise you that.' She then directed her next words to the rest of the group. 'The weather out there is horrendous this evening, and we've heard that the roads will be dangerous, so you're all invited to stay the night. We have several bedrooms, you can each take one. The man in the wheelchair is welcome to sleep in here tonight if he wishes, or we could carry him upstairs if he prefers. Anything you require, simply ask. My name is Irene, that's Agnes, and over there is Louise. We shall be staying up all night to make sure that you have anything you might need, at any hour.'

Vivian forced a smile back at the maid, and then returned to the others by the fireplace.

'I don't know about the rest of you,' Anna said, 'but I don't want to spend the night here, not again. Once was bad enough.'

'What choice do we have?' Harold said. 'Plus, it sounds like the weather's only getting worse out there. I don't think I can manage the journey back, and to be honest there's not much better waiting for me back at home. I'm so tired. I'd very much like to just sit here by this fire for as long as I can.'

Mark agreed with him. 'We've been through a lot tonight, I think a relaxing evening where we don't have to rush off home and get stuck in traffic in bad weather sounds good to me. I'm also intrigued to know for myself what a night spent in this place is like.'

'Seriously? Then you're madder than I thought.' Anna then turned to Vivian. 'What about you, Vivian? Surely you'd want to go home, after everything that's happened to you tonight?'

Vivian waved her hand in the air. The reflections of the flickering flames danced in her eyes. 'I'm quite exhausted, to tell the truth, so if they can promise me a comfortable bed and the ability to summon a maid for anything I might need at any time of night, then I'm prepared to give them a chance. Just so long as I'm nowhere near that dining room or any more water.'

Anna shook her head. 'I can't believe you'd all willingly stay here. Katarina, come on, be the voice of reason. What do you think? We should go, right?'

Katarina turned to look at Anna and looked apologetic as she answered, 'I know I wasn't very well the last time that we stayed here, but I did have such a good night's sleep. I felt much better by the morning. I don't usually sleep that well. So I'm happy to stay here for tonight, if everyone else is going to. Anna, will you stay too?'

'It looks like I'll have to now, won't I?' Anna grumbled. Her mind turned to Jelly – the poor cat would have to spend another lonely evening by himself in that apartment. Anna envied him.

Anna approached the maid Irene and said, in a quieter voice, so that the rest of her group wouldn't hear, 'Alright, we'll all stay, but we've heard about the Gray family that lived here and what happened to them, and I'd prefer not to sleep in any room where somebody might've had an agonising death, thank you very much.'

To Anna's annoyance, Irene seemed to find her request amusing. She wore a smile on her previously stern face as she told Anna, 'Not to worry, I'm sure that we can find at least one or two rooms for you somewhere in this house that might meet that criteria.' She turned to the rest of the group. 'You will find your rooms up the stairs and to the right, when you're ready to retire for the evening. Now, who here would like something to drink?'

Mark was lingering outside Anna's room. 'Goodnight then, Mark,' she told him.

Harold had remained downstairs in the drawing room, while the rest of the group had come upstairs to their assigned bedrooms. Each room looked like it had been carefully prepared well in advance, almost as if their impromptu sleepover wasn't entirely unexpected.

Vivian and Katarina had retired to their rooms for the night, so Anna and Mark were the only ones still up and about, and she was finding it difficult to get him to leave her alone and go to his room.

The drinks that they'd had earlier in that warm, cosy drawing room seemed to have put him in a romantic mood, but Anna wasn't having any of it. She just wanted to go to bed – by herself – and sleep away the hours until morning, when she could get away from this house.

Anna heard the chime of the grandfather clock echo along the corridor.

'Did I tell you about how my dad and my mom first met?' Mark asked, his voice slurring.

'No, and that's a story for another time, not tonight. I think it's time we both got to bed now.'

He nodded quickly and looked at her with eager eyes, like an excited little puppy, but she shook her head at him and pointed down the corridor. 'Mark, your bedroom's further down that way.'

'But your bedroom's right here!'

'Yes, it is.'

'So…' he said slowly and suggestively.

'So, I'm going to go into my room now. Alone. You go down the corridor, find the room with the door open, go inside, and get yourself some sleep. You're very tired.'

'Am I?' Mark seemed unsure.

'Yes, you just told me you were. So sleepy!' Anna faked a yawn.

'Alright,' he said, 'I suppose if I'm tired, I ought to go to bed.'

'That's right. Goodnight, Mark.'

'Goodnight, Anna, don't let the… What do they call them again?'

'Bed bugs bite?'

He pointed a finger at her face, and almost hit her chin with it. 'Yes! That's it! Bed bugs! You need to watch out for them, um, they bite!'

Anna put her hands on Mark's shoulders, turned him around, pointed him in the direction of his room, and then gave him a firm push. She watched him stumble along the corridor.

Mark stopped suddenly and burst out laughing. 'I'm wearing a bathrobe!'

Anna watched as he walked past Katarina's room and then kept on walking straight past his own room too. She rolled her eyes. 'Mark!' she hissed loudly, avoiding shouting so that she wouldn't disturb Katarina. He turned and started walking back towards her, but then suddenly seemed to get distracted and wandered off down an adjoining corridor. 'Damn it...' Anna said to herself. She realised that she was going to have to shepherd the idiot back to his room or he'd get lost up here and never find it.

She followed in Mark's footsteps, but when she turned into the next corridor, she couldn't see him. She kept walking until she finally found him in another corridor. He had his back to her and was staring at a big black door at the end of the corridor. She approached him and he turned around.

'Have you seen this big door?' Mark asked her. 'It looks special. I wonder what's behind it. Should we take a look?'

Mark looked disappointed when Anna shook her head. 'No, let's not. Come on, follow me, Mark, or you're going to get yourself lost.' She led him back to where his room was, and she gently pushed him inside. He flopped down onto his bed. Anna knew that she wasn't going to get any thanks, so she left his room and closed the door behind her.

Anna entered her own room, closed the door, and let out a sigh. She shook her head to try to clear away the fog of alcohol, and any thoughts of Mark that might still be lingering in there.

She watched the second hand make its way rapidly around the clock on the wall, while the minute hand crept ever so slowly onwards and the hour hand seemed to refuse to move even as she tried to will the time to pass faster with her mind.

It was now just after half past two in the morning. It wasn't the first time in recent weeks that Anna had still been awake at this time, only now it wasn't because she was working late. She couldn't seem to get to sleep; even the copious alcohol hadn't helped to send her off. The bed was comfortable enough, thanks to the efforts of Louise and the other maids, and the sound of the heavy rain from outside the window was also oddly comforting. But she still didn't feel like she could relax here in this house, and she couldn't seem to drift off to dreamland.

Ten minutes later, there was a soft knocking on her door.

At first, Anna thought that she might have imagined it, but then it repeated. Someone – or some *thing* – was outside her door in the middle of the night, trying to get in.

When the knocks repeated for the third time a few seconds later, she knew who it was. *Shave and a haircut...*

It carried the expectation of an answer.

She had a choice to make: to be alone, or not to be alone. It wasn't a hard decision.

When she went downstairs for breakfast in the morning, Anna found Vivian and Harold in the dining room, which was now completely dry and there was no sign of those sweets, although the table and the five chairs were now present again. They both still wore their bathrobes, as Anna did. Harold was voraciously devouring a plateful of bacon, eggs, black pudding and toast. Vivian was chewing slowly on a piece of bread. She seemed uneasy being back in this room again, and Anna couldn't blame her after what had happened last night. Anna greeted them and took a seat at the table.

One of the older maids – Agnes, was it? – laid some cutlery in front of her, and promised to be back shortly with Anna's breakfast.

'So, Anna, have you seen Mark this morning?' Vivian asked, between mouthfuls.

Anna swallowed. 'No, I don't think I've seen him since we were all together last night.'

Vivian was staring at her. 'I see,' she said, with a wink, before tucking into her breakfast. Anna hoped that Harold hadn't seen that wink.

'Ah, talk of the devil!' Harold said, and Anna felt a presence move behind her.

Mark took the seat next to Anna and said, 'Good morning, Anna. Everyone.'

'Good morning, Mark,' Anna replied, not meeting his eyes.

Mark fiddled with the belt on his bathrobe, while Anna started picking at the tablecloth. They looked up as Katarina arrived, greeted them all, and took her seat. She stared at Mark for a moment, and then at Anna.

Anna avoided Katarina's eyes. *Where was that damn maid with that damn breakfast?*

'How did everyone sleep?' Katarina asked.

'Good,' Anna and Mark chorused.

'The sofa in the drawing room was a little uncomfortable,' Harold answered, 'but at least the room was warm. So I can't complain.'

Vivian let out a sigh. 'I managed, I suppose. It was rather noisy last night, with the rain on my window, it got quite fierce at times.'

'I don't mind the rain,' Katarina said, 'but this old house has lots of strange noises. Lots of creaking and groaning. In the middle of the night, I was awoken by this very odd noise, like a kind of thumping sound, I don't know what it was. Oh, it didn't last long, but it was a little unnerving. Perhaps it was just a door banging in the wind, or something like that.'

'Or something like that,' Vivian said, shaking her head at the young woman, but with a smile on her face. 'Your bedroom was near Anna's room, wasn't it?'

Katarina frowned. 'Yes, it was. Why?'

'Let's talk about something else,' Mark said, hurriedly. 'Have they said yet when our clothes will be back? I'm getting tired of walking around in this bathrobe.'

'They should be ready shortly,' Harold answered. 'The maid said that they'd bring them to our rooms. When they do, if someone could, er, give me a hand, I'd be grateful.'

'Yes, no problem,' Mark told him.

Agnes returned with Anna's breakfast. She also brought cutlery for Mark, before telling him that she'd return shortly with his breakfast. Katarina told the maid that she wasn't hungry.

Vivian stabbed at her bacon with a fork and said, 'That was quite an eventful evening, I think we can all agree. For some more than others. But I'd very much like to be heading home as soon as we can.'

Anna ate her breakfast, and a few minutes later Handsworth appeared and told them that their clothes had now been delivered to their rooms, and that he was going to call the taxi company for them. He apologised again for what had happened, and told the group that he'd arranged for a plumber to come to the house, and promised that by the next session any problems would be taken care of.

The group waited politely for Mark to finish his breakfast, before they returned to their rooms and got dressed, finally ditching those bathrobes. Anna felt better wearing her own clothes again, and she had to give the maids credit – they looked immaculate, and smelled nice too. Even that small annoying stain on her shoe that she hadn't been able to remove herself was now gone.

They regrouped and waited outside the house for their taxis to arrive. The sun had started to come out and its warmth felt pleasant and reassuring on Anna's face. Patches of blue sky were breaking out of the clouds. She could also hear birds tweeting, as if reminding her that a world full of life existed away from Grimwald House.

When the first taxi arrived, Mark helped Harold inside the vehicle while the driver collapsed his wheelchair and put it into the boot. They waved goodbye to Harold as his taxi drove away and then the next taxi arrived, which Vivian took after saying her goodbyes.

As Anna waited with Mark, he took her to one side, out of earshot of Katarina, and asked her, 'Should we talk about—'

'No,' Anna said, firmly. 'We shouldn't.'

'Right.'

'I think it's for the best.'

'Yes.'

They waited in silence until their taxis finally arrived.

'I'll see you next week?' Mark said, phrasing it as a question, even though they both knew there was no question that they would be back here again.

'Yes, I'll see you then,' Anna replied.

Mark looked at Katarina. He seemed oddly nervous. 'Um, goodbye then, Katarina. I'll see you next week.'

'Goodbye, Mark,' she replied, with a smile. 'It was very nice to see you again.'

He nodded at her, then glanced at Anna before getting into his taxi. As it pulled away, Anna noticed that Katarina seemed to be staring at her curiously. *What's that look for? Does she know?* Thankfully, it wasn't long before the next taxi arrived, and Anna hurriedly climbed inside and shut the door. She wanted to be away from that girl's prying eyes, and this house, and everything that had happened here.

But the journey home gave Anna plenty of time – too much time – to think about what she'd done.

CHAPTER SIX

VIVIAN

Vivian took her coffee from the acne-ridden young man behind the counter and then looked for somewhere that she could sit and wait for her son's plane to arrive, but every table in the airport cafe seemed to be taken. She spotted an elderly woman seated at a table in the corner who was gathering up her things and putting them into her handbag, excruciatingly slowly, as if it were some momentous task.

Vivian walked over and stood very close to the woman, and coughed loudly. The woman looked up at her and said, 'Oh, I'm sorry, did you want this table? I'll only be a moment.'

Vivian tapped her foot on the floor. The other woman looked flustered and tried to move more quickly, but she was still agonisingly slow. Finally, she stood up from the table and said, 'There you go. Sorry, I'm not quite as quick as I used to be.'

Vivian forced a smile onto her face but as soon as the woman's back was turned, she threw it away. She sat down, put her coffee on the table and then took out her phone. She checked her messages. Still nothing from Daniel.

Her son was flying back from France to see her for the first time since his wedding was called off. Vivian was a little anxious. She wasn't sure what his mood would be. She knew from their phone calls that he'd taken the breakup very hard, and it had pained her to hear how broken he'd sounded. She'd wanted to put her arms around him and console him. He was still her son and it didn't matter how much growing up he might've done since he'd left home, she was still his mother and she knew that he still needed her. That would never change.

For the next few days, she'd have him back under her roof, and it was going to be so nice to have company again. Her house was very large and it often felt empty, and some days she'd have hardly anyone to talk to. Yes, she had cleaners who came once a week to take care of the house, but conversations with them could be difficult – she supposed that was her own fault for hiring people who could barely speak English.

Vivian wondered if Daniel might look any different to her when he stepped off the plane. Would he look like more of a man now, and less like the boy she still pictured him as? And what would she look like to him – a little older, greyer, more wrinkled?

She checked the time on her watch: 3.41 p.m. His flight had already landed by now and it was likely he was currently waiting in the baggage area, one of a crowd of people who would be staring intently at the hole in the wall waiting for their luggage to emerge, then desperately trying to catch hold of it while it circulated the carousel, before it could disappear back into that black hole. She wondered if Daniel had remembered what she'd taught him whenever they went on holidays – to tie a coloured ribbon around the handle of his suitcase, to make it easier to identify among the parade of bags and suitcases.

Vivian took a sip of her coffee and then cursed as it burned her lips. She blew on it before she took her next sip. From where she was sitting, she could see the Arrivals area and the line of expectant faces waiting there. There was no sign of Daniel yet though.

Her stomach was restless. She should have bought something to eat as well as a drink. She eyed a bacon bap sitting on a plate on the table next to her, seemingly abandoned while the two women at that table were deep in conversation. She caught snippets of their debate, some nonsense about contestants on a reality television show and which ones were cheating and with whom.

Her heart felt like it was beating a little faster than normal. She needed to calm herself down. Vivian was excited to see her son again, but she was also nervous. There was another feeling too, which one could call guilt, except that she knew that what she'd done had been for the best. She tried to push that feeling away, but it continued to linger on the edge of her mind.

Think of happier things. She had planned several special days with Daniel, including taking him to one of his favourite restaurants from when he was a child. The place was a little less upmarket than the restaurants that she normally took herself to nowadays, but she thought that Daniel might appreciate somewhere familiar, somewhere that held happy memories for him. Daniel's father, Vivian's first husband, had been out of their lives for many years now, but the last time they'd gone to that restaurant their family had been whole and happy. She could remember it well; Daniel and his younger sister Rebecca had played in the playground outside, even though they were probably a little too old by then to still be sliding on the slides and swinging on the swings. Even now, she could still remember how happy she'd felt watching them playing, laughing and enjoying themselves.

Vivian couldn't remember the last time that she'd heard Rebecca laugh as an adult, she was always so damned serious nowadays. It wouldn't kill her to have a little fun sometimes, nor to pick up the phone and call her mother once in a while, instead of it always having to be the other way around.

Daniel was different. She knew that some people called him a mummy's boy, but she had never seen that as a negative thing. In fact, she even felt a little proud of herself. Even when his father was still around, Daniel had always favoured his mother.

Since he'd moved abroad and taken that teaching job, they'd grown apart somewhat, and she missed him. He still called her two or three times a month, but afterwards she always found herself a little emotional and needing a trip to the drinks cabinet.

She checked her watch again, then her phone for messages, but still nothing. *Where is he?*

'Mother!'

Vivian jerked her hand in surprise at the voice by her ear, and almost threw her coffee over her son, who had seemingly appeared out of nowhere. She placed the coffee cup back on the table, and held her hand against her chest over her thumping heart. 'Daniel, you startled me! Don't do things like that, you could give your mother a heart attack!'

He grinned at her. 'Sorry, I couldn't resist! You were off in your own little world.' He gave her a kiss on the cheek and sat down next to her, placing two suitcases next to the table. 'It's good to see you.'

Vivian smiled back at him and reached out a hand to touch his face. 'Look how handsome you are!'

He looked embarrassed. 'Mother...'

She withdrew her hand. 'I'm sorry, I haven't seen you in so long, not in person. You're looking well. I've missed you!'

'I've missed you too.'

'Was the flight alright?'

'Yes, it was fine, although we almost missed the plane – we were a little late getting to the airport because our taxi was stuck in traffic as there'd been an accident. But we managed to make it in the end.'

Vivian frowned. 'I'm sorry, when you say "we", who do you mean?'

'Oh, right, well, I have some news.' He leaned back in his chair, beaming.

Vivian raised her eyebrows. 'Oh, I think I know that look – have you met someone? Is there a new woman in my son's life? Go on, you have to tell me!'

'Well...'

'There is, isn't there? Who is she? Please tell me it's that Sarah that you've mentioned. I saw pictures of her on the staff page of your school's website, she's quite lovely. Sorry, I was bored one day and got a little nosey. By the way, the photo they have of you on there could be better, you should see about getting a new one taken... Oh, I'm rambling on when you're dying to tell me all about your new girlfriend, I'm sorry, I'll shut up now.'

Daniel took a deep breath. 'This might come as a bit of a surprise, but we're back together – Arianne and I. We're still working some things out, but it's going well so far. I thought bringing her on this little trip might be good for us all.'

Vivian had heard the words that her son was saying, but she couldn't get her brain to accept them. *No, that's wrong! That's impossible! They can't be back together, they just can't...*

'I don't understand,' Vivian said, her heart racing again, 'Arianne called off the wedding, didn't she? You told me that she did?'

Daniel sighed. 'Yes, she did, and it was horrible, but we've put it behind us now. We've had a long talk about it, several in fact, and I can understand now why she did it. She was under a lot of pressure at work, there was the stress of arranging the wedding, and the financial problems her parents were having. I think it was all too much for her. She panicked. But then she had a change of heart, and she came back to me, because she still loves me, and because I still love her too.'

Vivian felt like she couldn't breathe. 'Daniel, please, don't you remember how upset you were when she left you? That awful girl ruined your life! She humiliated you! And now you're telling me you're just going to pretend that all of that never happened? No, I'm sorry, as your mother, I'm not going to sit by and let this happen all over again.'

Daniel suddenly thumped his fist on the table, startling her. 'Mother, please! Try to understand, we're together again now, and I'm sorry if you don't like it, but you are going to have to accept it. Look, Arianne's in the bathroom now but she'll be here any second, so you need to calm down and be civil to her. Can you do that? For me?'

Vivian's mind was racing as fast as her heart. She picked up the coffee cup and started drinking. She didn't care if it was still too hot. She finished the drink and then stared into the empty cup.

This was not how their reunion was meant to go. Daniel was supposed to be alone, vulnerable, and needing his mother again. Instead, Arianne – that witch, that conniving, deceitful little invader – had returned to plague their lives. Her promises to stay away had clearly meant nothing.

Vivian noticed Daniel studying her, probably wondering if she was about to cause a scene. She told herself to calm down. She would have to try to act like this wasn't the disaster it so clearly was.

Here she comes...

Wearing a nervous smile, Arianne arrived at their table. Daniel stood and kissed her cheek, then gave her his chair, and went to find another one.

'Hello, Vivian,' the young woman said as she sat down.

Once Daniel was out of earshot, Vivian glared at her and hissed, 'So, you're back in Daniel's life, despite what we'd agreed! Despite what you promised!'

'Vivian, please, I love Dan, and I still want to marry him.'

'I don't understand, what about your parents, their financial troubles, you said—'

'My father has a new job, so things are better now. They're not struggling so much anymore.'

Daniel returned with his chair and they stopped talking. His eyes moved nervously between the two women at the table. 'Everything alright?'

'We're fine, Dan, just catching up,' Arianne said, with a smile.

Vivian glared at her, and then she turned to her son and said, 'Daniel, we need to talk. In private.'

'Not now, Mother, we've only just stepped off the plane and we're both hungry and thirsty. Arianne, what can I get you?'

She waved her hand in the air. 'Oh, whatever you think I'll like. I trust you.'

With a boyish grin, he nodded and went to see what was on the menu, leaving the two women alone again.

'Vivian, I want us to get on with each other, for Dan's sake,' Arianne said. 'I want you to feel like I'm a part of the family. Like a daughter. That's all I want.' She reached her hand across the table, and when her dark skin touched against Vivian's pale fingers, Vivian pulled her hand away in disgust.

Vivian couldn't accept the thought of this woman being her son's wife, the mother to her grandchildren. It was intolerable. She had to do something about this. She'd tried to play nice before, and had even given this woman an easy way out, but Arianne had thrown that back in Vivian's face now. So Vivian would have to take things to the next level. She knew that there were people who could help her solve this problem.

Once she was back home, she'd have to make a call.

Vivian watched the two of them from her armchair. Daniel and Arianne were chatting away, talking over the top of one of her favourite television programmes, a historical documentary series that she watched every week. They were sitting on her sofa and they couldn't seem to stop touching each other: holding hands, stroking arms, interlocking their fingers... it was disgusting, and if they were to suddenly start kissing in front of her, if Arianne dared to put her tongue in Daniel's mouth, then Vivian felt she might be unable to resist the urge to grab the poker from the fireplace and drive it through that little bitch's skull...

'Anyone fancy a drink?' Daniel asked, interrupting her thoughts. 'I'll get them.'

'Nothing for me, thank you, honey,' Arianne said, and then looked at Vivian. 'Would you like anything to drink, Vivian?'

Vivian shook her head, told herself to control her rage, then stood up and announced, 'I'm going to bed.'

Daniel let go of Arianne's hand and stood up. 'Are you sure?' he asked his mother. 'It's only nine o'clock and the night's still young.'

'Yes, but I'm not. I need my sleep. I'll see you in the morning.' She looked at Arianne and told her, 'This is *my* house, I shouldn't need to remind you. There'll be no sleeping in the same room while you're under my roof. Daniel has his room. You will stay in Rebecca's room.'

'Of course, Mother, that's fine,' Daniel replied. 'I'll get her some sheets. Goodnight. I hope you sleep well.'

'Goodnight, Vivian,' Arianne said, in her irritatingly chirpy voice.

'Goodnight, *Daniel*,' Vivian answered, and then left the room. She made her way slowly upstairs, her legs aching, and went to the bathroom. In front of the mirror, she brushed her teeth and then spat out the toothpaste before also spitting out Arianne's name combined with various curse words.

Vivian stared at herself. It was almost like looking at that photograph of her mother that she kept out of sight in her cupboard. Perhaps she really was turning into her mother? Maybe it was inevitable, even though she'd tried to fight it all of her life. She could just imagine what her mother might say right now if she were still alive: "A *coloured* girl?! Cavorting with *my* grandson?! In *my* house?!" Then there'd surely be a slap to Vivian's face for allowing such a thing to happen.

In Vivian's youth, she'd been considered rather rebellious, very different to her strict mother, and she'd tried desperately to hold on to that adventurous spirit. She'd accepted that invitation to Grimwald House partly because she had wanted to experience something exciting, something with a little mystery and danger, but also because of the veiled threat that certain secrets from her past might be revealed if she didn't. She felt a desire to recapture some of that derring-do that she'd had when she was younger, to bring back the Vivian of her youth that did not shy away from new experiences. Certainly, she'd never had the opportunity to undress a mummified corpse before! There weren't many people who could claim to have had that particular experience.

The torrent of sweets and then water that had poured in from the wall in the dining room at that house had brought back long-forgotten memories, some good, some bad. She hadn't enjoyed almost drowning, but everything up to that point had been a refreshing change from her normal days. She had even enjoyed the company, particularly Harold – poor, unfortunate Harold – and it was quite amusing to watch the *will-they, won't-they, of-course-they-bloody-will* relationship play out between Anna and Mark. As for Katarina, what was there to say? The young woman was a little more tolerable than Arianne. But then, Katarina wasn't trying to steal Vivian's only son away from her.

Vivian left the bathroom and went to her bedroom, where she shut and locked the door, and then sat at her dressing table. She unlocked the top drawer and took out an address book. She knew that the phone number she was looking for was in there somewhere near the back of the book. Her second husband, who'd had dealings with various shady characters throughout his life, had told her to keep that number handy in case of emergencies. His exact words to her had been: "*Call that number if you ever have a problem that you can't get rid of any other way.*" She thought she'd understood what that meant, but she hadn't had to use it until now. She knew that there would be a financial cost to using it, and some might say a spiritual or moral one too, if you cared about that sort of thing. But she felt like she had no other choice. She'd already tried to get rid of Arianne the easy way, the least messy way. Vivian had known that Arianne's parents were in serious financial trouble and that they'd even been considering returning to wherever it was that they were originally from – somewhere in Africa, Vivian presumed. She had seen the opportunity to convince Arianne to leave her son alone in return for a generous sum of money that would pay off her parents' debts. All Arianne had to do was promise to stay away from Daniel, and in return, Vivian would send money to her parents. They'd already received two instalments, and she doubted that they'd ever bother to repay what she'd already given them. They certainly weren't going to be getting any more of her money now. But it wasn't the money that was the real problem. She would pay any amount if it meant keeping that girl out of her son's life.

Not long before the wedding was due to happen, Vivian had arranged a call with Arianne and had made the offer to her without Daniel's knowledge, and after a couple of days to think about it, Arianne had tearfully accepted. And then Daniel had called his mother, distraught, not able to understand why Arianne had suddenly broken off the engagement, and Vivian had tried to console him. He would never have to know that his mother was the reason that Arianne had left him. Vivian knew that he would get over that girl eventually and find a more suitable girl to marry instead – English, and white, of course – and they would have beautiful babies together, and all would be well again in Vivian's world.

But now Arianne had gone back on her promise not to continue to pursue Daniel. And Vivian could not allow that.

Vivian was shaking as she dialled the numbers into her phone. She misdialed on the first attempt and had to try again. She could hear it ringing, and she waited anxiously for someone to pick up.

The man's voice that finally answered was gruff and no-nonsense. 'Yeah? Who's this?'

'It's Vivian.'

'Vivian? Oh right, the wife of—'

'Yes. I was.'

'What do you want?'

'I have a problem that I need you to take care of.'

'What are we talking about here? A simple deterrent, or something more permanent? Because permanent costs extra. Quite a lot extra.'

'The cost is not an issue, you know who I am, you know I can afford it. I'm looking for a permanent solution.'

There was a pause as if the man was considering something. When he spoke again, he quoted her a figure. She baulked at the amount. 'That seems rather steep.'

'I can hang up if you want?'

'No, it's fine. It won't be a problem.'

'It'll be half up front, half when done, can't say fairer than that. In cash. I'll have someone meet you at the train station near you. Yeah, I know where you live. Get there by ten o'clock tomorrow and go to platform three. Bring a photo of whoever it is, and half of the cash.'

'I'll be there.'

The man then hung up on her. Vivian put the phone down and looked at her trembling hands. She clasped them together tightly to try to steady them, and looked up to see her reflection in the mirror.

'I'm doing the right thing,' she said, but her reflection did not look convinced, so she repeated, 'I'm doing the right thing. I'm doing the right thing.'

Vivian stood on platform three, watching a train depart for the second time in the last half-hour. Lots of people came and went, but none of them had approached her.

She wore sunglasses, a hat, and the least-fancy clothes she could find from her wardrobe. No one should be able to recognise her looking like this, not that anyone she knew would lower themselves to travelling by train with all the plebs.

A young bald man with tattoos and too much metal in his face bumped into her. When she admonished him, he told her to 'Piss off!' and all she could do was stare at him in shock. She thought about asking the man that she was about to meet if he'd consider taking on a second job for her, because she'd just found herself another person who she thought the world would be much better off without.

Vivian gripped her handbag tightly. She felt very vulnerable carrying around so much money. *Where is he? Why is he not here yet?*

Her heart was pounding in her chest now, and her armpits felt sticky. She wiped her brow. The noise of the trains coming and going, the crowds of people, the stink of dirty air, the heat – it was all starting to be too much. She was feeling light-headed. If her rendezvous didn't happen soon, she'd have to abandon the platform and try to find a bathroom, but the thought of stepping foot in a public bathroom made her feel even more queasy.

She noticed a man looking at her. He glanced around a few times and then approached her. 'Vivian?' he said.

She nodded. 'That's right.'

'Come with me.'

He led her away from the platform and over to a bench near to the ticket office. 'Sit,' he told her, and she obeyed, like a good dog.

If the man was trying not to look shifty, then he wasn't doing a particularly good job, as his eyes were darting all over the place. They finally settled down on Vivian. 'Show me the photo.'

Vivian took the photograph out of her handbag and passed it to the man. She couldn't help but glance at the photo as he studied it. She imagined that the image of Daniel it had captured was looking directly at her, keeping his arm around Arianne's waist as if he was trying to protect her from what his mother intended to do to her.

'It's the young woman who's the... target,' Vivian told the man. 'She's changed her hair since that photo was taken, she's not wearing it up like that anymore, but—'

The man gave her a look and Vivian chose to stop talking. 'Good-looking girl,' he said, pocketing the photograph. 'Shame, really. Anyway, where's the money?'

The packet had been burning a hole in her handbag ever since the bank, and she felt relieved to be getting rid of it. She took it out and passed it to him and he quickly pocketed it. 'I know I don't need to count this, right?'

'Of course not, it's all there,' Vivian replied. 'You have my word.'

'Next, I need you to arrange for this girl—'

'Her name is Arianne.'

'I don't care what her fucking name is, I just need her to be at the location on this piece of paper, at the time written underneath, tomorrow. Got it? Can you do that?'

Vivian took the piece of paper that he offered her and unfolded it. She'd barely finished reading the message on it when he suddenly snatched it out of her hand and stuck the paper into his mouth. She watched as he chewed it and then swallowed it. Then he grinned at her with teeth so bad they could be used as the *Before* picture in a dental hygiene campaign.

Then the man stood up. 'In two days we meet back here, same place, same time, and you'll give me the rest of the cash. Agreed?'

'Wait,' she said, grabbing his arm, then hastily letting go when he glared at her. 'How will you, you know, do it?'

The man gave a small laugh. 'Do you really want to know?'

Vivian thought for a moment and then shook her head. 'No, I suppose it doesn't matter, does it? The end result will be the same.'

The man turned away, and then he was gone, disappearing into the crowd of people, leaving Vivian alone on the bench with only an odd sense of guilt for company.

Vivian couldn't sleep. Her thoughts fluctuated between wondering if she'd made a horrible mistake, and knowing that what she'd done was for the best. It was a mother's duty to protect her son, after all, and that was what she was doing.

Vivian hoped that Arianne hadn't noticed that she'd been avoiding her, and Daniel too, for that matter. She'd found it difficult to look her son in the eyes. She had gone to bed early again, but she'd suspected that her chances of falling asleep were slim. She tried to occupy her mind by planning what would happen over the next few days. By tomorrow evening, Arianne would be gone, and Daniel would have no choice but to remain here with his mother, and she would take care of him. She wouldn't leave him, other than to return to the train station to pay off the remainder of the fee she owed, and also, of course, she would have to fulfil her obligation to attend the next session at Grimwald House.

There were two more sessions remaining, and Vivian felt like she could do without any more of those little tricks like the sweets and all that terrible water that were seemingly designed to remind her of her past, especially ones that might add to her current feelings of guilt. Nearly drowning in that room had brought back memories from long ago that she had tried so hard to forget. When Sammy Mitchell's body was found in the river just days after he'd been expelled from his school, Vivian began to have nightmares, putting herself in his place and imagining her own drowning. If anyone suggested a trip to the beach to see the sea, or even to take a walk near a lake or a river, she would decline. She couldn't look at the water without seeing her own lifeless body lying there, pale and cold and abandoned, just like Sammy's had been.

Vivian forced the memories out of her mind and tried to concentrate on the book she was reading about ancient Egypt, but none of the words on the page were sinking in, and eventually she dozed off.

She didn't resurface until several hours later, when there was a series of knocks at her door. She looked at her bedside clock. It was 7.25 a.m. 'Who is it?' she called out.

'It's Daniel. I brought you breakfast in bed.'

She raised herself up out of her bed, went to the mirror to check that she was presentable, and then opened the door.

Daniel came into her room, bringing a giant smile as well as a tray that held a glass of orange juice and a plate with slices of toast, bacon and an egg. Vivian had a flashback to when an eight-year-old Daniel had brought breakfast on a tray to his parents' bedroom, a seemingly sweet gesture but with an underlying motive: the boy had obviously wanted to make sure that his parents had reconciled after they'd spent most of the previous evening arguing.

She knew that having his father – her first husband – walk out on them had been devastating for Daniel, much more so than it had been for his sister Rebecca, and it had made him latch onto his mother even more closely, as if terrified that if he left her alone for just a moment then she might suddenly disappear from his life too. She'd seen their closer relationship as being the silver lining in that miserable cloud. Yes, their closeness may have caused Rebecca to drift away from both of them over the years, but that was a sacrifice that Vivian was prepared to make. Daniel was her favourite, after all. Even when Vivian remarried, Daniel was still the most important man in her life, and he always would be.

'Are you alright, Mother?'

She realised that Daniel was looking at her curiously. She smiled at him. 'Yes, I'm fine, just reminiscing. Thank you for this, it's a lovely gesture. Very thoughtful of you.' She sat back down on her bed as he brought the tray over to her.

'Actually,' he said, 'it was Arianne's idea. She's feeling a little unwell this morning, so I'm letting her rest. She thought this would be a nice thing to do for you.' After placing the tray on her lap, Daniel hovered by the side of the bed. His expression changed and he looked a little nervous. 'I know that you and Arianne don't always see eye to eye, but she is trying her best. I'm sure that once you get to know her, you'll love her just like I do. She's the most amazing woman that I've ever met. She's everything to me.'

Hearing Daniel declare his love for another woman like this, it was as if he'd picked up the knife from her tray and stabbed Vivian in her heart. She stared down at her breakfast and tore at her toast with her teeth. Then she looked back up at her son. 'I was thinking, perhaps Arianne and I should spend the day together, just the two of us?' she suggested. 'I thought perhaps I might take her to the Aviary to see the birds. Do you remember that place? We used to take you and your sister there when you were children. I do have somewhere that I need to go afterwards, I have to see a friend, but so as long as Arianne doesn't mind that, then I think this would be a good opportunity for us to get to know each other, like you wanted.'

Daniel looked surprised. 'You'd do that? Thank you, that would be great! I'm sure Arianne would love that. She loves animals and birds. This means the world to me, thank you for doing this.' He moved towards Vivian and wrapped his arms around her. She swallowed the remains of her toast and held her son.

They embraced for a long time. She didn't want him to ever let her go. And she really didn't want him to go and put those arms of his around that other woman, the one who didn't deserve him.

To Vivian's dismay, Daniel broke their connection. He had that big smile back on his face as he said, 'I'll leave you to your breakfast, and I'll go tell Arianne. I know she'll be so excited!'

Vivian watched Daniel leave the room with a spring in his step and no way of knowing that soon he would instead be hobbled by grief.

Because soon Arianne would be gone, and Daniel would turn to his mother to console him. Then it would just be the two of them again – as it was always meant to be.

Vivian watched Arianne. The younger woman looked like she was enjoying herself. She excitedly pointed out the birds on the branches in their cages, and Vivian smiled politely, pretending to be as interested as she was, but truthfully Vivian had only one thing on her mind, and it wasn't the tweeting and flapping of these noisy creatures. She checked her watch.

'Oh, aren't they wonderful?' Arianne exclaimed. 'All the different shapes and sizes, so many different patterns. And just look at all those colours! You can't help but love every last one of them. Whatever colour they might be.'

Vivian glanced up at that last comment, but Arianne was still staring at the birds, so perhaps she hadn't meant anything by it. Vivian could begrudgingly admit that Arianne's grasp of English was quite good, with only her accent giving away the fact that she didn't belong here. It was perhaps her one redeeming feature.

Vivian was aware that the time was now getting away from them, and that they absolutely could not miss their very special appointment. 'Arianne, we need to think about heading off now.'

Arianne wore a disappointed expression, pouting like a little girl, and it reminded Vivian of her daughter Rebecca who'd worn the same expression whenever she was told it was time to leave this place. But Vivian didn't want to think about Rebecca right now, or Daniel either. She wanted to focus only on what needed to happen next.

'Do we have to leave so soon? Can't we stay a little longer?' Arianne pleaded.

'No, I'm afraid not. I have somewhere important I need to be.'

'Oh, alright then.' Arianne waved goodbye to the birds and walked with Vivian back towards the entrance gates. 'I really enjoyed seeing all of those wonderful birds – Dan has some competition, I may have just found something that I love almost as much as your son!' She gave Vivian a smile that wasn't returned.

There is nothing in this entire world that you should love more than my son, you ungrateful little—

'I think I might suggest to Dan that we get a pet when we get back to France, perhaps a bird – what do you think?'

You aren't going back to France, silly Arianne, Vivian thought. *In fact, there's no point in making any plans for your future at all.*

Vivian caught sight of a little girl standing alone a few feet away from the entrance. She had her head down and appeared to be crying about something. Arianne spotted her too, and she approached the girl and then bent down to look the child in the eyes, and asked her, 'What's the matter, sweetheart?'

Between sniffles came the reply, 'I can't find my daddy!'

'Oh, you poor thing, it's alright, don't cry. We'll help you find him. My name is Arianne, and my friend over there, her name is Vivian.' She pointed to Vivian, who the little girl looked at warily. 'What's your name?' she asked the girl.

'Kimberly,' she sobbed. 'I want my daddy.'

'Where did you last see your daddy?' Arianne asked her.

The little girl pointed in the direction of the entrance just as a man came rushing towards them from the opposite direction, calling out, 'Kimmy! Kimmy!'

He scooped up the little girl in his arms, and she cried out happily, 'Daddy!'

Arianne stood, and smiled. The father held his daughter tight as he told Arianne, 'Thank you, I was going out of my mind for a minute there, I only turned away for a second and then she was gone, you know what kids are like.' He then said to the little girl, 'Kimmy, you don't run off like that, ever again, do you understand me? You scared Daddy!'

'I'm sorry, I'll never do it again, ever! I promise!' The girl started crying again, and her father hugged her close.

Vivian cleared her throat. 'Arianne, come on, it's time to go.'

They headed towards the car park, with Arianne casting glances back at the still-hugging father and daughter. 'That little girl was so adorable, and the way her father was with her, that's real love, isn't it? When I saw their faces the moment they were reunited, oh, I felt like I could just die!'

'Yes, you could,' Vivian muttered under her breath.

They spotted their car and approached it. Arianne had insisted on paying for a rental car so that she could drive. Vivian had bristled when Arianne had said that she was looking forward to trying to drive on the "wrong" side of the road again. Vivian was originally going to suggest that they hire a taxi, but then she'd realised that there was some benefit to the idea of as few people as possible knowing where they were going.

They got into the car and Arianne drove them out of the car park and onto the roads, where Vivian gave her directions. When Arianne asked what her appointment was about, Vivian told her that she was going to visit an old friend who needed her help with a personal matter, and that it wouldn't take very long, but that it was important.

'When we get back, I'd like to cook dinner,' Arianne suddenly announced, 'if that's alright with you?'

'Yes, I suppose so.'

'Vivian, I'm happy that we're doing this today, just the two of us. I feel like we can put things behind us, and start afresh. I want us to get along, and I know Dan wants that too. He loves you. And I love him.'

'Yes, I love him too,' Vivian told her. 'He's my son and I want the best for him and I'll do whatever it takes to make that happen.'

They continued driving, edging ever closer to their destination. Vivian noticed that Arianne opened her mouth as if to say something, then hesitated. Finally, she spoke. 'I want to have a baby. A little girl, that would be nice, a sweet little angel like the one we just saw.'

Vivian stared at the back of the van on the road in front of them. 'Oh.'

'I'm sorry, I shouldn't have suddenly said it aloud like that. Dan and I haven't discussed it yet, and we're not even married yet, so I know that you're going to say that I'm getting ahead of myself and that there'll be plenty of time for all that and that we have our whole lives ahead of us, but it's something that I can't stop thinking about.'

Vivian caught a few glances from Arianne, as if she was expecting her to reply to that. Instead, Vivian told her, 'Eyes on the road, please.'

'Sorry, I only wanted to know how you felt about that?'

Vivian shrugged. 'There's not much I can do about it, is there?'

'No, I only meant, it would be your grandchild, and it's such a big thing, and you know Dan better than I do, you're his mother – how do you think he might feel about it? What do you think he might say?'

'I think he would say that there's no need to rush into anything,' Vivian answered. 'You never know where life is going to take you, so I suggest you take things one step at a time.'

'I know, but it's exciting to think about. Although it's very scary too. How did you cope when you had Dan and Rebecca, especially after Dan's father left – that must have been so hard for you?'

'I dealt with it like I would with any other problem,' Vivian answered. 'You do what you have to do, and you keep going. Turn off at the next left and follow the road.'

The car turned and they headed away from the main roads, driving along a bumpy path that parted a field, and eventually they saw a farmhouse.

'Your friend lives on a farm?' Arianne asked curiously as they approached the building.

'This is where I was asked to come.'

Arianne parked the car and waited as Vivian got out and approached the farmhouse. She knocked on the door four times, as per the instruction on the sheet of paper that she'd been handed.

There was no response. Vivian checked her watch. This was the right time, the right location, and she'd knocked the right number of times. So where was he?

Suddenly there was a scream from behind her.

Vivian spun around and saw a man reach into the car and drag Arianne from it. He threw Arianne onto the ground, and as she continued screaming he pulled her up and dragged her over to a trough and banged her forehead on the metal – twice – before pulling her head up over the edge and then forcing it down into the water, which splashed out onto the ground. Arianne's arms and legs were going like crazy, but he was a big man and far stronger than she was. She wouldn't be able to fight him off, even if she was fighting for her life.

In Vivian's mind, she was fighting a battle of her own. As she watched Arianne being drowned, she couldn't stop thinking about Sammy Mitchell and his lifeless body in the river. She'd only been a child then, and had felt all kinds of overwhelming emotions when he had died, however she realised that she felt nothing for this woman dying in front of her. It was as if she was watching a television programme where a character was about to die, but she didn't care less about their fate. She'd rather change the channel and watch something else. But she couldn't seem to get Sammy's face and his dead eyes out of her mind.

Arianne eventually stopped moving, and the man picked up her lifeless body and carried it to the farmhouse. He kicked open the door, took her inside, and then closed the door behind him, so Vivian could not see whatever he was doing to the body in there.

Vivian eventually regained control of her own body and walked back to the car. She sat in the driver's seat and gripped the steering wheel hard, her knuckles white. It had been a while since she'd driven a car herself, rather than be driven by someone else, but it all came back to her quickly – like riding a bike. As she started the car and then drove away from the farmhouse, she had one hand on the steering wheel, and with the other she adjusted the controls for the radio until she found a station playing classical music, and she turned it up loud.

After all the anticipation, it had happened so quickly that it now felt a little anticlimactic. Strangest of all, she hadn't felt any joy watching Arianne die, even knowing that it meant that she and Daniel would finally be free of her.

For now, Vivian focussed on her driving and planning what she would say to Daniel when she reached home. She would tell her son about the horrific ordeal that she and Arianne had suffered: after they had left the Aviary, Arianne had told Vivian that she wanted to drive around and see some countryside, but after a while they realised they were lost and stopped to ask a man for help, but the man suddenly produced a knife and ordered Arianne out of the car. He then forced her into his own car and sped away, leaving Vivian all alone. After recovering from the shock, Vivian had managed to drive herself home in the rental car, distraught. Yes, she had her phone on her and in hindsight she should have called the police straight away, but she was in such a panic that all she could think about was coming home to Daniel.

Daniel would be so worried over the coming days, not knowing what might have happened to Arianne but fearing the worst. Vivian knew that Arianne's body was likely to turn up somewhere eventually, and then Daniel would finally be able to move on. Vivian would help him through it all, she'd be there for him, just like she always had.

Vivian was strong enough to do things for her son that no one else would. She was able to put aside any doubts that she might have and do what was necessary, whatever that might involve. She would do that for him. No one loved him as much as she did, and no one else ever could.

In the driveway of her house, Vivian sat with her hands on the steering wheel. It had been five minutes since she'd arrived home and she still hadn't left the car. She knew that she should go inside the house and tell Daniel about Arianne, but for some reason she couldn't seem to motivate herself to get out of the car. She felt a complete lack of energy. In her mind, she kept replaying what had happened. It was like a delayed reaction, and only now was she finally starting to realise what she'd done. Vivian couldn't seem to get the image of Arianne thrashing about in the water out of her mind. That damned girl, even in death she was still haunting her thoughts.

Vivian closed her eyes and took deep breaths. *Focus on Daniel. This is all for Daniel.* She needed to calm down and relax. A nice long soak in her bath would normally do the trick.

When she opened her eyes, she realised that something felt wrong. There was a heaviness, a strange pressure in the centre of her chest, and then she found it hard to breathe. She felt light-headed, and she was sweating. She felt sick. She started to panic. She looked at the house in desperation, it was so close – if she could just reach Daniel...

She pushed open the car door and tried to get out, but she fell headfirst into the gravel, and it scratched at her face. As she lay there, clutching at her chest, unable to move, Vivian thought, *After everything I've done, everything I've survived, don't you dare try to kill me with a bloody heart attack now!*

She then heard a voice, a familiar voice calling to her – it was Daniel, but he sounded so very far away. She hoped he was closer than he sounded. She heard him mention something about getting her to a hospital.

Good boy, taking care of your mother, just like I've always taken care of you. It's just you and me, Daniel, as it always should be. I love you. Please, don't let me die...

CHAPTER SEVEN

SESSION FOUR

Of all the things that Anna ought to be afraid of when she returned to Grimwald House – the decaying corpse in the hidden tomb, the ghostly piano player, the dining room that had tried to drown them, the untrustworthy Handsworth – it shouldn't have been the thought of seeing Mark again that worried her the most. Even now, a whole week later, she still couldn't understand how Anna-from-last-week had been so foolish as to allow what had happened between them to happen.

After several minutes had passed since the taxi had arrived at the house and Anna still hadn't made a move to step out, the driver called to her, 'We're here, you know.'

'I know we are,' she replied testily. 'Give me a minute, will you?'

Anna took a deep breath, then opened the door and stepped out onto the gravel. It was raining again, fiercer than ever. It hadn't rained all week, perhaps it had been saving itself for today. The taxi drove away, leaving her alone.

No one dashed from the entrance to rescue her with an umbrella, so she sprinted for the front doors, and used the knockers to try to get attention from inside. Anna wiped the rain from her face and tried to straighten herself up, just in case *you-know-who* answered the door. When the door finally opened, she saw Vivian's face instead.

'You're here, then. Come in out of the rain.'

Anna entered the house and took off her wet coat. She hung it on the coat stand by the door and eyed the umbrellas that sat there in their box all snug and dry while she was wet and miserable.

'I swear the weather gets worse each time we come here,' Anna grumbled. 'So, are we the first ones here tonight?'

'No,' Vivian replied, 'Harold and Katarina are already in the dining room waiting for us. No sign of Mark as yet, I'm sure you'll be disappointed to hear.'

Anna noticed that Vivian seemed a little subdued and her eyes were distant. 'Is everything alright with you?'

A soft smile appeared on the older woman's face. 'I'm fine. I had a... minor health issue, but it's nothing to worry about. But it's been a long and tiring week and I want to get this over with. I need to get back home, my son's staying with me so I don't intend to be spending the night here again this time.'

'I don't either, but we never know what to expect on these evenings, do we? Shall we go in and see the others?'

Vivian reached out a hand to grip Anna's arm gently but firmly. 'Anna, a word of warning, a piece of advice from someone who's been there too many times. Whatever it is between you and Mark, you should put a stop to it.'

'I'm not sure what you mean?'

'You've had your fun, but nothing good will come of pursuing it any further. You don't know this man, not really, even if you think you do. None of us here know one another very well at all, do we? We've been thrown together for these strange evenings, with no clue what the point of it all is. I think it'd be very dangerous for any of us to get too attached to one another. Just think about what I've said.'

Vivian released her grip on Anna's arm and went into the dining room, leaving Anna to consider her words. She took a moment before entering the dining room after her.

She saw Katarina standing next to Harold, and the young woman beamed a big smile at her. 'Anna, it's so wonderful to see you again! How are you?'

Anna tried to muster up a little enthusiasm and answered, 'I'm fine. How are you, Katarina?'

'I'm well, thank you for asking. Harold and I have been having a conversation about his injury. I think he's doing better. Don't you think he looks better?'

Anna looked at Harold in his wheelchair and nodded. 'I do. Harold, it's good to see you.'

Harold rolled himself closer to her. 'Hello again, Anna. I suppose we're just waiting for Mark now, aren't we?'

Anna was surprised when Katarina asked her, 'Anna, could I speak to you for a moment, in private?'

Anna nodded, and allowed herself to be led away from Harold and Vivian. 'What is it?'

Katarina looked a little sheepish as she said, 'I wanted some advice and I thought you would be the best person to speak to.'

'Oh. How can I help?'

Katarina leaned in closer and lowered her voice, almost to a whisper. 'It's about Mark.'

'What about Mark?' Anna felt her defences go up. *Does Katarina know about us?*

'I think he likes me,' Katarina answered. 'I mean, *likes* me, you know, in that way.'

Anna frowned. 'What do you mean?'

'Last week, when we all stayed here, after everyone had gone to bed, I found Mark outside my room. He asked me to take a walk with him, and we did. We wandered along the corridors, talking about this and that. We tried to be quiet so as not to wake you and Vivian. We came across that room with the big black door and he dared me to try to open it, but fortunately the door was locked – not that I would've gone in, anyway, I'm not that brave! I told him we should stop being silly and wandering around in the dark trying to find spooky rooms and that we should go back to our bedrooms, where we know it's safe. Mark was being very playful, and he offered to come into my room and make sure there were no monsters inside, and I agreed. So then we were alone together in my room, in the middle of the night.'

Anna felt a little unsteady as Katarina continued, 'To be honest, I think Mark had had rather a lot to drink, and you know how men can be when they're like that. I think he wanted some company.'

Anna shook her head. 'I'm sorry, what are you saying? Did you sleep with him?'

Katarina looked mortified. 'No, of course not! I barely know him! What kind of woman do you think I am?'

Yes, you're right, what kind of woman would do something like that...

'I'm not sure I understand, Katarina. What *did* happen?'

Katarina's eyes drifted away, and a smile crossed her lips. 'We sat on the bed and we talked for a while. Mark's really quite charming and funny, especially when he's had a few drinks. Of course, he's rather handsome too, anyone can see that. It was nice, talking with someone like that, feeling things that I haven't felt since...

'Oh, it's a little embarrassing, but I have to admit, I found myself very attracted to him. After we'd talked for quite some time, he then gave me a kiss – two, actually. He told me how beautiful I was and how much I impressed him. He was so very sweet, but I told him that he ought to leave before... Well, it just wasn't proper for him to stay in my room, we are guests in this house after all. And he did go, eventually, but it took some persuading! I hope he wasn't too disappointed.

'Anna, I know it's silly, but ever since that night, I can't stop thinking about him, I haven't been able to think of anything else all week! Am I crazy, or do you think the two of us could have something special?'

Anna placed a hand on the wall to steady herself as she tried to come up with a response. 'I think you're just getting carried away,' she said. 'I don't think it's real.'

'What do you mean?'

'I just mean that someone like Mark, he's a ladies' man, he's a charmer, he's a flirt. Especially when he's had a few too many to drink. I don't think you should take any of what he said or did seriously. It was just the alcohol talking.'

Katarina looked upset. 'No, you're wrong, I know it was more than that. There was definitely a connection between us.'

Anna wanted to shake her. 'No, there wasn't! And you need to be more careful, and less bloody naive, or lying bastards like Mark are going to take advantage of you. So just grow up, for God's sake!'

Katarina looked like she was about to burst into tears. She turned and ran out of the dining room and back into the hallway. As Anna watched her go, she heard Harold call out, 'Is everything alright?'

Anna didn't answer. She followed Katarina and entered the hallway, closing the dining room door behind her. She found Katarina sitting on the staircase, her head in her hands.

Anna tried to remind herself that none of this was Katarina's fault and that she shouldn't be so hard on her. It was Mark who was the bad guy in all of this, not this poor girl. Anna still couldn't believe that on the same night that Mark had come to her room and they'd had passionate – if drunken and clumsy – sex, he'd actually tried his luck with Katarina first – only, unlike Anna, Katarina had had the self-respect and willpower to turn the drunken lothario away.

Anna sat herself down beside Katarina and said softly, 'I'm sorry if I upset you. I didn't mean to be so harsh. I'm just angry with Mark. For what he did to you.'

'But he didn't do anything wrong!' Katarina sniffled. 'And neither did I.'

'I know you didn't.'

Katarina looked at Anna. 'I've not had very good experiences with men, Anna. Something very bad happened to me with a man that I thought I knew, someone I cared about. He wasn't who I thought he was, and he did something awful to me, to my body.'

'God, Katarina, I'm sorry.' Anna offered her hand to Katarina. She looked hesitant at first but then placed her hand in Anna's.

Katarina gave her a sad smile. 'It's alright, it's in the past, but for a while, I wasn't sure if I could ever feel that way about a man again. I had sworn to myself that I would stay away from men altogether, but that's quite a difficult thing to do, as I'm sure you'd understand. And then we were here in this house and Mark was being so nice to me and saying such sweet things to me, and I suppose I got swept away again. Oh, you must think I'm some silly little girl with a silly little crush.'

'No, listen to me,' Anna said, 'you're a good person. You're sweet, you're kind, and you're beautiful – my God, are you beautiful, I'm honestly so bloody jealous of you. I'm sure there are plenty of other men out there, *good* men, who would kill to be with someone like you. You deserve to be with someone who'll treat you right, but you have to trust me when I say that person's not Mark.'

'But how do you know that?'

Here we go. Come on, Anna, you can tell her the truth. Tell her what happened that evening after horny Mark left Katarina's room disappointed, tell her whose room he went to next. You have so many secrets, perhaps it'd help to unburden yourself of just this one?

Anna took a deep breath before answering. 'The reason I know, is because—'

She was suddenly interrupted by the front doors swinging open, allowing in the wind, the rain – and Mark. He heaved the doors shut behind him and shook himself like a dog. Then he spotted Anna and Katarina on the stairs. He waved at them, and after he took off his coat, he walked over to them and said, 'Good evening, ladies.'

Katarina raised her head and said, 'Hello, Mark.'

Anna narrowed her eyes. 'Mark.'

'Is, er, is everything alright here?' Mark asked, as his eyes darted between Anna and Katarina. Anna could swear there was a little fear in those eyes. *Good. Be afraid. Because I'm onto you.*

'We're fine,' Anna replied.

'What were you two talking about?' he asked. 'Anything interesting?'

'It's nothing, it's girl talk, it doesn't concern you. The others are in the dining room, you should go on in too. We've all been waiting for you to arrive. You're late.'

'Right. I'll go in now, then. Are you two coming?'

'Go on without us. We'll be there in a minute.'

'I hope so, the evening just wouldn't be nearly as interesting without you two lovely ladies.'

He put on that cheesy grin of his again, but Anna could tell that Mark was worried about something.

As she watched him go she thought, *You won't get away with this, you bastard.*

'The arms next?'

'Yes, the arms.'

Having had Vivian's confirmation, Mark stepped forward and started by unwrapping the left hand and lower arm of the corpse.

Almost as soon as Anna and Katarina had entered the dining room, the ticking had started and the secret door had revealed itself to the group, as if by magic, but it had remained closed. On the dining table there was a single solitary red rose in a vase in the centre, with a jug of water beside it. While Mark was busy trying and failing to pull the door open, on a hunch Anna had tried pouring the water from the jug into the vase – and wasn't too surprised when the door to the tomb had then suddenly opened. Their host was still playing games with them. They wasted no time going through the open door and into the tomb again.

Harold and Vivian were now focussed on the unwrapping of the body, seemingly keen to take their turns as soon as Mark was finished. Anna saw that Katarina was lost in thought, and wasn't paying much attention to the unveiling. Anna didn't like thinking that she was the reason that Katarina was upset, but at the same time, she couldn't allow her to go on thinking that a relationship with Mark was a good idea. Vivian had been right about him. Anna had to protect Katarina, and herself, from Mark. She couldn't allow the bastard to—

'Fuck me!'

Mark's sudden exclamation pulled Anna out of her thoughts. 'What's the matter?' she asked.

He stopped unwrapping and turned to face the group. 'I'm sorry, I apologise for swearing like that, but... well, see for yourselves.'

Mark pointed at the part of the body that he had unwrapped. Anna stared at it, trying to work out what had got Mark so rattled. She realised that the skin of the left arm and hand was quite different to that of the rest of the body – it was much smoother, much less decayed.

'Incredible!' Harold exclaimed. 'That arm appears to be so much better preserved than the rest of the body, even more than the chest area. Compare it to the legs and feet, it's like a different state entirely. The difference is extraordinary.'

Mark looked puzzled. 'From the lower parts of the body, I thought this thing was hundreds of years old, or even thousands, but there's no way that this is the arm of someone who's been dead for anywhere near that long.'

'Perhaps it depends on how it's been preserved?' Harold suggested. 'It's very odd, though. Here, let me go next.' He moved his wheelchair closer and unwrapped the right hand. He was breathing heavily and Vivian took over from him and unwrapped the lower right arm.

Anna went next, revealing the rest of the left arm. Once she'd finished, she stepped back, and looked at the body in disbelief. 'It's not far off looking like the arm of a normal, living person. That's pretty disturbing.'

'Katarina, you're up next,' Vivian said. She didn't respond, so Vivian pushed. 'What's the matter with you now, girl?'

Katarina woke from her daze. 'Nothing, I'm fine.'

'You're clearly upset about something, we can all see that. So what is it now? Too cold in here for you? Did you break a finger-nail? Did you get a spot of dirt on your lovely white dress? Come on, out with it, what's wrong with you?'

'Nothing's wrong with me!' Katarina yelled back.

Vivian seemed to find Katarina's outburst amusing. She looked at the others. 'She's completely useless. We'll have to do the rest of the unwrapping ourselves.'

'I'm not useless!'

Vivian turned back to face Katarina. 'Then why are you behaving like you are?'

'I can't, I...'

'You can't what? Spit it out, for God's sake.'

'I can't tell you, I'm sorry, it's... complicated.' Katarina glanced at Mark and then looked at Anna for help.

Anna decided that she should intervene. 'Vivian, leave her alone.'

Vivian sighed with frustration. 'There's clearly something going on with her, and I only wanted to know what it might be, but she can't even tell me that. I suppose if you ask a simple woman a simple question, you should expect a simple answer.'

'Hey, come on now, there's no need for that,' Mark said.

'I'll take Katarina's place,' Anna said. 'I'll unwrap the rest of that arm.'

'No, I can do it, just give me a moment,' Katarina said. She took a deep breath and then stepped closer. She stopped and eyed the body apprehensively.

'It'll be alright, there's nothing to be afraid of,' Mark said, giving Katarina a reassuring smile.

Katarina reached out and ripped the rest of the wraps from the remainder of the right arm, and then stepped back. She looked relieved, but also pleased with what she'd accomplished.

'Well done, Katarina,' Mark said, smiling at her. 'You see? Sometimes it's alright to take a chance and do something a little risky, a little dangerous, once in a while.'

As Katarina returned Mark's smile and they seemed to stare into each other's eyes for far too long, Anna could feel the anger building inside of her. *Does Mark think he can flirt with Katarina right in front of me?! That bastard, I'll kill him...*

Harold then made an observation that caused the rest of the group to stare at him. 'The more we unwrap, the less decayed it seems to be... so I'm just wondering what the head is going to look like when we unwrap that.'

'There are two possibilities, I think,' Mark said. 'One, she'll turn out to be a hideously ugly monster, or two, we'll discover that she was some gorgeous princess and they had to hide her away from the world because her face was just far too beautiful for any mortal man to look at. Who knows, she could be the most beautiful woman that we'll have ever seen... present company excluded, of course!' He grinned at Katarina, who smiled back, then he did the same to Anna, who did not. He only looked at Vivian when she coughed to remind him that she was there in the room too.

'So why don't we just get this over with and find out?' Anna said angrily. 'I'm sick to death of doing everything so bloody slowly, having to wait a week to come here each time and then doing this unwrapping one tiny little bit at a time, it's so infuriating! We should just unwrap the head now and be done with it all!' She stepped towards the body and started to pull on the wrappings around the head.

'Wait, Anna,' Katarina said, 'I don't think we should—'

'It'll be fine!' Anna told her. The wraps resisted her at first, but when she used more effort, grunting as she did so, Anna managed to tear a sliver of the wrapping away from the left side of the corpse's face.

Suddenly the candles in the room flickered violently, as if a strong wind had blown through the room, and a different kind of gong sounded, an angrier-sounding gong. Anna took her hand away and the candles settled back down again. She realised everyone was staring at her now, and feeling embarrassed and annoyed with herself, she withdrew.

'That was quite a silly thing to do,' Vivian said, shaking her head as if disappointed in Anna. 'What were you thinking? You don't want to make our host angry with us, do you? What possessed you?'

'I don't know... just forget it, will you?' Anna said, through gritted teeth. She noticed Mark was frowning at her.

The normal gong sounded, the candles went out, and the door reopened. They returned to the dining room and took their seats, and the door to the tomb closed, although it still remained visible. There was no meal waiting for them on the dining table, only that jug of water and the single red rose in the vase at the centre. Anna caught Mark staring at the rose as if this was the first time that he'd noticed it, and something about it seemed to be bothering him.

'I think I find this room even more disturbing than the one with the corpse in it,' Vivian said.

'After what happened last time that we were here, that's a perfectly rational thing to feel,' Harold told her, with a sympathetic look in his eyes.

'And look, no dinner for us again,' Vivian noted. 'We're going to starve. This is all becoming a little tiresome. Oh, I'll be glad when this ridiculous mummy farce is finally over. I think I've had quite enough now. I think I'd like to go home as soon as possible.'

'Has anyone seen Handsworth since we got here tonight?' Mark asked. 'I wonder where he's lurking this time.'

Suddenly there was a gasp from Katarina. 'I think there's something moving under this table!'

They all watched in surprise as Ebony the dog crawled out from under the table and wandered over to the door to the tomb. She started scratching at the door. Anna got up and walked over to the animal, and reached out her hand to stroke her, but hastily withdrew it when the dog started growling at her. 'What's wrong with you then, you silly thing?' she asked, but the dog didn't answer, so Anna gave up and went back to her seat at the table. The dog then got up and went back under the table. It started sniffing around Vivian before she kicked it away and barked at it, 'Go bother someone else!'

The dog then approached Katarina but she quickly brought her knees up to her chest, keeping her feet away from the animal, and hissed, 'Go away! I'm not in the mood!'

The others looked at her with some amusement, but Anna was not amused to see that Mark's eyes seemed to be focussed on Katarina's bare legs. She tried to distract his attention. 'Mark, shouldn't you be looking for handles in the walls again? There's probably another fun surprise waiting for us.'

Mark pulled his eyes away from Katarina and told Anna, 'I suppose I could, but I don't know whether to expect sweets or a wave of water to suddenly come rushing out of those walls at me again. So no thanks, I think this time I'm quite happy to just sit here, enjoying the company.'

He had a grin on his face again, and Anna hadn't wanted to punch someone so much in all her life, not even Conniving Connie from work. She hoped that whatever tonight's entertainment might be, it would wipe that grin off Mark's face.

'I have got quite an appetite though,' Mark said. 'I'm not quite sure what I want, but I know I'm hungry for something.'

To Anna, it seemed like every word coming out of Mark's mouth was designed to rile her up even more. *I know exactly what you're hungry for, and you're not getting it, not tonight, I'll make sure of that.*

'If I close my eyes,' Harold said, inhaling, 'I can almost smell a nice big steak cooking.'

Anna sniffed the air. 'I don't think you're imagining it, I can smell something cooking too.'

Vivian rubbed her hands. 'Then perhaps we are getting some dinner tonight, after all. The smell must be wafting in from the kitchen.'

Ebony emerged from the table and made a whimpering sound as Mark said, 'Is it me, or is the air in here getting a little hazy?'

Anna looked around. He was right. 'It's smoke! I think something's burning!'

The rest of the group looked around, alarmed. Mark stood up and rushed over to the door to the hallway, and put his hand on the doorknob. He quickly pulled his hand away, with a gasp.

'Well hurry up and open it then!' Anna shouted.

'I would if I bloody could!' Mark shouted back at her, startling her. 'That doorknob's red hot!'

Katarina got out of her chair and joined him. He warned her not to touch the doorknob. 'Oh no, look!' she cried out. She pointed at the base of the door, where they could all see smoke beginning to drift through.

'I think there's a fire out there in the hallway, that's not good,' Harold said. He looked down at his wheelchair as he added, 'That's not good at all.'

Vivian banged her fist on the table. 'What are they up to this time? Is this another one of their stupid little games? First water, now fire?'

'The smoke's coming in quite thick now,' Katarina noted, just as Harold started coughing.

'What do we do?' Anna found herself looking to Mark for help, much to her annoyance, but he had a panicked expression on his face and he looked like he was going to be no help at all.

Vivian tried her phone. 'No signal,' she told the others. 'I don't think anyone's coming to help us...'

'We're going to be trapped in here,' Harold said, 'and there's nowhere for the smoke to go, so I think we only have one option. We need to get the door to that tomb open again. That room's got to be more airtight than this one, it's been keeping that body preserved in there, after all.'

Anna saw that Mark was still standing there, not moving, and staring at the smoke. 'Mark, snap out of it and do something! Get the door to the tomb open!'

Mark finally sprung into action, and tried to slide the door open, but he was unsuccessful. 'I can't get it open! It won't budge!'

'Say we do manage to get that door open, and we all hide away in that tiny little room over there, then what?' Vivian asked. 'If there is a fire, even if the smoke doesn't get us, the fire eventually will. This whole house might be burning down, for all we know!'

'At least it might give us some time,' Harold said, 'and perhaps someone will report the fire and the fire brigade will get here in time and put it out? There are other people in the house, there are those maids and Handsworth – surely they'll call for help and get someone to come and rescue us?'

Anna wasn't convinced that they would be receiving any help from the staff, but Harold's suggestion of withdrawing to the tomb seemed to be their only option at that moment. She leaned across the dining table and tried pouring the water from the vase back into the jug, then back into the vase, hoping that action would trigger the door to open again, but it didn't work. 'Damn it!' She joined Mark by the wall. 'There has to be some other trick to opening that door, we just need to work out what it is!'

'I haven't seen anything in this room that would be of any help to us,' Mark told her. 'There's nothing special here, other than that bloody dog who won't shut up. Maybe you should ask that stupid animal if it's got any suggestions about how the hell we're supposed to get out of this?'

Anna looked down at Ebony, who was cowering near her feet and whining.

'There is something else unusual in this room,' Katarina called out, as she plucked the rose from the vase on the table. 'This single rose.'

'Just put it back,' Mark told her, rather forcefully. 'I don't see what use a damn flower is to us right now.'

Katarina met his eyes and held them for a moment. 'It's a symbol of love, Mark. It's beautiful.'

'Great. It's not going to save us from a bloody fire though, is it?!'

'Please don't shout at me, Mark,' Katarina said, looking hurt. She examined the petals with her fingers. 'It's lovely. I think I might keep it.'

'Oh do whatever you want, I don't care, we're all about to die in here!' Mark returned to the door and started banging on it impotently with his fist. Then he stopped, stepped back, and shouted at the door, 'Open the fuck up!'

'Yes, I'm sure that's going to work,' Anna said, rolling her eyes at him, 'that or "*open sesame*" – it's a toss-up, really.'

'Well, I don't know what else to do, Anna, so why don't *you* think of something, instead of just standing there and being so completely fucking useless!'

Anna stepped back at Mark's outburst. She'd never seen him like this before. It was like the true version of Mark had finally been revealed for everyone to see.

'Maybe this fire is all your bloody fault anyway?' Mark said. 'You tried to unwrap the head when you shouldn't have, and you pissed off our host, and now they're going to burn us alive. So well done, Anna, great job!'

Anna gritted her teeth. She stepped closer to Mark again and said, 'You know what, if we're all about to die here, then I want to say something to you, Mark – you're a selfish, lying bastard!'

'Thank you, that's very helpful,' he replied.

Lowering her voice, Anna told him, 'I know all about you and Katarina.'

Mark frowned and glanced across the room towards Katarina, who was trying to reassure a frightened Harold. 'What? What are you on about?'

'I know I was only your second choice that night, and that you would have preferred to have slept with Katarina instead of me. All the things you said to me, what you felt about me, they were all lies, weren't they? Tell me I'm wrong. Go on, lie to me again.'

'I don't know what the hell you're talking about!' he hissed at her. 'All this smoke's clearly affecting your brain. You're acting even crazier than you normally do. Why don't you do something useful and keep your bloody mouth shut for one second so that I can think straight.'

Anna's rage couldn't be contained anymore. The volcano wanted to erupt. She suddenly lashed out and struck Mark's face with a slap so hard that it knocked him backwards. His head hit the wall, and he put his hand to his face where she'd struck him, with a look of shock that was mirrored on the faces of the rest of the group.

'Anna!' Katarina gasped. 'What have you done?!'

'What is going on over there?' Harold said. 'You're supposed to be getting us out of here, not fighting! Did you forget we're all about to die in here?'

Mark took a step towards Anna, his eyes full of hate, clenching his fist, and for a moment she thought that he was going to strike her back—

Katarina quickly placed herself in between the two of them. She faced Mark and told him, 'Please, stop! We need your help! We're going to die if we don't find a way out of here! You don't want us to burn to death, do you? Help us, Mark. Save us!' She clutched the rose against her chest and pleaded, 'Save me!'

Mark stared down at the rose, transfixed. He looked lost. His mind seemed to have drifted away. Wherever he was, it wasn't here.

Anna could feel the room becoming much hotter now. She turned to Harold and Vivian and said, 'Please tell me that you've found something, anything?'

They heard a ticking sound and turned to see the door to the tomb suddenly begin to open. 'I don't believe it!' Harold said, speaking for all of them.

Anna stared as the impossible door slid open by itself.

Vivian's voice came from behind her. 'Don't just stand there, get inside!'

'Somebody grab the dog!' Anna yelled, but no one moved to help the animal, so Anna had to do it herself. As she approached Ebony, she told the dog, 'You'd better not bite me!'

Anna was relieved to be allowed to pick the dog up without resistance. She carried Ebony through the door into the tomb. Inside, she felt the bodies of the others as they moved around her. She could smell dust and sweat. She felt Harold's wheelchair bash into her leg, but she bit her lip and didn't cry out.

The door closed behind them. The only sound was Ebony's whimpering and their panicked breathing. The dim candlelight only just enabled them to see each other's faces, pale and ghostly in the dark. Unlike the previous times when they had been inside this tomb, this time none of them were looking towards the partly-uncovered corpse that stood behind them against the wall, they all had their eyes on the door, praying that they wouldn't see smoke rising from beneath it.

So far, so good, Anna thought. They'd waited a couple of minutes, and the smoke still hadn't penetrated the tomb. Perhaps this room was airtight, although that did mean that there was probably a limited supply of air in the room, and with six bodies all breathing hard, then it might not last very long. She decided not to share that morbid thought with the others and kept it to herself. She stroked Ebony. It wasn't the same as having Jelly here to comfort her, but it would have to do.

How were they going to escape this nightmare? No one knew that they were here in this house, no one would come looking for them. Anna could think of only one way out of this, but she knew that it could be very dangerous. She'd have to be absolutely sure before she attempted it. For now, she had to hope that it wouldn't come to that, and that their salvation might come from another source. Where was Handsworth when you actually needed him?

'We're all going to die,' Mark announced.

'That's not helpful,' she told him.

'I don't care. We never should have come here to this damned house.'

Anna did not disagree with him on that.

They had been squeezed into this little room together for around twenty minutes, according to Anna's phone, but it felt like a lot longer. Thankfully, there was still no sign of the smoke being able to penetrate their hideout, nor did it feel particularly warm in here. In fact, it felt just as cold as the previous occasions that they'd been in this room.

'When we get out of here,' Vivian said quietly, 'we should tell Handsworth that we'll refuse to come back here again unless he promises to get this deathtrap of a house safety checked first.'

'You're assuming that any of us are going to survive this,' Mark said miserably.

'Perhaps Mark's right,' Harold said, tapping on the arm of his wheelchair. 'Perhaps we're all doomed to be trapped in here with this corpse until we die from the smoke or the fire or lack of air. Perhaps someday long in the future, someone will open up this tomb and when they do, they'll discover not just that woman's corpse over there, but all our bodies too... Just think, we'll be a source of great mystery to whoever discovers us, just as that poor dead woman there is to us.'

'Oh, could we all please stop talking about that awful dead body!' Katarina said. 'You're upsetting... the dog.'

Ebony whined in agreement. Anna noticed Vivian suddenly looked unsteady and had her hand on her chest. She caught Anna looking and told her, 'I'm fine.'

When Harold spoke next, there was a sadness in his voice. 'I'm wondering then if this might be as good a time as any for us to get some things off our chests. If there's a strong likelihood that we're all about to die in here, then this might be our last chance. Who wants to go first?'

No one seemed to want to volunteer, so Harold said, 'Alright then, I suppose I'll have to go first.' They heard him take a deep breath. 'I've tried to enjoy life and all its pleasures. Perhaps I tried too hard. Not too long ago, my doctor warned me that I might not live past fifty if I didn't do something about my health.'

'Oh Harold,' Vivian said, 'I'm sorry.'

'It's alright, I'm just making my peace with things while I still can. You all should too. It's my own fault – too much smoking, too much alcohol, too much rich food, too little exercise. I didn't take care of myself. Since my doctor said what he said, I did try to cut down and look after myself better, but it's probably too little, too late.'

Harold looked down at his legs. 'I'm my own worst enemy, I realise that. My legs could be getting better, so that I shouldn't need this wheelchair, but... I'm not even trying. I sit there in my chair at home, and I know I should be trying to use my crutches so that my legs can get strong again, but I just can't seem to bring myself to make the effort. I think I've convinced myself it won't work and there's no point trying. I even cancelled the physiotherapy appointments my doctor made for me.

'What I've done to myself is bad enough, but what I've done to others is just as bad, if not worse. There are things I've done to people who trusted me, things I shouldn't have. I let them down. And I've lost my family because of the way that I've behaved in my life, I see that now. I think someone up there's punishing me, and I can't say that I blame them.

'So if I'm about to die here, then I need to tell someone that I am sorry for the things that I've done, not only the things that I did to myself, but also what I did to others. I want to say sorry for my greed and the poor choices that I've made. You have to believe me, if there were some way I could go back and change the things that I've done, then I would. In a heartbeat.'

Katarina placed her hand on Harold's shoulder. 'It's alright, Harold.'

He looked up at her. 'Do you think people can be forgiven for the things that they've done, if they're genuinely sorry for them?'

Katarina looked uncomfortable with the question. 'I... don't know. I hope so.'

Harold took off his glasses, wiped his eyes and then said, 'I'm sorry for getting so emotional. Forgive me. Someone else say something, please. Vivian, what about you?'

'What about me?' Vivian said, rather defensively.

'Is there anything that you regret? Anything in your life that you wish you hadn't done?'

'Other than coming here tonight?' She shook her head. 'No.'

'Nothing at all?'

'Nothing at all. Everything I've done, it had to be done, for the good of myself and my family. So no, I don't regret any of it.'

'Alright then,' Harold said, looking a little disappointed. 'Anna, what about you?'

All eyes turned on her and Anna felt uncomfortable in their gaze. She put on a smile and told them, 'Me? Regrets? No, of course not. None at all. *Non, je ne regrette rien.*'

'God help us, I think she's about to burst into song,' Mark muttered. 'I didn't think this situation could get any worse.'

Anna turned sharply and stared daggers at Mark. 'Actually, you know what, I do have one regret that I could mention, a very recent event, something that I shouldn't have done. I foolishly got intimate with a man who turned out to be a lying bastard. He told me all about how he fell for me the moment that he laid eyes on me, that I was special, but that was a lie. I know now that he would've jumped into bed with the first woman who'd said yes, and that I was nothing special to him at all. So I regret that, I wish I hadn't done it. And I hope it never happens to any other woman, because believe me, he definitely wasn't worth it.'

Mark glared at Anna, and Katarina looked at her curiously. Harold seemed oblivious to who Anna was talking about and said, 'Whoever that man was, he doesn't deserve you, Anna. I hope you can move on and find someone better. If we survive this, of course.'

'Yes,' she agreed, 'I hope I find someone better too. Don't worry, it shouldn't be too hard.'

Suddenly there was a loud bang on the door.

'What was that?' Katarina cried out.

'Sorry, that was me,' Mark said. 'I'm sick of being stuck here in this tomb with... that body. I need to get out of here.'

Harold turned to look at Katarina. 'Katarina, nice young woman like yourself, surely you haven't lived long enough to have any regrets?'

Katarina stroked the petals of the rose in her hand as she said softly, 'I have some, but none that I'd like to share. I'm not sure what good it would do, anyway. What has happened has happened, so it'd only be words, it wouldn't mean anything.'

'I see.' Harold seemed a little annoyed that so far no one else was prepared to reveal their secrets or apologise for their mistakes like he had, not even in the face of their imminent deaths. Anna, however, was more interested in what Mark was doing. He was staring at Katarina again, fixated on her and what she held in her hands.

'I do have a question for Mark,' Anna said. 'What's so special about that rose, the one that Katarina's holding? I can see the way that you're looking at it, it clearly means something to you. So what is it?'

Mark didn't answer, so Anna pressed, 'I saw how you reacted to it when you first saw it in the dining room – it was like you recognised it, and you seemed almost afraid of it, just as you're afraid of the fire out there. And also, now that I think about it, the last time we were here you behaved very strangely around that fireplace in the drawing room, like you couldn't bear to go near it. There's something about fire, isn't there, you're more afraid of it than any of the rest of us, aren't you? So come on, tell us your big secret, Mark. Tell the truth, for once.'

'Alright, enough!' Mark said angrily. 'I'll tell you, if it'll shut you up.' He took a moment, looked around the group, and then said, 'A few months ago, I was in a relationship with an amazing woman, her name was Leah. She was the sister of my friend John. I'd met her a long time ago when I was a teenager and she was still a kid. Even after she'd grown up, she'd always been out of reach, she was always with somebody else, or I was with somebody else, or she was off abroad somewhere, trying out another new career.

'Then one day we got chatting and she agreed to go on a date with me. One date became two, two dates became three, and so on. And then at some point, somehow, we were a couple. I even thought about marrying her someday, if you can believe that.

'We decided to go away together for a weekend, and we stayed at her parents' cabin in the woods. Leah loved roses, like the one that

Katarina's holding. I suppose most women do. So I surprised her with a whole bunch of them. She put a few around the cabin to decorate it.

'Anyway, we got into a fight about something, just some silly argument, and I stormed out. I needed to clear my head, I thought a walk in the fresh air would help. But it was dark, and it was cold, and I ended up getting lost in the woods. I couldn't find my way back to the cabin. I remember rehearsing in my head over and over what I was going to say to Leah to put things right, basically acknowledging that I was being an idiot. Anyway, I finally found my way back to the cabin, but when I got there...'

Mark took a deep breath before continuing his story. 'There was all this smoke. The whole cabin was on fire. The flames were so high, and so hot, and I couldn't get close. I didn't know what to do, we were miles from anywhere, and I'd stupidly left my phone and car keys in the cabin when I'd stormed out, so I couldn't do anything, I couldn't get help. So I just stood there as the cabin burned, I didn't know what to do, I was so scared. I've never been that scared in all my life. I watched the cabin burn, and Leah... she was still inside.

'I snapped out of it and ran off to get help, but I got lost, I didn't know where I was going. I must have wandered around for hours. I was so tired but I kept walking, and eventually I found a house early in the morning, and the people inside called the police and the fire service, and they went to the cabin, but by then it was far too late to save Leah. They found her body in the ruins, all burnt up.

'In the remains of the cabin, they found a single rose that hadn't burned. I took it with me. I couldn't let go of it, not even after it died. I don't know, perhaps I thought if I held onto it, Leah might somehow come back to me, and I could give it to her and tell her that I was sorry and that we'd be together again. Stupid, I know.'

'Oh Mark, you poor thing!' Katarina said. 'What a horrible story. You must have felt terrible. I'm so sorry that you had to go through something so awful.' She put her hand on Mark's arm.

'Thank you,' he said, putting his hand on top of hers and resting it there.

Ebony growled in Anna's hands and she told herself not to squeeze the animal so tightly. 'The rose, the fire – Mark, this is about you tonight, isn't it?' she said. 'This is meant to get you to remember things that happened in your past, like with Katarina's journal, Harold's piano and the money in the chairs, and Vivian's sweets.'

'And the water, don't forget about all that water…' Vivian said, her voice drifting away.

'Yes, that too,' Anna agreed. 'Look, if all of this is designed to get us reminiscing about our pasts, if they're trying to make us feel guilty about things that we might've done or not done, then I think whoever's behind this doesn't actually want us to die here. So I think that maybe that fire out there might not be what it seems.'

'What do you mean?' Mark asked.

'I mean, I've been wondering whether there's actually even any fire at all. I think this could all be another trick.'

'I think that's a dangerous thing to assume,' Mark said dubiously.

'What about the smoke?' Vivian said. 'There's the heat too. We're not imagining that.'

Anna looked around the group. 'I know it's dangerous, but I'm going to go out there, back into the dining room, and I'm going to try and open the door to the hallway. And then I'm going to prove that this isn't real.'

'Do you honestly think you're brave enough to go out there and risk your life just to see if you're right?' Mark said. 'Because I'm not convinced. You're acting brave, but come on, is that really who you are, Anna? Or are you just as scared as the rest of us?'

Anna ignored him. She looked at the door, then back at the group. 'I'm going out there. So, you all stay in here in this tomb with the dead woman, somebody take this crazy dog off me, and I'll go check if this madhouse is burning down around us or not. Alright, that might be the weirdest sentence that I've ever said in my life.'

'Be careful out there,' Harold told her.

'Thanks, I intend to, but I'm sure I'm right about this. And if I am, then I think all of us will want some pretty serious words with Handsworth, or whoever the hell he's working for.'

She handed Ebony over to Vivian, who scowled at the animal and held it at arm's length as if it was a bomb. Ebony gave her a low growl as if to tell her that the feeling was mutual.

Anna put her hand on the door, and was relieved to find that it didn't resist as she began to slide it open. 'I'll be back in a few minutes if I'm right, and if it turns out that I'm not, then it's been nice knowing you. Some of you, anyway.' She took a deep breath, slid open the door, stepped through into the dining room, and pulled the door shut behind her.

What the hell am I doing? Anna wondered. *When did I all of a sudden become the bravest member of this group? Or am I doing this just to try to prove that I'm right and that Mark's wrong about me, that I can be brave, despite what he thinks of me?*

Anna glanced back to check the door was still closed behind her and that no one was watching, then she pulled her blouse up over her head, taking it off so that she could use it to cover her mouth from the smoke.

The smoke was thick, and her eyes were streaming, but she managed to make her way across the dining room. To her surprise, the chairs and the table with the vase and the jug seemed to have vanished completely, but she didn't have time to think about that now.

She reached the door to the hallway and looked down at the doorknob. She held her breath, took the blouse away from her mouth, rolled it up and wrapped it around her hand, hoping to prevent her skin from getting burned when her hand made contact with the doorknob.

Bracing herself in case she'd made a dreadful mistake and she was about to feel a blast of heat and flame as the door opened, she squinted her eyes, then quickly turned the knob and opened the door.

When she hadn't been burnt to a crisp, Anna stepped into the hallway and took a look around. No fire, no flames, no smoke; the house wasn't burning down after all. She was right. It was just an illusion.

Anna turned and caught sight of herself in the mirror on the wall: sweaty, red-faced, and nearly half-naked. In a sudden fit of rage, she grabbed hold of an umbrella from the box near the front doors and swung its wooden handle at the mirror. The glass shattered. She panted as she stared at it, regretting what she'd done. She dropped the umbrella. She could almost feel the faces of the Gray family peering down at her from the portraits on the wall and judging her for her rash actions. 'What are you looking at?' she grumbled at them. 'Shut up, I've a right to be mad right now.'

She wiped the sweat from her face and then put her blouse back on. She wouldn't be at all surprised if there were cameras on her right now, their unseen host cackling with glee at the result of their latest prank. She still couldn't figure out what their host's intentions might be, and whether they had actually been in any real danger, or if this was all simply just smoke and mirrors?

Anna tried the front doors and was relieved to find that they weren't locked. She opened them wide and felt a cool breeze on her face. She hoped that the wind blowing into the house might help to dissipate the smoke that remained in the dining room.

She could see no sign of any staff rushing around in a panic about this supposed fire. She guessed they were all in on the joke. How she would love to get her hands on Handsworth right now...

She waited a few minutes, and then when she thought that the smoke had cleared enough, she made her way back through the dining room and reached the door to the tomb. Anna opened the door, and a small furry creature dashed past her legs. She wondered if Ebony might flee out through the front doors that she had left open, but she thought that if the dog did want to leave then it would be better off out there than being trapped in this house of horrors any longer.

'It's alright, there's no fire,' Anna told the group of confused faces that she saw inside the tomb. 'It wasn't real. You can come out of there now. It's perfectly safe.'

Vivian stepped out first, then helped Harold with his wheelchair, and Katarina followed next. Mark was the last one still in the tomb. Anna could see real fear in his eyes. 'Mark, come out,' she told him, 'there's no fire, just a little bit of smoke, which is clearing now. It was a trick, to wind us all up – especially you, it seems. Come on.'

Anna reached out her hand to him, and he tentatively took it. Feeling his skin on hers again for the first time since that night – not counting the slap, which she now partly regretted – brought a mix of feelings, and not all of them were bad. She tried to ignore them. She led Mark through to the hallway, where they found the others. When he saw them, he muttered, 'Where's that bloody Handsworth? If I find him, I'll kill him.'

'Join the queue,' Anna said. She noticed that Harold was breathing hard, his face red like a beetroot, and Katarina was stroking his arm, gently, trying to comfort him. Ebony the dog sat on the stairs, regarding the group curiously.

Vivian stared at the broken mirror in the hallway. 'That's all we need, more bad luck. Oh, let's all just go, I don't feel well, and I'm so tired, and I've had quite enough of this nonsense.' She helped Harold towards the front doors. She stopped in the doorway and regarded the heavy rain outside.

To no one's surprise, a few minutes later the first of the taxis had started pulling up to the house to take them away. Mark was looking in the direction of Handsworth's office, and Anna knew that he was considering going after Handsworth, so she put her hand on his arm.

'Mark, I'm just as angry as you are, but I think we've all had enough drama for one night. The taxis are here, so let's just go home. We only have one more of these sessions and then we're done.'

Mark gave her a look. 'Based on these four sessions, how do you think the fifth one's going to go? What's going to be our host's grand finale? It could be something painful from your past next time. So what might that be?'

'I don't want to think about it,' Anna answered, 'and I don't really care right now, I just want to go home. I'm not even going to gloat that I was right about the fire and you were wrong. All I want to do is go home to my bed and get back to my life and forget all about this craziness for as long as I can. Come on, let's just go.'

Mark glanced at Katarina, then took Anna to one side. 'Listen, what you were saying earlier about Katarina—'

'Forget it, it doesn't matter right now.'

'But—'

'I mean it, I don't care about any of that right now. Look, I'm sorry I hit you, I probably shouldn't have done that. But I'm leaving now. We're all getting in those taxis and getting away from this bloody house before anything else happens to us. So are you coming with us, or are you staying here in this house by yourself?'

Mark considered for a moment before he answered, 'I'm going.'

They rejoined the rest of the group by the front doors. Everyone looked tired and miserable.

'So,' Anna said, trying to break the awkward silence, 'this was great, wasn't it? Lots of fun. We should all do this again sometime. How's next Friday for everybody?'

Nobody looked amused.

Chapter Eight

Mark

Mark felt like he was on top of the world. He took a swig of water and then wiped his mouth with his glove. His left eye was itching so he removed his sunglasses to rub it and was almost blinded by the brightness of the sun. The icy air was stinging his face, but it was worth the price to be here and to see this incredible view.

He watched a bird fly over his head and then glide between the snowy peaks of the mountains, soaring on the wind. It came to rest on a distant peak, near a dark brown patch that might've been a nest. Mark envied the bird for its ability to travel so fast, especially since he knew that he would have to take the long, slow way down the mountain, walking all the way down to the valley and the crystal-clear lake below. When his far more adventurous friend John had invited him on this trip, Mark had jokingly suggested that they bring a wingsuit, because he quite liked the idea of soaring through the air like a bird. However, John had laughed at him and told him that there was no way that he had the balls to do something that brave, and Mark knew that he was right. Reaching the top of this mountain had felt like a tremendous achievement and he was proud of himself, but his reverie was broken when the guide behind him called out, 'Alright, everyone, can you finish taking your photos and then gather round now, please! We'll need to start making our way back down.'

Watching the rest of the tourists in his group milling around, some of them a good few decades older than himself, Mark felt his sense of accomplishment begin to dwindle away. He had to remind himself that he was not here because he wanted to feel like some great adventurer or to live up to the memory of his father. All he'd done was climb to the top of this mountain to escape from his problems, and it hadn't even been a climb, more of a long, slow walk. Many others had done it before him, probably several dozen even just today. No, the real reason he'd ventured up here was that he wanted his body and his mind as far away as possible from Grimwald House.

After what had happened in that last session, he felt like he needed this escape. Yes, the fire hadn't been real, but the thought of it was burned into his brain and he couldn't stop thinking about it. From up here, it was hard to imagine that a place as grim as that wretched old house could even exist in the same world as these beautiful white mountain peaks, green valleys and blue skies.

If there was one thing that he *would* like to take from that place and bring here, then it was Anna. He thought that she would like this view, and how peaceful it was up here – if you could ignore the small groups of gabbling tourists slowly making their way up and down the mountain. They hadn't exactly parted on the best of terms, and Mark regretted losing his temper with Anna in their last session. She also seemed to have got a bee in her bonnet about Katarina. But in spite of how things currently stood between them, Mark thought that he still might be able to win her over. He found Anna fascinating. She was a new, exciting challenge, and one that he knew would be a lot harder but also a lot more fun to conquer than this mountain. Perhaps after they'd completed their one remaining session at Grimwald House and they were free of their obligations, he and Anna could arrange to meet up and see where things might go from there? That thought excited him. Alright, so the sex that night they'd spent together hadn't been anything special, from what little he remembered of it, but they could work on that.

In some ways, Anna reminded him of Leah, although he knew that no woman could ever truly match her, she'd been one of a kind. He suddenly felt a pang of guilt again, which he had by now become an expert at pushing away. The events at Grimwald House had reawakened powerful memories, thoughts and feelings that he had tried very hard to put behind him.

He told himself to stop thinking about that house. He wanted to be right here, right now, enjoying this view.

A hand smacked him on the back so hard that it hurt and he winced. He turned to see his friend John looking at him. 'Enjoying the view, are you? It's not bad, is it? I've seen better, though. It's not like going on a *real* climb. You're only seeing the tourist version of Scotland and its mountains.'

Mark glanced at the other tourists and replied, 'This is just fine for me, thanks. It's about my level.'

'You know, if you were in better shape and were more adventurous, you'd see that there's a whole wide world out there, and so much that you haven't seen or done yet. I could tell you some stories, believe me.'

'Yes, *Dad*.'

John smiled. 'You mock me, but your father – now he was a good man, and brave, too. And he put all his money to good use. It's a bloody shame you don't take after him more.'

No, Mark thought, *I don't take after him, and if you knew what he was really like, behind closed doors, then you'd know that was a good thing.*

'What are your plans for tonight?' John asked.

Mark shrugged. 'Nothing in particular, why?'

'Me and some of the blokes are meeting up later, not far from here. I know they're not the kind of posh crowd that you usually hang around with these days, but give them a chance. There'll be a blazing fire, food, drink, and good company.'

'A blazing fire?' Mark looked down at his feet in the snow.

'Shit, sorry, I didn't think.' John reached out his hand to Mark.

Mark batted it away. 'It's fine. I'm fine.'

'I wasn't trying to bring us down, you know.'

'I know.'

John scratched his head. 'So, are you in, then? I think it'll be good for both of us. It's important to me that you'll be there. You can share my tent. It'll give us a chance to talk about things.'

Mark smiled. 'Spending the night getting cosy with a bunch of strange men I don't know, in the dark, in the middle of nowhere? I think that sounds more up your street than mine.'

'Ah, fuck you – not that I ever would.' John grinned at him. 'You're not nearly as good-looking as you seem to think you are. Look, are you gonna come with me tonight, or not?'

'Yes, fine, I'll go.'

'Good man. It'll be worth it, you'll see. You said you wanted to take your mind off whatever it is that's got you wound up so tight recently. I promise this'll do it.'

'Gentlemen, are you with us?' their guide called out, and they could see that the rest of the group was now waiting for the two of them. Mark received another smack on the back from his friend and they went to rejoin the group and begin their descent.

The mountains seemed to take on a different form under the star-filled night sky; they were more mysterious and forbidding, dwarfing every-thing around them like silent, unmoving giants.

The air was so very cold that Mark found himself grateful for the campfire and the warmth it provided, although he still sat further away from the fire than the rest of the group did.

When Mark and John had arrived they were immediately offered beers, and they'd both taken one and joined the group in sitting down on the chairs arranged around the fire. The flickering flames of the fire lit up their five faces, but Mark didn't recognise any of John's friends.

He and John rarely moved in the same social circles any more; their lifestyles were very different. Mark had plenty of money, but John sometimes struggled, and he always refused Mark's help when it came to money. Mark guessed it was a matter of pride for him.

John had introduced Mark to the others, but after the third beer, he'd already forgotten their names. He knew he was unlikely to see any of them again after tonight anyway, so what did it matter? He decided to think of them as Big Beard, Red Head, and Grumpy Face – that was easier than bothering to remember their actual names.

Mark realised that Red Head was staring at him curiously, and then the man asked, 'What do you do for a living, then?'

'I'm a special agent for the government,' Mark told him. 'Think James Bond, but better looking. I spend my time jetting around the world, and I spend my money on cold beer and hot women.'

Red Head frowned. He looked unsure whether Mark was being serious or not. Mark gave it a moment before putting him out of his misery. 'No, I'm joking. I'm sort of between projects at the moment, but I've got plenty of things lined up. I'm not lying about the hot women, though, I've got plenty of those lined up, too.'

Red Head laughed at that and clinked his bottle against Mark's. It was all about judging your audience, Mark knew. He then realised that John seemed to be glaring at him for some reason.

'I've learnt never to believe a word this git says,' John told the rest of the group. 'He's so full of himself, and so full of shit, because the only thing that Mark's good at is spending money, and he's got his dad to thank for all the money he's got. Don't think he's actually worked a day in his life, lazy sod.'

'Alright, I think that's enough,' Mark said with a nervous laugh, not quite able to tell if his friend was joking or not. 'I love you too, John.'

'Nah, I'm only kidding,' John said. 'I didn't mean all that. But I do know you, I know you better than anyone. Remember that.'

Big Beard grinned at them. 'Ah, this is the life, isn't it? A bunch of blokes being blokes, getting drunk, telling bad jokes, making up shit. And let's not forget the embarrassing confessions. Speaking of which...' He looked at Grumpy Face. 'Tell Mark here about the time you fell through the snow into that hole and ended up having to use it as a loo.'

Grumpy Face, who looked considerably older than the rest of the group, said, 'Hey, it wasn't my fault, as I've said a hundred times before. I was young, I was stupid. My mates had told me to eat something to get me warmed up inside, you know, before I started the climb in the snow.'

John grinned. 'They got you to eat what, exactly? What was it called again?'

'The Burner,' Grumpy Face muttered. 'Hottest curry they had. Nearly set my insides on fire. I was stuck in that hole for at least an hour. You can guess the rest.'

Big Beard and Red Head laughed at that, and Mark joined in. 'I heard they renamed that area from White Peak to Brown Peak after that, in his honour,' Big Beard said, shaking with laughter.

'No, they didn't!' Grumpy Face grumbled. He looked at Mark. 'That's not true. It's a lie.'

'Speaking of hot food, who's hungry?' John asked.

Mark watched as sausages were cooked, and his stomach rumbled in anticipation. This was proving to be a nice distraction from everything. He was glad he'd accepted John's offer to come here. It was also good to see John almost back to his old self again, considering the tragedy with his sister Leah had only happened a few months ago and was still relatively fresh in both of their minds.

Mark found his eyes drawn to the fire. He felt conflicted as he watched the flames dance. He couldn't deny that there was an alluring beauty to them, even though he knew they could be dangerous. He'd had the same kind of love-hate relationship with John's sister Leah.

He glanced across at the three tents. He would be sharing one of them with John tonight. That'd be fine if the man wasn't such a snorer, as Mark had discovered on a previous camping trip a couple of years ago. Mark knew there was a very good chance he might not get a good night's sleep tonight.

Mark woke up sweating. He opened his sleeping bag, but he was still hot. He was only half-awake, and half-sober, but he knew that the heat was strange considering that they were out here in a tent in a valley near snowy mountains at night, and it had been so cold earlier.

He looked across at John's sleeping bag. It was empty. 'John?' he called out, but there was no answer. Mark decided he would have to get up and check on his friend, just in case John had wandered off drunk and had decided that it would be a great idea to try climbing a mountain on his own in the middle of the night.

Mark yawned, then reached for the door of the tent. He could feel the heat far more intensely now. It was almost as if the campfire had somehow been picked up and repositioned, and was now burning directly outside his tent. He carefully pushed his head out of the tent. He looked up, and in his daze, struggled to understand what he was seeing.

John was standing there, staring down at him. In either hand, he held a flaming torch.

Mark rubbed his eyes. 'John, are you alright? What's going on?'

John's face seemed to hold none of the levity that it had held earlier that evening. He looked deadly serious when he answered Mark's question. 'I know, Mark. I've known for about a week or so now.'

'You know what?' Mark asked, frowning at his friend.

John took a deep breath. 'After Leah died, I put her laptop away in the loft at our parents' house, along with the rest of her stuff. I couldn't look at anything that belonged to her, it was too painful. But a week ago I went back and dug it out, and started going through what was on her computer – her files, her photos, her emails. I don't know, maybe I thought it would somehow make me feel connected to her again. I think I was also trying to reassure myself about her state of mind, that the fire at the cabin was just some random bloody accident, and not what some people claimed. I know there were rumours that she'd caused the fire herself, that she was depressed and doing drugs again, but I never believed that.

'Then I found an email that Leah had sent to one of her friends, and in it she said that she was really scared. I've never heard my sister say she was scared, ever, not even when we were kids. Leah was a rock. She was always a tough one. But in that email she said that she'd seen a very different side of someone she thought she knew, and that she was afraid of what they might do to her. She didn't say who it was, but I know she was talking about you, wasn't she? It's so obvious now. Was she going to leave you? Is that why you did it? Is that why you killed my sister?'

'What?!' Mark gasped. 'I didn't kill Leah! What are you talking about?' Mark tried to move further out of the tent, but John stepped closer, forcing him to back off, the torches in his hands dangerously close to the material of the tent. 'John, come on, why don't you go to bed and sleep this off. You're drunk, and you're imagining things, you're making up crazy stories that you know aren't true!'

'Don't fucking lie to me!' John screamed at him, surely loud enough to wake the other men in their tents. Mark expected them to come out to see what the commotion was all about, but there was no movement from their tents at all. Where were they?

John caught Mark's glances at the other tents. 'They won't hear us. After you went to bed, I took them some pills. They thought they were gonna get high, but instead, they'll be out cold for hours. They won't see or hear anything that happens. I brought you out here for a reason,

Mark. There's nobody else for miles around, and everybody knows what this place is like. Accidents happen.'

John held one of the torches closer to Mark's face, and he recoiled in fear. 'The flames scare you, don't they?' John said. 'Good. You know something, even when I thought your story about what had happened to Leah in that cabin was a bit sketchy, I still never believed that you could have anything to do with her death. I thought: no way, my friend Mark, he's a good man, a bit of a playboy, and maybe he secretly thinks he's better than the rest of us, but deep down he's got a good soul, and there's no way in hell that he'd ever do anything to hurt my sister. He wouldn't kill Leah, no, because he loved her. He's not capable of something like that.

'But you had me fooled, didn't you? I think you started that fire yourself! Why the hell did you do that to her? You were supposed to be in love, for God's sake! Go on, admit it, tell the truth for once in your life, you sick bastard!'

Mark tried to raise himself up. 'John, please—'

'Sit back down! You know, I keep thinking about all those times I came to you when I was down after she died, and you pretended to be my friend. You and me, we shared that grief, you said we'd help each other get through it, but it was all a lie, wasn't it? All that time, I bet you were laughing at me behind my back. I was such a bloody idiot!'

'Come on, you can't believe any of that!' Mark protested. 'You *do* know me! Maybe I'm not perfect, I can admit that, but you know that I'd never hurt Leah. I loved your sister, I always have done, more than any woman I've ever met, and that's the truth. I didn't kill her, I swear. It was just a terrible accident!'

'Stop lying to me!' John raged. 'You didn't love her! I don't think you're even capable of that! You're a bloody monster! You're sick in the head!'

'Put down those torches and we can talk, we can sort this out,' Mark pleaded. 'Come on, you're my friend, John. You're my best friend.'

John held the torch even closer to Mark's face. John had tears in his eyes as he said, 'Tell me the truth, right now! Tell me that you killed my sister! I need to know the truth, I can't stand not knowing anymore. So just tell me!'

Mark gazed at the flame with fear. He looked into John's angry eyes. 'Please, stop this now, before you go and do something stupid!'

John shook his head. 'There's only one way to stop you from hurting anybody else.' He then threw one of the torches at the tent, and it caught fire, the flames moving rapidly across the surface. 'This is for Leah! I know she'd want to see you burn for what you did to her. So fucking burn!'

As John raised his arm to throw the second torch, Mark lunged at him and knocked his former friend backwards, where he landed in the muddy grass. He kicked dirt over the torch John had dropped, to put out the flame.

Mark could feel the intense heat from the tent behind him, the flames engulfing it and everything inside it. John was back on his feet now, and his fist flew out towards Mark's jaw, but Mark recovered in time to twist his body out of the way, and he grabbed hold of John and with all of his strength, he shoved him towards the burning tent.

The fire swallowed John whole. Mark released his grip and managed to pull himself away. As the flames consumed the body of his screaming friend, Mark suddenly realised that both of his own arms were now aflame, and the fire was tearing the skin from his arms. 'Oh shit!' he cried out in horror. Fighting the almost unbearable pain in his arms, his heart racing, his eyes streaming, Mark scrambled away and ran towards the lake below. He ran faster than he ever had in his life. The minutes were long and agonising. Finally, he reached the lake and plunged his arms into the freezing water, crying out in pain.

Mark tried to focus his mind away from the pain, and on working out how he would tell his story. He'd tell everyone that there'd been another terrible accident, and that John had tragically died in a fire, just like his sister Leah had. He would say that, just like last time, drugs had been involved, and that he felt cursed to watch the troubled people that he loved die and not be able to save them. People would feel sorry for him and tell him that someday he'd be able to put this awful tragedy behind him and go on with his life, and they'd be right, he would.

Mark knew that he could convince everyone that this wasn't his fault, that he'd done nothing wrong and that what had happened was simply an unfortunate accident, and they'd believe him. He was sure that it would work. After all, he'd done it before.

CHAPTER NINE

SESSION FIVE

This is it. The final session. Soon, all of this madness will be over.

Knowing that this would be the very last time that she would have to make this journey to Grimwald House gave Anna some small sense of relief, but she still had to survive this final evening and whatever their mysterious host had planned for them.

Jelly had been unusually fussy tonight and making strange noises. The stupid cat had kept getting in her way as Anna had tried to leave her apartment. Perhaps he had an inkling of where she was going and was trying to stop her? *Sorry, Jelly, perhaps you should have tried harder.*

Anna would have loved to be back home with him instead of here at Grimwald House. Was it sad that her happy place was her apartment, sitting on her sofa by herself with a drink in one hand and Jelly's fur in the other and watching trashy TV?

There were many things about Grimwald House and these sessions that she would not miss. The corpse in the tomb, of course, but also the weird staff who worked there, and the bizarre torments that their host seemed to enjoy inflicting upon them.

And Mark, of course. She'd be happy never to have to see him again, wouldn't she? She was hardly the first person to have had a one-night stand with a stranger who turned out not to be who they'd seemed, and Anna knew that she shouldn't be letting it affect her so much, but Mark had said some things that evening – lines that she was sure he used with all of his conquests – and they'd worked, they'd struck a nerve. He'd played on her loneliness and her desire to be appreciated. She hadn't realised how much she'd missed having someone pay her that much attention and tell her that she was interesting and beautiful. It had been a long time since anyone had said anything like that to her. So she'd fallen for it, like a fool. She knew now that he'd said the same things to Katarina. Why couldn't she stop thinking about him, even now after finding out what he was really like? Anna hated this power that he had over her.

Mark, on the other hand, was probably fine, and it was likely he hadn't given her any thought at all since their last meeting. He might even have been with other women since that night. Why did that thought make her so angry? And what about his story, the one about losing the love of his life in that horrible fire – should she hate Mark less now that she knew the tragedy he'd endured? Should she forgive his behaviour? She wasn't sure what to feel.

Between these thoughts of Mark and the strange events at Grimwald House, and how tired she'd felt lately, Anna had started to let her work suffer. She'd found herself being extra snippy with colleagues who'd quite rightly pointed out some of the silly mistakes that she'd been making. So for the sake of her career and her sanity, she needed this to be over so that she would never have to think about Mark or this house ever again.

There were other reasons why she was particularly anxious about tonight. For one thing, they would be unwrapping the final parts of the body in that tomb, and she had no idea what was supposed to happen when it was fully uncovered. At the end of the evening, would they be told who that dead woman had been, and why she was so special? And would their mysterious host finally be revealed? Would there be some kind of reward for their efforts? The only reward Anna wanted was to never have to come back to Grimwald House ever again.

Another concern Anna had was that so far each session had included events that had seemed specifically designed to remind a particular participant about their past, dredging up bad memories for some unexplained purpose. Was it her turn next, and if so, what would they dig up from her past to upset her like they'd done to the others? She'd be quite happy to be spared any painful memories this evening. She didn't need anyone judging her for things that she might've done. She tried to remind herself that this was all just some kind of game, and she shouldn't be letting it get to her like this.

The weather was fierce tonight, but she'd come prepared this time: she wore a heavy coat and carried an umbrella. When the taxi finally arrived at the house and she stepped out, she realised her mistake almost instantly; the umbrella blew inside out and its ribs broke in the relentless wind. Anna fought against the wind to gain control of the useless item, but she was fighting a losing battle, and a sudden gust wrenched the umbrella out of her hand and carried it away. She swore as the wind and rain beat her face, but she managed to push her way to the front doors as she heard the taxi drive away. The light from its headlights lingered a little longer on the road past the gates, before that too faded away.

Anna took hold of the knockers and banged on the doors. She waited a minute before banging them again when she'd had no answer. *This damned house needs to be dragged kicking and screaming into the 21st century and get itself a bloody doorbell!*

She checked her watch. She was roughly on time, perhaps a few minutes late. Someone was bound to be here already. She imagined the rest of the group were likely to be as keen as she was to get this evening over with. So where were they? She banged on the door again.

'Come on, somebody let me in!' she shouted, but her cry was lost in the wind.

Anna wanted to be inside, out of the weather, even if Grimwald House wasn't exactly her idea of a safe and comfortable place. Anna banged again and waited some more. She kept checking her watch. She was definitely late now. No other taxis had pulled up since hers had gone. Perhaps the group hadn't bothered to wait for her and had already gone through to the dining room or the tomb and they couldn't hear her at the front doors?

There was a loud snap from somewhere to her left, and she turned to look at the woods. Was someone out there? Perhaps the strong winds had broken a branch off a tree. She switched on the torch setting on her phone, but it gave only a tiny amount of light to help her see, and the bad weather diminished its usefulness. She decided that she wasn't prepared to venture into those dark woods alone to investigate. Instead, she started walking around the left side of the house, fighting the wind and the rain, looking for a way inside, until she reached the back of the house.

Anna stopped and stared. A five-sided glass structure with an angled roof protruded from the back of the house like some kind of unsightly mole on its backside. She realised that this must be the conservatory, and it might offer a way into the house. She found a small door and tried it, but it was locked. She tried to peer inside through the glass, but it was too dark to see much of anything. She held her phone against the glass, and with its light she could just about make out the dark silhouettes of giant leaves belonging to whatever exotic plants were growing inside. She tried tapping on the glass and then banging on it, but she knew it was unlikely to get anyone's attention, not unless someone was standing there in the dark among the plants, listening out for her.

What the hell was she supposed to do now? She was cold, wet, shivering, and miserable. She wanted to close her eyes and make a wish to be out of the cold and the rain and be inside the house where it was dry. She told herself to be sensible, and to think straight; surely there had to be something that she could use to break the glass and force her way in? Alright, so Handsworth and their host might not appreciate another act of vandalism after she'd broken one of their mirrors when she was here last time, but then again, a little cracked glass seemed fairly insignificant compared to what she and the rest of her group had been put through. And it wasn't like she couldn't afford to pay for the damage.

Anna looked around, but nothing she could see immediately stood out as particularly strong enough to shatter that glass. She needed something hard, metal – perhaps a shovel might work? There must be one somewhere. She decided to break away from the house and try investigating the garden; there was bound to be a tool shed somewhere for the gardener. Someone had to look after the grounds, they wouldn't look after themselves. Of course, the shed might be locked, but she'd cross that bridge when she came to it.

It was hard to see anything with the rather pitiful light from her phone. She told herself to be careful, because the last thing she needed was to fall over in some muddy ditch. She could imagine the look on everyone's faces if she turned up covered in mud. They'd all laugh at her, Mark shaking his head at what a mess Anna was while he wrapped his arms around beautiful Katarina's perfect body—

Focus, Anna!

She bumped into something hard and braced herself before looking down, hoping that she hadn't stumbled across a gravestone, because that would unnerve her even more, and her nerves were in a pretty rough state already.

To her relief, she discovered that it wasn't a gravestone, but some kind of water feature: a small tower of rocks, with a Jelly-sized gargoyle sitting at the top spewing out water. She gently stroked its ugly stone head and said, 'Sorry for disturbing you, you go back to sleep now and forget I was here.'

She stared at that strange little winged creature. There was something oddly familiar about its big round eyes, its horns and pointy ears, and its mischievous expression. A name suddenly came to mind: *Girrock. Girrock the Gargoyle.* Where did she know that name from? Then it came to her. It was a character she remembered seeing in a film that she'd watched as a child, a film that she'd seen at the cinema with her father on the day that—

She heard a shout.

Anna waited, breathing hard, refusing to move until she could establish what it was that she'd just heard. Had it come from behind her, from the house? Or was it from somewhere up ahead of her? She couldn't be sure. She started to wonder if she'd imagined it. Was her mind playing tricks on her?

Another shout, and this one was definitely coming from behind her, from the direction of the house. And this time, she was sure that it had said her name. She turned around quickly. Her heart was pounding. Who was calling out her name in the dark?

Then she saw a dark shape, a strange figure, creeping around near the house. There was something odd about the way that it walked. Suddenly the shape moved away from the house, and started coming towards her...

Anna wasn't sure what she should do. Should she wait and see who it was? What if they weren't friendly and intended to do her harm? She could turn and run, but where would she run to? Or she could try to fight them, but with what? Her phone would be a pathetic weapon. Inside the house there were plenty of possible weapons: she could grab a knife or a rolling pin from the kitchen, or the poker from the fireplace in the drawing room – anything that she could do some damage with. Even an umbrella from the box by the front doors would be better than nothing. But out here, with nothing but her phone, she felt completely defenceless. She couldn't even call anybody to come and help her, because even if she could get a signal she had no idea what the phone number for Grimwald House was, and anybody else that she could call wouldn't reach her in time before—

The stranger was now almost upon her, their long coat glistening in the rain. She still couldn't see their face. They moved with a jerky motion against the wind. Anna's whole body was shaking, and not just from the cold. She couldn't assemble her thoughts into some-thing coherent so they flew all over the place. She imagined that this creature was a man-sized gargoyle come to life, perhaps the parent of the smaller one that she'd accidentally bumped into here in the garden, come to take its revenge on her for disturbing its child's slumber. Or perhaps it was that mummy, having escaped from its tomb, and it was now intent on pulling the flesh from her body just as she'd ripped the wraps from its body...

'Oh God!' Anna cried out, as the thing came ever closer to her. She braced herself for whatever it might want to do to her, and as it reached out to her with its long arms she squeezed her eyes shut and wished desperately that she were anywhere else but here...

'—coming around, finally. See?'

'Looks to be in a right old state, poor thing.'

'Get her coat off. Is she bleeding, or is that just—'

'Help me to help her up.'

Anna felt a pair of arms go under her armpits, and then she was being lifted up and carried across a room and lowered onto a sofa. Fuzzy images swirled in her brain, refusing to clarify themselves. She could feel warmth, and when she turned her eyes she saw an orange ball of fire, like a small sun. It gradually came into focus and she realised that she was looking at a fireplace with a burning fire. Something hard touched her lips and then she tasted water. She swallowed it and her sore throat thanked her. It also helped keep the bile down that was threatening to force its way out. Anna turned her aching head too fast and it made her feel dizzy and sick. Some of the blurry shapes had now become people: a young man, an older man with a moustache and a walking stick, and a middle-aged woman. She didn't recognise their faces. They wore elegant clothes: the woman a long red dress, the two men sharp suits.

'Where am I?' Anna croaked, wishing that the frog currently residing in her throat would hop off and that it would take the blinding pain in her head with it. She eyed the strangers around her warily. 'Who are you?'

'We were wondering the same of you, young lady,' the older man with the moustache and beady eyes said. 'Can you tell us your name?'

The other man, who was considerably younger than his friend, looked at the others and then said, 'Perhaps she's had an accident? She doesn't look well. I think we ought to call for a doctor.'

'Anna,' she managed. 'My name is Anna.' She realised something was missing, and looked around on the floor but couldn't find it. 'Has anyone seen my phone, I think I lost it?'

She looked at the confused faces staring back at her and then took in the rest of the room. She realised that she was in the drawing room inside Grimwald House. The woman in the impressive red dress approached her, knelt by the sofa, and placed her hand on Anna's leg. She gave her a reassuring smile and said, 'It's a pleasure to meet you, Anna. My name is Vanessa. It's alright, you're safe now.' The woman turned her head away and coughed several times. It sounded like a nasty, painful cough. She recovered, and continued, 'You were outside in that dreadful weather, apparently you were unconscious. It's lucky Handsworth found you when he did.'

'Handsworth?' Anna said, groggily. 'Yes, I did see someone out there in the garden before everything went black, that could've been him. Is he here? I don't see him...'

'He's gone to fetch you some towels,' Vanessa answered. 'You might also want to change into some new clothes to replace the wet clothes that you're wearing – which, if I may say, are quite unusual. Now, if these two gentlemen here were actual gentlemen, they'd have introduced themselves by now and greeted you properly.' Vanessa looked pointedly at the two men.

'You're quite right, Vanessa,' the man with the walking stick said. 'Many apologies. My name is Charles, and this young man here is Henry.' He held out his hand for Anna to shake it and seemed disappointed when she didn't.

'Delighted to meet you,' Henry said. She noticed he had his arm in a sling, and didn't offer her his hand.

Anna tried to sit up. 'I'm sorry, I don't mean to be rude, but I don't understand what's going on. Where are the others? Where's Mark, and Vivian, and—'

The door opened and she stared as Handsworth entered the drawing room carrying some towels. He walked over to Anna's side, handed her a towel, and said, 'Thank goodness you're alright.' From the expression on his face, he didn't seem that pleased to see her, despite his words. 'You were unconscious when I found you out there in the garden. Who are you? Why are you here?'

Anna rubbed her face with the towel and looked at him quizzically. 'What do you mean? You know who I am. You know why I'm here. I came for the final session.'

'Oh, so you're not one of the staff?' Vanessa said, looking surprised. She turned to Handsworth. 'I thought you'd said that we were the only guests who had been invited to these sessions?'

'You are,' Handsworth confirmed. 'I'm afraid I don't know why this woman would be here.'

'What the hell are you talking about?' Anna tried to stand up, but her unsteady legs told her to think again, so she dropped back down onto the sofa. 'I'm not sure what's going on here, but this isn't funny. Oh, wait a minute, is this another one of your games? It is, isn't it?'

'This is no game,' Handsworth told her.

'It *is* all a game, though, isn't it?' Henry said softly. 'Or at least, it seemed like one at first, before...' He drifted off as he stared down at his broken arm.

Vanessa then had another painful coughing fit, and strained herself to apologise, 'Oh, please excuse me.'

'There should only be five guests, there are only ever five,' Handsworth muttered. 'Why were you out there in the garden?'

'Because no one had answered the front doors,' Anna replied. 'I didn't know where anyone else was, I thought they were all here inside the house somewhere but weren't answering the door for some reason.'

'But how did you come to be at Grimwald House in the first place? Do you remember how you got here?'

'Of course I do. A taxi brought me. I remember the journey, it took a couple of hours, longer than usual because the weather got so bad on the way.'

Charles looked surprised. 'Only a couple of hours? Then you must live quite close. It usually takes the better part of a day for me to get here, this place is so damned remote.'

'And for me too,' Henry agreed.

Vanessa looked at Anna curiously. 'You mentioned earlier that you were invited here. By whom?'

'I don't know for certain,' Anna replied, with a glance at Handsworth. 'My group, we all received invitation letters, and whoever sent them just signed them with the letter "H" and promised mysteries, secrets and revelations, to lure us here. Then we all had to sign a contract, with ink and blood, and we had to come back here every week until the final session, which was meant to be tonight.'

Charles nodded. 'Yes, we all received similar invitations, and on our first night here we all signed that contract too.'

Anna looked at Handsworth. 'Please, tell me what's going on here. Why don't I recognise any of these people? Do you have more than one group? Did I get the day wrong? No, I'm pretty sure I didn't.'

Handsworth thought for a moment, and then he asked her, 'This may sound like an odd question, but what year do you think this is?'

Anna glanced at the others before answering. 'Why would you ask me that?'

'Humour me, please.'

'Alright, but I haven't gone completely mad, I know what year it is. It's 2023.'

The others looked at her like she'd told them that she was an alien from another world. Charles laughed at her.

'No, my dear, it's not 2023,' Vanessa said, smiling at her like she was a silly little girl who'd made a childish error. 'I'm afraid that you're off by a whole century. This is the year 1923.'

Anna frowned at her. 'It's what? Say that again?'

'It's 1923.'

'You're joking.'

'No, I'm afraid that I'm not.' Vanessa shook her head. 'It's 1923, and King George the Fifth is on the throne, and you're here with us at Grimwald House, which is... somewhere in England, don't ask me where exactly, I have no idea, the route here was so very long and complicated! Oh, you look so bewildered, is none of what I'm saying familiar to you? I'm just trying to help you remember.'

Henry looked at Anna with sympathy and said to the others, 'Poor woman, she must have hit her head out there. She's damaged her brain. I think we ought to call for a doctor.'

'My brain is just fine,' Anna said, 'and I know what's really going on here. I'm sure you all think this prank is hilarious. You've put a lot of effort in this time, haven't you, Handsworth? Hiring these actors to act like it's 1923. I suppose it would explain why you're all dressed in such strange, old-fashioned clothes.'

Charles looked offended. '*Old-fashioned?!*'

'I want to know the truth,' Anna said, ignoring him. 'I want to know what's happened to my friends. Where are they?'

Vanessa held Anna's hand and said, 'Did you honestly think that you were in the year 2023, dear?'

'Yes.'

'She believes she's travelled here from the future,' Henry said, chuckling, 'like something from a science fiction novel. I think she's been reading too much H.G. Wells.'

'Surely this is good material for your own books that you're writing?' Vanessa said to Henry, with a smile.

'No,' Henry said, shaking his head, and looking down at his arm. 'I shan't be writing anything anymore. But let's be clear, Vanessa, the poor woman's only imagining all of this. She's not really from a hundred years into the future.'

Anna shrugged. 'Right now, I'm starting to wonder what planet I'm even on. I don't know what's real or not. Maybe I did hit my head out there in the garden? I can't tell if this is just another elaborate trick or not. If not, then this is insane. Or maybe *I'm* insane.'

Henry and Charles were looking at her like they agreed with that assessment of her mental state. She noticed that they kept their distance from her, and only Vanessa was brave enough to be close to her.

'Alright,' Anna said, 'I'll play along with this madness for a second. Let's say that this really is 1923 and that somehow I've gone back in time. If that's true, then how is Handsworth here too?'

Charles frowned at her. 'What do you mean?'

Anna stared at Handsworth. 'I *know* Handsworth. I met him in 2023. That's how I recognised him. How can he be there in 2023 and also be here in 1923? Oh wait, am I supposed to believe that he's one of Handsworth's ancestors? Maybe his grandfather?'

Handsworth looked annoyed now. 'I think it's time to admit to us – and yourself – that what you think is real, is not. This is a delusion.

You are not from the future. You are simply a troubled young woman, who has somehow wandered into our lives this evening, and you need help. There are places for people like you. I can have someone come and take you there. They will help you get better.'

Anna glared at him. 'Answer me this then, Handsworth – I heard you say that there should be five guests here, right?'

'That's correct,' he said, nodding.

'I know my vision's still a little shaky, but I can only see three people in this room, other than you and me,' Anna said. 'So where are the other two?'

Vanessa answered her question. 'Unfortunately, one of our party was feeling rather unwell this evening and excused herself, and I believe the other went to check on her. I'm sure they will be back shortly, and then you can meet them.'

'I think we should warn you, you may be a little taken aback when you see them,' Charles told Anna. 'Neither woman is quite what you might expect. One of the women has a disfigurement, of a sort, and the other, well, let's just say she doesn't quite fit in with the rest of us here.'

'Charles, please...' Henry said, looking annoyed.

'What? I'm only speaking the truth.' Charles started chuckling. 'Don't mind Henry here, I think he has something of a soft spot for our young friend!'

'We can't blame her for feeling unwell,' Vanessa told him. 'Not everyone here has as strong a constitution as you, Charles, and with certain recent events, I think a queasy stomach is perfectly under-standable. This house makes me feel rather uneasy too, and I must confess, I've said a prayer or two before coming here. I've never felt particularly safe here.'

Henry coughed for attention and then said, 'Look, this is all very fascinating, but this isn't progressing the evening. We should continue on to the dining room, and endure whatever our host has planned for us this time. I'm sure we'd all like to conclude this evening as soon as possible. Let's get on with it and unwrap the final piece of that damned puzzle.'

'Ah yes, the final piece,' Charles said, 'what we've all been waiting for.' He didn't look too excited at the prospect. 'Hold on a moment – what if the evening has started already? What if Anna here is part of the entertainment?'

Vanessa raised an eyebrow as she turned to look at him. 'In what way do you think this young woman might be our "entertainment"?'

'I only meant that perhaps she's another part of our host's games, like the other little tricks we've seen in each session,' Charles answered. 'A woman claiming to be from the future? I believe this is just one more odd and unexpected thing to encounter in this strange house, something that's meant to surprise and confuse us all.'

'I'm not an odd thing,' Anna protested, 'and I'm not anybody's entertainment. Maybe it's not me who's delusional, it's you? Maybe the trick's on all of you. I know who I am, where I am, and *when* I am. I know why I'm here. I was invited to unwrap that bloody mummy in that tomb, for God knows what reason. I just want to finish this last session and be done with it all.'

'You know about that odd body in there?' Charles asked, rubbing his moustache.

'Yes,' Anna said. 'My group were invited here, like you say you were, in order to pick apart that mummy in there.'

'It's a ghastly thing, that body,' Henry said to himself, staring into space. 'I saw more than enough dead bodies when I was fighting in the Great War, and then with the Spanish flu too, enough to last me a lifetime, so I don't need to see any more, thank you very much.'

'The Great War?' Anna said, puzzled for a moment. 'Oh right, I'm supposed to believe you were a soldier in the First World War now, am I?'

Henry seemed puzzled. 'Why did you call it the "*First* World War"?'

Anna hesitated before answering him. *If these people really do think they're in 1923, as ridiculous as that is and as deluded as they must be, then of course they wouldn't know what was to come...*

'Nothing,' Anna said. 'I didn't mean anything. I don't know what I'm saying. Ignore me.' She noticed that Henry suddenly looked very troubled.

Charles grinned and nudged Henry's good arm. 'I think you came to the wrong house if you're skittish about death, Henry. It's not only the body in the tomb – this place has seen its fair share of gruesome events, of that I'm sure.' He looked at Handsworth. 'Yes, we've already heard the story about that poor family who died here, the Grays, and their daughter who was never found. One of your maids told us about it. I wouldn't be too surprised to find out that this house has a long and sordid history, more than we know. Perhaps this place is haunted? There could be ghosts roaming the halls here. What do you say to that, Handsworth?'

Handsworth gave a polite smile. 'Every house has its history, Charles, and any house that is more than a few decades old is bound to have had one or two deaths in its past. This house is no worse than any other, despite what you may have heard. I know some of the younger maids enjoy telling tales, they're worse than old wives, but come now, you're a rational man, I'm sure that you don't believe in such things as spirits and apparitions, do you? You're quite safe here in this house, I assure you.'

'Hmm,' Charles said, unconvinced.

'Please, gentlemen, that's enough talk of ghosts and death,' Vanessa chided them. Then she turned back to Anna. 'Now, I'm sure once you get out of those wet clothes, and perhaps have something to eat, then you'll feel a lot better. Here, let me get you something, I saw bread rolls in the kitchen. How would you like that?'

'Yes, that's a good idea,' agreed Charles. 'Handsworth, could you speak to that wonderful cook of yours, and see to it that we all have something to eat, and soon?'

'I think I ought to remain with our new arrival,' Handsworth replied. 'I should keep an eye on her.'

'I doubt she'll be much more trouble. Now, Handsworth, be a good chap and do as we've asked, would you? We are guests here, after all, and it's your duty to see to our needs. I think we could all do with something to eat. How about it? I have no doubt we'll need our strength for whatever other strange events might transpire this evening.'

'Very well,' Handsworth said with some reluctance. 'I would request that you all remain in this room for the time being, and keep a watchful eye on this woman. See that she doesn't go anywhere. I may have more questions for her.'

'That's fine,' Charles said. 'She's staying right here.'

Handsworth looked at Anna before leaving the room.

'Try and rest for a moment,' Vanessa told Anna, who agreed with her suggestion. Charles and Henry began talking out of earshot of Anna, while Vanessa gently stroked her arm and gave her a reassuring smile.

A few minutes later, Handsworth returned and told the group that some food would be served shortly. In his hand he held a plate with a selection of bread rolls, which he offered to Anna. She was a little reluctant to take anything from him, but Vanessa – and Anna's grumbling stomach – persuaded her to take one.

She ate the roll and felt a little better. Handsworth left the room again and closed the door behind him. Not long after he'd gone, Henry said, 'Oh, I think I can hear the others coming now.'

Anna heard female voices from the hallway outside the room. Henry went to open the door and called out, 'Hello again, ladies. Come on in and join us. We have a surprise for you.'

Anna could hear what sounded like a young woman's voice in the hallway, but couldn't make out what she was saying. Then she heard an older woman's voice cry out, 'This is very... unexpected! Who on earth is she?'

'Her name is Anna,' Charles answered. 'She was found outside in the garden.'

The older woman's face suddenly appeared in Anna's eye line, giving Anna a fright as she peered down at her with one glass eye and another that seemed permanently only half-open. 'And what does Handsworth have to say about this new arrival?'

'I think he's as much in the dark as the rest of us,' Charles answered, 'but then, you never can quite tell with that chap.'

'This nonsense had better not disrupt our evening. It's getting late and we have much to do.'

Apparently, Anna was a burden to this party. She spoke up. 'I don't want to be here either, you know.'

'You appear from nowhere and expect us to believe that you haven't come to cause trouble?' the old woman with the odd eyes scoffed. 'So what are you, then? A thief? Hoping to steal something valuable, were you? Well, my dear, you chose the wrong house.'

'Mary, she knows about the unveiling,' Henry told her. 'She knows about the corpse in the tomb and why we're all here. How could she know about that?'

'What?!' Mary seemed furious. 'I knew this woman was trouble, the moment that I laid my eye on her. We should get rid of her.'

'Steady on,' Charles said, 'what do you mean by that, exactly?'

'Send her back outside, out into the rain,' Mary suggested. 'If Handsworth or anyone else asks, we'll simply say that she ran off and that we couldn't stop her.'

'I'm not sure about that,' Henry protested. 'She could catch her death out there.'

'This evening's far too important to be spoiled by this unwelcome woman,' Mary told the group. 'We don't know her. We can't
trust her. Whatever her motives are for being here, I'm quite sure
that they will not be good. After everything that we've all been
through, I'm not prepared to let her ruin things now, and you
shouldn't be either. So cast her out. Lock the doors. Let her die
out there, for all I care, it's of no consequence to me.'

'No, no, I won't be a party to anything like that,' Vanessa
protested. 'This is getting out of hand. Mary, please—'

'Useless bloody idiots! I'll do it myself then,' Mary said, shaking
her head at them. She then grabbed hold of one of Anna's arms.
Anna tried to pull away from her, but the woman refused to let go,
so Anna scratched at the woman's face, feeling the glass eye against
her fingernails. Mary then slapped Anna's face, hard, in retaliation.
Then she slapped her again, and again.

As Anna closed her eyes to fight the tears, desperate to escape
this pain, but too weak to fight Mary, she suddenly felt something
powerful pulling at her, trying to drag her away from this room
and away from Mary, Vanessa, and the others...

From somewhere far away, she thought that she could hear a
familiar voice. It sounded like Katarina's voice. It was very faint,
but it was calling out, 'Oh! Is she alright? Someone, help her!
She's—'

Anna tried to focus on the sound of her friend's voice. She
thought it could be a lifeline in the darkness, something to help
her find her way back.

When she opened her eyes again, Anna found that her whole world
had changed. Everything was blurry but she now appeared to be deep
in some kind of jungle, lying on the ground, looking up at the giant
leaves of strange plants. She could hear distant voices all around her,
saying words that she didn't understand. She imagined that there
might be an angry tribe hiding among the bushes and trees, coming

closer, armed with spears, intent on killing or perhaps even eating this invader to their territory...

Anna was soaking wet again, although it didn't appear to be raining in this jungle. Her head ached, and she felt sick. Suddenly a face appeared in front of her, a beautiful, familiar face.

'Anna, it's me, it's Katarina, can you hear me? I was so worried about you!'

Anna's brain fog refused to completely clear, but she could now see where she was. She was lying on the floor of the conservatory at the back of Grimwald House, and not in a jungle after all, although she was surrounded by strange-looking plants.

Katarina was kneeling beside her, telling her that she was going to be alright, but she looked concerned. Anna's eyes roamed the room and she could see Vivian and Mark. Curiously, Mark now had bandages over both of his arms – had he hurt himself somehow? What had she missed?

Anna realised with relief that she was back where she expected to be, with the people that she knew, rather than Vanessa and Mary and those other strangers who had tried to convince her that she was in the past. Maybe it had all been a dream?

Handsworth was here as well, wrestling with the door that led out to the garden. The wind was howling as he tried to pull the door to a close. Vivian took over from him and told him to go and check on Anna. Handsworth knelt beside Anna and examined her, and then said, 'We should bring her through to the drawing room so that she can get warm by the fireplace.'

Anna felt nauseous, drowsy and confused. The world didn't seem real. These weren't entirely unfamiliar feelings, but normally there'd be alcohol involved and she was sure that she hadn't had anything to drink tonight.

'Anna, are you alright? Are you with us? Do you know where you are?' Mark asked. He seemed surprised when she suddenly burst out laughing, finding his questions hilarious.

'Handsworth found you in the garden, unconscious,' Vivian told her. 'What on earth were you doing out there?'

'I took a nap and had the strangest dream, you won't believe me when I tell you about it.' Anna pointed at Handsworth. 'You were in my dream too.'

'I'm not sure that we should move her too much, she could be injured.' That was Harold's voice, but from where she was lying, Anna couldn't see him.

Anna did not agree with his assessment, and told the group, 'Actually, please go ahead and move her, because she's wet and she's bloody freezing!'

'You heard her,' Mark said. 'Handsworth, I can't pick her up with my arms the way they are. You'll have to do it.'

Anna then felt herself being lifted up by strong arms and carried away from that jungle. She stared up at the ceiling as she was being carried through the house. She thought that she could smell food cooking. 'Is it dinner time already?' she asked. 'I'm starving! I feel like I haven't eaten for a hundred years!' She giggled to herself. They passed the kitchen but although the door was open, she couldn't see anyone inside.

She could see a portrait on the wall of that family, the Grays, who used to live in this house. 'Hello again, how are you?' Anna said, but they didn't answer her back, which annoyed her immensely. The father and the mother looked directly at Anna, their faces blank, while the handsome son was staring off at something beyond the frame of the painting. Anna was convinced that their daughter – Helena, was it? – was now giving her an evil look, so Anna stuck her tongue out at her. 'That's fine, I don't like you either!'

'What's that? What did she say?' a man's voice called out through the fog in Anna's brain. Was that Mark? Where was he? She couldn't see him. Oh, she liked Mark. He was lovely. No, wait, she didn't like him now, she remembered – or did she? It was hard to think with everything so swirly in her head.

'I was talking to Helena, not you, Mark, so you shush!' Anna said. She turned her head and saw Mark and his bandaged arms. 'Why are you dressed like a mummy now?' she asked him. 'Are we going to unwrap you too?'

'I think she's delirious,' another man's voice said. Was that Harold? *Oh, poor Harold, and his poor legs!* It upset her to think about what had happened to him. She hoped that one day soon he would spring up from his wheelchair onto his two good legs and dance around, happy and healed.

Anna was carried across the hallway and then through into a brightly-lit room and lowered onto a sofa near a fireplace. 'That's better,' she mumbled as she felt the warmth of the fire. She saw a young maid enter the drawing room, carrying a pile of clothes in her arms, before laying them down next to Anna.

'That's very nice of you,' Anna said.

'We'll get you changed now, Anna,' Vivian said, as the maid left the room. Then she turned to the others and said, 'Could you gentlemen give us ladies some privacy, please?'

Mark and Harold left the room, both looking worried. Handsworth seemed reluctant to leave, but Vivian stared at him until he finally made his way out, closing the door behind him. 'Katarina, bring me that dress over there. Yes, the red one. We need to get her out of these wet clothes and into something dry.' She turned to Anna. 'You're in quite a state, aren't you, Anna? Look at you, you're soaking. Why were you wandering around outside in the rain? You could've caught your death out there, and we wouldn't want that, would we?'

'It's not my fault, no one answered the door, I think you were all having a party without me,' Anna said. 'I couldn't get into the house. I went around the back, trying to find a way in, but I couldn't. And then I think someone chased me around the garden. Was it Handsworth? Were we playing a game? I can't remember. I think he was about to catch me, but then I made a wish and I escaped and when I woke up I was somewhere I wasn't supposed to be, somewhere very strange. Maybe it was just a dream, but it felt so real that I don't think it was.'

'Go on then,' Vivian said, sounding a little annoyed. 'Tell us where you think you went.'

'It was here, in this drawing room, but it wasn't the same, because there were different people here, other guests, not us.'

'That's not likely,' Vivian said. 'We haven't seen anyone else here, have we?' She looked at Katarina, who shook her head, looking puzzled.

'No, you don't understand, it wasn't just different people, it was...' Anna took a deep breath. 'They told me that the year was 1923.'

Katarina's eyes went wide, but Vivian just said, 'I see.' She got up and stood next to Katarina. 'I'm sorry, Anna, I'm not quite sure what to say to that. Katarina, I'll finish changing her clothes while you go out into the hall and try to explain to the others what's going on. Tell them I think Anna here might be delirious, perhaps she was out in the cold for too long. Handsworth ought to call for a doctor. Or perhaps that should be a priest? I don't know, all this is beyond me – secret tombs, mummies, and women who think they can travel through time! It's utter madness.'

'I'm not lying about this,' Anna grumbled. 'It's the truth.'

'Perhaps you're not lying and you really do believe what you're saying,' Vivian said, 'but be rational, isn't it far more likely that you imagined all of it? You're clearly not well, are you? I think all that's happened is that you've dreamt up a little fun fantasy to take your mind off how unwell you are. And I also think that – Katarina, why are you still here?'

Katarina seemed unwilling to leave. 'I think I should stay with Anna, she might need me.'

'Will you please just do as I ask?' Vivian looked at her sternly. 'Oh, just for once, try not to be so bloody useless!'

As Katarina approached the door to the hallway and looked back at Anna with concern, Vivian muttered under her breath, 'Useless girl! They're all alike, aren't they?' Then she turned back to Anna. 'I'm going to remove your clothes now, is that alright, Anna? I hope these clothes fit. This dress looks a little old-fashioned, but I think that's the least of your problems, isn't it?'

Anna nodded, and soon she was undressed. She could see that despite Vivian's outburst, Katarina was still lingering, and staring at her with curiosity, but right now she didn't care. In fact, with the warmth of the fire, and how tired she was, she felt like she could just take a nap while Vivian dressed her in that oddly familiar red dress. She let herself drift away...

When she awoke, she was relieved to find that she hadn't gone anywhere. She was still here in the drawing room with Vivian.

But something felt different. Something was wrong.

'Anna! Snap out of it, for God's sake!'

Vivian was leaning over her, a worried look on her face. She grabbed Anna's arms and shook her. Anna tried to push her away, but she was too weak. 'You have to wake up, now!' Vivian hissed at her. 'Something's happened, something terrible!'

Anna could see how scared Vivian appeared to be, and it scared her too. She forced herself to sit up and try to pay attention. Whatever was going on, it seemed important, and something she needed to be present for. She would try not to close her eyes and drift away again.

'What's going on?' Anna asked drowsily.

'You'd been asleep for something like half an hour, so we'd all gone through to the dining room, while the maid Louise was supposed to wait here with you. We were all there in that room, talking, and worrying about you. I'd explained to the others that I thought you might be suffering from some kind of head injury, especially since you'd told me that crazy story about going back in time to 1923, and Katarina was acting so distraught, and Mark and Harold were arguing about what we should do, but then Handsworth appeared and said that they'd prepared some big feast for us for our final day, and he insisted that we carry on and eat our meals while we waited for you to wake up, rather than let all that food go cold, and we had just started sitting down at the table to eat when...'

'What?' Anna asked. 'What happened?'

Vivian seemed to be far away when she answered. 'The hidden door appeared straight away, almost as if the tomb was eager to invite us in. But it was so strange, because that door wasn't in the same place as it had been before in our previous sessions – this time, it was on the *other* side of the dining room!

'When Mark opened the door, we could see that the tomb was there, almost as if that entire room had somehow transported itself from one place to another, as impossible as that seems. Then the ticking clock started up, so we decided not to wait, and we went into the tomb without you. We thought that if we finished unwrapping the rest of the body, including the head, then that would be it, our job would be done, then we could all go home and never come back to this house again. So we started unwrapping the final parts of the body, and when we finished...'

Vivian's eyes returned to meet Anna's and she looked at her with a fierce intensity. 'At first, I thought it was another trick, another clever illusion. But it wasn't. It was real. We've been lied to, Anna, right from the start.'

Seeing someone as strong as Vivian look so scared terrified Anna. 'What do you mean? I don't understand!'

'I can't...'

'Vivian, what did you see? Tell me what the hell's going on!'

Vivian pulled away from her and stood up. 'I think you need to see it for yourself,' she said solemnly, 'and then you can tell me that I've not lost my mind.'

Vivian offered Anna her hand to help her to her feet. 'This way, come with me,' Vivian said, and led Anna out of the drawing room and into the hallway.

'Where are all the others?' Anna asked.

'I don't know where they are,' Vivian answered, her voice so quiet that it was almost a whisper. 'Please, keep your voice down.'

They entered the dining room cautiously. It was bare; if there had been a banquet laid out for their final meal, as Vivian had claimed, then it had miraculously disappeared along with the table and chairs. Anna could see the door to the tomb in the wall, and it seemed to be in the same position that it had been in their other sessions. The door was partly open.

'It's moved again!' Vivian gasped, shaking her head. 'I swear, Anna, that's not where the door was when we were in here earlier.'

Anna approached the door, with Vivian following just behind her. As they reached the doorway, Vivian whispered a warning in Anna's ear. 'Try not to scream when you see it.'

Vivian then pulled the door, sliding it fully open. The tomb inside seemed empty save for the mummified corpse at the other end, only barely visible in the candlelight. Vivian helped Anna inside the room, but then let go of her, and quickly stepped back out. She kept her hand on the doorframe as she urged Anna to go forward. 'Go on further in, go closer, and see for yourself, Anna.'

Anna stepped forward and could now see that the final wraps had been removed from the body. She couldn't yet make out any details of the head in the dim light, so she moved closer until she was mere inches from the dead body.

Now she was able to make out the face: the eyes, the nose, the mouth, even the hair – it was all there. The skin looked so smooth and fresh. The face was so incredibly well-preserved, the woman could have been alive and only sleeping.

And that face, it was so very familiar…

'No!' Anna gasped in horror, shaking her head. She took a step back. 'Oh my God!'

'No, not God,' a voice said from behind her. 'In fact, I think this room is about as far from God as one could get.'

Anna turned around slowly, her whole body cold with dread.

Vivian stared back at her with bulging eyes, her face contorted, her skin pale, her mouth gaping. To Anna, she looked like a ghost, frozen in the moment of her death. But she wasn't dead. Not yet.

Someone was holding Vivian up against the wall, their hands clasped around her neck, squeezing, choking her – before those hands finally released Vivian and she dropped to the floor. The impossible figure in front of Anna turned towards her and smiled a terrifying grin. Then it began to fade, becoming almost transparent, and floated up a few inches off the floor.

Anna shook her head in disbelief at the spectre coming slowly towards her. 'No!' she gasped.

Even though Anna's mind was screaming at her that this couldn't be possible, that it had to be an illusion, she knew in her heart that what she was seeing was real – the mummified corpse in this tomb, and the ghostly apparition that had strangled Vivian in front of her, both shared Katarina's face…

Anna was becoming used to the world not making any sense. Boyfriends who said one thing and did another. Colleagues that behaved like they were your best friends while secretly gossiping about you and plotting to usurp you behind your back. The sudden death of her father, all those years ago, and what that had done to her family. Closing her eyes and opening them to find herself in a whole different place, even a different time. And now, discovering that a long-dead body locked away in a secret room in a strange old house somehow had the same face as someone that she knew, someone that Anna cared about, and whose beauty and youth she had even been jealous of. But it wasn't jealousy that she felt as she looked at Katarina now. It was terror.

Somehow, Katarina and the corpse in this tomb were the same person, but it was as if they'd been split into two separate entities. How could that even be possible? It was another thing in this insane world that did not make any sense to her.

Anna saw the murderous intent in the eyes of Katarina's spectre, which had now solidified again, and she was holding a knife in her hand.

'Don't fight me, Anna,' Katarina told her. 'It'll all be over soon.'

Anna tried to turn away from Katarina, but when she did, she saw the corpse with the same woman's face staring back at her. She felt like she was in a horror movie, trapped between a ghost and a mummy. Whichever way she looked, the view was terrifying. So she decided she didn't want to look at any of it. She shut her eyes, and tried to concentrate and think of something else, anything else but where she was and what was about to happen to her. She desperately wanted to escape from this insanity...

Anna opened her eyes. She felt woozy and her head hurt. She looked up at the corpse standing against the wall in front of her. She was still in the tomb, her wish to escape hadn't been granted.

But there was something very different about the body. She realised with a shock that it wasn't the same person, it wasn't Katarina anymore. And this corpse's face was missing a particular feature. It was missing an eye.

When she turned her head away from the corpse, Anna found herself looking into the surprised eyes of an old woman – or at least, one eye, as the other was false and made of glass.

'Mary!' Anna gasped. Both the spectral figure in front of her, and the corpse behind her, were no longer Katarina. Instead, they were now Mary, that horrid old woman who had attacked Anna when she'd woken up in what was supposedly 1923. On the floor, Anna could see a body, but it was not Vivian anymore, now it was Charles, and he looked back at Anna with lifeless eyes. She fought the confusion in her mind and realised where she must be – or *when*. So she hadn't dreamt it after all, she really had somehow been sent back to 1923, and now she was back there again. She'd escaped the nightmare of her own time only to end up facing a similar nightmare here in the past.

'You can scream if you like, but no one will be able to save you,' Mary told her.

A wave of pain hit Anna, and her head felt like it was going to burst. Anna couldn't stop herself and she vomited on the floor.

'How disgusting!' Mary said, her nose turned up. 'I have to say, I'm quite surprised to find you here again after you vanished from the drawing room so suddenly earlier. I don't understand how you were able to do that, to be here one moment and then gone the next. Perhaps I shouldn't find it so strange, since I know very well that this house is full of so many odd things. But still...

'You were not the one I had expected to be my sacrifice, no, I've had my eye on someone else for some time – yes, my one good eye! Hah!

Speaking of eyes, I suppose there's no need for the illusion any longer, is there?

Mary's form began to shimmer and then became transparent, like Katarina's had. Anna's jaw dropped as Mary's glass eye fell out of her head, leaving behind an empty socket, and then it rolled across the floor, picking up some of Anna's vomit as it went, before it finally came to a halt against Charles's boot.

'I shan't be needing that false eye of mine soon anyway,' Mary said. She seemed amused by the look of disgust on Anna's face. Then the old woman's form began to solidify again, and she picked up a bloodied knife from beside Charles's body and pointed it towards Anna.

'Now get up, my time is very short, and since my intended sacrifice has hidden herself away somewhere, it seems that you will have to take her place. Perhaps you'd like to take some solace in the fact that you're saving her from having to endure this nightmare, this curse, like I have for so long. You'll have plenty of time to consider that. You see, your death won't be the end of it, far from it. In a way, you've been delivered to me in my time of need. Whatever reason brought you here, you can be the one to die for me. You will be my sacrifice!'

Anna could see that the door to the tomb was open, and she thought that she could see the dining room, her way out, but Mary blocked her path. Anna was trapped between the woman with the knife, and the corpse that shared the same face. There was nowhere she could go. She tried to throw a punch at Mary, but the old woman swatted Anna's fist away, and then grasped Anna's throat with her hand.

Anna screamed for help, but she knew that it was futile; no one would be coming to save her. Mary raised her knife above Anna's head, the vicious metal glistening in the candlelight as it hovered there, about to end her life.

Anna heard a gasp, and was shocked to see a familiar face suddenly appear in the doorway. Katarina stepped into the tomb, her eyes wide, her body shaking. 'Mary, stop this, please!' she cried out. 'Don't hurt this woman! Leave her alone!'

'Katarina?!' Anna cried out incredulously. She couldn't understand what she was seeing. *How can Katarina be here in 1923? What the hell is going on?!*

Anna met Katarina's eyes, but there was no sign of recognition on the younger woman's face. The door to the tomb suddenly slid shut behind Katarina, trapping her inside with them.

Mary's eyes darted between Anna and Katarina. She looked torn. 'Decisions, decisions...' she muttered. She pointed the knife at Anna, then at Katarina. 'I only need one of you to be my sacrifice. Blood is blood, I suppose it hardly matters too much who it comes from. So which shall it be?' She looked at Anna and said, 'I don't believe in coincidences, so for you to be here, whoever you are, right now, that must mean something. Perhaps it's you who's meant to die here?'

'No, stop!' Anna begged, as the knife came closer.

'Then you have to make a choice,' Mary told her. 'You can die here, and allow Katarina to live. Or you can go, leave this place, and allow me to kill her instead of you. Whoever dies here now will take my place here in this tomb for the next hundred years. They will be cursed, just like I was. So decide now, and quickly, or I will decide for you.'

Anna could see Katarina's terrified face, so different from the hard face that had threatened her before, and she suddenly realised that she already knew the outcome of this moment in time. She'd already seen whose body was destined to take Mary's place in this tomb for the next hundred years. So really, there was only one option, wasn't there? It just so happened to be the one that benefited Anna. And if she took it, then that didn't mean that she was being selfish, or cowardly, it was just the way that things were meant to be. Wasn't it?

'I'm sorry... I'm so sorry, Katarina, I have to go...' Anna said, and turned her head back towards the mummified corpse and then closed her eyes, and as she tried to ignore Katarina's screams she thought to herself, over and over again, *Take me away from here! Take me back...*

When she opened her eyes again, she realised that she was lying on the floor, still in the tomb, but when she looked up she saw that the corpse had Katarina's face once more. She was back in her own time again. But in no less danger.

Katarina's spectre looked down at her curiously. 'So where did you just fly away to, little bird, all of a sudden? Oh, of course! I know already, don't I, Anna? You sent yourself back to 1923, you were here with Mary and me in this tomb on that awful night, weren't you? And this, right now, is the moment that you returned yourself to when you escaped and left me there. Oh, I understand it all now!'

That makes one of us, Anna thought. She got to her feet and stepped back as Katarina moved towards her, brandishing her knife. Anna's eyes fell to the corner of the room, and instead of seeing the body of Charles, she now saw Vivian again. 'Vivian!' she cried out in despair.

'Oh, don't worry, Vivian's not dead – at least, not yet.'

Anna dreaded the answer to her next question. 'What about Harold and Mark, what have you done to them?'

'I haven't done anything to either of them,' Katarina answered. 'I think they're still here somewhere in this house, although I shouldn't get your hopes up about seeing either of them again.'

'I don't understand any of this!' Anna cried. 'You, and Mary, what the hell are you? What is this all for?'

Katarina smiled. 'I can help you to understand, Anna. I think you deserve that much.' She gave Vivian a sharp kick, and she began to stir. 'Wake up, Vivian!' Katarina said, in a sing-song voice. 'It's time for everyone's secrets to come out. Including yours.'

Vivian's eyes opened. She rubbed her throat as her eyes wandered the room, growing wider as she realised where she was and saw Katarina's spectre and her corpse. 'No!' she gasped.

'I thought you should be awake for this, Vivian,' Katarina said. 'You might find what I have to reveal very interesting.

'Anna, as you now know, I was here a hundred years ago, with Vanessa, Charles, and Henry, on the night that Mary was freed from this tomb. I was just another foolish guest who'd been invited to this house, but I didn't know the real reason that I'd been invited. You see, Mary had been trapped in this house for a century, just a spirit, with her physical body hidden here in this tomb, waiting to be freed. She wanted to be restored to life again, and to do that she had to kill one of us and curse that person to take her place for the next hundred years. On that final evening, in our last session, Mary revealed herself to us all. Henry and Charles, they died quickly. Vanessa died next, she was on her knees and praying to God, but that didn't save her.'

'Those people I met... they were all killed?' Anna said, shaking her head in despair. 'I can't believe it...'

'Yes, it was very sad, although remember this all happened a very long time ago,' Katarina replied. 'After they died, I was the only one left alive that night. I hid, hoping that Mary wouldn't find me. Mary was becoming desperate, she had so little time left to make her sacrifice. Then I heard someone calling for help here in this tomb, it was a woman's voice, and so I thought that perhaps Vanessa had somehow survived after all, and I knew that I couldn't just leave her here to die, so I forced myself to be brave and I came into the tomb to try to help. But then I saw you, Anna! I had no idea how you came to be there with us that night, or who you were, but I wasn't just going to leave you to die at Mary's hands, I needed to try to save you if I could.

'But then you suddenly vanished again, just as you'd done earlier that evening in the drawing room before Mary revealed herself to my group. I now realise that you escaped back here to this time, right now. It's quite incredible.'

Vivian stared at Anna. 'So you weren't making it up, then. You really were back in the past with those people. I'm sorry I didn't believe you.'

'Oh yes, Anna was there in 1923, it's true,' Katarina said. 'As for how, well, she's a very special woman, but we'll get to that in a moment.' She looked at Anna. 'Do you want to know what Mary did to me after you left me there all alone with her? First, she beat me, then she dragged me over to her corpse, and then she cut me with her knife – this very knife, actually.' She stared down at the knife in her hand. 'She cut me so many times, there was so much blood, so much pain... and then finally, here in this room, I died. Sometimes I wish it had ended there, but it didn't.'

Vivian swore in disbelief as Katarina continued, 'Yes, my blood was spilled on Mary's corpse, and that rejuvenated her. Her spirit and her body became one again, whole, for the first time in a hundred years. But the opposite happened to me, I floated away from myself, I became... this. I could do nothing but watch as the maids prepared my body, covering it with salt to dry it out, wrapping me from head to toe in bandages, and finally placing me in this tomb, like a hideous mummy from a horror story. They told me that doing all these things to my body was important and that without it I might disappear into nothingness. Sometimes I think that might have been preferable to existing like this.'

Katarina pointed past Anna, towards the unveiled corpse behind her. 'Can you understand what it's like for me to look at that thing, knowing that it was once me? It reminds me that I'm not really here, I'm not really alive, I'm only a shadow, an echo of who I once was. I wandered this house, lost, for so long. I was trapped. A prisoner. You cannot imagine the terrible loneliness, the despair, what it's like to be a part of the world but also be so very far apart from it at the same time. To crave a connection, anything to make you feel like you truly exist and that you haven't simply imagined yourself.' Her bottom lip was quivering. 'Although, I suppose I was never completely alone here in this house. There were the maids, but they come and go over the years, and usually avoid me, even sweet Louise. There was also Ebony, who I would sometimes find scratching at the wall near my tomb. I suppose she could smell my body in here. She's a good dog, most of the time, but there is only so much meaningful conversation you can have with a dog, isn't there? On rare occasions there are also certain other visitors that come here, but I have to admit that they frighten me, so I try to avoid them. And then, of course, there is Handsworth.'

'Handsworth. He lied to us, didn't he?' Anna muttered. 'He knew exactly what was going on here. I never did trust him.'

Katarina nodded. 'Oh yes, Handsworth's always been a part of this, I think since the very beginning. Those paintings on the walls of his office, supposedly of his ancestors? They aren't, of course – they're all of him. I have no idea how old he truly is. Or what he truly is. Nevertheless, while I was trapped here, Handsworth helped me not to drift away and forget myself completely. He talked to me. He was even kind enough to read books to me when I couldn't touch or turn the pages myself, and he also told me stories of his own experiences. I do envy him, he's travelled all over the world and seen so much that I haven't. I loved hearing about exotic far-off lands, countries that I'd never even heard of before. And he guided me, he helped me to understand what I am, just as he did for Mary and all the others before me, and just as he will do for all the others to come.' She looked at Anna. 'Just as he will do for you, too, Anna. This is my hundredth year, and only now do I have the chance to free myself, as Mary did. Once the sacrifice is made, I can live again, and be whole again. More than that, once I'm freed, I'm going to live forever, like Mary and all those before her! A reward, for everything that I've endured. And I've endured so very much.'

Anna's head was spinning with all these revelations. 'All of this, these sessions, the things that have happened to us in this house, and unwrapping that body – it was all part of some kind of ritual to release you from this curse, wasn't it?'

Katarina nodded. 'Yes, in a way, but these little gatherings have several purposes, one of which is to allow us to choose our sacrifice from the people who come here. As each of you took the bindings from my body, you began to restore my physical form, but there is also power in your emotions too, in your thoughts, and your feelings. This house, it brought all your memories and fears to life – Oh, let me tell you, it's so wonderful when that happens, it creates this kind of *energy*, it's hard to describe in words. The house absorbs most of it, it feeds on it, but I took some of that energy within me, too, and it made me stronger.

'During our first session, I could finally begin to touch and feel things again, in this form, for the first time in so long. It was fleeting at first, only for mere moments, and it took a lot of concentration. I had to be careful not to let any of you touch me if I wasn't ready for it, because then you would have realised that I wasn't really here. I couldn't even step outside into the rain with you, because it would pass through me if I didn't concentrate hard enough! I had to try so very hard not to let you all see the truth about me. I was always here before you arrived, and when you all went home in your taxis I stayed behind, because I couldn't leave this house, even if I would have given anything to be able to go with you.'

Anna's thoughts were chaotic but she forced herself to ask, 'If you're a... spirit, or whatever the hell you are, then why did you look so ill on that first night when I stayed here with you?'

'I *was* ill, in a way,' Katarina replied. 'I was weak, drained from the effort of appearing real to you all. Everything takes so much effort, even just walking around and going up those stairs was a struggle, to seem as if I was physically touching each step as I went. Sitting in those chairs in the dining room, and lying down on that bed upstairs – even just breathing in and out! I wasn't used to the immense amount of concentration it requires. When you stayed with me that night, Anna, I didn't actually sleep, I only pretended to. I continued to play the innocent, weak young woman that you all thought I was, in each session that we shared. I let you take care of me. I spoke very little, to allow you and the others to do most of the talking. That was so hard, I wanted to say so much, after all these years of being alone! However, doing so helped me to understand you all so much better.'

Katarina reached her hand out to one of the candles and extinguished the flame with her fingers, then smiled at Anna. 'As each day passed between the sessions, I grew stronger and stronger, and while parts of my physical body in this room slowly began to heal, in this form I started to feel things again – not just physical, but emotional too. When I saw Mark, I felt things I hadn't felt for such a long time. I had almost forgotten what it's like, that desire for... connection.'

Anna had a sudden realisation. 'That night you said Mark came to your room wanting to sleep with you, you turned him down because you knew that if he tried to touch you too much, then he might start to realise that you weren't real. That was the real reason you told him to stop, wasn't it?'

Katarina suddenly looked a little sheepish. 'Actually, I lied to you about Mark. He never tried to touch me. He never even came to my room that night. Oh, he did look at me once or twice, but no more than most men do. He seemed far more interested in you, Anna. I suppose I was jealous of his interest in you and of how very close you two had become. I'm sorry I lied to you, but I have to say, I don't think that things would have worked out between you two. Mark needs to be with someone who truly understands him and his pain.'

Anna now felt a pang of guilt for how she'd treated Mark. It had been based on a lie.

Katarina sighed. 'These feelings of being connected to the world again, even just partially, they weren't enough. It was only a taste of freedom, of reality. Imagine being so desperately thirsty and having someone tease you with only a few drops of water on your lips. I needed more! I wanted to be whole again, and to make that happen I knew that I had to choose someone to die for me and to take my place in this tomb, just like Mary did. It's the only way.'

'But why me?' Anna asked. 'Why any of us – Mark, Harold, and Vivian? Why did you choose us?'

'No, you don't understand, you were chosen by the house. We all were.' Katarina looked at the ceiling, the walls, and then down at the floor. 'The house selected us, and Handsworth sent those letters to invite us here. Good people don't get invited to Grimwald House. We were all chosen because of the bad things that we've done in our lives – the sins that we've committed, the evil that we've done.'

Anna shook her head. 'No, that's nonsense. You can't tell me that Harold's a bad person, nor Mark, not even with all his faults. They're not evil.' She glanced at Vivian. 'None of us are. We don't deserve this.'

Katarina raised an eyebrow. 'It's interesting that you believe that. From the moment you signed your names in ink and put your blood on the contract to agree to attend these sessions, certain events were set in motion. The house made sure of that. Past deeds and old secrets were brought to light, with sometimes tragic consequences, like Harold and his poor legs, for example, and Vivian's heart attack, and poor Mark burning his arms.'

Anna looked at Vivian. 'You had a heart attack?'

'Yes,' Vivian admitted. 'I survived it, thanks to my son's quick actions. But that was simply caused by stress, it wasn't anything that "the house" made happen. She's talking about this place like it's a living thing, but it's only a wretched old house, that's all it is.'

Katarina tutted. 'Even now, you still can't grasp the truth of what you're a part of, can you? You can't even begin to imagine what this place really is, and what secrets it holds behind its many doors.

'Do you think what happened to Mary and I was unique? It wasn't. This has happened for hundreds of years, perhaps more. And it will happen for hundreds more. These gatherings of guests who come to this house and take part in this ritual to unveil the body and reunite it with the spirit has been going on for centuries. Vivian, you told us about those Victorian parties where groups would gather to unwrap a body, well, it has been going on for far longer than that here in this house, in one form or another. Even I don't know quite how long, but I do know that it was going on well before the unfortunate Gray family lived here.

'Louise told us the story of the Gray family, didn't she, Anna? How that poor family all died here in this house on that night long ago, and that their adopted daughter Helena then went missing. But I don't really think Helena actually got away, do you? I don't think anyone could ever truly escape from this house, not when it has decided that it wants you.

'This is the incredible, terrible power of Grimwald House. It *is* alive. It thinks. It decides. It chooses who and what it wants. It curses and gifts as it sees fit. And it knows each one of us, and all our secrets.'

Anna realised now that the sensation she'd felt of being watched when she'd first arrived at Grimwald House hadn't just been her imagination playing tricks on her, it was real; this house was somehow alive, and it was some ancient, malevolent thing. And it wanted her. It wanted all of them.

Katarina stared down at the knife in her hand. She ran her finger along the blade. Then she looked at the body behind Anna and grimaced. 'But you have to understand, the house itself didn't create the evil that lies inside of us, it was already there, and the things that we'd done were always going to catch up with us sooner or later, the house just made it a little sooner. The house has shown me your whole lives, and all your worst moments. I've seen it all. We've all done terrible things, myself included. So perhaps it would only be fair that I admit my own terrible sins, before we discuss yours?

'From our previous sessions, you probably considered me a woman of few words, didn't you – I'm proving you wrong now, I know! But the truth is that I used to talk a lot, back when I was alive – too much, some might say. Yes, I was something of a gossip. I suppose I still am, perhaps I haven't learnt my lesson after all! But I loved discovering people's secrets, and I would write them down in my journal, and then I would share them with other people. Everyone loves to hear gossip, don't they? Scandalous rumours, secret affairs – I discovered and shared them all. I couldn't stop myself. And then one day a friend of mine paid the price for my addiction. Poor Jane was strangled by her husband because I'd believed she was having an affair and I just couldn't keep it to myself, and her husband heard the rumours that I'd spread. But I was wrong, I'd made a mistake. And she died because of it. Because of me.'

Katarina's eyes stared off into space, not seeing Anna or Vivian any-more. 'That was my secret shame that led me to accept the invitation to come to this house. I didn't know back then that my life was suddenly about to change in such a horrible way. It was 1923, just a few days after the first session here where I'd met Mary and Vanessa and the others, and I'd arranged to meet with a man that I knew named William Taylor. I'd first met him on the day of my friend Jane's funeral, and over time we had become friends, and then something more. I soon discovered that William was not a good man at all, and I'd been very wrong about him. He was a monster. He attacked me that night, he drugged me and then cut the toes from my left foot, and then he lied to the police and blamed another man, an innocent man.' She stared down at her left shoe, with sad eyes, then at the corpse behind Anna. 'Soon my body will heal fully, and my missing toes will grow back, once the sacrifice has been made. I will be whole again then, for the first time in a hundred years.

'But back then, after what William had done to me, and what he did to those other women, I decided that I couldn't let him get away with it. So... I cut off his fingers to stop him from hurting anyone else. Oh, there was so much blood! He nearly died, but he didn't. Do I feel guilty about what I did to him? Perhaps I should, but then I remind myself of what that man took from me and the other women, and then I don't feel so bad.

'So there you have it, those are my sins – or at least, the ones that I committed before I became trapped in this house. Oh, I know that there will be more to come. Starting with your death, Anna, I'm afraid.'

'Katarina, I'm sorry for what that man did to you,' Anna said carefully, 'and maybe I'd have even done the same if I were in your shoes and someone did that to me. But all this pain and death has to stop, it can't carry on! Let me and Vivian go. Let us leave this place. End all of it, so no one else has to suffer.'

'I can't do that,' Katarina said, shaking her head. 'I have to make the sacrifice, or else I'll be trapped here for another hundred years, and I couldn't bear it, not again, no!' She had desperation in her eyes, and she took a moment to calm herself before she continued. 'So you can't leave. And besides, I'm not finished yet, Anna, far from it, there's much more to tell.

'For example, shall we talk about Harold? Don't you want to know his secret? You all thought he was a good man, but you were wrong. As you know, Harold did not take good care of himself, and it was the same with his money – rather ironic, with him being an accountant. Realising that he needed to make a lot of money quickly to pay off his debts, he chose to betray his clients, selling information to their rivals, even working with his own estranged daughter in his latest scheme, someone who has committed her own fair share of bad deeds. The melody that we all heard coming from the room upstairs, the one that seemed to fascinate Harold so much, was a song that he learnt from his father, and he used it to sing to his daughter Erin as a child to help her sleep. I'm afraid that Harold will never get the chance to mend his relationship with his daughter now. And with his failing health, the truth is poor Harold would likely have been dead in just a few years anyway, even if he hadn't been chosen by the house to come here. It's all quite sad, I suppose.'

Katarina turned her head and looked down at Vivian. 'As for Vivian here, I thought she was going to have another heart attack when the last bandages were removed and she finally saw my face on the body over there! Although, perhaps when you hear what she's done, Anna, then you'll think that she *should* die.

'You see, Vivian paid a man to murder the woman her son was in love with, sweet Arianne, purely because she didn't have the right colour skin. I suppose you must have hated me too, Vivian, for the same shallow reason?'

Anna gasped, staring at Vivian. 'My God. Tell me that isn't true, Vivian. Did you really do that?'

Vivian didn't answer and just glared at Katarina.

'Then there is also the matter of Sammy Mitchell,' Katarina said. 'Do you remember Vivian telling us about him, Anna? He was her admirer, the boy who brought her all those sweets when she was a child. It was Vivian who told a teacher that Sammy was stealing those sweets from the shop for her. Vivian's friends had been teasing her about having a boyfriend who wasn't white and had threatened to tell her mother. They didn't believe Vivian when she said that she wasn't interested in him and had only strung him along so he'd keep giving her the sweets that she wanted. Poor Sammy was then expelled from his school, although that didn't stop him from continuing to pursue Vivian, nor her friends from continuing to tease her about him, and I suppose eventually one day Vivian decided that she'd had enough.

'She arranged to meet him at a park nearby, on a bridge over a river, one that many young lovers used to meet at. She demanded that he leave her alone for good. They argued, and they fought... and then Vivian pushed him off that bridge into the water.

'Sammy couldn't swim, but Vivian could, and she could have tried to help him, but she deliberately chose not to. Instead, she let him drown, because she thought that would solve her problems. So you see, Arianne was not the first person that Vivian had caused the death of. They both died because of her disgusting prejudices.'

Vivian finally spoke, ignoring the looks that she was getting from Anna. 'How can you know any of this, it's not possible! No one knows this!'

Katarina smiled. 'There you go, underestimating me – and the house – again. Do you want to pretend that anything I've said isn't true?'

Vivian stared down at her hands, and after a moment, she said, 'No, you're right, it's all true. What's the point in denying it? Yes, I let Sammy drown, I had no choice, he wouldn't leave me alone. I couldn't be seen with someone like him. He was ruining my life. And as for Arianne, she was an evil girl who wanted to steal my son away from me. She was going to ruin his life. My Daniel deserves so much better. So I only did what was necessary, and I don't regret any of it.'

Katarina gave a little laugh. 'You can keep telling yourself that, if you think it will make you feel better. But I can *feel* the guilt that you try to hide, and so can this house.'

Anna stared at Vivian, but the older woman refused to look her in the eye. Anna had always felt a little wary of Vivian, but she could not have imagined that she would be capable of these things.

'So, shall we talk about Mark next?' Katarina said. 'I'm sorry to say that he's also done very bad things too, but I don't think that they were entirely his fault.

'Mark lied to us when he said that he couldn't save his girlfriend Leah from dying in that fire. When he found out that she was cheating on him, his anger took hold of him and he lost control and tried to strangle her. In a panic, seeing her body and knowing the trouble that he would be in, Mark started a fire to try to cover up what he'd done. When he left her there in that burning cabin and ran away into the woods, he hadn't known that Leah wasn't actually dead. She was still alive. If he hadn't started that fire then he might still have been able to save her. It's such a tragic story.

'Only a few days ago, Mark had a terrible fight with Leah's brother John, who was his best friend, and John was killed, in another awful death by fire. Mark's arms were quite badly burned, but he'll recover, he's strong.

'Poor Mark, he's been searching for someone, anyone, to fill the void that his beloved Leah left behind. I think he just needs the right person to help him and then he'll be alright again.'

Anna felt overwhelmed. All this deceit, all these terrible tragedies – if it was all true, then Anna hadn't known these people at all. She'd let them get close to her, particularly Mark, who she'd now found out was a murderer. She felt sick. She managed only a few words. 'I can't believe this. This is all too much.'

Katarina smiled at Anna, but instead of being reassuring, it was terrifying in the glow of the candlelight. 'I know this is a lot to hear all at once, and it's probably quite overwhelming for you. However, there is only one more person's sins that we need to talk about. Yes, finally we come to you, Anna. Of course, I know all about your past, and all the people that you've hurt.'

'What do you mean, what people?' Anna said guardedly.

'Oh Anna, shall we be honest – you've only had such great success in your life and your career because you had an unfair advantage over everyone else, and you abused it. You're only successful because you've caused so many others to fail, and you did that without a care for how it might affect their lives and the people around them. Did you ever stop to think how many of your victims lost their jobs, and even their marriages, because you damaged their careers with your actions? Are you going to deny this, or will you admit your sins?'

Anna felt Vivian's eyes on her. She knew that she could try to deny what Katarina was saying, but she seemed to know everything already and was prepared to reveal it, so Anna decided that if her so-called sins were going to be exposed here and now, then she would rather explain them herself. She knew that she could justify the things that she'd done. But she still found herself trembling as she spoke.

'You wouldn't understand,' Anna said, 'you don't know how difficult it's been for me, I've had to fight hard – very hard – to make my business a success. I worked so bloody hard, and I put my health at risk sometimes, but it still wasn't enough. I realised that you can't be a successful woman in this world by playing nice and by always doing the right thing. So yes, sometimes I had to get a little ruthless to get what I wanted, what I needed. What I deserved.

'Anyone in my situation who found themselves with an... ability like mine would've done exactly the same thing, and anyone who says they wouldn't is a liar. So I'm not going to apologise.'

'What are you talking about? What ability?' Vivian asked. 'I don't understand.'

'Go on,' Katarina said. 'Tell us. Let it out, Anna. I promise you'll find it cathartic to shout it out, to finally unburden yourself of your biggest secret, your biggest sin.'

'No... I can't,' Anna said, shaking her head.

'Then I will,' Katarina said. 'You see, Vivian, Anna isn't like anyone else, she's very special. She has a rare gift. You know that she travelled back to 1923 and then returned here, well, that wasn't the first time that she's done something like that, to move herself from one place to another. Far from it. Come on, Anna, you can admit it now. Tell the truth. Be free.'

Anna saw Vivian's incredulous reaction, and she realised that there was no point trying to hide her secret any longer. After all these years keeping it to herself, being so careful not to reveal to anyone else what she knew she was capable of, this was the moment where it would all come out into the open. There was no escaping it now. Anna would have to admit what she was. A freak. Abnormal. Something *wrong*. She took a deep breath.

'Alright... yes, what Katarina's saying about me and what I can do, it's true. I know it must sound insane, Vivian, believe me, I do, but I can focus my mind and think about a place that I've been to before, and if I concentrate hard, then I can... *move* myself there. Sometimes it works, sometimes it doesn't. It's a bit like sleepwalking and waking up somewhere entirely different from where you were, except that it happens almost instantly.

'But I can't control it very well, and it's always risky, it's always disorienting, and usually it hurts and makes me feel sick. Sometimes I even black out. Don't ask me how exactly it works, or where it came from, or why I have it – because I don't have the answers to any of that. But what happened to me tonight, not just physically moving myself from one place to another, but actually going *back in time* – I've never done that before, that's new, and it's bloody terrifying.'

'This is absolute madness,' Vivian said. 'Do you expect me to believe any of this?'

Anna shrugged. 'Vivian, with everything else that's happened, and with what's happening right now in this room, is my ability really the most bizarre and unbelievable thing that you've heard all night?'

Katarina laughed. 'I expect it's not! So, what did you do with this wonderful gift of yours, Anna, once you realised that you had it? Shall I tell Vivian?'

'No, don't, please...' Anna said, but she knew that it was futile and that she wouldn't be able to stop her.

'You abused it, in many different ways, didn't you?' Katarina said. 'For example, you've used it to eavesdrop, to spy and to steal, and even to plant incriminating things in the offices and homes of your rivals. Many despicable acts like those, and more.'

'No, that's not fair,' Anna protested. 'What I did, it doesn't make me a terrible person. It's how the world works, you have to use any advantage that you have, because no one's going to help you, they're all out for themselves. I'm no worse than anyone else.'

'I'm not sure if you're trying to convince us or yourself,' Katarina said. 'But there's more to it, isn't there? People got hurt in other ways because of your ability. For example, shall we talk about what happened to your father?'

'No, just shut up!' Anna shouted. 'Enough! Nothing that I've done makes me a monster, and I don't deserve to be here with killers like Mark and Vivian. I haven't murdered anyone. We're not the same at all!'

Katarina shook her head, as if disappointed in her. 'Oh, Anna, I think out of all of us, it's possible that *you've* ruined more lives and hurt more people than anyone else. Even if, as you say, you haven't actually killed anyone, and we say that your father's death was simply an accident.'

Then Katarina's face changed. She looked angry now, as she raised the knife to Anna's throat. 'Except, of course, you *have* killed someone, haven't you? You killed *me*! You may as well have held the knife that killed me yourself, because you're the reason that I died that night, all those years ago! You vanished, ran away, and you didn't try to save me from Mary, you let her kill me. I could have escaped, I could have lived, instead of being cursed to remain in this house for a century! What happened to me was your fault!'

Katarina was shaking with rage now. 'That first session when you came here with Vivian and Mark and Harold, I recognised you straight away. At first I couldn't believe it, you were the same woman that had appeared back then at the night of Mary's unveiling, a hundred years before. The same woman that had left me to die in this tomb! Handsworth recognised you too. I suspected then that you were meant to be my sacrifice, and as each session progressed, I became more and more certain of it. If nothing else, this will give you the chance to atone for what you did, abandoning me to die like that. You're going to save me this time. So goodbye, Anna, I wish I could say that it won't hurt when you die, but I'm afraid it will. But I'll try to make it as quick as possible, I promise.'

Vivian tried to get up, but with her free hand, Katarina pushed her back down onto the floor. Anna knew that she should try to use her ability again and send herself away from here, but she couldn't seem to focus her thoughts, and she couldn't take her eyes off Katarina's face as it came closer, an eager, crazed look in the dead woman's eyes as she brought the knife closer to Anna's throat...

'Stop!'

Handsworth appeared in the doorway. He stepped into the tomb and saw Vivian on the floor, who looked up at him in fear. His eyes then found Anna, and as he stared at her he told Katarina, 'Enough! Do not kill her!'

Katarina reluctantly lowered her weapon and said, 'Why? She's my sacrifice! I chose her, Handsworth. She's going to make me whole again!'

Handsworth placed himself between Anna and Katarina and said, 'I've felt the full strength of her power now, and it's... intoxicating. Anna used her ability again, didn't she? She travelled through time, and I felt it. I *tasted* it. The energy, the power that she has, it's incredible!

'Katarina, you and I first saw Anna in 1923, and we never discovered who she was and where she came from, or where she went after that night. And then a few weeks ago, she arrived here as just another invited guest, looking exactly the same as she had a century before. As soon as I saw her again, I realised that there was something very powerful in this woman. I thought at first that perhaps she was ageless, immortal, but now I understand that she transported herself through time. What an incredible power she has! I wanted to take her that first night when she slept here, but for its own hidden reasons, the house would not let me have her then. But now I understand why – it was because she had yet to fulfil her purpose: to go back and play her part in your destiny, Katarina. But now that that's done, I'm going to take her.' He reached out his hand towards Anna. 'The house has amplified your ability, Anna, evolved it, and guided you towards your full potential. Not just the ability to move across distances, but to move through time as well. Can you imagine the possibilities? This is far too special a gift to be lost to a simple sacrifice, when any blood will do. We can do so much more with this wonderful gift of yours. I can do so much more with it.'

'Both of you keep calling it a gift, but you're wrong!' Anna said. 'It's painful, it's dangerous, and unpredictable. It doesn't always work when I want it to or the way I want it to... and people have been hurt because of it. It's a curse, if anything. A burden that I never asked for.'

'You ungrateful child!' Handsworth shouted at her. 'It *is* a gift! A wonderful, powerful one! Even if you're too small-minded to appreciate what you've been given.' He turned his attention back to Katarina. 'I'm taking her to the Black Room, where we can harness her power. Do not try to stop me.'

'No, you can't take her there!' Katarina protested. 'Please, Handsworth, I need her!'

Handsworth seemed suddenly taller as he stared down at her. 'Are you going to defy my will? Or the will of the house?'

'No, of course not,' she said, with fear in her eyes.

Handsworth pointed towards Vivian, who recoiled. 'You can have that one instead, or kill the man Mark, if you wish. They will all have to die tonight anyway.'

'No, not Mark! Not him! I can't!'

'You *can't*?'

Katarina looked pained. 'I thought – I hoped that once I was free, once I was whole again, that perhaps Mark could come with me, and we could be together, and we could be happy.'

Vivian spoke up. 'You stupid girl, do you really think that Mark or anyone else would ever want to be with you? You're not even real, you're dead. You shouldn't even still exist.'

'Shut up!' Katarina shouted back.

'No, Vivian's right,' Anna said, 'Mark isn't going to love you, and you said it yourself, he killed the last woman that he loved, and then his best friend too, so what makes you think that he would treat you any better than he did them?'

'You're wrong! I understand him, I'm the only one that does. I accept his mistakes, and I know that he would accept mine.' Katarina put her hand to her breast. 'I know him better than anyone does. I can love him. I'm the only one who ever truly could.'

'Then you're insane!' Vivian spat at her. 'Perhaps you two *do* deserve each other. I hope you have a long and miserable life together.'

Katarina ignored her and said to Handsworth, 'Please, leave Mark alone. I need him. After everything I've endured, I deserve some happiness. Take Anna, if you must, but let Mark live. Promise me that you won't hurt him, Handsworth. Please!'

'Oh, very well,' Handsworth said. 'I promise not to hurt him. Kill Vivian instead, she will take your place, and she will be a guest of the house for the next hundred years.'

Vivian opened her mouth to protest, but no words came out. She looked like she was in pain, and was clutching at her chest.

'Time is running out, Katarina,' Handsworth said. 'The window will close shortly. You've wasted far too much time explaining yourself to these people, revelling in revealing all of their petty sins, when you should have been making the sacrifice. You talk far too much, you always have done. These people should all already be dead by now! You *must* make your sacrifice, now, before it's too late. Or do you want to remain trapped here for another hundred years?'

'No, of course I don't!'

'Then get on with it.' Handsworth grabbed Anna's arm and dragged her past Katarina and Vivian and threw her out into the dining room. Anna looked back into the tomb and saw Katarina standing over Vivian, the knife in her hand.

Vivian reached out her hand towards Anna. 'Don't leave me here to die!' she cried out. 'Anna, please, come back! Help me!'

'I can't...' Anna said. 'I'm sorry!'

'Anna!' Vivian screamed.

'Be quiet now!' Handsworth ordered, and he reached out his arm, which seemed to stretch further than should be humanly possible, and he slid the door to the tomb shut, sealing Vivian's fate. The door vanished into the wall.

'Vivian! No!' Anna cried, but she had no strength left to fight as Handsworth grabbed her and dragged her from the dining room and out into the hallway.

Anna's foot caught on something, and when she looked down, she saw that it was Harold's wheelchair. It lay on its side. There was no sign of Harold himself. The wheel that she'd caught her foot on spun uselessly. She wanted to think that perhaps Harold's legs were suddenly better and he'd decided that he didn't need the use of his wheelchair anymore, but she suspected it was more likely that he hadn't got out of that chair voluntarily.

'Stop dawdling!' Handsworth was terrifyingly strong, and he was able to pull Anna along the hallway and up the staircase with just one hand in a matter of seconds. At the top of the stairs, he turned left, and they passed the master bedroom that she'd stayed in with Katarina on that first night.

She heard the grandfather clock chime ominously in the distance, and then suddenly gasped when she saw someone lying down on the floor in the corridor up ahead of them. As they approached, she realised who it was.

'Harold!' she cried out. He was just lying there, not moving, as if he had no energy to move. What was wrong with him? How the hell did he get up here? She really hoped that he hadn't crawled his way up the stairs and along the corridors to get here, because the amount of effort that would've taken, the amount of strain that would have put on his body...

As Anna got closer, she saw with horror that Harold's eyes and mouth were open, his face pale, and there was no life in his eyes.

Harold was dead.

'No!' Anna screamed. 'Harold! Oh God...'

Harold had his hand outstretched towards the music room, and Anna could hear that ghostly piano melody again, coming from behind the door. Had he been drawn up here like before, powerless to resist the lure of that music, almost like a siren's song? *Oh, Harold...*

Handsworth dragged Anna away from Harold's body. As he pulled her along the corridors, Anna kicked out, occasionally hitting one of the doors. She hoped that someone would hear her, perhaps one of the maids, but no one came out to help her. All the curtains had been opened now, but she could see only darkness outside the windows, as if nothing else existed in the whole world apart from this house.

'Where are you taking me?!' Anna cried out.

'To the Black Room, of course,' Handsworth answered. 'Don't worry, you won't be alone. There are others in there, special people, people with powerful abilities a little like yours, Anna. Every once in a while, the house senses someone out there in the world with a gift, a power, and sends me to try to find them and bring them back here. Sometimes my task can take days, even weeks. It's a big job, but sometimes I have help. I've been to so many distant places. Oh, the things that I've seen...'

They turned into a corridor and at the far end Anna could see the big black door that she'd seen before, but now it appeared to be two or three times the size of all the other doors. Handsworth dragged her towards it, produced a large black key from his pocket, and started unlocking the door. His grip on Anna was incredibly strong, and as much as she tried to struggle, she couldn't free herself. Whatever was waiting for her behind that black door, she would not be able to escape from it.

Handsworth pulled open the door, and when Anna looked through the doorway she could see nothing but darkness. She closed her eyes and tried to wish herself away from here, but Handsworth's grip on her body was so painful that she couldn't concentrate.

Suddenly a voice called out to her from the black void and sent a shiver down her spine. She opened her eyes and stared in fear at the darkness ahead of her. Who – or *what* – was in there, waiting for her?

'It's time,' Handsworth said, and pushed the screaming Anna through the doorway and into the Black Room.

CHAPTER TEN

ANNA

Silence.
  Darkness.
  Cold... so cold.
  Abandoned.
  Afraid.
  Monkeys.

At the zoo, three-year-old Anna had loved the monkeys, especially the spider monkey that had pressed its face against the glass. She'd pressed her own face against the glass too and then placed a kiss on it that she hoped the cute little monkey could somehow feel, despite the barrier between them.

The monkey had then dashed away, disappearing into the branches and leaves in its little prison, and young Anna could no longer see him, and she started crying.

Her parents had taken her to see the lemurs next, and she'd quickly forgotten all about the tiny spider monkey that had won and then broken her heart. *Fickle little Anna!*

Grown-up Anna, the Anna that was shivering and scared in the Black Room in Grimwald House, wouldn't find it so easy to forget the creatures staring at her from inside their glass prisons. These weren't animals, they seemed human, but almost like a bad artist's impression of what a human being should look like; they were far too thin, and their skin looked pale and stretched tight across their bones. Many of them were hunched over as if they'd forgotten how to stand like a human being should. These strange creatures all seemed fascinated by Anna and called out to her as she passed by their glass cages.

Handsworth pulled her forward. The prison seemed never-ending. She couldn't begin to count how many of these creatures were trapped in this place. She looked back at the doorway – it was still open, but it was fading into the distance now, and there was no way she could get to it as Handsworth's grasp on her was too tight.

She looked up. High up above – impossibly high, if this was still a room contained within Grimwald House – she could see a kind of lightning storm, but one that flashed a multitude of different colours. Each flash brought the sound of groans of pain that echoed around this hellish place.

Anna saw and heard a frenzy of heads, fists and feet thudding against the walls of the glass cells, pounding like the heart in her chest, and then she heard a chorus of anguished cries, growing louder and louder.

Handsworth stopped and put one of his hands on the nearest cell. He looked at Anna and said, 'Do you feel that? Can you feel its energy?'

Anna felt something, a feeling of being pulled forward, not just by Handsworth, but by something even more powerful.

'Each one has a power, like you do,' he told her. 'Something special. Unique. Valuable.'

'What are you doing to them?'

Handsworth grinned at her. 'They're here to sustain the house. To make their contribution. And soon, you will too. The house takes some energy from the guests who attend our little sessions, from their fear and their guilt, but from those here in the Black Room it takes something even more special. These people have abilities far beyond normal men and women, just like you do, Anna. The house keeps them alive here for much longer than their natural lifespans. Gradually, over the years, it syphons their powers, storing them away for its own purposes. Whenever the house senses a soul with a special energy out there in the world, I bring them here. And in return, I am rewarded.'

'How are you rewarded?' Anna asked, but immediately regretted asking that question.

'I'll show you, shall I?' Handsworth grinned at her and then reached to pull down a lever by the side of the nearest glass cell. The cell split open to reveal a hairless, emaciated woman crouching inside. The old woman stared up at Handsworth and Anna in terror.

Anna wanted to reach out and help her but Handsworth held her back. With one hand, he lifted the old woman out of her cell and held her in the air, her thin legs wavering about a foot off the floor. Anna watched in horror as Handsworth placed his mouth against the woman's forehead. He then made disgusting sucking noises for several seconds before he finally released the woman and her drained, dead body crumpled to the floor.

'My reward,' Handsworth said, licking his lips. 'For each new one I bring in, I am allowed to take one of the older ones for myself. I take whatever little they still have left in them. A treat, for my hard work.'

'You're a monster!' Anna spat at him, tears in her eyes.

'I am merely a servant who serves his master well. I deserve a little reward now and then, don't I? Now come along, Anna, there's an empty cell just up ahead that's waiting for you.'

Handsworth took her a little further until they came across a glass cell that was empty. He pulled the lever and it opened wide.

Anna screamed as Handsworth pushed her inside the cell, and then he pulled the lever, and as the cell slowly encased her she realised that she would be trapped here forever in this glass tomb...

There was a sudden flash of light from high up above and Anna felt something like a pulse of electricity flow through her body. Then there was another flash and another pulse, and another, and each time it felt like she was being pulled apart from the inside.

The pulses stopped and she collapsed in her cell, gasping, her arms and legs banging on the hard glass. Her insides felt like they were on fire.

After several long seconds, the pain began to recede, and Anna knew that she had to take this opportunity to try to transport herself out of this cell and away from this house while she still could. She closed her eyes and thought about her apartment and her daft cat. She pictured herself sitting there on her sofa, safe and free, and far, far away from the nightmare that was Grimwald House.

But when she opened her eyes, she was dismayed to find that she was still in her glass prison in the Black Room. Handsworth was looking at her curiously through the glass. 'Trying to escape?' she heard him say, his voice slightly muffled by the glass between them. 'Your ability won't work inside your cell, Anna. And eventually, over time, you will lose it altogether. The house will drain your power from you, just like it is doing to all the others kept here in this room.'

Anna banged on the glass, and screamed at Handsworth to let her out, but he just shook his head and smiled. He seemed to be enjoying her suffering. Anna rested her head against the glass of her cell and sobbed. *Please, God, don't let me be trapped here! I'm sorry for everything that I've done, I'm so sorry, but don't do this to me, please! Help me ! Save me!*

Anna gasped as she saw Handsworth suddenly fall forward, hitting his face on the floor in front of her cell. She was shocked to see Mark standing behind Handsworth, the poker from the drawing room fireplace in his shaking hand. Mark was gritting his teeth, his face contorted, as if he were fighting intense pain.

Handsworth clutched at the back of his head, and Anna could see blood. He turned and shot a look of pure evil at Mark – who then swung the poker a second time, striking Handsworth across the forehead. Handsworth collapsed to the floor as Mark looked at Anna in her cell and shouted, 'Anna! How do I get you out of this?'

She pointed at the side of her cell, where the lever was. Mark nodded and pulled the lever, and Anna's cell split open and she fell to the floor, only inches away from Handsworth. She gasped with relief. She was free!

'Get up, now!' Mark screamed at her. 'We have to get out of here! Move!'

With immense effort, Anna managed to pull herself up onto her feet. Leaving Handsworth moaning in pain on the floor, she and Mark ran as fast as they could. Anna stumbled several times, trying to ignore the cries of the creatures in their glass cells as Mark urged her onwards. The doorway was still open, and through it she could see the corridors of Grimwald House, the dim candlelight acting as a beacon for them to follow, a way out of the darkness.

Once they were through the doorway and back into the corridor, Mark shouted, 'Anna! Help me close the door!'

Anna helped him and they forced the black door shut. She realised that there was no key in the lock and turned to Mark. 'Handsworth still has the key, this won't stop him!'

'Then let's not hang around,' Mark said.

As they moved along the corridors, trying to find the staircase that led back downstairs, Anna stared at Mark's bandaged arms. 'What happened to your arms?'

'Don't worry about me, I'll be fine.'

'Mark, it's Katarina, she's—'

'I know already. I saw it. I can't think about that right now, about what she is.'

'How did you find me?' Anna asked.

'I was with Vivian and Harold in the tomb downstairs, and when we found out what Katarina really is, there was all this panic and confusion... I didn't know what to do, there was so much chaos. I got out of there, but Katarina followed me, so I ran up the stairs to get away from her. I don't know where she went then, but she didn't come after me. I was lost in these corridors for what seemed like bloody hours, but then I heard you here with Handsworth, so I followed you and watched him take you into that room. What the hell is that place, Anna?!'

'I think it *is* Hell... or something close,' Anna replied. 'Mark, I don't understand – why did you come back for me? You should've just tried to get away.'

'I couldn't just leave you there to die, I had to try to save you.' He looked out through the windows and then told her, 'We should try to get to the woods.'

There was a sudden flash of lightning and a roar of thunder, and through the windows the crisscrossing branches of the trees were illuminated and appeared to Anna as a giant spider's web, awaiting a fly or two to ensnare. 'I'm not sure the woods are such a great idea.'

'Then what else do you suggest?' Mark asked, exasperated. 'We can't stay in this house, we have to get out of here, and we have to do it now!'

'Alright, alright, let's go,' Anna said, and they moved quickly along the corridors, making several wrong turns. Eventually they reached the corridor where Harold's body lay.

'Don't look at him, Anna. Poor Harold, he didn't deserve this.'

Anna couldn't just ignore the body on the floor. She knelt and touched Harold's arm, and looked into those dead eyes one more time. 'Perhaps we *do* deserve this, all of us,' she said softly.

Mark knelt in front of her. 'What do you mean?'

She looked up at him, then back at Harold's body. 'Katarina was right about us. We're all terrible people, and the house knows it, even if we don't want to accept it. We're monsters.'

'Speak for yourself.'

Anna looked him in the eyes. 'Mark, I know about Leah, and your friend John. I know what really happened to them. Katarina told me everything. She told me you killed them. It's true, isn't it?'

Mark stared at her, his mouth open, and for a moment she thought that he was going to try to deny it. But instead he said, 'Yes, it is true, but you have to understand that it wasn't my fault, it was theirs. I didn't want either of them to die, I cared about them both. I loved them both. I still think about Leah every bloody day. I never stopped loving her. I didn't mean to kill her, and I didn't mean to kill John, either. I'm sorry that they had to die, I am, but what was I supposed to do? It happened, there's no changing that. And I couldn't tell anybody the truth or I'd have ended up going to prison, and what would be the point of ruining my life as well? So yes, I lied, because it was better for everyone to think that they were just accidents. It's not like confessing what I did would bring either of them back to life, is it?'

'You know, Vivian warned me about you, I should've listened to her.' Anna shook her head at him. 'Somehow, she knew what kind of a man you are. Even when Katarina told me about the things that you'd done, there was a part of me that didn't want to accept it. I knew you were a liar, but I never realised what you really were... a murderer. You *are* a monster, Mark, just like Handsworth, even if you can't see it.'

'Fuck you, Anna,' he spat at her, 'don't you dare judge me. You don't know, you weren't there. I'm not a bad person. For Christ's sake, I just saved your bloody life! I didn't have to do that. Maybe I shouldn't have bothered, maybe I should've just left you there in that room with Handsworth?'

Anna saw Mark's eyes move past her and fixate on something else. When she turned her head to follow his gaze, she could see that there was someone standing in the corridor up ahead of them. It was the young maid, Louise. She stood with her arms outstretched as if she was trying to block their path. She might have looked comical had the situation they were in not been so desperate.

'Get out of our way!' Mark warned her, and he started to raise the poker he held, but the effort seemed too much for his damaged arms, and he cried out in pain and dropped it. He looked at Anna pleadingly.

Anna picked up the poker and extended it towards the girl. 'Louise, move aside!' she called out. 'We don't want to hurt you!'

Louise did not move. 'You can't leave,' she told them. 'I'm sorry, but you can never leave. The house wants you. Don't fight it. You don't need to be afraid.'

Anna stood up and approached Louise, but she still refused to move out of the way, so Anna raised the poker and swung it and struck Louise's left arm, hard. The girl screamed, clutching her arm, then turned around and ran away.

'It's her own damn fault, we did warn her,' Mark said. 'Now, are you going to come with me and we'll try and escape this house together, or would you prefer to stay here and keep on judging me for things that you don't understand?'

Reluctantly, Anna agreed to follow Mark, and they continued on unobstructed until they reached the top of the staircase. The dead head of Gerald the stag looked down on them with its blank, impassive eyes, and offered them no help. Anna kept glancing behind her, convinced that at any moment a furious Handsworth would come lunging out of the darkness towards them, reaching out with those impossibly long arms of his... but for now there was no sign of him or any more of those maids.

Suddenly Anna heard a voice calling out to her. She couldn't tell where it was coming from, but it sounded like a woman's voice, and it said, 'Anna, don't be afraid, everything will be alright.' She raised the poker and looked around frantically. Was that Louise – had she returned to try to stop them? Was Anna going to have to strike her with the poker again?

'Anna, what is it? What's wrong?' Mark asked her. It seemed as if he hadn't heard what she'd heard. Perhaps she'd only imagined it?

Anna shook her head and answered, 'It's nothing, let's keep moving.'

They took a few more steps down the stairs before they both froze, having heard a deep, angry growling, which seemed to be coming from somewhere downstairs.

'What the hell is that?' Mark said, and his question was answered when a creature on four legs slowly crept into view at the bottom of the staircase, and then turned its head to look up at them. It opened its jaws and drool dropped onto the floor.

Anna put her hand on Mark's arm, and stepped forward. 'It's alright, it's just Ebony.' She took another step forward, but the dog then bared its teeth at her, and Anna retreated back. She realised now that Ebony looked different, she stood more steadily on her legs, and she appeared somehow *bigger* than she had before.

'We have to get past that thing,' Mark said. 'Any ideas?'

'Funnily enough, I didn't bring a bone or any dog biscuits with me, so no, I don't know what to do. Ebony seems different this time. She looks bigger, more dangerous.'

'Try and hit it with the poker, scare it off.'

'I think that'll just make her even angrier.' Anna thought for a moment, and then said, 'Mark, I'm about to do something, something that's going to look very strange to you, and you won't understand it, but I need you to stay calm, alright? Please, trust me.'

Mark looked confused. 'What are you talking about?'

Anna took a deep breath, and then pictured the kitchen in her mind. She closed her eyes, and concentrated hard. *Please work, please work...*

When she opened them, she was standing in the kitchen, with the poker still in her hand. She steadied herself against one of the cupboards as a wave of pain hit her. She heard a distant voice cry out, 'What the hell?!' *Sorry, Mark, I'll have to explain later.*

Anna forced herself to try not to think about the fact that her whole body felt like it was on fire, and grabbed some meat off a hanging hook. She tried to ignore the disgusting feeling of cold flesh in her hand,

and took the meat out into the hallway. She dropped the meat on the floor and stood there in the dim candlelight, with the poker raised in her hand, and shouted, 'Ebony! Come here, girl! It's Anna! I've got something tasty for you! Ebony!'

She waited, and then a few seconds later she heard a scratching sound, and then she saw movement in the darkness up ahead. The dog slowly crept towards her. Ebony's head was tilted to one side as she looked first at Anna, and then at the meat in front of her. She approached the meat and sniffed it a few times. Then she looked up at Anna. And then she opened her jaws hungrily.

Anna closed her eyes, and pictured Mark, and Gerald the stag, and the staircase, and wished herself away from the vicious hungry dog...

She was falling. She opened her eyes as she tumbled down the staircase. Mark tried to catch her, but failed. She let go of the poker, which banged on the floor just a second before her body did.

Lying there on the floor at the bottom of the staircase, she couldn't stop her body from convulsing. The pain was incredible, worse than it ever had been before, as if something was very wrong with this ability of hers – had the house done something to her while she was in that cell in the Black Room?

Mark followed her down to the bottom of the stairs and once her body had stopped shaking, he helped Anna back up onto her feet. 'What the hell just happened to you?! You vanished, right in front of me!'

Taking several deep breaths and trying to force herself to focus, Anna said, 'I don't have time to explain it to you now, we have to get out of here!'

Anna picked up the poker from the floor while Mark tried the front doors, but they were locked, and there was no key in the keyhole. 'We need another way out,' he said. 'The conservatory! There's a door to the garden. Anna, we have to try!

'Alright,' Anna agreed. 'Let's go.'

'Wait... what about that dog? It'll be in our way.'

'Hold on.' Anna carefully crept along the corridor to the left of the staircase. She saw Ebony biting into the meat that she had brought her from the kitchen. Ebony looked up when she saw Anna, but then went back to chewing on the meat.

'I think she's busy, at least I hope she is,' Anna told Mark. 'Follow me, we'll go past her. *Slowly.*'

'Oh shit,' Mark said, as he followed Anna. They slowed when they came close to Ebony, who looked up at them, but didn't move from her spot.

'Good girl,' Anna said softly. 'Such a good girl. You're going to stay right where you are, and you're not going to eat us, are you?'

She glanced at Mark, who looked terrified. She took his hand and guided him past the dog. They continued on until finally they reached the conservatory at the back of the house. Mark stood in the doorway, looking back to check that Ebony hadn't decided to pursue them. 'Hurry up!' he hissed at Anna.

'Here!' she called out when she found the door to the garden, hidden behind the plants. She was relieved to see that the key was still in the lock. She stopped and looked at Mark. 'Wait, we can't leave Vivian here with Katarina, she's going to kill her! Vivian will take her place and be trapped here for a hundred years, like Katarina was. We can't let that happen to her!'

'You want to go back?!' Mark said, incredulously. 'Are you mad? Look, I'm sorry for Vivian, but I don't want to risk my life trying to save her. And I don't want to risk yours, either. Never mind the dog, neither of us is strong enough to take on that undead bitch Katarina, are we? And not Handsworth, either, whatever the hell he might be. I don't think that poker you're holding is going to be enough to take them down for good, do you? We have to leave Vivian behind and save ourselves. You know Vivian would do exactly the same if she was in our position.'

Anna hated his logic, but she reluctantly agreed, and took hold of the key in the door and turned it. The wind and rain tried to force themselves inside as Mark and Anna pushed their way out through the doorway into the garden. 'Come on!' Mark yelled, as they fought against the weather.

Mark suddenly cried out in pain.

'What is it?' Anna asked him. 'What's wrong?'

'It's my arms, and this bloody wind and rain, it hurts like hell. But I'll be alright. We have to keep moving!'

Anna guided him from the garden around to the side of the house, towards the low wall and the small iron gate, beyond which was a path leading to the woods. The wind swept through the trees, rustling the leaves, and it sounded like the gentle waves of the ocean. It reminded Anna of the white noise machine that she had by her bedside at home that helped calm her thoughts at night and helped her to relax, but this noise had the opposite effect. The hissing woods seemed as if they were warning her off, and she had her doubts as to how much safety they offered. Were they making a mistake by going in there?

Still clutching the poker in one hand, with the other she pushed the gate open. It resisted as if no one had used the gate in years, but she managed to defeat it.

Anna paused when she heard what sounded like a scream from somewhere behind her. She thought that maybe she had only imagined it, that it was just the wind, but when she looked at Mark and saw the fear on his face, she knew that he had heard it too. She looked back at the house, but couldn't see anything. Then she heard the scream again. It flew down to them on the wind and chilled her body far more than the cold night air. Then her eyes caught something moving high up on the roof of the house. She stared, trying to make it out. A dark shape rolled like a wave across the roof, then suddenly seemed to melt away.

What the hell was that?!

'We should go!' Mark said, desperately.

Something slithered down the wall of the house and dropped to the ground. It unfolded two long arms, stretching them out towards them as it began creeping closer.

Mark was shaking his head. 'I'm not seeing this. No, I don't believe it. I'm going crazy. Yes, that's the only explanation. None of this is real.'

Anna wished that she could live with Mark on his isle of denial, but she knew that this was all real, and they were in terrible danger. That thing, whatever it was, was coming for them.

'Run!' she screamed at Mark, and they ran towards the woods. They were both exhausted but they knew that they couldn't stop, they had to keep moving, or else that thing chasing them would catch them, and she didn't like to imagine what it had in store for them when it did.

A flash of lightning helped her see a little more of the path ahead through the mess of trees. Anna felt the soft carpet of wet leaves beneath her feet and hoped that she wouldn't stumble across an out-stretched root or fallen branch that would send her flying, because if she did fall then there was every chance that she might impale herself on the poker that she carried in her hand.

Thorny things scratched and stabbed at Anna's arms and legs and tore at the dress that she wore, and she knew that she was probably bleeding, but she couldn't do anything about that now. All that mattered was that she kept moving.

Mark suddenly stumbled and fell to the ground, moaning, causing Anna's heart to stop. 'Get up!' she yelled at him. She tried to help him but he was agonisingly slow to get back up onto his feet. She daren't look back and see how much closer their pursuer might be now.

'I can't take much more of this!' Mark moaned.

'We don't have a choice!' she told him. 'We have to keep moving!'

Anna's foot landed in a puddle of water and she winced. The rain had finally started to ease off and they weren't under such constant at-tack from it anymore. Their path was illuminated by rays of moonlight that had managed to eke their way through the web of branches above them. A twig snapped under Mark's foot and at the same moment he cried out, 'Anna, let me go!'

'What?!' she cried, in disbelief.

'Let me go! I can't go on, the pain in my arms is too much, I think I'm going to—'

Then Mark collapsed to the ground again, and stopped moving. He was silent. Anna stared down in shock, the moonlight making his face look as pale as that of a corpse in a morgue.

'No!' she screamed at him. 'Get up!'

Anna grabbed hold of Mark's shoulders and shook his body, but he didn't respond. Had he abandoned her, with that *thing* coming for her? She heard a screeching sound and turned her head.

Something incredibly long flew out of the darkness towards her and punched her in the chest.

Anna flew backwards through the air until she smacked her back against a tree. Then her stunned body sunk down towards the roots. In her daze, she was reminded of a bird that once struck the glass doors of her parents' dining room and broke its wing, the one that her father had had to put out of its misery, which had caused a very young Anna to refuse to speak to her father for days, until they took a trip to the zoo and she fell in love with the monkeys and forgot all about that poor bird.

As Anna lay there, a broken bird herself now, her chest stinging sharply with every single breath that she took, she knew that she must have cracked several of her ribs, but she was far more concerned with the horrific thing taking form in front of her. She watched as its long arms folded back into its bulbous body and then a head sprouted, but it had no features on its face, as if it was a blank slate waiting to discover who it was meant to be.

The creature made disgusting squelching, cracking sounds as it shifted its body around, until finally it stopped transforming, and now it looked down at her with Handsworth's face.

'Anna,' he hissed, 'it's time to stop running.'

'Oh God!' she gasped, as a hideous hand delicately brushed the strands of wet hair away from her face. Fingers from another hand ran themselves slowly and gently down her neck and then against her chest, and then down to her ribs. The fingers started moving in circles, and she felt a warmth inside her, and then the pain she'd been experiencing seemed to fade away. Her ribs no longer hurt. It was as if she'd been healed.

Handsworth smiled as he knelt down in front of her. 'Come with me, Anna, back to the house. You know there is a place there for people with gifts like yours. No one will care about your sins there. You'll finally have peace, and you'll never be lonely again.'

He reached out *another* hand – an impossible *third* hand – and offered it to her to take.

A noise came from behind Handsworth, causing him to swivel his head completely around – without turning his body. Anna saw Mark stumbling towards them. 'Leave her alone!' Mark shouted. He picked up a branch from the ground, and with an agonised yell he threw it at Handsworth, but it bounced off the monster harmlessly.

Handsworth's head swivelled back around and he gave Anna a horrific grin full of sharp crooked teeth before he extended a fourth arm down to pick up the branch from where it had fallen. He raised it up to his face and opened his mouth. He ran an impossibly long tongue along the wood, making disgusting slurping noises, and as he did so, the branch caught fire. The flames were unnatural colours: black, green, and purple.

Handsworth raised the fiery torch high above his head, the flames flickering shadows across his long face. Anna saw that Mark was frozen in place, staring at the torch in the creature's hand, seemingly mesmerised by those flames. Mark didn't even attempt to struggle as Handsworth reached out an arm and clasped his fingers around his neck.

'No!' Anna screamed, but she could do nothing but watch as Handsworth dragged Mark closer, to within inches of that distorted body of his, and then touched the flaming torch against Mark's head.

Mark's body convulsed in Handsworth's hands as the fire took hold of him. It swept across his whole body in an instant, and he burned away to nothing in front of Anna's eyes. It happened so fast that he didn't even have the chance to scream. So instead, Anna screamed for him.

Handsworth dropped the torch, and then brushed the ash of Mark from his hands. He turned to Anna and grinned at her. 'Oh dear, Katarina will be upset about this! But I won't tell her if you don't.'

Her eyes streaming with tears, Anna stared at the monster and cried, 'What the hell *are* you?!'

'I am Handsworth. I am a part of the house, I always have been, and always will be. You don't need to fear me, Anna, so long as you stop fighting and come with me back to the Black Room. I don't wish to hurt you. You don't have to die like Mark and the others. The house can take away all your pain and all your loneliness, you just have to let it. You'll be free of the "burden" of your power, this gift that you say you don't want. It will be your donation to our cause. Don't be afraid.'

Anna felt nothing *but* fear in this moment, staring into that creature's soulless eyes as its face came closer to hers. She spat in his face.

Handsworth hissed at her angrily. Then Anna felt his long, sharp fingernails press against her left cheek, but they didn't stop when they hit skin, instead they began to dig further and further into her face, and then they were suddenly pulled downwards, tearing her cheek open. She screamed at the intense pain.

After an agonising few seconds, Handsworth finally withdrew his hand from her face. She put her hand against her cheek, and when she took her hand away she could see that her fingers were covered with blood.

She looked up at Handsworth with pure hatred for what he'd done to her face, and what he'd done to Mark and all those poor souls in the Black Room, and suddenly she knew what she had to do. But it would take all of her strength to do it.

In the split second before she acted, Anna saw Handsworth's demonic eyes shift down to her right hand, which she'd buried in a pile of leaves. As she brought her hand up, the leaves fell away and revealed the poker that she held. For a brief moment she thought she saw a flicker of fear in the monster's eyes – before she screamed 'Fuck you!' and drove the poker straight into his eye, then out through the back of his skull.

Handsworth howled in pain, falling back from her, grasping at the poker embedded in his head. He wrenched it out with a sickening tearing sound. Then he threw it aside and glared down at her with his one good eye. There was a gaping hole where his other eye had once been.

Anna knew that she'd won only a small, temporary victory. She'd hurt Handsworth, but she hadn't defeated him. She'd angered him, and might have even pushed him to decide that she wasn't worth the hassle and that he should just kill her and be done with her. But Anna hadn't expected to be able to kill Handsworth with the poker, only to stun him long enough so that she'd be able to enact the next part of her hastily conceived and insanely dangerous plan. She forced herself up onto her feet, and took a deep breath.

Then Anna fought against every instinct that she had and threw herself forward and wrapped her arms around Handsworth's slimy body, embracing him, fighting the urge to scream as she did so. She shut her eyes tight, and concentrated her mind, and pleaded with the universe not to let her die.

The flashing lights were so bright that they hurt her eyes. When they stopped, Anna saw multiple versions of herself, circling around her. Then she saw her mother, her sister and her brother. They didn't move, they just stared at her and said nothing. And then she saw her father. She reached out to him, but he turned away from her. Her family vanished, and everything went dark.

Then fragments of her life began to play out in front of her eyes like scenes from a movie. They played far too quickly though, and at first she struggled to make any sense of them, but she then started to realise that what she was seeing were all the moments in her life when she had used her ability, her power.

One moment in particular played out before her now, and had slowed down, letting her relive every second of it. She knew what this was. She had never forgotten this moment.

It was the first time her "gift" had manifested. And it was the worst day of Anna's life.

It had started out as a good day; her father had taken her shopping for her birthday present in the morning and then on to the cinema in the afternoon. Her mother had meanwhile taken Anna's brother and sister with her to prepare a party for Anna at her aunt's house that evening. So it was a special father-daughter day, which suited Anna just fine.

Little Anna had made the mistake of drinking too much pop and eating far too much popcorn and was feeling sick, so even though the film about the friendly gargoyle named Girrock hadn't finished yet, she'd asked her father if they could go home. She felt miserable that she'd ruined their afternoon, and when they left the cinema and headed towards the car park across the street, her father had insisted on holding her hand as they crossed the road and she'd got irrationally angry with him, and pulled her hand away from his, yelling at him about how she wasn't a little girl anymore and how embarrassing it was for her to be seen holding hands with her father at her age.

Her father had shaken his head at her and told her, "*Well, that's tough, Anna, because you're my daughter and it's my job to keep you safe, whether you like it or not!*"

She'd then closed her eyes and wished she was back at home in her bedroom so that she could cry without anyone seeing her do it, and when she'd opened her eyes again, suddenly she somehow *was* back home in her room, with no memory of how she got there.

A short while later, a policeman came to the door and asked to speak to her mother, and when Anna explained that her mother wasn't home yet, he called her on the phone and they waited together until she got back.

Anna remembered sitting in the living room and listening as the policeman explained what had happened to her father, that he'd been hit by a car while crossing the road, and that unfortunately, he had died. The driver had told the police that Anna's father seemed to have just stopped in the middle of the road for no reason and wasn't looking at the traffic, and the driver wasn't able to stop in time.

Anna's mother was angry at her for running away from her father, but she was relieved that Anna hadn't been hurt in the accident too. But her mother never knew the full story, she didn't know that Anna hadn't just run away but that she'd actually vanished from the spot, sending herself back home in the blink of an eye, leaving her father shocked and terrified, and his confusion had resulted in him being hit by that car that he hadn't seen coming.

She had caused the death of her own father because of the ability that she had been given and her inability to control it.

And now, fearing for her life in the woods outside Grimwald House, Anna had used her power again. The visions of her past faded away and she could now see where she had sent herself; it was exactly where she'd intended to be. It was also the last place in the world that anyone would want to be.

Anna had pictured the Black Room in her mind and focussed on sending herself and Handsworth here. She knew that it was incredibly risky and could so easily have gone wrong, but miraculously, her plan had worked. She looked at the monster and he seemed very disorientated, even more so than she was. She knew that she might have only a few seconds before Handsworth recovered, and she had to take advantage of his confusion.

She immediately pushed herself away from Handsworth. She felt sick, and weak, but she couldn't afford to allow herself to indulge in her pain right now.

As she moved through the Black Room, Anna paused briefly to pull the lever by each glass cell, before running on to the next one. Five, ten cells now, all beginning to open. She heard a cry and knew that Handsworth was coming for her.

She opened more of the cells, and glanced back to see a few of the creatures tentatively stepping out of their cells.

Suddenly something fast and hard and powerful struck her in the back, and she fell to the floor. She looked back as Handsworth approached her, roaring in anger, raising an arm to strike her again...

Then he suddenly stopped, and looked around. She thought that she could actually see fear in his eyes. All around the two of them, things that were once people came ever closer, reaching out and moaning the name '*Handsworth!*' over and over again.

While Handsworth was distracted by the approaching creatures, Anna fought her way through the crowd to get away from him. They didn't seem interested in her at all, they were only focussed on Handsworth, so she tried to be gentle as she pushed them aside, not wanting to inflict any more pain on these poor creatures, but she knew that she had to get past them or Handsworth would catch her. Handsworth had no such qualms about hurting them, and she turned to see him drive a fist through the chest of one of them, before swinging his arm around and decapitating another.

The creatures wailed but still they converged on Handsworth, and now she couldn't see him for all the bodies that surrounded him. She could hear squelching, ripping sounds. Handsworth was making a horrible noise, a terrible cry of agony, yet at the same time, the sound of his pain was like music to Anna's ears.

She suddenly realised that one of the creatures had broken away from the crowd. Anna stopped and stared. It was a woman, or what was left of one; she was withered, naked and had no hair on her body. Anna didn't get the sense that this woman wanted to harm her.

Anna was shocked to realise that she recognised this poor woman. She'd seen that face before, but it had been much younger and much more full of life, in the portrait on the wall downstairs in Grimwald House, the one of the Gray family and their adopted daughter...

'Helena?!' Anna gasped.

Suddenly a long black arm punched its way out of the mass of bodies, and then Handsworth forced his way out. As the creatures tried to pull him back in, he lifted his head and saw Anna and screamed with rage. He fell to the floor as he pulled himself away from them, and then started to raise himself back up onto his feet.

Helena turned to face Handsworth. They stood facing one another for several seconds. Anna feared that at any moment Handsworth would reach out his arms and tear Helena apart, but for some reason he didn't. Instead, he shook his head once, then again, and scratched at his head as if there were bugs crawling in his hair. Eventually he stopped and just stared at Helena, as if transfixed by her. 'Yes,' he said, although no question had been asked as far as Anna could tell. Then he reached one of his hands deep inside his body, and pulled out a small object covered in a kind of black goo and handed it to Helena. She then held the object towards Anna, who cautiously approached her.

Anna reached out and took the object that Handsworth had dug out of his own body, and when she wiped the slime from it, she could see that it was the key to the black door. Somehow, just for a moment, Helena seemed to have been able to control Handsworth, and she'd forced him to give her the black key.

Helena suddenly stumbled, as if drained by the effort of what she'd done. A man that looked as worn and fragile as Helena stepped away from the crowd of creatures and approached her and helped her back onto her feet. They stared at each other and then they embraced, before they both turned and looked at Anna. At first, she wondered if perhaps this man might be a member of the Gray family, either Helena's father or brother, but his face didn't match any of the portraits that she'd seen. From the way the two of them were now looking at each other and holding each other, it seemed more like they might be lovers. Anna watched as the man then released Helena, and after a final glance at Anna she returned to the crowd.

Handsworth was shaking his head as if awaking from a daze, and when he saw Anna and the black key that was in her hand, he screamed at her. Suddenly the man that had helped Helena stepped between them, and with a huge amount of effort he raised his hands high in the air and cried out as he clapped them together and a ball of fire appeared in the air over his head. Anna watched in shock as the man brought his arms down, holding the fire in his hands without burning himself, and then held it out towards Handsworth, who backed away in fear.

The man forced Handsworth further back towards the mass of bodies. Many hands reached out and grabbed Handsworth and pulled him back inside, and he vanished from Anna's sight, screaming out her name. The man with the fire in his hands gave Anna a nod before he stepped back into the group.

Anna looked down at the key in her hand. Thanks to Helena and her friend and their strange powers, she had what she needed. This was her chance, she had to take it. She ran back to the black door, trying to block out the cries of agony from Handsworth. She stepped through the doorway and into the corridor.

From somewhere deep inside the Black Room, she could still hear Handsworth screaming out her name. Anna tried to ignore it as she put the key into the lock. She turned the key and locked the black door, and to her amazement, the door immediately vanished before her eyes and was replaced with a blank wall. That horrifying room had hidden itself away somewhere in the walls of Grimwald House, just like the door to the tomb downstairs had. She still held the key in her hand, and clenched her fist around it.

Anna was desperate to get out of here. She ran through the corridors, not allowing herself to think, focussed on nothing else but escaping this house. Each time she turned a corner, she found herself in another identical corridor, with more rows of closed doors. This labyrinth felt like it was never-ending, which didn't make any sense; the house was big, but it couldn't be *this* big. But then, after seeing the Black Room, Anna knew that there was no reason to assume that the rest of this house would play by the rules of reality. It seemed as if the house was rearranging itself, fighting her, trying to prevent her from escaping. Was there any way out of this madhouse?

As much as she feared the pain she knew it would bring, she decided to try to use her ability to escape. She closed her eyes and tried to concentrate and send herself away, she didn't care where, she didn't even care *when* – just some place far from here.

It didn't work. When she opened her eyes, she was still in Grimwald House, and nothing had changed. What was going on? Why wasn't it working now, when she needed it the most?

Frustrated, angry, and willing to try anything, Anna looked down at her shoes and tried clicking her heels together three times and wishing herself back home, but she wasn't too surprised to find that that didn't work either.

There was nothing else she could do, she just had to keep running and hope that eventually she'd be able to find a way out of this maze, or else she'd be trapped in this house forever.

Anna felt like she'd been lost up here in this labyrinth of corridors for an hour or more, before she turned a corner and finally saw the staircase again. She gasped with relief, almost unable to believe her eyes. She moved quickly down the stairs. At the bottom, she stopped and looked towards the dining room. Should she go in and try to find the hidden door to the tomb, and try to save Vivian? But what if Katarina was still in there too, what might the crazy dead woman do to Anna if she saw that she was not in the Black Room like she was supposed to be?

Anna chose instead to keep going. The front doors were still locked, but she knew that there was another way out. She passed the kitchen, and while there was no sign of Ebony the ravenous dog, Anna decided to move slowly and carefully, trying not to make a sound. She continued on to the conservatory. She had difficulty locating the small door to the garden as there were so many plants in her way that it was like fighting her way through an overgrown jungle. Eventually she found the door and forced it open.

Anna ran out into the garden, and didn't stop running until she reached the woods.

She leaned against a tree for support, and tried to control her breathing, her head pounding. In her hand, she still held the key to the Black Room, and she wasn't sure what she'd do with it yet. The side of her face still hurt from where Handsworth had clawed at it. She didn't want to think about how badly scarred her face might be.

She shivered, and looked down at her torn dress, the one that Vivian had changed her into when her own clothes were wet. Something about it was very familiar. She suddenly remembered where she'd seen this red dress before: back in 1923. Vanessa, the woman who'd been kind to her when she'd travelled back to that time, had been wearing this same dress on that night, in her final session. The night that she'd died.

It was yet another reminder that Anna had failed to save any of the other people that she'd met at Grimwald House. Vanessa, Henry and Charles had all died. So had Harold and Mark, she hadn't been able to prevent their deaths, or the terrible fate that awaited Vivian. She felt useless – no, worse than that, she felt guilty, because she'd survived when none of the others had, and because she should've tried harder and done more to try to help them.

She placed her hand on the wet ground and said softly, 'Good-bye, Mark. I'm sorry.' She had been so angry with him, but it was hard to completely hate someone who had given their life to try to save yours, even if they had done terrible things.

At least she'd taken revenge on Handsworth. She hoped that those creatures in the Black Room would tear that bastard apart so that he'd never be able to harm anyone ever again. She felt more guilt when she thought about Helena and those other poor trapped souls, and wished that there was a way that she could help them. Perhaps she should go back inside the house and try to find the Black Room again and open the door to let them out, but what if Handsworth was still alive in there? She couldn't risk freeing him too.

Anna could *feel* that the house still craved her and her power, like it was pulling at her, trying to draw her back in, and she was terrified of ending up in one of those glass cages in the Black Room forever. She knew that she needed to stay out of the house's reach. But what about Vivian? Could she allow herself to abandon Vivian to her fate, like she'd done to Katarina in 1923? Could she live with herself and with the inevitable nightmares if she didn't even try?

She knew that Vivian could be dead already, her body being wrapped in that tomb, her spirit doomed to wander the house, and Anna would have no way to save her. And then there was Katarina, who wasn't human anymore, she was something else, something even more dangerous.

Maybe she should try to get help, but who would believe her crazy story? No, she was on her own. There was nobody else who could save Vivian. She had to at least try. She had to be brave, and stop thinking about herself, just this once.

Anna fought the part of her brain that was screaming at her to stay where she was, to stay safe, and not to go back inside that house. She closed her eyes, and pictured the tomb in her mind. She would try to send herself directly into the tomb, as dangerous as that would be. *Concentrate, Anna...*

But it didn't work. When she opened her eyes, she was still in the woods. She tried again.

Still here. She tried to send herself to the dining room, the drawing room, the kitchen, the conservatory, the bedrooms – but nothing worked. She couldn't seem to transport herself back inside Grimwald House at all. In desperation she tried thinking about other places, faraway places like her apartment, her office, and her childhood home, but it didn't work. She remained where she was in the woods outside the house.

Anna felt a terrible sensation of emptiness now. It began to dawn on her that she might have lost her ability for good. It was the one thing that had made her special, the one thing that had given her an edge over everyone else, in her life and in her work. And now it was gone. What would she do without it? Who would she be without it?

Anna knew now that Katarina had been right about her and what kind of a person she was. Whoever or whatever had decided that Anna should have this ability, they had made a mistake, they should've realised that she couldn't be trusted with it. Surely there were better people, more reliable, more responsible people, that would have used it only for the right reasons, or would have known better than to use it at all?

And now God or whoever it was had seemingly taken that ability away from her, so perhaps she was finally being punished for the things that she'd done. She'd proved that she wasn't worthy of this power.

Anna looked around at the woods. If her ability had now failed her, then how on earth would she get home? She had no idea where she was. She'd lost her phone, so she couldn't call anyone even if she did know her location. She could pick a direction and start walking, but she had no clue where she might end up. These woods looked like they went on forever. She could be lost out there for days, and might starve to death. What if there really were wolves in these woods, or something even worse?

Suddenly she heard a noise coming from the front of the house: it sounded like tyres on gravel. Could this be her salvation? Perhaps it was one of those taxis that had brought her here before, or just someone who'd taken a wrong turn. She could plead with them to take her away from this place, and if they refused, then she would steal their vehicle from them. She had to get away from this nightmare. Whatever it took, she would do it.

I'm sorry, Vivian. I'm so sorry, but I can't stay, I can't help you. I have to go. I hope you can forgive me.

Anna took a deep breath, and ran.

A rumble of thunder preceded a sudden downpour, the rain fighting its way down between the leaves atop the twisted trees and running along their outstretched fingers that crookedly pointed towards the dark sky.

As more vehicles began to arrive, the rain hammered Grimwald House and hailed on its windows, slithering down the glass, looking for a way to penetrate its walls, but its efforts were futile.

A lone figure stood watching from the woods as the weather grew worse. Anna wiped the rain from her eyes as she watched more people arrive at the house, each one brought by a separate taxi.

When she'd heard the sound of the first car as it had approached the house, she'd hoped that it might indicate a means of escape, until she'd crouched behind the low wall and watched someone with a very familiar, distinctive face step out of the vehicle.

Anna had recognised Mary immediately – that face, and that false eye, were unmistakable. Somehow, Mary was here in 2023, one hundred years after she'd been freed from her tomb, and she was no longer a spirit or a corpse, but a living, breathing human being again. Or, at least, something that looked like one.

In the tomb, Katarina had told Anna that she believed she would be given the gift of immortality once the sacrifice was made, and that her body would also be made whole again and her missing toes would grow back. If Mary was restored in a similar way when she was freed a century ago, then why hadn't her missing eye grown back, why did she still have that false eye now? Anna's imagination provided a horrible answer: perhaps that awful old witch had grown so accustomed to looking down on people with that intimidating, unreal eye of hers, that after her real eye had grown back she'd decided to cut it out and replace it with a false one again? Anna shuddered at the thought.

The other people now arriving at the house after Mary, however, were unfamiliar to Anna. There were men and women, some young-looking, some as old as Mary. They showed no signs of wariness as they walked towards Grimwald House, it seemed quite familiar to them, as if they'd all been here before. The maid Irene greeted them at the front doors, and seemed to recognise them, smiling and chatting with them as they entered the house.

After observing them for a while, Anna began to realise who these strange people must be and why they were here. They had to be Mary's predecessors, people like her who'd been entombed in this house, kept prisoner for a hundred years, and then freed, brought back to life by the sacrifice of other guests. They were all a part of this terrible cycle that had been going on for God knows how long. There were so many of them; the house must have been building its little army of cursed souls for centuries, perhaps even millenia. Anna knew that it couldn't be a coincidence that they had all come to Grimwald House on this night. They must have come to greet Katarina now that she had finally escaped her imprisonment. Now that she'd become one of them.

Anna wondered if they were all expecting to find her own body there in the tomb, rather than Vivian's, since she was apparently meant to be Katarina's sacrifice. And had anyone noticed yet that Handsworth had gone missing? What would Katarina and the others do once they discovered what Anna had done and that she was still free?

It was Katarina who scared Anna the most, more than Mary or any of the others. Now that she was reunited with her body, how dangerous might she have now become? What if she took all of that anger and frustration from a hundred years of torment – including her fury at what Anna had done to her by abandoning her – and brought it out into the world with her? What terrible things might she be capable of?

Anna wanted to burn this terrible place to the ground while Katarina and her predecessors were all gathered together inside of it, to get rid of them all, but she suspected that these people, and Grimwald House itself, would not die so easily. If these people really were immortal, if they could live forever, did that also mean that they couldn't be hurt, that they couldn't be killed?

Crouching there in the cold rain, Anna couldn't stop herself from sneezing. She ducked behind the wall and hoped that no one had heard her. The bright red dress that she was wearing that had belonged to Vanessa did not exactly help her blend in to her surroundings. She had to be very careful. If these people discovered that she was watching them and intended to do them harm, then who knows what they might do to her? There was an army of them, and she couldn't take them all on by herself. To defeat them, she would need an army of her own, but it wasn't as if the police or military would accept her insane story.

Anna had beaten this house and escaped from its clutches, trapping Handsworth in the Black Room, hopefully forever, but it still felt like she could not truly escape from it. She was still tied to this house. She stared at the key to the Black Room in her hand. She couldn't let Katarina or Mary or any of the others obtain it, she couldn't allow them to free Handsworth from his prison.

She touched her other hand to her cheek and felt the unfamiliar rough edges of the slashes that Handsworth had made in her face with his fingernails. She was glad that she didn't have a mirror to see herself and the damage that he'd done to her.

Anna tried again to wish herself away from here, but her ability still wasn't working. She would give anything to be able to send herself back to her apartment right now, and curl up on her sofa with Jelly, and watch television and eat chocolate and forget all about this nightmare. Or perhaps if she'd been able to move herself through time again, then she could have sent herself back to that very first session on that first evening and she could have tried to warn Mark, Harold, and Vivian about what was to come, although she doubted that any of them would have believed her. Anna wanted to be able to go back and scream at her past self to ignore that invitation letter, to get rid of it, to burn it. She would plead with herself not to go to that first session, to stay away from Grimwald House, because that naive Anna had no idea of the terrifying things that she was destined to experience there. There were horrors here beyond anything that even her wild imagination could have dreamt up – she'd make new friends but then lose them in horrific ways, and all of her sins would be uncovered, and she'd be forced to confront the terrible things that she'd done.

Was it even possible to change the past anyway? Her trip back to 1923 had not just been some random thing, she knew that the house had guided her to that specific point in time with Mary and Katarina in the tomb so that she could play her part in Katarina's fate.

Something caught Anna's eye. She noticed that there was a solitary taxi still parked near the front of the house and there didn't seem to be anyone around it. If the keys were inside, she could try to steal that vehicle and drive away before anyone realised what was happening. She knew that she would be spotted easily in this red dress if anyone happened to be watching. But she also knew that she had to try.

Anna waited until she was sure that there was no one around, and then she sprinted for the car, banging her elbow as she dived down behind the boot. She waited there, her heart pounding, desperately hoping that she wouldn't hear any cries to suggest that she'd been seen.

She cautiously approached the driver side and lifted her head to peer inside the vehicle, hoping to see the key still in the ignition. She froze when she saw a man lying down on the back seat, seemingly asleep. Or maybe he was dead? She watched his chest and saw it rise and fall. The driver was only sleeping. She might've preferred to find him dead.

What should she do? The driver would wake up the second that she tried to enter the vehicle, and he'd try to alert the others. If he pressed the horn, then it would all be over for her. She could turn around and run back to the woods, but what if this was her only chance to escape? She decided that she needed a weapon. She looked down at the Black Room key in her hand. It would have to do.

Anna tapped the key against the window, and then ducked down. She waited a few seconds, but there was no sign of activity, so she tapped on the window again. This time, she saw the taxi shake slightly, and then one of the doors slowly opened. She hid behind the boot and waited.

She heard shoes crunch gravel, and peered around the side of the car. The driver stood there, his back to her, turning his head slowly. This was her chance.

Anna got to her feet and quickly approached the man from behind, then she raised the key and pressed the cold metal up against his neck, digging it into his skin. 'Don't move, don't say anything, or I swear to God I'll cut your throat with this knife and you'll bleed to death, right here!'

The man froze, and raised his hands as if surrendering. 'What do you want?' he growled.

'Just the keys to your taxi,' Anna answered, 'but I will kill you if I have to. If you think I won't, just know that I've already seen several people die here tonight, so one more is not going to bother me all that much.'

'Alright, alright, I believe you.'

'Give me the keys!'

The driver took the keys from his pocket slowly, and held them out. Anna took the keys with her left hand, her other hand keeping the Black Room key pressed against the man's neck. 'Start walking, and don't look back,' she told him. 'Don't you dare turn around, or I *will* kill you.'

The driver did as he was told, and as he walked away, Anna pulled open the door and sat down on the driver seat. She turned the key in the ignition and felt a wave of relief as the engine started. She yanked the door shut, dropped the Black Room key onto the passenger seat and put her hands on the steering wheel.

Anna pressed her foot to the pedal and drove the taxi past the driver and out through the gates, convinced that at any moment some invisible poltergeist would fling those gates shut to prevent her escape. But she made it through, breathing a sigh of relief as she drove out onto the road, almost unable to believe that she was finally getting away from that house.

As the rain beat down heavily on the windscreen, she activated the wipers, but the view was still blurry and dark, even with the headlights on. She looked at the rear view mirror, and for the first time she could see the bloody claw marks in the side of her face from Handsworth's attack. She tried not to let herself cry.

Anna glanced at the Black Room key lying on the seat next to her. She decided that she would take it and bury it somewhere safe, somewhere far away from here, where no one would ever find it, so that Handsworth would remain trapped forever. He would never again be able to go out into the world and hunt down any more "special" people with abilities like hers. No one else would have to suffer the agony of those poor souls in the Black Room.

She thought about Vivian again, dead or dying in that tomb. In a century's time, would a new group of guests arrive at the house to free Vivian, while she chose someone to be her sacrifice and take her place, just like Katarina and Mary had done? Would that same horrific loop keep repeating on and on and never end?

There had to be something that Anna could do to stop it all. She couldn't just go and never look back and pretend that none of this had happened. She owed it to the others that had died here to find a way. But what could she do on her own, against all that evil? She needed help, but she had no idea where to get it. For now, all she could do was keep driving and put as much distance between herself and that terrible place as possible.

Anna saw Grimwald House recede behind her in the mirror. She thought that she could feel the house watching her, that she could feel its rage and its desire to draw her back inside. But she would not let it take her, she would not let it win.

Yes, you know my secrets and my sins, Grimwald House, but now I know yours too. I know about Katarina, and Mary, and all the others. I know about Handsworth and the Black Room and the people that you're keeping prisoner in there. And I don't know how, but somehow I'm going to find a way to stop you. For Vivian and Harold. And Mark. And all the others whose lives you've taken. This isn't over.

Epilogue

Vivian felt trapped. Isolated. Alone. Abandoned.

This was nothing new, of course. She'd felt this way every day since she'd escaped from Grimwald House.

The whole thing seemed so surreal now, like a dream or a nightmare, or something that had happened to someone else and not to her. Even now, she still couldn't quite believe that she wasn't still there in that tomb, thinking her life was about to be over. Or perhaps she *was* still there in Grimwald House, and her body was wrapped from head to toe in bandages, and she was only imagining this life that she thought she was living now?

Since she'd returned home after that final session, she'd barely left her house at all. Every time that she'd tried to go outside, she'd have a panic attack and have to go back inside and take deep breaths to try to calm herself down. She thanked God for the wonder that was online grocery shopping, or she might've starved to death.

Vivian touched her hand to the water in the bath in her bathroom, and quickly pulled it away to prevent the heat from burning her skin. 'Too hot, too hot,' she muttered to herself, and turned the cold tap to cool the water down. She stared at her wavering, distorted reflection in the water as she waited for the bath to fill. That face looked so old and worn that it was almost unfamiliar to her now. Where was the strength and vitality that she'd had in her youth? She looked and felt as if she'd aged another ten years or more in the few months since she'd escaped from Grimwald House.

Vivian had spent most of her days since that fateful night alone, except for the company of the people in her television programmes and books, but they didn't know her, and they didn't care about her. The weekly visit from her cleaning ladies had become the depressing highlight of her week, and even then, any conservation was difficult and disappointing.

No one called her on the telephone anymore. She had been quite used to going months without hearing from her daughter Rebecca, but not hearing from her son Daniel anymore was painful. Even when she plucked up the courage to call him, he refused to speak to her. That was her own fault, of course, because in a moment of weakness Vivian had foolishly confessed to Daniel what had really happened to his girlfriend Arianne.

Vivian knew that there was still a part of Daniel that loved his mother, in spite of the awful things that he'd said to her after she'd confessed her involvement in Arianne's death, because he could have gone to the police and told them what his mother had done but he'd chosen not to. However, Daniel had told her that he never wanted to see or speak to her ever again.

Vivian still believed that the things that she'd done were for the best, even if Daniel wouldn't understand, but she thought now that perhaps she should've just kept quiet and taken her secrets with her to her grave. This was the price of honesty, it seemed: a life of loneliness and misery. If so, then perhaps it was better that those kinds of secrets stay hidden. But it was too late now.

She blamed her experiences at Grimwald House for her sudden irrational need to confess the truth to her son. Thinking about that awful place and what had happened made her feel ill. And angry. She'd been abandoned there; not one of her fellow guests had come back to try to rescue her from that tomb and that crazed dead woman with the knife. Not Mark, not Harold, and not Anna. No, they'd all been quite happy to leave Vivian to her fate. She knew that she should never have allowed herself to think of those people as anything but strangers who would only care about themselves. If Anna and the others did survive that night and escape from Grimwald House, like she had, then Vivian hoped that they were suffering just like she was. And if they weren't, then she had a few ideas about what she might be able to do about that. Not one of them had tried to save her, they'd all left her there to die in that tomb. It was therefore rather ironic that the person that *did* actually save her life that night was the same person that had originally intended to end it.

Even now, Vivian still couldn't fathom why on earth Katarina had let her escape, especially considering what that would mean for her own fate – to be trapped in that awful house again for another hundred years. *Why did you let me live, Katarina? I don't understand. Why couldn't you kill me?*

Vivian wasn't sure if Katarina herself even understood why she'd been unable to make the sacrifice. In the tomb, when Vivian had been convinced that she was going to die, the young dead woman had started arguing with herself, seemingly fighting some kind of internal battle over whether she could actually commit the act or not. Vivian hadn't been able to do anything but watch it play out and wait for the outcome. Finally, Katarina had put her knife down, and she'd told Vivian, "*No, I can't do this... not even to you.*" Then she'd opened the door to the tomb and ordered Vivian to leave, to find a way out of Grimwald House and to go and never look back. She'd told Vivian that others would soon be coming, bad people, and that if she wanted to live then she had to get out of that house as soon as she could.

Vivian had made her way to the conservatory at the back of the house and out into the garden, and then into the woods. It was dark and cold and wet outside, but she'd been determined not to go back, only forward. She'd been afraid that at any moment Katarina would change her mind and come after her to drag her back to that tomb, so she kept walking throughout the night, fighting her fatigue, forcing herself to keep going. She'd felt like she was walking in circles and was completely lost, with no idea which direction to go in. She had begun to believe that she'd never see anyone ever again, that she was doomed to die out there all alone and miles from anywhere. It wasn't until sometime the following evening when, utterly exhausted, hungry and thirsty, she'd finally found her way out of the woods and stumbled across a farmer working in a field, who took her back to his house and allowed her to use his telephone to call a taxi to take her home. When she'd asked the farmer what he knew about Grimwald House, he'd told her that he'd never even heard of the place.

Vivian had on several occasions since that day tried to work out where exactly Grimwald House was. But all the internet searches that she'd tried, and even the private investigator that she'd later hired, were unconvinced that the house even existed at all. But she knew that it must be out there somewhere.

Vivian snapped out of her daydream when she suddenly realised that her bath was now nearly overflowing, and she quickly turned the taps off. She then lifted her legs over the sides of the bath and stood with her feet and ankles in the water, then gradually lowered the rest of her body down into the water, which wrapped her up in a warm, comforting blanket.

Vivian laid her head back, let out a deep breath, and tried to relax. She stared up at the glass ceiling, which reflected her miserable glare back at her. She had no desire to look at herself, it would only make her feel worse. She closed her eyes and tried to think of something more pleasant. She thought of her children Daniel and Rebecca when they were young, playing on a playground, waving at her.

There was a sudden crash from somewhere downstairs, which jolted her back into the real world. *What on earth was that?!* There was no one else in her house, she was alone. She wondered if she'd left some windows open, and she remembered opening a few earlier because the house had smelled funny – had she forgotten to close them? Perhaps it was a sign of dementia, on top of all her other problems? She thought she could feel a breeze, and she could hear the fierce wind howling outside.

She didn't want to leave this comfortable bath to go and investigate that noise, and frankly, if it was a burglar, then she was happy for them to take whatever they wanted, because she didn't care anymore.

Vivian listened for a while, but couldn't hear any more noises, so she decided that it must have been the wind, or her imagination playing tricks on her. She closed her eyes and allowed herself to settle back into the comfort of the water and her dreams.

When she opened her eyes, Vivian could see her reflection in the mirror in the ceiling again, and she told it, 'Go away, no one wants to look at you anymore, you ugly old thing.' She realised that the water had now gone cold. She must have dozed off. She was shivering. The air was cool too, her own fault for leaving those windows open. She reached over the side of the bath for her towel, and wiped her eyes, and then glanced up again at her reflection, and it was at that moment that she realised that the Vivian staring back at her from the mirrored ceiling above was not alone.

There was a woman crouched at the end of that other Vivian's bath.

Vivian blinked her eyes and tried to understand what she was seeing. That reflection was *wrong*. There was no one else in her bathroom but her. She blinked her eyes again, but still that strange impossible figure would not go away.

Vivian let out a gasp that threatened to develop into a scream – but a moment later, the woman in the mirror vanished, as if she was never there. Vivian let out a nervous laugh, but for some reason it suddenly hurt to laugh, and then it hurt to breathe. Her chest felt tight, like it was being squeezed, and there were sharp pains in her chest which started spreading to her arms, her back, her neck, her jaw... She started to panic. Something was very wrong inside her, she could feel it. She tried to stand up in the bath, too quickly, and felt dizzy, and she reached for the sink to steady herself but her wet hand slipped and then her legs gave way and she fell backwards, shouting out in pain as her legs twisted awkwardly beneath her and her back struck the end of the bath.

Her heart was beating too fast. Vivian clutched at her chest. *No, no, no!* She couldn't have a heart attack, not now, not when she was alone and couldn't get help...

Vivian knew that she needed to call for an ambulance, but she couldn't seem to move her body to raise herself out of the bath and get to her phone. There was no Daniel here to save her this time, and even if he were here, he might have chosen to leave her to her fate after what she'd done to Arianne. Daniel didn't care about her, Rebecca didn't care about her – was there no one left who cared if she lived or died?

Her body slowly began to slide further down into the water, and eventually the water went up past her neck. She couldn't seem to summon the energy to keep her head above the water and she started choking and sputtering as her whole face was submerged and the water began to force its way up her nose and down her throat and into her lungs. An image flashed into her mind: Sammy Mitchell, thrashing about in that river, pleading for Vivian to help him while she just stood there and watched and didn't try to save him.

Please, don't let me drown!

Vivian was unable to move any part of her body now. Another image came into her mind: Arianne, fighting for her life as her head was being shoved down and submerged in that water at the farm-house. But this time, Arianne did not die. In her mind's eye, Vivian saw Arianne somehow push her attacker away from her and pull her head out of the water. Then she turned and began crawling her pale wet body towards Vivian, one slow step at a time, thrusting her fists into the muddy ground as she dragged herself towards Vivian, her eyes full of hate, her mouth open wide as if silently screaming...

The mental image evaporated and as Vivian stared up at the surface of the water, she suddenly saw a face looking down on her from above, its features blurred by the water. The figure was illuminated by the bathroom lights, giving it a bright aura, and Vivian thought that perhaps she was looking up into the face of an angel who'd come to take her from this world and on to the next. But as the face came closer, Vivian saw that it didn't look like what she thought an angel's face should look like. The strange woman that she'd seen in the reflection in the mirror was now here in the room, and her indistinct face was now just inches above Vivian's head, and with a sinking feeling, she suddenly realised who it must be.

Somehow, Arianne had returned from the dead, and had come to punish Vivian for her sins. Vivian realised then that no angel would be coming to take her to heaven, because heaven didn't want her, not after everything that she'd done.

Vivian's pain was becoming unbearable now, and she knew that she was dying, and no one was coming to save her, certainly not the creature that must be Arianne, who seemed content to float above her and not reach out its arms to save her life and to instead just watch her die. The wavering surface of the water unfairly divided their two worlds; Vivian could not breathe trapped in her underwater prison with no air, but on the other side of the divide was all the air that anyone could ever want, yet she knew that the apparition she saw there would not even need it. This was a dead woman. A ghost.

Vivian's sight had now faded away completely, although she could still see images in her mind, and she imagined a bright sunny day in a park with Daniel and his wife Arianne by his side, and their two children, Vivian's grandchildren, a boy and a girl, who were playing on a playground just like her own son and daughter used to, and it was the most wonderful thing that Vivian had ever seen, and as Vivian made her last futile struggles for air, that happy picture in her mind began to disintegrate and all that she was left with was an image of Arianne's angry face staring at her accusingly, before that faded too.

As the darkness took over her, Vivian thought she could now begin to understand the horror of what she'd done, the pain and terror that Sammy and Arianne must have gone through when they'd died, and all the lives and potential happiness that she'd destroyed because of her own selfishness and prejudices. But she knew that it was too late now to make amends for all the harm that she'd caused. Far too late.

There was nothing she could do now but die.

As Vivian's life drifted away in the bathroom, in her bedroom a sudden gust of wind blew through the open window, toppling a bottle of pills and scattering a collection of papers that had been on Vivian's desk. Five of the pages that had fallen on the floor were of a different colour to the rest, and on each page was a list of handwritten notes. One was titled *Private Investigators* and had a list of contact details, another page had the title *Grimwald House* along with a rough drawing of the exterior of the house and a description of its surroundings.

The other three pages had notes divided under subheadings including *Physical Appearance, Estimated Age, Family and Relationships*, and *Career*. There was also a section headed *Current Address* which was empty on each sheet. The final section on each of these three pages was a list of much more detailed notes, some highlighted, that were under the heading of *Secrets and Vulnerabilities*.

At the very top of each of these three sheets of paper was a single name:

Harold (surname unknown).
Mark (surname unknown).
Anna Harper.

A figure entered the bedroom and stopped to look at the sheets of paper now scattered across the floor.

It seemed Vivian had been busy – she'd written down everything she could think of about Grimwald House, and about the other guests that she'd been there with. She'd apparently even hired private investigators to try to locate the house as well as her fellow guests. Would anyone ever find these notes, all these secrets that Vivian had recorded, and would they understand what it all meant?

Katarina reached out her fingers and tried to pick up the papers from the floor, but she knew that it was futile. Her fingers passed through the paper like she wasn't there. Although she had recently discovered a way to reach out into the world, Katarina still couldn't physically interact with anything, and she could only be away from the house for brief periods of time. She knew that she would have to return to her prison soon. By failing to sacrifice Vivian in that crucial moment in the tomb, Katarina had condemned herself to another excruciating century of imprisonment, and unless something were to change, these fleeting excursions would be all that she would see of the outside world for the next hundred years, until she finally got another chance to make a sacrifice to free herself. Since that disastrous evening and her failure to do what was expected of her, Katarina had suffered greatly for her moment of weakness, but now that Vivian was finally dead, perhaps the house might be appeased just a little and it wouldn't need to punish her quite so much anymore?

'Is it done yet?' came a voice from the doorway. Louise stood there looking anxious, her eyes darting around the room.

'Yes, it's done,' Katarina answered. 'Vivian is dead. She's in the bathtub.'

Louise glanced towards the bathroom. 'Oh. I shan't be taking a look in there, then. I don't think I want to see her. So, I suppose that just leaves Anna now, doesn't it?'

Katarina looked away. 'Yes, I suppose it does.'

'As I've said before, Anna's proving difficult to find, even harder than finding Vivian was.' Louise sighed. 'We still don't know Anna's full name yet, or where she lives, or anything about her, really, and with Handsworth still missing it's not going to be easy to locate her. But you know the house won't be happy until it has her. It still wants her.'

'Yes, I know that, but I'm sure you will find her eventually.'

'I really think we ought to be getting back now, miss. I'm worried about you. You know you shouldn't be out here for this long away from the house, we just don't know how it might affect you.'

'Yes, yes, fine.' Katarina sighed. 'I do appreciate your help, Louise, you know I do. And I appreciate the risks you're taking for me. I know how painful this can be for you when we do this, and if there was some other way—'

'It's alright, I can stand the pain. I don't mind.'

They stared at each other for a moment, before Katarina took one last look around the room and then told the girl, 'I think we can go now. Are you ready for me?'

Louise nodded. 'I'll just need a moment to prepare myself, and then I can take you back inside of me. Then we can go back to the house.' She hesitated, seeing all the papers strewn across Vivian's bedroom floor. 'What are all those notes? Are they anything important? Did you find anything useful?'

Katarina glanced down at the sheet of paper on the floor that was titled *Anna Harper*, and then answered the girl's question with a smile. 'Oh, no, these are nothing, nothing important at all. You can take me home now, Louise. Take me back to Grimwald House.'

A Note from the Author

Thank you for reading The Unveiling. I hope you enjoyed this book. If you have the time, please consider leaving a rating or review to help other readers discover this book.

You can claim a free ebook and stay up to date on my new releases by visiting www.pauldturner.com and signing up to my newsletter. You can also use the 'Follow' button on Amazon to be notified whenever I release a new book.

The rest of this note contains spoilers so please avoid reading it until you have finished the book.

The Unveiling is my first full-length novel and I began writing it in May 2022. The story was inspired by an article I read about Victorians who would get together for parties and witness a mummified body being unwrapped for entertainment. What if that strange practice was still going on today, at a house seemingly hidden away from the world, and you received an invitation that suggested someone knew your darkest secrets and was going to reveal them, whether you attended or not?

From that seed the story grew and branched out to show how the lives of the guests begin to fall apart between the sessions due to their past actions. By the end of the book we've found out what each of the characters has done to deserve the bad things that are now happening to them and how their actions have affected the people around them. Because, after all, nobody innocent gets invited to Grimwald House.

I also wanted to hint at a much bigger story going on behind it all involving the mysterious house itself, which takes on a character of its own, and has a history that suggests these aren't the first people to be drawn there to suffer terrible fates, and won't be the last. As soon as I had finished writing The Unveiling, I realised that there were more stories to tell and that this wouldn't be the last time that I'd need to go back to that creepy old Grimwald House in my mind. There are plenty more dark secrets lurking behind its walls, and they aren't going to stay contained in that house forever... Wish me luck!

Thanks again for reading.

Paul D. Turner

ABOUT THE AUTHOR

Paul D. Turner writes thriller stories that sometimes include paranormal or science fiction elements. He enjoys creating stories that twist and turn and focus on troubled characters who don't always get everything right. He is inspired by writers such as Stephen King, Jeffery Deaver, Mark Edwards and Gillian Flynn.

Paul has worked as a librarian and website developer and has a degree in Business Studies. He lives in the West Midlands in England.

Visit www.pauldturner.com and sign up to the mailing list to download a free ebook by Paul D. Turner and to be the first to find out about his new releases.

facebook.com/pauldturnerauthor
instagram.com/pauldturnerauthor
goodreads.com/pauldturner